I0599968

MAGICA RIOT: FULL BLOOM

MAIDENSONG MAGICA
BOOK 2

KARA BUCHANAN

STORM
MAIDEN
STUDIOS

Copyright © 2025 by Kara Buchanan

All rights reserved.

Published by Storm Maiden Studios.

No part of this book may be reproduced in any form or by any electronic or mechanical means, including information storage and retrieval systems, without written permission from the author, except for the use of brief quotations in a book review.

Absolutely no portion of this book was created or edited with generative AI technology. I feel the technology is harmful and unethical, and besides, no AI could come up with Hikari.

Also, while I'm at it, no part of this book may be scanned or otherwise analyzed by generative AI technology. Keep your grubby techno corp hands off my gals.

ISBN (digital): xxxx

ISBN (hardcover): xxxx

ISBN (paperback): xxxx

ACKNOWLEDGMENTS

I would not be here today without the help of some very special people.

My story editor, Rowan Church, whose efforts have made every Maidensong Magica story better. She has made me a better writer, and I am eternally thankful.

My copy editor, Stephanie Buchanan, who makes sure these sentences are polished. She has saved me from myself many times.

My artist, Amber Dill, who takes the images in my head and brings them to life. In a world that is increasingly devaluing art, Amber shows why a skilled artist is worth their weight in gold.

My audiobook narrator, Emma Martello, who transforms the *Magica Riot* audiobooks into something truly special through her acting ability. It's impossible for me to write without hearing her voice in my head.

And, finally, my readers. *Magica Riot* launched from zero and became a magical girl story loved by all kinds of people, a magical girl story that embraces trans identity and queer love. Every time you read about my girls, you give them life.

Thank you.

-Kara

For all the magical girls out there, in public or in secret.

OVERTURE

Jade Evergreen
Portland, Oregon
March, 1981

OVERTURE

THE PERILS OF POLYBIUS

Jade Evergreen sighed with relief and returned her lockpicks to her backpack. She brushed back her wavy red hair from the glasses in front of her green eyes and pulled out a pair of flashlights, and handed one to Catherine. Slowly, Jade swung the door open and peered inside. The interior of the arcade was dark and still. Even the windows along Belmont let in very little light, mostly blocked, as they were by game cabinets.

"Let's go," Jade said, "and be careful with your light."

"Yeah, yeah," Catherine said. "This ain't my first time."

They made their way inside, and Jade shut the door behind them. Stardust was larger than she expected, and it was crammed full of game cabinets alongside several pinball machines, arranged in snaking aisles that tried to make as much of the modest space as they could. With everything powered off, finding Polybius in here would have to be a matter of going cabinet to cabinet until they stumbled across it.

As they made their way down the first aisle, their flashlights held low and out of view of the windows to the street, Catherine spoke softly in the darkness.

"So, what are we gonna do when we find this thing?"

"I don't really know yet," Jade said. "I guess we try to look the cabinet over and see if there's anything strange about it."

"Strange like how?"

Jade shook her head. "If I knew that, I'd already know what to do."

Games and pinball machines passed beneath Jade's flashlight beam, decorated with all sorts of artwork to tempt the eye of potential players. Some she'd heard of, and some were completely new to her; she'd never spent much time around arcades, and she was now realizing how varied it was.

For a moment, she wondered if Polybius was a myth, just some kind of ghost story passed from student to student.

And then, she saw it.

Polybius sat in a corner at the back of the arcade, ever so slightly isolated, as if the other cabinets were afraid of it. It was in many ways the least-decorated cabinet in the room, which had the effect of making it look *more* mysterious, even creepy. The cabinet was solid black, the only decorations being a double stripe of ghostly cyan along its side and the word POLYBIUS on the front, the title in blocky lettering. A minimal set of controls sat on the shelf beneath the screen, just a joystick and a few buttons, with two coin slots beneath that.

It was very real, but what was it?

"There's our mystery game," Catherine said.

Jade stared at Polybius for a few moments longer. Something felt strange about it, a sensation that was also oddly familiar, in a discomforting way.

"Let's check it out, but be careful," Jade said.

"You aren't scared of that thing, are you?" Catherine asked. Jade noticed the tension in her voice; it sounded less like a tease and more like a genuine question.

"I don't trust it," Jade said, "so I don't want to let it surprise us."

She and Catherine approached the cabinet and shined their flashlights on it. There was one more detail on the front of the unit, small enough that Jade hadn't noticed it before: the words *Sinneslöschen Inc.* written above the coin slots. She'd never heard of any company called Sinneslöschen before. Still, it was something, so she pulled out her notebook and wrote it down.

"What are we lookin' for, anyway?" Catherine asked.

"I'm not really sure," Jade said. "Anything that looks suspicious, I guess?"

"Do you see anything like that?"

"Hmm. Not yet. Let's see if we can pull it away from the wall a little."

Jade and Catherine grasped the sides of the cabinet and pulled. It was surprisingly heavy, but with some effort, they were able to pull it back enough to move around behind it.

At first glance, the back of the cabinet was even less interesting than the front: a single sheet of particle board spray-painted black, without so much as a manufacturer's label. She sighed and let the beam of her flashlight drift down, and then she suddenly understood why the device felt so heavy.

The particleboard stopped two thirds of the way down the cabinet; the final third gleamed at her in the flashlight beam. It was some kind of heavy, solid-looking metal, painted black to match the rest of the cabinet. The metal was secured with thick, industrial-sized bolts. A trio of heavy power cables snaked out of a port at the bottom of the cabinet and ran over toward the wall before disappearing behind the next set of games.

Most curious of all was a rectangular hatch in the center of the metal panel. It featured a cylindrical lock unlike anything Jade had ever seen before. In the center of the lock, a small crystal glowed dimly in the darkness of the arcade.

Across from her, peering down from the other side of the cabinet, Catherine let out a long, low whistle. "Whatcha make of this? I've never seen anything like it."

"Me neither," Jade said. "One thing's for sure: This isn't any normal arcade game."

"Even I can see that," Catherine said.

Jade studied the heavy metal section some more. "If this thing can really mess with people's heads, I bet whatever is inside there is what does it."

Catherine shook her head. "I'd believe this thing can do anything, and that's kinda scary."

"It is. Also …" Jade trailed off.

Catherine looked at her curiously. "What?"

"It makes me feel *weird*." A shiver went up Jade's spine. "Like, physically weird. Like it knows something in me."

"Jade, that's kinda freaky."

Jade nodded. "I know. I need to know what's in there."

Catherine shined her light on the strange cylindrical lock. "I'm not sure even *you* can pick that thing."

Jade studied the lock more intently and reached out to touch it. As her hand neared the cylinder, she felt a warm sensation, and it all came into focus in her mind.

"What is it?" Catherine asked. "You just kinda stopped."

"I think it's a magic lock," Jade said. "I feel it. Hold on."

Jade laid her hand on the lock cylinder and concentrated. The feeling of magica was even more intense, and as she focused on it, a surge of power built up in her hand. A moment later, with a small flash of green light, the cylinder rotated with a heavy *clack*.

"Be careful," Catherine said. It almost sounded like she was concerned about more than the lock.

"Don't worry," Jade murmured as she gingerly pulled on the metal latch.

After a few tugs, the hatch popped open. She swung it down, and a sickly cyan glow poured out of the interior of the cabinet. She exchanged a nervous glance with Catherine, and then leaned down to peer inside the cabinet.

A cluster of glowing crystals mounted to a box of electronic parts sat in the middle of the cabinet, connected by bundles of wires to dozens of circuit boards, and to one of those thick power cables on the outside. Jade recognized the crystals immediately; they looked like the ones in her guitar. Not *exactly* the same, but pretty close. The ones in her guitar sparkled clean and clear, like faceted jewels. These looked hazy, their glow dull and clouded.

A set of lenses was mounted above the crystals, aimed up toward the game cabinet's screen. Whatever this strange crystal device was for, the entirety of Polybius appeared to be built around it.

Catherine was already reaching the same conclusions as Jade. "What the heck? That looks like—"

"Yeah, it does," Jade said. "Whoever this Sinneslöschen is, they've got a lot to answer for."

She wondered if any of these components could be removed; if she could get a better look at them, they might reveal something important. The natural place to start was the crystal device in the center, so she slowly reached her hand inside the cabinet to take hold of it.

Just before her fingers could grasp the device, a loud, repeating *beep* sounded from a speaker somewhere in the depths of the cabinet. A moment later, the internals of Polybius lit up with power and activity. Jade yanked her hand out and fell back onto her butt, surprised by the sudden activation of the cabinet.

"Hey, you okay?" Catherine asked, also stepping back from the now-running game cabinet.

"I'm okay," Jade said. "It must have some kind of alarm on it!"

"That's probably not good, huh?"

"Probably not! Whoever's running this thing might know we're here!"

Catherine ran around toward the front of the cabinet. "Did the whole thing turn on? Or was it just..."

She trailed off, and for several long moments, Jade didn't think anything of it. She recomposed herself and got back up on her knees as she peered back inside the cabinet.

"I wonder if we can just pull the power, or if this thing's set off an alarm somewhere else," Jade said. "What do you think I should do?"

Catherine didn't answer, so Jade called out again.

"Cathy? You okay? I asked if you think I should try to pull the power cables?"

Silence. Slowly, a new dread crept up inside Jade, and she stood and walked around toward the front of the cabinet.

What she saw there made her freeze.

Catherine was staring directly into the screen of Polybius, her eyes glassy and vacant. A tiny bit of saliva beaded up in the corner of her slack mouth. Cyan and white light bathed her in swirling flashes and patterns as the sound of the game blasted out into the room.

Jade's breath caught in her throat and her heart raced. *No. No, no, no! This can't be happening!*

She ran to Catherine's side and tugged on her arm. "Cathy? Cathy? Come on, snap out of it! Stop looking at it!"

Catherine didn't respond. She kept gazing into the screen, growing more and more empty-looking by the second. Her body had locked up, fighting Jade's pulls with leaden weight.

Jade's stomach turned, and her legs went so weak that she felt as if she might collapse.

This is all my fault.

Panic roiled inside her, cold and clammy. In desperation, she gave Catherine's arm a tremendous pull. This, finally, snapped Catherine away from the cabinet. The pair toppled over backward, and Catherine fell into Jade's arms.

"Cathy! Cathy, come on, wake up!" Jade shouted as she cradled Catherine and stroked her face, trying to think of anything she could do to wake her up. Catherine simply laid there, blank and empty, though Jade could at least tell she was alive from her slow and steady breathing.

Jade looked back up at the cabinet, still blasting out some kind of wild pattern of light from its screen. The thought occurred to her that maybe, if she could understand what it was doing and then deactivate or destroy the cabinet, she might free

Catherine from its grasp; gently, she laid Catherine down on the floor, got back up, and approached Polybius.

She knew the game was dangerous, but there was little choice left. As the screen came into view, she chanced a look into it, hoping that her magical abilities would let her break away from it if she felt it trying to take her over.

Curiously, she didn't feel *anything* happening. She walked closer and allowed herself to stare directly into the screen, and the mystery deepened.

Polybius looked to be playing itself. A little ship, represented by a blocky white triangle, blasted away at similarly blocky enemies as it flew through and around a series of patterns and shapes. Jade wondered if this was some sort of protection against tampering; if someone messed with the cabinet, it could subdue them with the brainwashing effects.

Except Jade wasn't feeling brainwashed at all. Instead, she felt something else, something instantly recognizable.

Magica.

Behind the mesmerizing graphical patterns, the screen was blasting out an absolutely ridiculous amount of magical energy. She could sense it in her mind, attempting to erase things, capture her, feed her new thoughts. It was as if the Maidensong had inoculated her against this kind of magical virus.

The feeling was different from the power she was used to; where the magic of the Maidensong was beautiful and melodic, this was crude and atonal, a raw beam of magic drilling into the brain of whoever played the game. It truly felt like magica wielded by somebody with no understanding of how magica actually *worked*.

In that instant of realization, the components inside the cabinet and the multiple power cables made a kind of sense to her. There was a tremendous amount of technology inside Polybius, all designed to blast energy into those crystals and feed the magica out through the screen. She wondered if the game's mind control abilities were simply what the crystals did when shot indiscriminately full of power. But who would want to try that in the first place? And why blast regular people?

Power. If she yanked those cables from the wall, she could turn it off and break the magical beam.

She ran around to the back of the cabinet and followed the trio of power cables. They disappeared behind more game cabinets, and she grabbed each one in her way and shoved them away from the wall as she followed the path of the cables to their destination.

Unfortunately, the cables disappeared into a heavy metal box mounted to the wall, their connections hidden inside. The cables themselves were also were massive, with silver mesh armoring much of their length. Whoever had built Polybius, and whoever had installed it, did *not* intend to let their precious mind control game get tampered with.

Jade stood there, trying her best to control the panic in her as she weighed her options. There had to be some way to shut this thing off. She was so consumed by the problem that she almost didn't notice the air in the room turning chilly, until a wind whipped up around her out of nowhere.

Jade spun around. Tendrils of black mist snaked past her, carried on that impossible wind. The mist swirled around in an ever-tightening vortex, gradually forming a humanoid shape.

Along with the mist, Jade could sense a tremendous surge of magica. This was not her own, nor the crude atonal energy of Polybius. It was cold, sinister, but also accomplished, melodic, even beautiful in its own way. It rattled Jade to her core. She tensed, like a prey animal catching a whiff of a predator.

A woman's voice, dark and alluring and utterly confident, echoed out of thin air. There was no escaping it; it seemed to emanate from every corner of the empty arcade.

"What sad, rudimentary display is this?"

Jade ran back over and kneeled at Catherine's side as she looked around and tried to determine the source of the voice. "Come out and show yourself!"

"I do not accept demands from lesser beings," the mysterious voice said, *"but I will reveal myself to demonstrate my superiority!"*

The tendrils solidified, and from them emerged a woman of some species that was decidedly not human. She towered over the cabinets; by Jade's eye, she must have been at least seven feet tall, her height emphasized by the regal way she carried herself. Her skin was an elegant gray, like a shark. It showcased a form that was curvaceous and toned, an embodiment of whatever power she drew upon. Her ears were elven, long and pointed, and framed a face marked by turquoise eyes, an imperious nose, and smirking lips that wore black lipstick. Turquoise hair puffed up from her head and cascaded down the long black dress she wore, a dress that clung to her shape and was slit high, revealing both of her thighs.

In her right hand, she held a staff as tall as she was. It was made of dark wood, burnished until it gleamed, and topped by a golden sigil of geometric rings and inky black crystals.

Jade had never seen anything like this woman, and it pinged some deep-down terror inside her. She knew instantly that this being was as dangerous as she was striking. Sweat beaded up on Jade's forehead, and a very real part of her screamed at her to run away as her heart pounded.

But she couldn't run, not with Catherine in trouble. That wasn't an option, so she buried the fear, as deep as she could, and willed herself to stay.

The woman looked down at Jade, regarding her with visible disdain. "Does this satisfy your curiosity, child?"

Jade's blood turned to ice at the sound of her voice. Every muscle in her body strained against her, begging to flee.

She swallowed, and tried to slow her breathing.

"No!" she eventually answered, her voice shakier than she'd hoped. She forced herself to summon a bit more confidence, and tried again. "I want a name!"

The woman chuckled. "Perhaps introductions *are* in order. You, dear girl, find yourself in the presence of the seventh-generation diviner of the twelfth-dimensional House of Marelia. The keeper of the arcane dark arts of the Undertow. Life-sworn wielder of the Staff of Sorrows. The one, and only, Cosmic Sorceress Makula!"

Jade's stomach turned as she realized how out of her depth she now was. This was no possessed deck of cards or mindless slime monster. The aura of power this Sorceress Makula exuded was undeniable. Jade's situation was instantly a million times worse than it had been moments before, and her mind raced as she tried to think of what to do next.

Maybe she could buy some time to think.

"Did you do this?" Jade asked.

"Did I do *what*, exactly?" Makula shot back.

"This!" Jade shouted, as she pointed back at Polybius. She felt tears building up in her eyes, but she didn't slow down. "Did you make this thing? Did you brainwash all those kids? Did you hurt Catherine?"

Makula looked at Polybius, and Catherine's motionless body, then back at Jade. She laughed. "Child, your babbling makes no sense. I would not craft such mediocre magica."

Jade was overwhelmed, gripped by panic for Catherine and deeply scared of what Makula might do, but somehow she knew the sorceress wasn't lying. Every note of magica that surged around Makula felt refined and precise, completely unlike the ragged and blunt Polybius magica.

"Alright, then who did?" Jade asked.

Makula stepped closer. "How am I to know? I have been tracking this pathetic, reckless use of magica across the dimensions, seeking to put whoever unleashed it back in their proper place. This species of yours is out of its depth! I will set this right, and I will go through *your* pathetic frame to do so, if I must!"

"That thing has been hurting innocent people, taking their minds," Jade said. "If you destroy it, what's going to happen to them?"

"It has already taken victims?" Makula asked. "Well, then, they would die, I assume. I'm not especially concerned about a handful of inferior, non-magical beings."

"You're not even going to *try* to help them?"

"Why go to the effort, when grinding that device into dust would be so much simpler?"

Makula's callous disregard for the game's victims made Jade boil inside, her fear sparking into anger.

"That's despicable," Jade said, glaring back at the sorceress. "How could you let all those people die? They haven't done anything wrong!" Her eyes glanced down at Catherine's mesmerized body, and she took a deep breath, stood up, and stared Makula down. "Only a monster would hurt people like that. And...I'm going to punish you for it!"

"You?" Makula laughed. "*You?* What could you do to a being of such magnificence as myself? What power could you *possibly* wield that would be anywhere near my own?"

Jade wiped her eyes behind her glasses and raised her right hand skyward. "Let me show you!"

With a flash of magical light, a microphone laced with glittering green crystals materialized in her hand. She lowered it to her mouth and shouted the phrase the song had taught her that first day it had called to her when she'd been reawakened as her new self.

"Maidensong harmony power...go live!"

In the span of a heartbeat, her body shined, engulfed in radiant light. Magical energy swirled around her and lifted her off the floor of the arcade. Suspended in the air, she slowly twirled as her street clothes vanished, piece by piece, shattering into glowing shards that flew off her body. Ribbons of green magica flowed across her, wrapped her up, and left a new outfit in their wake.

A silky white blouse formed on her torso, with billowing ruffles cascading down the chest, secured in the center by an emerald crystal. Joining it was a dark green skirt with wide pleats that hung down to her mid thigh. Matching boots with wide cuffs materialized on her feet, reaching up to her knees. A long jade coat with golden braided epaulets, like something a 19th century naval officer would have worn, draped down her chest, fastened in place with gold buttons.

Her hair lengthened and swooped to the side, piled high atop her head and flowing down in a torrent of radiant auburn. Behind her glasses, a streak of dark emerald makeup splashed across her eyes, and glistening earrings popped into existence on her earlobes.

She touched back down on the floor of the arcade with a solid *thump* of her boots. The sensations of magica were familiar to her now, and she embraced them fully. The Maidensong's power surged into her body from the cosmos itself, chasing away fear and doubt. Whatever Sorceress Makula's fearsome abilities might be, Jade had her own. As the magical whirlwind faded around her, she stood up straight and tall, pointed at Makula, and shouted the final words of her transformation.

"I am a guardian of song and heart! Agent of malevolence, be silenced by the song of Jade Evergreen!"

The sorceress stared back at her, and after a moment, smiled broadly. "How fascinating! It would appear there are humans who have connected with true magica again! Even if it is still through a shaper as *pedestrian* as the Maidensong."

That was strange; what did Makula mean by "connected with true magica *again*"? Not that it changed Jade's immediate job.

"I'm connected to it, alright," Jade said, "and I'm gonna use it to teach you a lesson!"

Makula pointed the tip of her staff in Jade's direction and laughed. "Try it if you wish, and let us see if those words will mark your grave!"

The tip of the staff glowed with intense energy. Jade realized she'd perhaps been a little hasty diving straight into combat, but there was nothing to be done about now. First things first: Get Catherine out of harm's way.

She hefted Catherine's hypnotized form up in her arms, spun around, and took off running in the direction of the arcade manager's office, zigzagging as best she could. A blast of magica arced out of Makula's staff and sizzled past her, slamming into a nearby pinball machine and blowing it into a thousand pieces. Jade didn't dare look back; once Catherine was relatively safe, she could face Makula properly.

Her muscles burned as she pushed herself harder, flying toward the manager's office at top speed. *No time to slow down now.* She braced herself, shielded Catherine, and smashed straight into the door with her shoulder. Her magical girl strength blew the door off its hinges, sending a shower of splinters into the room. She slid to an emergency stop before she crashed into the office's far wall.

She chanced a look back. As she expected, Makula was closing the distance. Jade set Catherine's body down on the floor behind the manager's desk. She reached out and touched her cheek, then took a deep breath and stood up.

Time to be a hero.

She strode back out of the office, directly into the path of the angry sorceress.

"Running will not help you, girl," Makula said, charging her staff for another attack. "You must fight or perish!"

Jade smiled back at her and nodded. "Okay. Deal!"

She summoned her guitar into her hands. It materialized from a cloud of sparkling energy, its strings replaced with six glowing strands of magica.

Makula fired, and Jade rang out a chord. A wave of magica rolled out of the guitar and shot across the room at Makula and into the sorceress's blast. The shot from the staff deflected up into the ceiling, and the rest of Jade's wave crashed into Makula and knocked her back across the arcade floor.

After steadying herself, Makula grinned back at Jade. "That is more like it, human! You're actually giving me something to fight!"

"If you like that," Jade said, "get a taste of *this!*"

She fretted a chord and held her guitar out by the neck with her left hand. With her right, she ran her fingertips across the strands. They crackled with energy as she pulled them back. An arrow of glittering emerald magica slid out of the aether, nestled in the strands.

She smirked, took aim, and loosed the arrow at Makula.

It sliced through the air, trailing sparkles in its wake. The arrow shot straight for Makula's chest. The sorceress, however, was faster than Jade expected.

Makula held up her free hand. With an intense flash of energy, a glowing disc of intricate geometric sigils appeared at her palm. A split second later, Jade's arrow crashed into this sigil disc. A blast of green exploded from the arrowhead and shoved back against Makula's shield. While the sigils protected her from the magical explosion, it didn't stop the force. Makula flew back into a row of game cabinets and groaned as her body smashed the wooden frames to bits.

The sorceress scrambled back to her feet and shot an angry glare at Jade. "Very well, child. I'm done holding back!"

Makula whipped her arm and swung her staff around. A long arc of energy sliced out of it from it across the room.

The attack was simply too fast and too big to dodge.

Searing force slammed into Jade's chest. The the percussive shockwave that followed knocked her back across the room and she smashed into a pinball table. The machine crumpled, sending glass shards flying up all around her. She gasped, the wind knocked from her lungs as she crashed to the floor atop a mangled pile of pinball components.

The world spun. She shoved her way up from the mess and wiped the debris from her face. A trickle of blood rolled down her forehead and streaked her hand.

Makula was upon her in seconds. "As I suspected! You put up a decent fight, but you are no match for a true master." She gestured over at the Polybius cabinet. "Now, I shall put you down, then deal with that crude mockery of magica."

Jade raced for a solution, anything that could stop the inevitable—and then, she felt something under her right hand. Something cold, metallic, and round.

"I might not be a master of magica," she shot back, "but I *am* a pinball wizard!"

With every ounce of her remaining strength, Jade hurled the metal ball at Makula's grip on her staff. Her aim was true, and the ball cracked into the sorceress's hand.

Makula shrieked, and the staff flew out of her grasp. It smacked the floor on the other side of the room and clattered away, out of sight.

That was just the surprise she needed. Jade scrambled to her feet and brought her guitar up. She nocked another magical arrow, aimed at Makula's leg, and let it fly. The arrow stabbed into Makula's shin with a flash of magica and knocked her to the floor as she shrieked in pain.

Jade wasn't about to let the advantage slip away. She forced her battered body up and ran over to Makula before the sorceress could stand. She fretted a new chord on the guitar and pulled back the energy strings. A trio of arrows shimmered into existence, aimed directly at Makula's face.

"Don't even *think* about moving," Jade said.

"Oh, well done," Makula said. "Color me impressed, girl."

Jade pulled back her ethereal strings a little more. "I'm not just a girl. I'm a magical girl."

Makula laughed. "Before you loose those arrows, *magical* girl, you might want to consider what you're about to do."

"What are you talking about?" Jade asked, eyeing her suspiciously.

"I'm simply saying that I can help you."

"Help me? You've been trying to kill me!"

Makula shrugged. "Clearly an incorrect decision on my part. You've shown you're at least slightly more clever than the non-magical nobodies that inhabit this worthless dimension. And you still have to help one of those unremarkable little people, don't you?"

"Stop trying to get inside my head," Jade said.

"I'm just trying to make you think, magical girl. Your little companion lying in that room over there is in real danger. And I can sense that you're worried."

"Shut up!"

Makula grinned. "Yes, that's it, isn't it? You *care* for that poor wretched thing."

"She's my ... friend," Jade said, quieter than she meant to. "You were going to let her die. You were going to let all of them die!"

Makula shrugged. "And now I'm not. That has to count for something."

"Hardly," Jade muttered.

"The fact is," Makula purred, "only *I* know how to save them." Her voice dropped to a whisper. "How to save *her*."

Jade had no reason to trust this Sorceress Makula, but she was out of options.

"Talk," Jade said, "and do it quickly."

MAGICA RIOT: FULL BLOOM

Claire Ryland
Portland, Oregon
Present Day

SIDE A
FAMILIAR FACES

CHAPTER 1

My hands flew across the keys of my purple Korg keytar's angular body. Sweat rolled down my forehead and the band's amplifiers roared from the back of the stage. Cass and I locked eyes, our solos intertwined and snarling, her twist-out hair bobbing with every beat.

To my left, Nova attacked her drum kit. Her arms were a blur as she rolled through her toms and snare. Her foot smashed the kick drum pedal.

Hana thumped the beat on her bass. She raised her leg and planted her boot on the top of Nova's kick drum. Her ponytail swayed as she bobbed her head and unleashed her megawatt grin on Nova.

The pent-up energy of the crowd was palpable in the air of the Daedalus Theater. As we came to the final notes of our last encore, I waited for that energy's release.

To my right, Sara spun as she rang out thick, overdriven chords on her guitar. As she twirled to face the crowd, she reared back and banged her head and torso. The final chord rang out, and Nova crashed down on her kit and brought the song to a stop.

The final notes hung over the room, quickly drowned out as

the crowd of twelve hundred people erupted in cheers, screams, and applause. I looked across the stage, completely over-whelmed. There were so many people here.

And then, for a moment, my head spun.

In that instant, I saw a memory of the cosmos. The faces of every magical girl who had ever existed and would ever exist. Limitless dimensions and world lines stretching out into corners of existence that nobody had ever seen before. The grand universal torrent of magica that connected it all yet lay beyond the reach of most people.

The room pulled away from me, and I felt as though I were falling into creation.

Four weeks ago, I'd seen *everything* in the span of a heartbeat. Flashes of that moment had danced across my mind in the days since Magica Riot saved the world, but they'd never been this intense.

The energy of our performance tonight must have turned up the dial. I'd unlocked the true powers of magical girls, but as far as I could tell, nobody else had experienced what I had. They felt the surge of magica from the Maidensong that day, but they hadn't gotten my cosmic revelation. That was something I had to carry alone.

I wasn't entirely sure what to do with that.

Before the moment could overwhelm me, I forced myself to slow my breathing and look away from the crowd. My focus shifted to Sara. She glanced over her shoulder and grinned at me, then turned back to the audience.

"Thank you, friends!" she shouted into her microphone, still catching her breath as sweat dampened her short red hair. "We have been Magica Riot! Be good to each other! We love you, Portland!"

I glanced from her to Cass, Hana, and Nova, and we exchanged nods. With a moment's concentration, we called upon our magica to send our instruments back to the aetheric plane, drawing another wave of cheers and gasps from people in the crowd.

As we headed toward the stage access door, Nova gave me a nudge.

"I'm so flammin' glad I don't gotta pack up a dang drum kit ever again! We shoulda gone public as magical girls way sooner!"

I laughed. "All the other drummers out there are going to be jealous."

"Maybe," Nova shrugged, "but they don't gotta fight monsters, so I figure it's a fair trade!"

I reached the stage door and opened it for her. As she walked through, Hana caught up and smiled at her.

"You'd rather fight monsters than lug around a drum kit?" Hana asked.

Nova nodded. "Fightin' creeps is way more fun!"

"I suppose you've got a point," Hana giggled.

As our rhythm section exited the stage, Cass walked up and I held the door open for her.

"How are you doing after all that?" she asked. "Gotta be the biggest rush on stage you've had so far."

"I was nervous, yeah, but I feel great," I said, honestly. "I'm not used to seeing so many eyes on me, but that was a blast."

Cass grinned. "That's what I like to hear! I'm glad you're feeling it. Me, I haven't played a show that good in a long time!"

She walked through the door and off stage, and finally, Sara followed. As she passed me, she gave me a smile, though I couldn't help but notice the tears in her eyes.

I knew she had to be full of complicated emotions right now. Tonight was Magica Riot's biggest musical triumph in two years. It was also the first show since we had all discovered that Sara's girlfriend, Iris, wasn't actually dead. Even though Iris was alive, she was still being occupied by the entity known as Bloom.

The same Bloom who had disappeared with Iris's body and mind after we saved the world.

To come so close to having the love of your life back only to feel her slip away again for some unknown period of time? It was entirely understandable that Sara would be delicate right now.

I stepped through the stage door and let it close behind me, muffling the crowd. Nova, Hana, and Cass were headed for the green room, but Sara stood there by the door, waiting for me.

"You did great, Claire," she said. "I needed to tell you that."

"That means a lot coming from you," I said. "Are you okay? I saw—"

"Yeah, I'm okay," she said. "It's just been a long time since we had a show go *that* well. Takes me back, y'know?"

I nodded. "Yeah. I hope I did justice to Iris's parts."

"Without a doubt," Sara said. "You two are different, but you're both good at what you do in your own ways. You learned to be your own magical girl, and you became your own musician, too."

"Aw, thank you. Maybe Iris can tell me that herself one day, if everything goes well."

She sighed. "I hope so." Then, she re-centered herself and motioned in the direction of the green room. "Let's go finish up. The others would never forgive us for skipping out on the victory party."

We made our way down the creaky wood hallway to the green room. The moment I stepped through the door, a pair of warm arms wrapped me up and held me tight.

My girlfriend—and Magica Riot's new band manager— Hazel Hoffman gave me a kiss, then broke away and beamed at me. "You all did *great!* Did you hear that crowd? They were eating it up!"

On the other side of the small room, Hikari Tomori, our new computer expert, nodded imperceptibly. They brushed their cyan hair away from the glasses in front of their amber eyes, and the faintest hint of a smile flashed across their face. When they spoke, it was in their usual monotone mumble. "For sure for sure you executed the maximum amount of rock allowed by physics and perhaps even a little more considering the magical nature of things I doubt anybody out there was disappointed in the quantity or quality of said rock."

"Yeah, the Magica Riot family's back on top, and I flammin' love it!" Nova shouted as she toweled off the sweat from her face. She draped the towel across her shoulders beneath her twintail hair, ran over, and put her arm around me, squeezing so tightly that I worried I might crack a rib. "And Claire cutie's finally got a real show to be proud of!"

"I still can't believe I got through it," I said, "but it feels good, yeah! Even if the stage fright was a little rough."

"Oh, don't worry," Hazel said, "you'll have plenty of other opportunities to work on that stage fright! I've actually got a surprise for you girls that I didn't want to tell you about until after the show tonight, because I didn't want to add even *more* anxiety."

From the back of the room, our team commander, the tough former rancher Meredith McCoy, let out a hearty laugh. "It's been a pain keepin' this from y'all, but I promised I wouldn't spoil the big news."

"Well, don't keep us hanging," Cass said. "Let's hear it!"

Hazel stepped to the center of the room, cleared her throat, and grinned. "Magica Riot's the most famous band on Earth now, right?"

"That's right," Hana said. "At least, for now, while we're the only public magical girls."

"Exactly," Hazel nodded, "and you just played your biggest show so far, yeah?"

"Right ..." Cass said.

"So what's the next step?" Hazel asked. "What's bigger in Portland than the Clarion Room and the Daedalus Theater?"

"Well, there's the Schnitzer, and the Keller," Sara said.

"Yeah, aren't those, like, twenty-five hundred seats? Three thousand?" I asked.

Hazel's grin broadened. "You need to think bigger! Way bigger!"

Nova made the connection first. "Wait a flammin' minute, babe! You ain't talkin' about—"

"I am," Hazel said. "What do you girls think about playing the Rose Garden Arena?"

The room went quiet for a moment before Cass spoke again. "Are you serious?"

"I'm very serious," Hazel said. "I'd been working on something at the Keller, but it was tracking to sell out so fast, the promoter and I worked out a chance to move it to the arena instead. You girls are *hot* now."

"How long do we have?" Sara asked.

"A month," Hazel said. "Short notice for something like that, but it's all about the numbers. There's that much demand to see the magical girl band that saved Portland."

"That makes sense," Hana said. "We showed the world that literal magic exists. That's bound to pique some curiosity!"

I shook my head in disbelief. "That's incredible, Haze. A little terrifying, but incredible."

"You girls are ready for it," Hazel said. "You're Magica Riot. This isn't even close to the most impossible thing you've done!"

"Can't argue with that," Cass laughed.

The commander walked over and stood beside Hazel. "Now understand, the final say's up to you girls. We want y'all to be comfortable with this. If you think you're ready, though, this'll be the biggest thing you've ever done, musically speakin' of course. And it'll give us some major income on top of what the Alliance spends on us. Always good to have some breathing room."

Sara looked to each of us. "What does everybody think?"

"Don't gotta twist my arm, babe," Nova said. "You couldn't keep me off that stage!"

"I agree with Nova," Hana said. "It's a wonderful opportunity!"

Cass nodded. "No way I'd miss this, boss."

Sara's attention fell to me. "And how about you, Claire?"

It would have been a lie to say I wasn't nervous about the idea. Twelve hundred people was one thing; if I walked onto a stage with fifteen or twenty thousand watching me, would I even be able to move? Would I remember to breathe? Would I have to transform into Riot Purple just to summon up enough courage?

On the other hand, it *would* be an amazing opportunity for the band, and after I'd made myself step up as a magical girl, I really didn't want to let them down as a performer. I took a deep breath, exhaled, and spoke.

"I think we should do it. Not saying it won't be a lot of work, but I think it's worth it."

"Yeah?" Sara asked.

"Yeah. Everybody's right. It's a huge chance to show the world who we really are again. We're magical girls, but we're also people."

Hana nodded. "A very important thing to show."

"That settles it, then," Sara said. "I feel the same way. Commander, Hazel … let's go for it."

"Yes!" Hazel exclaimed, pumping her fist. "You girls are going to do great!"

Hikari perked up from their laptop again and nodded. "For sure and I can't wait to get my hands on that arena's sound system do you know the kind of power one of those things puts out think about the possibilities think about all the laws of decency I can break with my engineering skills I'm gonna make you girls sound like a magical thunderstorm it's gonna be truly awe-inspiring and frightening and maybe even a little bit horny but you know in an auditory sense."

"See, it's even got the Hikari seal of approval," Nova said. "It's gonna be a big cutie crew party!"

"I'll start finalizing everything tomorrow," Hazel said.

Cass grabbed her bag from the floor and motioned for the exit. "Alright! I say we go have ourselves a celebration."

"I agree with that," Hana said. "Mom and Dad said they'd keep a private table open for us at the restaurant, if we wanted one."

"Sounds perfect," Sara said. "What do you say, Claire?"

I smiled. "Yeah. I could use some food. Let's go."

After dinner, we all hopped back into Vancent Price, the dark-gray extended-length 1993 Dodge van that had been transporting magical girls since the days of Portland's original protector, Jade Evergreen, and had seen more than his fair share of action.

I settled into the plush bench seat, upholstered in what I could only describe as "bordello red" cloth, and enjoyed the happy, warm combination of a full stomach and Hazel snuggled up against me. The sensation was pleasantly domestic, and I let my mind wander to thoughts of many happy days to come as Sara drove us around and dropped people off.

"Okay, here we are," Sara said, breaking my train of thought as she pulled Vancent up to the curb. "Hazel, does this look right?"

"Yeah, that's my apartment over there," Hazel said. "Thanks!"

I slid over and opened Vancent's double side doors, and stepped out to make room for Hazel as she exited. She took my hand, gave it a squeeze, and looked in my eyes.

"You okay?" she asked. "You seemed a little quiet."

I nodded. "I'm okay, yeah. Just having nice daydreams, I guess."

"What a coincidence," she said. "So was I." She leaned closer. "I'm so proud of you. You got through that show, and you did great."

"Aw," I blushed, "thanks, Haze. It felt good to finally do it."

"I'll bet," she said. She grinned and gave my hand another squeeze. "You know, if you're too tired to go the rest of the way to your apartment, you could just crash here."

I laughed and protested instinctively. "Oh, you don't have to do that, Haze. I know you're tired, too. I'll just head home. I should check on my apartment, anyway."

Hazel gave me an odd look and nodded. "Okay! We'll see." She smiled, leaned in, and kissed my cheek. "Goodnight, Claire."

I managed to croak out a "goodnight" as she turned to head up to her apartment. I returned to the van, only to find the rest of the band blocking the side doorway, giving me disappointed looks.

"Claire, what are you doing?" Cass asked.

"Um, going home?" I replied, as if I were unsteadily answering a teacher after being called on in class.

"Is that really the best course of action here?" Hana asked.

"I mean, that's where my bed is," I said.

Cass shook her head. "*Claire.* I ask again, what are you doing? Get up there and celebrate with her!"

"Didn't we already do that?" I asked.

"*Celebrate,*" Cass repeated.

Slowly, realization crept up on me. "Oh. *Oh!*"

Sara laughed. "You're such a useless lesbian. It's impressive."

"I just didn't want to bother her!" I protested.

"Pretty sure she's already bothered, if ya get my drift, babe," Nova said.

Cass grabbed the doors to pull them shut. "Go have fun, alright?"

"Consider it an order," Sara added.

"Understood," I said, already feeling the redness in my cheeks. "Thanks."

Hana giggled. "Goodnight, Claire!"

Satisfied that I'd been thoroughly educated, Cass closed the doors. Sara shifted Vancent into gear and pulled away from the curb. I stood there for a moment, more than a little embarrassed, before I turned and dashed up toward the steps to Hazel's apartment.

She was waiting for me by her door, her green eyes sparkling mischievously behind her shaggy blonde hair. "Mmhm. Thought so!"

"Yeah, sorry," I said, nervously rubbing the back of my neck. "I'm not so good at picking up on things."

"It's okay. I'll just have to make my signals a little more obvious!"

Before I could say anything else, she took my hand, pulled me close, and kissed my lips. Her kiss was warm and needful, and I felt my nerves melting away instantly.

With her lips on mine, she reached back with her free hand, opened her apartment door, and guided me inside. As the door shut, she broke our kiss, locked the door, and turned her gaze back to me.

She grinned. "C'mon, rock star. Let's *really* celebrate."

Her hands moved slowly and with purpose, taking me and guiding me toward her bedroom. Like every moment with Hazel since I'd come out, it felt exactly right. She made me feel safe and desired and cared for in ways I hadn't thought possible.

I closed my eyes, even as I felt joyful tears well up in them. Hazel fit me so well that it was hard to believe we hadn't been together for years. And, for a moment, I had the thought that I could see myself living like this, together with her, every single day. Maybe that was something we could talk about sometime.

For now, though, there was this moment.

———

The next morning, we made a slow, giggly breakfast together, and then it was back to business. Hazel had a meeting scheduled with the promoters about ticket prices, and I actually did need to check on my apartment.

I left her place and walked to the nearest Cycleburg station, where I grabbed an e-bike and set off for my apartment in Northeast, off Sandy Boulevard. The morning sky was cloudless and boldly blue, contrasting off the green of the trees passing overhead as I followed bike lanes and routes north across Burnside and into my part of town.

The whole way north, I felt like I was flying. That warmth from the night before carried over so effortlessly into the morning after. Spending time with Hazel—whether it was carefree or that happily harried time when we both had to be responsible adults—was so *right*. I'd found somebody who truly cared about me for who I really was, somebody who, despite my cluelessness, I cared about just as deeply.

It was so easy to imagine moving in with Hazel, or her moving in with me. Just making this *us*, with no asterisks. The thought made me feel fuzzy, and a huge grin broke across my face.

I pedaled faster, and laughed out loud to the city that had given me a life that was so much better than I'd ever dared to dream.

In short order, I reached my neighborhood. After stowing the bike at the nearest dock and walking the rest of the way to my apartment, I climbed the stairs and walked to my door, where I found an agitated figure trying to open the lock. I yelped, falling hard as I stumbled back.

All of this noise drew the attention of my mysterious guest, and as they turned around, I caught a better look at their long violet hair and their disheveled, but strangely familiar, clothes. They faced me and gazed down with unearthly red eyes and a wild expression, and I finally realized who it was.

"Bloom?!"

CHAPTER 2

There was no mistaking her: Menagerie Bloom, former leader of a trio of corrupted consciousnesses occupying the bodies of magical girls, who had very nearly unleashed Mistress Rennia and unspeakable ruin upon the world. After an unexpected impact with Vancent Price that woke up Iris's mind inside her, Bloom had grown a conscience and betrayed her sisters to help Magica Riot prevent that global cataclysm.

Now, she stood outside my apartment door, looking like a stray cat.

"Claire," she said, attempting to affect the theatrical voice she'd always used, but sounding weak and shaky. "I see you do actually return to your home. I was beginning to think you had taken up permanent residence in that drab underground tin can of yours!"

"Bloom, what the hell are you doing here? I thought you'd vanished to go figure yourself out."

She grumbled. "Are you aware that your grotesquery of a society requires currency to obtain even basic necessities?"

The thought of Bloom being turned loose in America with no

money hadn't occurred to me before. I clamped my hands over my mouth.

"Oh shit, you didn't have any money," I whispered between my fingers.

"Precisely," Bloom muttered. She stumbled forward, straddling me and leaning in closer. "It pains me to ask a *magical girl* for assistance," she said, chewing on the words like drywall, "but I require some things. A chance to bathe. Water. Food. Something called 'hormones.' And ... to talk about the next steps for me and this accursed do-gooder sharing my physical form."

"Bloom, I—"

"Claire, I am starving," she said. "We can talk once I'm not on death's door, okay?"

———

I brought Bloom inside and let her take a shower, telling her to take her time. While she cleaned up, I decided I needed to put together a meal for her. I wasn't exactly a professional chef, but I could feed somebody. The only question was *with what?*

My first obstacle was the basic matter of supplies. I'd been spending a lot of time with Hazel at her place, and as a consequence I'd let my grocery shopping atrophy a bit. I dug through my cabinets and the fridge, pulling together as much as I could. I hoped to get around my lack of knowledge about Bloom's tastes through sheer variety.

Some things were easy. I poured her a bowl of cereal, opened a bag of chips, gathered up some fruit that was still fresh, and threw together a quick sandwich. What if she needed more, though? I had some leftover rice that I'd made, so I brought it back to life and tossed some instant teriyaki noodles over it, along with some shredded cabbage that was still good.

It all looked pretty solid. It'd help her, which was the important thing. I was feeling rather proud of myself until a thought occurred: What about allergies? Did Iris's body have any? Would Bloom even know about them? What if I made her sick, and I—

The sound of the bathroom door opening kicked me out of my anxiety spiral.

Bloom emerged from the bathroom wearing my bathrobe, her hair wet, looking significantly more clean and calm than before.

"Feel better?" I asked.

"Mmph," she mumbled as she walked over to my couch and sat down. "From the smells in here, am I correct to assume you prepared food?"

"I did, yeah," I said as I brought the various offerings to the coffee table and laid them out for her, along with a pitcher of water and a glass. "I made a bunch of stuff, just to cover all the bases. Not that I had too much in the kitchen. Um, anyway, please, go on and eat."

She looked over the offerings, nodded silently, and dove in with ravenous energy.

I sat in a chair across from her as she guzzled the water and inhaled the food I'd set before her. Some minutes of furious eating followed before either of us spoke.

"So, um, is it good?" I asked.

She paused, and considered the question. "I do not know. It could be vile. I have no idea what I like yet."

A defense of my modest cooking skills flared up inside me. "What do you mean *vile?*"

"No matter," she said with a dismissive wave as she looked up at me and swallowed a bite of cereal. "I got quite some distance from your city before I realized I was experiencing an entirely new set of sensations. Apparently, Mistress Rennia's magica had frozen the biological processes of this body, so that it could serve the singular purpose of enacting her will."

"That means you never had to eat?"

"No eating, drinking, sleeping," she nodded, "none of the complicating factors of your human existence."

"I guess that explains how you and Burst and Blaze could be so dedicated to the cause."

"Precisely," she continued. "When Rennia was sealed away, the magica broke and those urges slowly returned. I do not know what food or drink I enjoy. I suppose I could call this food inoffensive, if I must."

"That's a start. If anything stands out to you, I can get you more of it."

Bloom frowned and stared deeply at the plates and bowls before her, and pointed at the cereal. "If pressed, I would say these crisped orbs bolster my dark heart."

"So you want more Peanut Butter Crunchlins?"

She nodded. "If you wish to express it in more pedestrian terms, yes."

"I can do that," I grinned. I got up, retrieved the box from the kitchen, and refilled her bowl before I sat back down. "So, um, where have you been while you've been dealing with these new needs?"

"I went northwest," she said, "until I found myself in a place called Astoria, sleeping on rooftops and stealing stale bread from a bakery to survive. And, I would like to add, feeling awful about it, thanks to this damned conscience festering in me."

"I don't think you need to feel bad about stealing food to live," I said as I reached over and refilled her glass from my water filter pitcher.

She frowned. "Not all of the people I have encountered on my travels would agree with you. Your society and its rules are terribly complex, and quite often infuriatingly nonsensical!"

I nodded. "You aren't wrong. You mentioned Iris's conscience. Does that mean she's alright? What does she think of all this? I remember when she popped up before, it caused you a lot of pain."

"She is dealing with things surprisingly well, considering the circumstances. She's very much still alive. In fact, she's getting stronger inside me by the day. And I no longer experience the distress I did when she became active before. I believe that was a side effect of Rennia's magica. With that gone, Iris is free to be as quiet or loud as she likes. That does mean she and I are a bit blurrier than before." She sighed. "This has all become rather complicated."

"*Become* complicated? Wasn't it that way before?"

"As Iris grows stronger, things in here—" she tapped the side of her head "—become more noisy. Indistinct. The wall between our consciousnesses becomes more permeable, and I experience more of her mind as if it were my own. And all the while, I'm trying to figure out what I even am now."

"How's that been going?"

She sighed. "Menagerie Bloom was a remorseless agent of chaos. Bloom, the creature before you, is a blend of that being and Iris Carr. Or perhaps she's a creature *colored* by Iris. It is hard to explain."

"Wow," I said. "That sounds like a lot to get used to."

She nodded. "Indeed. My sense of self is a mess, Claire."

"I know how that feels," I said. I sat back and nodded. "How can we help?"

Bloom leaned closer to me. "I want out. I want my own body. I want to be free of this confusing existence. And with Rennia gone, well, you magical girls are my best option, as loathe as I am to admit it."

"I know we'll do anything we can." I sat forward again and looked Bloom in her eyes. "You know that means going back to the Vault and meeting with everybody. Um, are you okay with that? You didn't seem to be last time you were around Sara."

Bloom frowned. "I expect it will be awkward, yes, but I have nowhere else to go. Perhaps it makes me weak, but that is my situation."

I shook my head. "It's not weak to ask for help. And helping's what magical girls do. I might still technically be the new girl, but I know that much."

Bloom laughed and rolled her eyes. "Corny as always." She

looked down at the empty plates and bowls before her and nodded with satisfaction. "Your food was *appreciated.*"

"You're welcome," I smiled.

Bloom leaned even closer. "Now, speaking of this body's needs … do you have any of those hormones I asked about?"

"Oh! Yeah, I do," I said, as I got up and grabbed my backpack off the floor near the front door. I dug around in it and pulled out a bottle of small blue pills. "Estradiol, coming up. Take two and put them under your tongue."

I handed her the pills, and she took them, slipping them beneath her tongue as I instructed. After a few moments, a satisfied look crossed her face. "Ah, yes, that's it. This body has been lacking that sensation."

"Um, stop me if this is a little personal, but I didn't realize Iris was, y'know, like I am. Trans, I mean."

"I think it simply never came up," Bloom said. "I've learned a lot of things from Iris and her memories. I had no idea such a subject was so fraught in human society."

I sighed. "Yeah, that's one way to put it."

"It is baffling," she said. "What concern is it to anybody but the individual what form they were given at birth, and what form they desire now?"

I nodded. "Human society has a lot of problems."

"So it would seem," she laughed. "Perhaps I should still try to rule over you people. I could, at least, avoid your many mistakes!"

I smiled and shook my head. "Let me get you some clothes, so we can head to the Vault. And no world-ruling, okay?"

She smirked. "No promises."

I managed to find some clothes that Bloom could tolerate. She settled on a pink T-shirt with mesh sleeves, a black skater skirt, and black thigh-highs, which was the most "tough" look I had in my wardrobe. We each also put on sunglasses, something that had become useful to Magica Riot since our unplanned magical girl reveal during the Rennia incident. They helped anonymize us, and in Bloom's case, with her red eyes concealed, she looked downright "Portland" with her borrowed outfit and violet hair.

With Bloom dressed, we walked from my apartment down to the Hollywood MAX station to board a Blue Line train headed downtown.

"Claire, do you not have your own conveyance?" she asked as I paid for her with my Hop card.

"I don't, no. This is Portland. I like to walk, and ride bikes, and take the bus, train, or streetcar."

She nodded. "I see. Perhaps it is understandable, given your propensity for hurling wheeled vehicles under your control into other people."

"Hey, I did that *once*," I laughed as I led her to a seat in the middle of the train. "And I really don't want to keep up with my own car. It saves me a lot of money. Besides, I left that kind of thing back in Texas."

Bloom considered this. "I am surprised that your Starlight Alliance doesn't reward you with riches for your work."

"Hey, *keep that down*," I said, attempting to hush her. "We're trying to be a little subtle right now. And you know that magical girls don't work for personal gain."

A handful of other people boarded the train. A few moments later, the doors closed, and we pulled away from the station. A casually dressed mother and her young daughter took the seats in front of us, and as the MAX picked up speed, the girl turned around in her seat and stared directly at Bloom.

Bloom stared back at her for several moments before acknowledging her with a smile. "Yes? May I help you, young one?"

"I like your hair," the girl said. "It's pretty!"

Bloom's smile grew into a broad grin. "Ah, I see you are a

child raised with taste. Perhaps your society is not entirely hopeless."

The girl's mother glanced back at us. "I'm sorry if she's bothering you. She loves purple."

"It's totally okay," I said. "We don't mind."

Bloom leaned forward. "If you fancy purple, child, what do you think of the purple magical girl who appeared in your city recently?"

I tensed. "Hey, uh, we don't need to—"

"Riot Purple?" the girl asked. "She seems nice!"

My tension immediately flipped over to delight. "Aw, you really mean it?"

The girl beamed. "Yeah! But … I think my favorite's Riot Blue! She's funny!"

Bloom burst out in uproarious laughter, loud enough to attract curious looks. "Well now, Claire! How does it feel to be usurped by the drummer?"

I chuckled nervously, and shrugged. "Honestly, that's fair. It's Nova we're talking about."

———

Bloom and I got off the MAX at the Old Town station, which put us beside Waterfront Park. We made our way past the crowds of people there, some of whom were simply enjoying the sun and the river, and some who were sightseeing around the area where Magica Riot had fought the invading Pandora Corruption army just four weeks before.

After we slipped past one of the construction crews repairing the damage from the battle, we took off our sunglasses and entered a maintenance door beneath the Burnside Bridge, descending into the old tunnel system that led down to the main entrance of the Vault.

At the security door, I activated the locks with my wrist link and waited as the heavy steel door slid open. Beside me, I noticed Bloom seemed to stiffen up, as if being back here made her tense.

"Um, are you okay?" I asked.

"I am fine," Bloom said. "I simply have some … *conflicted* feelings about this place."

"That makes sense. We did have kind of a bad fight down here."

Bloom shot me a sideways look. "A fight I won, I would like to point out. But there are Iris's feelings to consider, as well. This place holds meaning for her."

"And you feel that, too."

"Indeed." She stood straight, as if puffing herself up. "I must also face the others again. Claire, I …" She trailed off, the words caught in her throat.

"What?"

"Do not let me be captured."

"We're not going to capture you," I said. "I promise. It's going to be okay."

She took a deep breath, exhaled, and looked over at me. "I will hold you to that promise."

I smiled back at her. "Please do."

By then, the door had opened, and I led Bloom into the main corridor. The Vault's vast size stretched out before us, occupying two blocks of space beneath downtown Portland. At the moment, the corridor was quiet and empty, the rest of the team clearly occupied in other rooms.

I opened a comm channel to the facility's command center on my wrist link. "Commander? This is Claire, um, Agent Ryland. Could you assemble everybody? Something's come up, and we need to talk."

After a few moments, Commander McCoy responded. *"Agent Ryland? What sort of thing's come up?"*

"Um, something … Bloom-shaped," I answered.

There was a pause, and then the commander replied. *"Right.*

Got it." Another beep on the wrist link, as the line shifted to all users. "*Attention, attention. Agents Ward, Coates, Hasegawa, Nova, Barrera, O'Carolan, and Tomori. Report to the command center, ASAP.*"

"And so, I returned, and made my way to Claire's residence," Bloom said, concluding her tale of the last four weeks to the assembled team. "The rest should be obvious."

The room was quiet for a few long moments. Cass was the first to break the silence.

"So, have you had any sort of contact with Rennia in the last four weeks?"

"None whatsoever," Bloom said. "Believe me, magical girl, if Mistress Rennia was reaching back out to me, you would have found out by now."

"What about Blaze and Burst?" Hana asked. "They got away before we sealed the dimension gate."

"Nothing," Bloom said, as she shook her head. "I have no idea where my former sisters are, and I do not care. They were not especially fond of me when we last spoke."

Hikari nodded. "Yeah I think Bloom is being honest the sensor grid hasn't picked up anything there hasn't been so much as a flavor-blasted cheese puff of Menagerie vibes anywhere in Portland."

"Those girls are probably still dangerous," Commander McCoy said. "For all we know, *you're* still dangerous."

"I am always dangerous in some fashion, my dear commander," Bloom smiled. "I simply pose no danger to you or your city anymore."

I stared at Bloom, noting the change in her personality. She'd been vulnerable, even downright *human*, back at my apartment. Now, she'd switched back to her old ways. That wall of bluster and arrogance had gone back up. In a way, it made it clear she was feeling better now, but I wondered why she'd chosen me of all people to expose that softer side to.

The commander stared back at her. "That so?"

"I'll be saving my rage for those who wrong me directly, for the foreseeable future," Bloom said. "I trust that won't be anybody from the Starlight Alliance. We do have a mutually beneficial opportunity here, after all."

Sara looked up from her thoughts. "Yes, we do. You want your own body."

"And you all want your precious Iris back," Bloom said. "You, Sara Ward, most of all."

Sara nodded. "You're right."

"Well then," Bloom said, smiling back at her, "I should think my freedom for her life is a fair trade."

The commander sighed and turned to me. "Agent Ryland, she came to you first. Is it your honest assessment we can trust Bloom?"

I took a deep breath and nodded. "I think she's sincere, yeah. Bloom isn't Menagerie Bloom anymore. Whoever she is now, she's better than that."

"Why thank you, Claire," Bloom said. "That is, sincerely, the nicest thing anybody who's smashed my skull with a van has said to me."

Sara took a step closer to her. "Just know that we'll be keeping an eye on you. If you do anything to hurt Iris—"

"Oh, *please*, girl prince," Bloom shot back, "I have no more interest in hurting your girlfriend than I do in hurting myself. Which, of course, is the same thing for now."

"I have your word?" Sara asked.

"For whatever you think it's worth, you do," Bloom said. "As long as you all hold up your end of the bargain, I shall be on my best behavior. Do you magical girls do a pinky swear or something similarly cringey?"

"You don't gotta be a jerk about it," Nova said under her breath.

The team's resident physician and biologist, Dr. Marisol Barrera, raised her hand and stepped forward. "All of this will be academic if we can't find a way to separate them. Bloom, that's going to involve me doing a lot of tests on you."

"I expected as much," Bloom said.

"To be perfectly clear, I mean *a lot*," the doctor continued. "Nobody has ever done anything like this before, in all of the Alliance's recorded history. We will truly be operating beyond the edge of known science, medicine, and thaumaturgy."

Bloom frowned. "Yes, yes. Can you do it?"

"I don't know if anybody can do it," the doctor said, "but I will put all of my knowledge and the combined knowledge of the Alliance into being the first person who does."

"Aye, it'll be one monumental task," magical weapons armorer Saoirse O'Carolan said as she stepped forward beside the doctor, "but I'll help as much as I can. I've got engineering talent. I can adapt tools to do the job."

Hikari moved to join the doctor and Saoirse. "Yeah uh hi I don't think we've ever really met before but uh I have computer skills some might call mad if there needs to be programming or data crunching I can throw my brain sauce at it until it's nice and tasty I want to help I'm always up for mixing coding with mad scientist stuff."

"You see, Bloom?" Hana asked. "You're in the best hands for this in the world!"

Bloom's usual smirk curdled into a grimace. "That's not especially calming for my nerves, but so be it. When do we get started?"

"Let's you and I head down to the medical bay," Dr. Barrera said. "I'll get comprehensive starting points and decide on a path of action from there."

The commander nodded. "Sounds like a plan. Let's all get to work and see if we can't solve this problem."

CHAPTER 3

Bloom's first day in the Vault did indeed consist of a lot of time in the medical bay. While Dr. Barrera ran tests on her, the rest of the band and I and spent our day practicing some possible songs for the arena show and running combat drills in the training room.

I knew all of us were dealing with Bloom's return in our own ways, but the one that hit me the hardest was Sara. She'd opened up a lot after the fight with Rennia, regaining some of the warmth and good mood that the other girls had told me about from the band's old days. Seeing Bloom—still occupying Iris's body—walk back into her life had caused her to visibly regress to the serious demeanor she'd had during the dark days after Iris disappeared. The smile I'd gotten so used to on her face had vanished, replaced by the frown I knew too well.

I could only imagine the emotional rollercoaster she must have been going through.

After practice, as evening rolled around, it became obvious we all needed to figure out what Bloom's living situation was going to be.

It wasn't a surprise that she didn't want to live in the Vault, despite Dr. Barrera's insistence that she could make it comfortable. Though she wouldn't say why, I had to imagine the Vault reminded her of her Menagerie days. No, Bloom said she had made her decision already, and stubbornly stuck with it.

With *me*, rather.

Cass gave us a ride out to my apartment in Vancent Price and dropped us off. As the van drove away into the slowly deepening summer darkness, Bloom and I climbed the steps up to my door.

"You should feel honored to be blessed with my cohabitation," Bloom said.

"I totally do," I said, not entirely sarcastically, as I unlocked the door. "Why did you want to stay with me, anyway?"

She seemed to consider this for a moment. "I suppose it is because I feel completely unintimidated by you."

"Really? Why?"

Bloom stepped through the door and into the living room as I followed. "I admit, we have had our clashes, and you performed admirably. However, I now realize you have an unthreatening softness, like a prey animal. I think it rather unlikely you will hurt me in quite the same way again."

I couldn't help but smile a little at her blustery wall coming down again. "I'm not planning to. Just be good."

"Yes, yes, no global domination for the foreseeable future," she said as she plopped herself down on the couch. "This furniture shall be my domain, I think. It has a pleasing texture. Now, I trust there is a meal forthcoming?"

"Trying to figure that out," I said, as I looked through the kitchen. Bloom's earlier binge had emptied what few groceries I had. "Um, I'm a little low on, well, everything. Think I'll run down to the co-op and stock up. I don't suppose you'd like to come?"

She laughed. "The illustrious Bloom does not trouble herself with the mundane. Also, the relentless barrage of tests your doctor performed on me has sapped much of my remaining vigor."

"You know what? That's fair. Okay. I'll be back in a bit, then. Don't blow up the apartment while I'm gone."

Bloom stretched out and settled into the couch. "As long as you procure more of those crisped orbs, I shall engage in no such activities."

Satisfied that my apartment would still be there when I returned, I left and set out for the local grocery co-op. As I began my walk, I pulled out my phone and made a call. After a few seconds, it connected, and my favorite voice answered.

"Hey, rock star," Hazel said. *"How were things at the Vault today? I got busy working on logistics for the arena show and just stayed at my place."*

"Hey, Haze," I said. "Things were interesting. Um, this is going to sound a little random, but are you busy? I need some help with grocery shopping, and we need to talk."

"That sounds ominous. Is everything okay?"

"Everything's okay. I'm just, well, shopping for two, and that's what I need to talk to you about."

A few seconds of silence passed before she spoke again. *"Claire Ryland, did I get you pregnant?"*

"What? No! How would that even ... uh, you're going to have to keep trying on that. I did sort of pick up a stray, though. Can you meet me at the co-op?"

"Sure thing," she said, through riotous laughter. *"I'm on my way."*

———

A few minutes after I reached the grocery co-op, Hazel arrived on an electric Cycleburg bike. She locked it to a nearby dock and bounded up to me with a grin on her face.

"Did you get a cat?" she asked.

"Not exactly," I said. "C'mon, I'm basically out of food. I'll fill you in as we go."

We entered the co-op and I took a basket and headed for the

produce aisle, with Hazel beside me. I grabbed a head of lettuce as I started my explanation.

"Okay," I said. "Bloom's back."

Hazel's eyes went wide. "Excuse me? *Bloom* Bloom? Menagerie Bloom?"

"Yeah. Well, without the Menagerie part, but yeah. She was waiting for me at my apartment this morning."

"Wow. Is she okay?"

"She was in bad shape at first. Apparently, her biological processes restarted."

Hazel nodded. "Oh yeah, that'll happen."

"She'd never had to eat or drink or sleep, so she was having some trouble adjusting," I said. "She was looking a little rough. I let her take a shower and fed her, and then took her to the Vault."

"How'd *that* go?"

We turned onto the cold foods aisle and I picked up some more almond milk before I continued. "Probably like you'd expect. Some tension with Sara, understandably. Everybody being a little on edge. In the end, though, we're magical girls. We want to help her. So Dr. Barrera did some tests on her, and we all agreed to work on getting her and Iris separated."

"I'm glad to hear that," Hazel said with a warm smile. "I'm guessing that since you're 'shopping for two' now, Bloom's not doing the whole evil thing, and she's living with you?"

I nodded. "You nailed it."

Hazel stepped away, grabbed some large cartons of coconut water from a cooler, and came back. "This'll be good for her. So, you need help taking care of your new roomie?"

I paused. "Well, first, I wanted to make sure you were okay with it. Um, me and Bloom living together."

"Of course I am," she laughed. "Why wouldn't I be?"

"I mean, your girlfriend just brought home another girl."

"Claire, please," she said, as she shook her head. "I don't get jealous that way."

"You don't?"

"No way! You've got a magical consciousness thingy inside another girl living in your apartment! That's rad as hell. Besides, I *want* Bloom to be okay. I want you to help her! And I want to help you help her."

I smiled, feeling warmth in my chest at Hazel's deep reserves of kindness. "That's really sweet of you, Haze."

She grinned. "When you brought me into this whole magical girl world, I signed up for all of it. I'm here with you through everything." Her grin became more mischievous, a look I was quite familiar with by now. "And hey, I'm never going to be mad about more cute girls hanging around."

I felt a blush creep into my cheeks. "Now *that* doesn't surprise me at all."

"You know me," Hazel laughed. "What else do you need? Let's grab it and get back to your place. I want to see her!"

"There's a bunch more stuff on my list," I said as I led us down one aisle in particular. I stopped and grabbed three boxes of Peanut Butter Crunchlins off the shelf. "Most importantly, this."

"Sounds like somebody's got a craving," Hazel said.

I laughed. "Haven't you heard? Crunchlins bolster a dark heart."

———

We finished shopping and went back to my apartment. I unlocked the door and we stepped inside, both of us laden with grocery bags. "Okay, Bloom, I'm back, and I've got all the food we—"

I stopped. Bloom lay on the couch, her eyes closed, snoring softly. She was out cold.

"She's asleep," I said, my voice dropping to a whisper as I brought my bags into the kitchen. "Can't say I blame her, after the day she had."

Hazel walked quietly in and sat the grocery bags down on the counter as gently as she could before tiptoeing over to the couch. "Aww, look at her! Claire, she looks so *cute!*"

I smiled. "Good thing she can't hear you say that."

"Poor thing must be exhausted," Hazel said. "I should let her sleep. I'll definitely see her tomorrow at the Vault."

"You don't want to spend the night?" I asked.

"I don't want to have her wake up to a surprise guest, not without getting her permission to be here. I'm sure we'll do the slumber party thing sooner or later, so let's just let her get comfortable with everything first."

"That makes sense," I nodded. "Thanks for, well, everything, Haze."

"Always, rock star. You and me are in this together." She leaned in and gave me a long, soft kiss on the lips. "I'll see you tomorrow."

"See you tomorrow."

I walked Hazel back to the door and saw her out. Before she left, she paused. "Take care of her. I bet you're the closest thing she has to a friend."

"I've been thinking that myself," I said. "I'll take care of her, don't worry."

Hazel smiled. "Later, tater."

After I shut the door, I returned to the kitchen and put the groceries away as quietly as I could. Once that was done, I walked over and checked on Bloom.

She was incredibly peaceful, a description I never thought I'd use for her. In that quiet moment, Bloom reminded me of the image of Iris I had gotten when she'd come to me in that magica-induced dream a month before. She looked human and vulnerable, and I felt an even stronger sense of duty to take care of her.

I slipped away, retrieved a spare blanket from the closet, and returned to drape it across Bloom as she slept. That done, I moved quietly to my bedroom and climbed into bed. I was pretty exhausted myself after the day's revelations, and I knew it was only the beginning.

————

With Bloom's presence in our lives re-established, we all settled into a new routine.

At the Vault, Bloom underwent a barrage of tests with Dr. Barrera in the morning. When not in the medical bay, she prowled around the facility, regaling everybody with tales of her time with the Menagerie or talking with Saoirse and Hikari about possible technological solutions to the Iris situation.

I got the feeling that she enjoyed having people to talk to again, even if she'd never admit it out loud.

Meanwhile, the band focused on rehearsal. The big concert at the Rose Garden Arena loomed in the distance, and none of us wanted to be unprepared for our biggest performance yet. We had time to hone our skills, but the calendar days ticking away made sure that low-level anxiety kept bubbling up in me.

After a week of that relative normalcy, the universe decided it was time to shake things up again.

We had just finished combat practice, followed by rehearsal. I was wrapping things up in the music room when a strange feeling came over me. It gnawed at me, less an idea and more a hazy memory, or a dream I'd had as a child. It moved like smoke away from my grasp. But, even in its haziness, it felt comforting and warm.

There was something else accompanying the feeling: a tiny fragment of a melody I was sure I'd never heard before. So why did it sound so familiar? It wasn't a song. Not yet. But there was something there, something that felt *important*. It just needed to be shaped, and it could become something beautiful.

Without consciously realizing it, my hands danced along the keys of my keytar, playing what little there was of the melody. I rolled it over and over in my hands, feeling it snake between my fingers. There was definitely something there.

"Hey babe?" The voice belonged to Nova. "You okay? Whatcha playing?"

I'd spaced out. I shook myself from my concentration and looked up at her. "Oh, it's nothing. Just an idea I heard in my head. Thought I'd try to get it out."

"That's cool! You wanna be alone or something? I was gonna go down to the armory and see if Saoirse could tweak somethin' on my drums, so I thought you might wanna come with!"

"Yeah, that sounds good, I'll—"

Suddenly, our wrist links lit up with an incoming alert. I looked down at mine and tapped the screen. A yellow alert dialog box popped up that read *"INDETERMINATE MAGICA EVENT"* over a small map of Portland, with an arrow pointed toward a spot across the river from downtown on the inner east side.

I'd seen the sensor system call things an "unknown" event, and I'd seen identified ones. "Indeterminate" was something new.

"The flam's this?" Nova asked.

"It's vague," I said. "What causes an 'indeterminate' signal?"

Right on cue, the commander called from the other end of the facility.

"Agents Ward, Coates, Hasegawa, Nova, Ryland, and Tomori, report to the command center. We have an alert."

I raised my wrist and answered the call. "Got it, commander. Nova and I are on our way."

CHAPTER 4

In the command center, Commander McCoy, Hazel, Sara, Cass, and Hana stood looking up at a map of Portland displayed on a tight array of bare CRTs that lined the entirety of one wall. Hikari sat at their computer terminal, their face lit by the glow of the displays.

The commander greeted Nova and me with a nod as we entered; I noticed, for the first time, that she'd changed into a blue and gray jumpsuit, an outfit I'd never seen on her before.

"That's a good look, commander," I said as Nova and I joined the rest of the team.

Nova grinned and nodded in agreement. "Yeah! Real fancy-style of ya, big boss!"

"Thanks," the commander said. "We just got these from Alliance HQ for everybody. Snazzy, huh?"

She turned and showed us the shoulder. A circular patch with a field of rainbow-hued stars and a purple streak was sewn to it. Around the outside edge of the patch, lettering read STARLIGHT ALLIANCE - THE POWER OF HARMONY FOR ALL HUMANITY.

"Now, as to the alert, I'm sure y'all have seen it by now," she continued, and gestured to the map.

"We have, commander," Sara said. "Inner east side?"

"Yep. It's centered over Tempest Brewing, at Seventh and Lincoln."

"Any idea why it's called an 'indeterminate' alert?" Cass asked.

"That, we don't know," the commander answered. "Agent Tomori, do you have anything to add from a tech perspective?"

Hikari gave us a small wave. "Yeah uh so going by what I've seen about how the sensor system was programmed it says indeterminate when it's like a partial match to something in the database but it can't get any closer than that so whatever it is it's like kinda maybe something we know and kinda maybe something we don't if that makes sense."

"Something we know and something we don't," Hana said. "That could mean almost anything."

"Yeah for sure I think it's gonna need the up close and personal touch if you get my meaning you know in the magical girl punch kick rock out energy blast sense," Hikari said.

"Right," Cass said. "So it's time to roll."

"Flammin' magic weirdness," Nova said. "We'll figure it out, babes!"

Sara nodded. "Alright, let's head out and see what's going on."

Hazel looked at me with a nervous smile. "You girls be safe, okay? There's no telling what's going on from that reading."

"Always, Haze," I said. "We'll be okay."

I hoped that whatever was out there wouldn't make a liar of me.

We walked out of the command center and headed in the direction of the garage. As we passed the medical bay, the door slid open, and Bloom—still putting back on the clothes she'd borrowed from me—stumbled out and stood in our way.

"So, off to get a little action, are we?" she asked.

"We don't know, exactly," Sara said. "There's an unknown reading out there."

"Could be nothing," Cass added.

Bloom grinned. "Well then, if you're facing the unknown, why not take a little something unknown for yourself?" She pointed to herself with her thumbs. "Couldn't you use a sixth pair of eyes?"

Dr. Barrera appeared in the doorway. "Bloom, we still have more tests to do today."

"I'll submit to whatever tests you want, *later*," Bloom said.

Sara shook her head. "Whatever Dr. Barrera says, goes."

"Oh come on," Bloom said, throwing herself at us. "I've been in this glorified rabbit warren for days now! Let me get a little fresh air and violence, too!"

"We aren't about violence, Bloom," Hana said. "Not unless it's needed."

"Yeah, if we gotta punch a creep, we will, but it ain't the goal," Nova said.

"Whatever, whatever," Bloom said. "Still, safety in numbers, and all that. Claire, what about you? Can't you lean on your band leader here?"

I stammered out an attempted answer. "Well, um, I don't know if that's really—"

"You know," Dr. Barrera interjected, "it actually might be beneficial to let her get some fieldwork in. She *does* have Iris's experience, after all. If she takes a wrist link, we can get some quality sensor data on her bio signs in real-world scenarios."

Bloom smiled at Sara smugly. *"Whatever Dr. Barrera says, goes!* See? Once more, our goals align!"

"Alright, fine," Sara said, "but if you get reckless, I'm pulling you out. We need to keep you and Iris unharmed."

"Don't worry, girl prince, I won't break your girlfriend," Bloom shot back. "Now, hook me up with one of your fancy little wristbands."

Dr. Barrera returned to the medical bay, and a few moments later, emerged with a spare wrist link. She fastened it around

Bloom's left arm and tapped a sequence of prompts on the screen to activate it.

"Bloom, you're online now," she said. "Most of what you'll need will be self-explanatory via the on-screen commands."

Bloom swooned theatrically while cradling the link in her other hand. "Oh, goodness gosh! I'm official now! Are we going to have a sleepover to celebrate? Maybe do each other's nails?"

Cass laughed. "Usually, we save that for after the fight."

"If we're all done here, we have an alert to deal with," Sara said. "Magica Riot ... and Bloom ... move out!"

———

Tonight was my turn at the wheel of Vancent Price. Cass sat in the front passenger seat, with Sara and Bloom sitting awkwardly together in the second row and Hana and Nova in the third. With the "indeterminate" alert reading growing stronger, I guided Vancent across the Burnside bridge and south down Martin Luther King, Jr. Boulevard toward the source.

We reached the brewery, and I pulled up to the curb and parked. As we got out of Vancent, I could hear the crowd noise of a typical Friday night at a Portland brewery drifting by on the breeze.

Sara led us through the brewery's front door and into the main room. As I'd expected, the place was packed. Tables were full of guests, and the bar in the center of the room was busy as well. Out on the patio, the picnic tables were all occupied by people drinking and having a generally spectacular time of it.

It would have been a completely unremarkable scene for any given Portland brewery, except for the robots.

Circulating through the crowd were several robotic dogs, their bodies rectangular and made of metal and plastic. Four slender legs extended down from the corners, while the front carried a head covered in camera lenses and other sensors. I recognized them from *The Hermes*, one of Portland's alt-weekly newspapers. Those reports had talked about them being used by the military or police and equipped with weaponry, but these dogs had some kind of storage box mounted to their backs.

Another robot stood behind the bar. This one was humanoid, rather than canine. It was gray and black, with a boxy body and articulated limbs topped by a smooth "head" with a glowing light bar across its face, likely concealing even more sensors. The bar's actual human bartender stood beside it, looking visibly annoyed.

The sight was unexpected and confusing, and I wasn't the only one feeling that way.

"The flam is all this?" Nova asked.

Cass frowned at one of the dog bots as it passed us. "Did we miss the robot apocalypse while we were stopping the magic apocalypse?"

"I've seen these robots on the internet," Hana said. "Rhapsodyz makes them."

"Rhapsodyz? The tech company in Beaverton?" I asked.

"Yeah, that's the one," Sara said. "They have a robotics division, along with a division for basically everything else."

Beside me, I noticed Bloom looking pale.

"Bloom?" I asked. "You okay?"

"I'm fine," Bloom said. "Just a bit ill, is all. You don't feel that?"

"Feel what?"

Her face turned sour and she ran a hand across her stomach. "This place is noxious. Like something curdled in the fabric of space."

I tuned out the noise and buzz of the crowd and focused. Somewhere down deep, I *did* feel a little discomfort. It was as if there was a sound outside of my range of hearing, but which I could sense in my body, a sound that was severely out of tune.

"Yeah, I do feel it a little," I agreed.

Bloom stared back at me in disbelief. "A *little?* My stomach feels like it's being pulverized!"

"I feel it, too," Cass said. "It's subtle, but it's there."

Hana shot Bloom a sympathetic look. "Poor Bloom. I'm sorry you're so sensitive to it, whatever it is."

Sara raised her wrist link and called up the scanner. "These readings are strange, like they're blurry. I'm not picking up anything more definitive now that we're here."

"Maybe that's because of all the robots," Hana said, checking her own link. "There's a lot of interference here."

"Let's report back, and then start asking around," Sara said. "One of the customers or the bartender might have noticed something."

Cass raised her wrist link and opened a comm channel back to the Vault. "Commander, this is Coates. We're on-site. Nothing unusual yet, except for some robots."

"Robots? Did I hear that right?" Commander McCoy answered.

"They're serving drinks," Cass said. "Tech bro stunt, probably. We're investigating."

"Acknowledged. Stay on the alert, and be ready for anything. Don't go hot unless you need to. McCoy out."

"Alright," Sara said. "Let's see if we can get some answers."

The six of us walked up to the bar and waited as the bartender, a shorter guy with a soft face framed by a full beard, stepped around his robotic companion to come greet us.

"What can I ... oh, hey, you're Magica Riot," he said. "Wild to see you here! You come for drinks, or something else?"

"Something else, actually," Sara said. "Has there been anything unusual happening here tonight?"

The bartender glanced back at the robot behind him. "You mean other than these overgrown aluminum cans making a mess of things? Naw, been a pretty normal night."

Now that we were closer, I realized the robot at the bar was actually bartending, or at least *trying* to bartend. A couple of customers were attempting to order drinks from it, and it wasn't going well.

"I don't even have all that," one of the customers said, the irritation in her voice obvious even from down the bar.

"I apologize, citizen!" the robot chirped back in a processed, clearly AI-generated voice. "I require a valid government ID and copy of your birth certificate, with clearly marked legal name and sex assigned at birth, to serve you!"

"No, you *don't*," the bartender shouted back at the robot, before calling to the customer. "Friend, I'm so sorry. I'll be right with you."

"That robot seems pretty awful," Cass said.

"And flammin' gross, too," Nova said. "What's the deal?"

"These things are 'a promotional installation by Rhapsodyz,'" the bartender said, applying air quotes liberally. "Showing off their whole 'Future of AI 8K Metaverse' thing, whatever that is."

Hana watched the customer arguing with the robot for a moment. "Seems like the future may not be fully baked."

"They're the worst," the bartender said, as he motioned to the robot working alongside him. "This jerk isn't serving trans customers. The dogs are supposed to be carrying food around in those little boxes on their backs, but the QR codes don't work half the time, so you can't get the food out. And they keep wanting to see proof of American citizenship. It's weird."

Cass shook her head. "I heard that Rhapsodyz CEO had gotten in with some real bad political crap, so I guess I shouldn't be surprised."

Nova made a disgusted face. "Sounds like a dang loser!"

"Excuse me, booze jockey," Bloom said. "Why do you not simply destroy these robots?"

"Uh, well, I honestly wouldn't mind that," the bartender answered, "but Rhapsodyz paid the owners, like, thirty thousand dollars to host this, so I've been told not to touch them."

Cass laughed and shook her head. "Boss makes a dollar, you make a dime, babysitting robots on company time."

"Tell me about it," the bartender sighed.

"Other than robots, there's been nothing else strange here tonight?" Sara asked.

"No, nothing else," the bartender said. "Why do you ask? Is there something we should—"

Our wrist links lit up with a new, urgent alert. I looked down at the screen, which now glared with a much more specific warning that nevertheless left me confused.

"Um, hey, what's a Marelian Incursion Event?" I asked.

Sara's eyes went wide, and she looked around the room, muttering under her breath. "Not now. Please, *not now!*"

The brewery darkened and the air turned chilly. Black tendrils of mist snaked their way around the edges of the room, slowly reaching toward the center. Customers screamed in shock and ran away from the mist, more than a few dashing out the brewery's front door.

"Aw, flam," Nova said, "I ain't seen *this* in a while!"

"What's going on? What is this?" I asked.

"I'm lost as well," Bloom said. "Iris recognizes it, but the memory is hazy."

"It's a big problem, is what it is," Hana said.

Cass tensed and raised her fists. "I knew I had a bad feeling. We need to go hot, boss."

"Agreed," Sara said as she stepped forward and raised her hand high. With a flash of red magica, her thaumatite-encrusted microphone materialized in her grasp, and she brought it down to her lips. The rest of us followed suit with our own mics.

"Transformation ready!" Sara shouted into her mic. "Maidensong harmony power ... go live!"

"Aw, beans!" the bartender yelped as he dove behind the bar.

I felt time slow as the Maidensong rang out through my mind and heart, saturating me with a massive surge of magica. Sara, Cass, Hana, Nova, and I were engulfed in rainbow energy and shot up through the dimensional barrier, ascending to the Celestial Stage. A gigantic glowing sigil appeared beneath us, and the intricate crystal lattice dome above the stage shone in the darkness of space.

Our street clothes blasted off our bodies in a torrent of light, replaced piece by piece with our magical girl costumes. Black skirts trimmed with our respective colors materialized on us, followed by our jackets and bows.

I felt the euphoria of transformation wash over me, and as my black fingerless gloves formed on my hands and my boots on my feet, I joined hands with the other girls, the final blast of magica tinting our eyes and hair with our colors.

Echoing across the cosmos, the voice of the Maidensong itself spoke the completion of the transformation. *"THOSE EXALTED BY THE MAIDENSONG SHALL WIELD THE POWER OF HARMONY."*

The five of us were again wrapped in rainbow light and shot back through the dimensional barrier. We blasted in a Technicolor torrent down to the brewery, re-emerging into the physical world as if we'd been standing there the entire time.

"We are the guardians of song and heart," Sara said. "Guardian of Lyricism, Riot Red!"

"Guardian of Melody," Cass yelled, "Riot Yellow!"

"Guardian of Rhythm, Riot Green!" Hana shouted.

Nova posed beside her. "Guardian of the Beat, Riot Blue!"

"Guardian of Harmony, Riot Purple!" I said, my voice far more forceful than before. "Servants of the darkness, be silenced by the song of Magica Riot!"

Beside me, Bloom snapped her fingers. A torrent of angry crimson magica swirled around her, and moments later, she emerged from it in her black corset dress, gloves, and boots.

"And their superior, the illustrious Bloom!" she shouted.

"Superior?" Cass asked.

Bloom shrugged. "We didn't exactly rehearse this part!"

A moment of silence passed before an echoing voice, its timbre warm and rich, danced around us from all sides, as if the mist itself were speaking.

"Well now! This is a reunion I've been looking forward to!"

The tendrils of black mist swirled together more tightly, like spider silk around its prey, and took a humanoid shape. Gradually, the shape solidified, until it finally coalesced into a woman unlike any I'd seen before.

I had never been great at estimating heights, but she must have been at least seven feet tall. Her face seemed almost chiseled, striking and beautifully cold, her figure curvaceous and strong. She had shark-gray skin, smooth and youthful; however, something about her expression told me that if she was any age at all, it was probably in the hundreds of years. It was impossible to tell.

Her ears were long and sharply pointed, elven, definitely not human. She had eyes of vivid turquoise, which matched the color of the voluminous, swept-back mohawk atop her head. She wore an immaculately tailored black suit that accented every one of her intoxicating features, accompanied by a red shirt unbuttoned most of the way down her chest, revealing cleavage that went well beyond "ample." Polished black boots gleamed on her feet.

A moment after she appeared, a staff as tall as she was materialized in her right hand. The staff was made of deeply burnished wood, topped by a complicated array of patterned gold rings and inky black thaumatite crystals.

The woman raised her other hand, turning it back and forth in front of her eyes as if inspecting herself. Then she looked at us and smiled, her velvet black lips curling up in a way that would have been alluring if it weren't so chilling.

"Magica Riot, my old friends," she said, her voice luscious, but growing more pointed. "You once again find yourself in the presence of the seventh-generation diviner of the twelfth-dimensional House of Marelia. The keeper of the arcane dark arts of the Undertow! Life-sworn wielder of the Staff of Sorrows! The one, and only, Grand Cosmic Sorceress Makula!"

I gulped and whispered to Sara. *"That's* Sorceress Makula?"

Sara nodded to me before turning her gaze back to our new guest. "What do you want, Makula?"

"Still gettin' over the last time we kicked your dang butt and sent you crawlin' back to the Undertow?" Nova asked.

"There'll be time for that shortly, my dears," Makula said. "I still have some introductions to make."

In the span of a heartbeat, she vanished in a cloud of mist and reappeared directly in front of me.

I froze, not sure if I should try to run. She leaned down close to my face and cradled my chin in her hand as she stared into my eyes. Even from simple visual observation, I could sense the tremendous magica in her, resonating in those sparkling eyes.

"You wear the costume of Riot Purple," Makula said, "but I don't know you, pretty girl."

"Um, I'm the new Riot Purple," I said. "Claire."

She smiled. "Ah, that explains it. And it also explains *this* one." She moved toward Bloom, who stepped back and glared at her.

"How *dare* you approach me?" Bloom snarled. "Back, or I shall—"

Makula leaned in and placed a finger on Bloom's lips. "I never forget a face, Iris, but there's something else at play." She sniffed the air beside Bloom's head, and nodded. "Oh, there is *quite* a story here. A hero, trapped. An evil, torn from its master, given the curse of morality. And you ..."

"Bloom."

"Yes. Magica itself, given life," Makula said, nodding. "What a fascinating creature you are, Bloom! Roughshod craftsmanship, but such ambition!"

"Who are you calling roughshod?" Bloom asked. "I was created by Lord Mistress Rennia herself!"

"Ah, Rennia! I am familiar with her as a servant of the great corruption, yes," Makula said. Her eyes scanned Bloom's face, the curiosity plain in her expression. "And you are another fascinating example of that same power. Far more intricate than those mindless creatures you call the Pandora Corruption. So many secrets to unlock."

"That's enough," Sara said. "Why are you back in Portland?"

Makula shook her head as she paced back and forth in front of us. "It's shameful what inferior beings have been doing with magica here yet again. There must be something about your soggy, moss-besotted city that compels you to dabble in things you should not touch."

"The flam are you talkin' about?" Nova asked.

"Feigning ignorance will not help," Makula continued. "I sensed the ripples in the cosmic torrent, all the way back in the Undertow. Corruption magica run rampant, wielded with no understanding. And you magical girls! You and your Maiden-song are behaving so irresponsibly."

I made the connection quickly. "You mean our true powers."

"That's what you call them?" Makula asked. "But yes, quite astute, my new Riot Purple."

Cass scowled at her. "There's nothing irresponsible about our new powers."

"Not at all," Hana said. "We used them to save the world."

Makula ignored her and continued. "You humans are again wielding magica like a blunt club. Look at these senseless, inelegant automatons. Like handing a bomb to a child! How dare you sully the most sublime force of the universe in this way!"

"We didn't have anything to do with these bots," Cass said. "They're just some crappy tech company's new toys! They don't have any magica in them!"

"I beg to differ, Riot Yellow," Makula said. "The stink of amateurish magica saturates these things! Not that they will prove to be a challenge for me."

One of the robot dogs wandered between us and Makula, and she grinned. With a single, fluid motion, she brought the head of her staff down onto the robot's back and blasted it with magica, severing its metal frame and sending it flopping to the floor with a metallic *thunk*, completely inert.

"As expected," Makula said. "Truly pathetic. Now, for the rest …"

She raised her staff and swirled it around above her head. A wave of magica rolled out across the brewery, and in its wake, all the other robots seized up, went dark, and fell over.

At the same moment, I felt the strange sensation we'd noticed fade away. It wasn't just me, either, as Bloom looked visibly relieved and less nauseous the instant the robots went dead.

The prospect that Makula was right about the robots, at least, was suddenly more believable.

Makula looked down at us smugly. "There! Your sad little automatons pose no challenge!"

"We had nothing to do with this!" Hana shouted back.

Makula laughed. "You expect me to believe this is only a coincidence? Oh well, truthfully, it matters not who created these beings. I put them back in their place, and now I shall do the same to you!"

"Try it, sorceress, and you'll be very sorry!" Bloom threatened as she summoned Iris's keytar.

I was about to call down my own keytar to fight, but suddenly, I was no longer in the brewery.

CHAPTER 5

I was alone.

The brewery had vanished. Instead, I stood inside a huge cylindrical chamber. I ran over to the wall and pounded on it, and hollow metallic sounds echoed through the space.

"Hello?" I called out, unsure if anybody could even hear me through the metal, or if there was anybody *to* hear me. "Red? Yellow? Green? Blue? Um ... Bloom? Is anybody there?"

Silence. I reached down and tapped my wrist link to open a communication channel, but a glaring red error message greeted me.

COMMUNICATION ERROR. UNABLE TO PING CENTRAL SERVER.

Alone, *and* out of communications range. Wherever I'd wound up, I would have to escape on my own.

I glanced around the chamber. The entire space was smooth and featureless, with no obvious exits. My gaze moved up along the curved metal walls until I reached the top, which was similarly featureless except for a circular hole cut into the exact center of the chamber's ceiling, one sealed with some kind of hatch.

Okay, that was a start. It'd be simple enough to reach it, not that I knew exactly what to do once I got there.

I concentrated and summoned a circular sigil of magica beneath my feet, calling upon the spell that let us launch ourselves into the air. With a bit of mental calculation, I judged the height up to the hatch. The sigil's intricate geometric patterns and symbols spun up, and a moment later, I shot upward toward the hatch.

Moments later, I reached the ceiling as my momentum slowed. I summoned another sigil to stand on and reached up to examine the hatch. There had to be some way to open it.

There wasn't, of course. I wasn't *that* lucky.

I thought for a moment. Whatever metal this was, it probably couldn't hold up to a charged blast of magica. I could use my keytar, and—

Mid-thought, the portal opened. A circular tunnel rose upward, fading into darkness.

"Huh," I said out loud.

I couldn't see where the tunnel led, but it was the closest thing to an exit I had. I prepared to launch myself with another sigil.

And then, the sound of gurgling filled the tunnel.

An instant later, a rampaging torrent of foamy, amber liquid blasted me in the face. The force smashed into me and tossed me off my sigil. I plummeted back to the floor and landed hard. The liquid poured down on top of me in an unceasing torrent.

I rolled out of the way and got up on my knees, coughing and trying to catch my breath. The taste in my mouth was unexpected, bitter and frothy with a distinctive floral note. And that's when it hit me: The liquid was beer.

I was inside an enormous keg.

The beer gushing into the keg was steadily filling it, so escape became more urgent. Leaving through the hatch was now out of the question, so I considered my options. There was only a single route left that seemed obvious, so I decided to take it.

I summoned my keytar from the aetheric plane and aimed at the wall of the keg. I played the chorus riff from "Charlatan," the chugging syncopation charging the keytar for a powered-up blast.

With any luck, this wouldn't end with me being hit by a ricochet. I took a deep breath, and fired.

My magica sliced through the metal wall and left a jagged hole behind. Beer sloshed over the edge of the hole, spilling out into whatever lay beyond and ending the danger of drowning in the world's most alcoholic swimming pool.

My good luck briefly re-established, I ran over to the hole and peered out.

A levitating path made of wooden brewing barrels extended away from the giant keg. Spiraling rings of floating bricks encircled the path, forming a tube leading off to whatever lay at the end.

There appeared to be no other options; apart from the path, there was nothing but inky blackness surrounding the giant keg. It definitely felt too easy, and I suspected I was doing exactly what Sorceress Makula had wanted me to. That didn't change the fact that it was my only way out.

I stepped out onto the first barrel, checked that it would hold my weight, and made my way along the path.

The floating barrels were stable, and I made the trip in short order. The final barrel hovered in front of a heavy-looking wooden door with an iron knob. I grasped the knob and swung it open, and for several long moments, all I could do was stare.

Beyond the door lay a view that was simultaneously awe-inspiring and completely impossible. A cavernous outdoor space with a long, perfectly straight brick path extended out through mid-air, ending in a round brick structure. There was a sky, but it was *below* the path; an endless blue full of fluffy white clouds drifting by beneath me, and apparent sunlight filtering in through them from farther below. Above me lay an enormous field, from which massive plants grew down toward me, dozens of feet tall in narrow columns planted evenly along the field.

The longer I observed them, trying to make sense of any of the things I was seeing, the more clearly I saw that some of the plants were *moving*.

Not walking around, but whipping over and attacking something on the "ground" that I couldn't see, as if they were all fighting some invasive animal dashing through the field. Whatever was causing this was approaching me, and as I watched the action getting closer, I started to hear the distinctive sounds of magica blasts and laughter.

Suddenly, a shot of red magica lanced through the air above my head, and I watched a series of plants collapse above me and fall up onto the ground. Standing there in the center of the scorched plants was a figure in a black corset dress, gloves, and boots, with long violet hair.

Bloom.

She fired another shot from Iris's keytar into more of the plants and cackled at the top of her lungs. "Ha! Take *that*, you … uh … *photosynthetic freaks!*"

"Bloom?" I called out. "Can you hear me?"

She looked "up" at me down on the sky path. "Claire? What the barren blasted hells are you doing up there?"

"I was going to ask you the same thing!"

"Ah, well, alright then," she said as she nodded. "Do you know where we are? We seem to be in the ass-end of madness!"

I shook my head. "I don't know, but I'm guessing Makula is involved."

"Most likely. Wait a moment!"

Bloom summoned a magica sigil beneath her and launched herself down toward the path in the "sky." Just as she neared me, she slowed and started to fall back toward the ground.

I reached out to grab her hand. The instant we touched, she reversed course and fell to the path, smacking into the brick surface with a thud.

"Aaaa! What was that all about? Are you trying to wreck this radiant form of mine?" she asked.

"I didn't do anything!" I said. "Me touching you must have, I don't know ... reversed your gravity, or something!"

She got up, dusted herself off, and shot me a withering look. "You must be more careful. I've still got Iris's body, after all. If anything happened to it, I know all of you goody-goodies would be devastated."

I was starting to get a little irritated by her constant dismissal of the idea that we wanted to help her, too, not just Iris, and my annoyance got the better of me.

"I know you don't think much of magical girls," I said, staring her square in the eyes, "but is it really so hard for you to believe that we care about *you*, too? I've stood up for you more than once now!"

Bloom stepped close to me and pressed her face close to mine. Her red eyes glared at me. "I'm not naïve, Claire. I saw how Sara and the others looked at me in the Vault. I'm little more than—" She stopped herself, frowned, and recomposed. "When, and if, the time comes to remove me from this body, you had best believe I'll be finding a way to come out on top. I'm not going to let anybody do otherwise to me."

In situations like this before, when I'd been closeted, I'd always backed down. Ever since I'd become a magical girl—and *especially* since our true powers unlocked—I'd felt the confidence grow stronger in me. And so, in a way I'd never done before, I let Bloom have it.

I moved closer to her and refused to break eye contact. "Sara has understandable reasons to feel scared. It doesn't mean we aren't going to help you. We all want to. We're magical girls, Bloom. That's what makes us different from villains like Rennia."

She snarled. "Don't you *dare* speak Mistress Ren—"

"We're only having this delightful conversation because we defeated Rennia in the first place," I interrupted. "All of us have gone way off-book here. Nothing's guaranteed, but if there's a way to save both you and Iris, we're going to do everything we can to find it. So let us help you, damn it!"

Bloom silently fumed for a moment. "I thought you magical girls didn't use such naughty words."

"We don't around Nova," I said, "but Nova's not here right now. I am. And I want you to know that I understand not wanting to let other people tell you how to live. I'm going to try my best to give you the same freedom I found. I just need you to make an effort to trust us."

I half-expected her to punch me, but after a few more moments of silence, she laughed. "I have to admit, Claire, I'm impressed. You've grown such a backbone in the time I've known you."

"It's part of being a magical girl."

She sighed. "Well, magical girl, how about we find ourselves a way out of Makula's brewery funhouse? I'll make no progress on my freedom if I'm stuck in here fighting the flora."

"Deal," I said. I looked back up at the giant plants above us. "What *are* those things, anyway?"

"They're hops," Bloom said. "Giant hop plants. Giant *evil* hop plants."

"You know what hops are?"

"I don't, but Iris does. I think she's a beer aficionado. Now, why there are massive hop plants trying to kill us, neither of us have any idea."

"It's all making a little more sense to me, actually," I said, and pointed back in the direction I came. "I just escaped from a giant keg. It's like somebody took a bunch of things from the brewery and turned them into some kind of fantasy world with no rhyme or reason."

"So we know this Makula is no brewer," Bloom said. "How do we escape this place?"

I motioned toward the circular structure at the end of the path. "We can't go back the way I came, and I really don't want to fight a bunch of giant hop plants, so I think we move forward and check that place out."

"Seems as good an idea as any," Bloom said. "Lead the way, magical girl."

"You don't want to go first?"

She shook her head. "I wouldn't want to deprive you of being the brave hero, now would I?"

I couldn't help but laugh. "Okay, fine. Let's get mov—"

I paused. In the brewery, Bloom had been in obvious discomfort. Here, in this odd place, she seemed fine.

"Are you feeling okay?" I asked. "You weren't doing too great back at the brewery, but you looked like you felt a lot better after Makula killed the robots."

"I feel perfectly fine now, yes," Bloom said. "I can only assume that whatever vile energies affected me came from those accursed automatons."

"That makes me wonder what's inside them," I said.

Bloom laughed. "Your bloodlust is admirable! Perhaps you will find out. For now, onward into the unknown, magical girl."

We reached the circular building and walked in through its open wood door. The space inside was made of brick and wood that matched the interior of the brewery. Three more heavy wood doors lay along the wall opposite the entrance; all three were closed, and I felt a twinge of dread about what might be waiting behind them.

"Which way?" Bloom asked.

"I don't know," I said. "You think this is one of those things where if we choose wrong, we'll get killed?"

Bloom frowned at the doors. "I'd like to see this Sorceress Makula try! I swear, when we encounter her next, she *will* feel pain!"

As if in response, the trio of doors creaked open.

"Claire, do you see this, too?" Bloom asked.

I sighed. "Yeah. Yeah, I see it."

Three hulking, clanking robotic forms stepped out of the

doors. They were taller than us, maybe even slightly taller than Makula herself was. Their components looked familiar, but it took me several moments to identify them.

They were made of brewing equipment. Torsos constructed from brewing tanks. Arms and legs assembled from pipes and hoses and valves. Heads formed by dials and levers.

And all three were now heading directly for Bloom and me.

Bloom summoned Iris's keytar again. "They want a fight, Claire."

"I think you're right," I said as I called down my own keytar. "Do you know any songs?"

"I've had 'Like You' stuck in my head since that day we invaded your Vault," Bloom said. "With Iris's guidance and our body's muscle memory, I'll more than keep up."

"Right," I said. "Stick with me, and let's do it! One, two, three, *four!*"

I played the opening riff of "Like You" as Bloom joined in on the chord progression. She was shaky at first, but I could feel her starting to lock in as she drew upon Iris's experience.

The trio of constructs bore down on us, their pipe arms raised in unthinking aggression. I tensed and leapt into an attack run with Bloom hot on my heels. As I played, magica surged through my keytar. With luck, I could string together a series of moves in coordination with Bloom to bring all three creatures down at once.

Fortunately, whatever strange place Makula had transported us to hadn't dulled the power of the Maidensong flowing through me.

We ran at full speed toward the construct on the right as the others shifted their path to follow us. I aimed at the construct ahead of us and loosed a charged burst of magica from my keytar directly into its chest, as Bloom fired her own shot at its head.

The fully charged twin shots smashed into the construct and blasted out the other side, sending ragged metal pieces flying as it crashed to the floor. Without missing a beat, I shoved off with my right leg and changed direction, flinging myself at the construct on the left as it lunged for us.

"Bloom," I shouted, "hit the legs!"

"With pleasure!" Bloom laughed.

Behind me, I heard Bloom fire another shot that streaked past me and sliced into the construct's legs. It tried to shift its weight to compensate, but tripped up and stumbled toward me. As the distance between me and the construct shrank, I shifted my grip on my keytar and swung it out ahead of me. The glimmering purple energy blade within it materialized from the body, glowing and ready to strike.

I sliced up into the second construct as it fell forward onto the blade. Rending metallic sounds filled the air as I shoved the magical blade through and ripped apart the construct before it could react.

That left only the third construct. It moved a bit more cautiously now after what had happened to its companions, but it still advanced on me. As it neared, it pulled back its arms to strike.

I shifted course toward my sole attacker. The numbers were on our side now, and one more trick occurred to me to finish this once and for all.

"Go for it!" I shouted to Bloom. "I'll distract it and hit it from behind!"

"Right!" Bloom answered.

With my left arm, I reached out and summoned a magica sigil. I carried a lot of momentum now, and as I flew into the sigil, that momentum transferred. The sigil spun up and released its magical energy. I launched into the air at tremendous speed, angled toward the construct.

It was all too fast for the mechanical monster to react. I streaked through its arms and soared up above its head. The construct tried to swing around and attack me, exactly as I'd hoped. I summoned another sigil to stop my flight and fired my keytar down into its face.

Bloom took the opening I'd given her. She leapt up, straight at the construct's chest tank. With a roar of fury, she raised Iris's keytar above her head. Her muscles flexed as she jabbed it down into the construct's chest, forcing the neck of the keytar through the metal.

A tremendous surge of magica exploded from Iris's keytar. The raw force tore through the tank and shredded it into a spray of debris. The construct, torn and twisted, stumbled and fell to the ground. With one last cacophony of smashing metal, the final construct collapsed into a lifeless heap.

I dropped back to the ground. Bloom, still standing on the remains of the tank, withdrew the keytar and laughed.

"It's been far too long!" she shouted. "Claire, find me more things to kill!"

"Um, well, just keep that urge limited to monsters," I said.

She jumped down off the debris and landed in front of me, grinning from ear to ear. "If I must!"

I turned and looked over the remains of the constructs. Whatever challenge Makula had meant for us, we'd pretty seriously beaten it. What was supposed to happen next?

"You seem troubled, Claire," Bloom said.

"I just hoped that maybe we'd get transported out of here when we beat those things," I said. "What *else* has she got planned?"

Bloom looked past me and nodded. "Maybe that's the answer."

I turned around and followed her gaze to the trio of doors the constructs had come from. The doors on the right and left had closed again, while the center one was still open.

"It could be a trap," I said.

"Possibly," Bloom said, "and if it's a trap, we shall kick its ass, too. Don't go timid on me now, Claire."

"Fine," I said. "I'm ready to get out of here."

As we walked toward the center door, I nudged Bloom's arm.

"Hey, um, just remember to stop the cussing if we get back around Nova."

"Yes, yes," Bloom said. "I'm well aware. Don't worry. I will behave." She let out a soft chuckle. "You know, Iris is actually sorry she used to tease Nova about that."

"She is?"

"Indeed. I still don't know how you girls deal with all these *feelings*."

I laughed as we reached the threshold of the doorway. "For what it's worth, you seem to be doing okay with them."

Bloom grumbled. "I suffer in silence for the good of the mission. Now, let's do this already."

"On three," I said. "One, two …"

"Three!" Bloom shouted.

The two of us stepped across the threshold, and the world went black.

CHAPTER 6

s instantly as flipping on a light switch, Bloom and I appeared back in the world as we knew it. We were in the brewery's patio area, and we were very much not alone.

Sara, Cass, Hana, and Nova were locked in a fight with an enormous version of the constructs that Bloom and I had just fought. This one appeared to be made of most of the brewery's equipment and some of its structure, a hulking assembly of tanks, pipes, bricks, wood, and kegs that towered over everything else. It had to be twenty-five feet tall, and had fists made of bundles of kegs that together must have weight hundreds of pounds.

The band played "Down in the Lilies," with Hana and Nova firing off destabilizing spells in an attempt to slow the construct while Sara hacked at it up close and Cass fired shots from her guitar from a distance. Nothing they did seemed to be making a difference; as I watched the fighting for a few moments, I noticed a shimmering gleam on the construct's body every time one of the other girls struck it.

A barrier of magica.

"This doesn't look great," I said to Bloom. "Let's get in there and see if we can help."

Bloom grinned. "That is a very tasty-looking target indeed! I look forward to ripping it to pieces!"

We ran up and fell in beside the other girls. I summoned my keytar and synced up with everybody else on "Down in the Lilies," and Bloom played along as best she could using Iris's muscle memory.

Nova looked over and realized we were standing beside her. The relief on her face was obvious. "Purple, babe, you're back! We were so flammin' worried!"

"I am back, too," Bloom said. "Thank you ever so much for the concern!"

"Hey, we're all glad you're both here," Cass called out. "We're just a little preoccupied!"

"Makula has been keeping us busy," Hana said.

Sara dodged an attack from one of the construct's keg fists and rolled over in front of us, popping back up to block yet another attack with a magica sigil. "What happened to you?"

I looked past the construct at Makula, standing behind it with her staff, cackling at us.

"She sent us on a trip. It's hard to explain."

"Allow me, Claire," Bloom said, as she fired shots from Iris's keytar at the construct. "Makula trapped Claire in a giant keg, threw me to the mercy of some evil plants, and set us against a trio of this thing's smaller siblings!"

"Alright, I guess it's not *that* hard," I said as I fired my own blasts at the construct, "but it was weirder than that sounds."

Makula noticed Bloom and me and shouted at us from behind the construct. "Ah, there you are! Welcome back to the festivities, my new acquaintances! I see you girls passed my test!"

Bloom pointed at Makula. "I am not about to let you teleport me all over creation to play your little mind games, sorceress! I was created to lead the armies of corruption, and I'll have you show me respect!"

"So, you didn't enjoy the taste of my wares?" Makula asked. "In that case, I'm happy to provide you with a more powerful libation!"

The construct rushed us, powered through Hana and Nova's area effect spells, and pulled back one of its enormous keg bundle fists to strike directly at Bloom.

"Watch out, babe!" Nova shouted.

She and I dove to our right, in front of Bloom, and summoned magica sigils to dull the impact, just in time for the keg fist to slam into Nova, Bloom, and me at full force. Even with a shield in front of us, pain consumed me as we flew backward. We smashed through a nearby brick wall into a storage room, and came to an unceremonious stop in a stack of bags that burst open beneath us in a hurricane of brewing hops.

After several long moments, the sound of Bloom groaning snapped me out of my daze. She pushed herself up on her elbows and shook off a load of hops and dust. "I am truly coming to loathe this accursed plant."

Nova rolled over and spit a hop from her mouth. "For flammin' real! This is gonna make me hate beer before I've even had any!"

I managed to sit up, and peered back through the hole we'd made in the wall. Sara, Cass, and Hana were still engaged with the construct, and every one of their attacks glanced off its barrier. From this distance, I noticed for the first time a similar gleaming shimmer around Makula.

She had a barrier up, too.

Keeping two barriers up while also powering that huge construct would require a lot of magica, and concentration. That meant there was a weakness.

I nudged Nova. "Hey. You feel like causing a blizzard, Blue?"

"Always, babe," Nova grinned.

"Okay. Hit Makula. Soak up the magica she's using for her

barrier. It'll pull from the construct, and then we can hit it. Win-win! I think."

Bloom laughed. "Color me impressed, Claire! You're thinking like a fighter!"

Nova punched her own palm and nodded. "Let's do it to it, babes!"

A moment later, we summoned launch sigils and shot across the patio directly toward Makula.

Our reappearance on the field of battle surprised the construct, and it couldn't redirect its bulk in time. I recreated my move from the fight in the other world and used a sigil to stop and quickly change direction. I soared and landed behind the construct. As Bloom landed on ground in front of it, Nova shot past and stopped directly in front of Makula.

Makula glared at Nova with suspicion. "And just what do you think you're doing, my young Riot Blue?"

"You missed a whole dang bunch of stuff while you were gone," Nova said, "so you ain't got a clue what's about to happen to ya! Eat my drums, ya flammin' jerk!"

"What are you going on about, child?" Makula sneered. "I've fought magical girls for decades! I very much doubt you can surprise me."

Nova grinned and reached out her hand. "That's what you think! Beat Stream Blizzard!"

Nova's holo drums materialized in front of her again and, as she played hard to the beat of "Down in the Lilies," the Maiden-song's power surged into her. Above Makula, dozens more glowing blue drums appeared; in a mass of rippling azure magica waves, they rained down their power upon her, slam-ming into the barrier Makula had conjured around herself.

The barrier shimmered and roiled and fought against the onslaught, but Nova's special attack was relentless. It was all Makula could do to keep up and maintain her protective shield; as I watched, I noticed the barrier around the construct start to falter.

The opportunity had come. I fired, sending a charged magica bolt shooting from my keytar. It smashed the construct's chest tank and blew a hole in the metal. Beer gushed from the wound like blood.

The barrier had fallen.

"Smart thinking!" Sara shouted.

"Thanks!" I shouted. "Now, everybody hit it! Big ending!"

"With pleasure!" Hana shouted back. She slapped her bass and sent a huge green shockwave flying into the construct, knocking it for a loop.

Bloom leaped up onto the construct's tank. As she'd done with the smaller version, she shoved the neck of Iris's keytar against the giant's body and fired down into it. Her attack blasted a chunk out of the construct's chest. It staggered around, clearly losing its ability to stand.

Cass blasted the construct with her guitar, and I saw Sara rush in to attack it up close. I moved to join her, and summoned back the keytar's blade as I played a multilayered chord to boost it with extra magica.

Sara and I attacked the construct's legs. Our instruments cut straight through the pipes and bricks with a single swing and sent debris flying. The construct attempted to swat us away, but it was heavily damaged by that point. It toppled over and slammed hard into the patio's paved floor.

"Time to end this," Cass said as she rung out a thick, over-driven chord on her guitar. "Maidensong Melody Severance!"

The rest of us rolled away as she played a shredding, complex guitar solo. She levitated from the ground and crackling yellow magica arced from her and generated eight copies of her guitar, orbiting her in a ring from head to foot. Her shredding picked up the pace, snarling viciously, as those guitars fired.

Rapid-fire bolts of magica blasted out of them and lanced down into the helpless construct. With the barrier down, the brewing hardware, tanks, and kegs stood no chance. The magica shredded them with ease, and as the attack continued, the giant's form disintegrated into a mess of debris.

The magica glow in the construct's dial and gauge eyes went out, and Makula laughed.

"You magical girls, as meddlesome as ever! You will be sor—"

She did not complete her sentence, as Nova's drum blizzard hit one final crashing end, overwhelming her barrier. Makula yelped and fell to the ground as Nova dissolved her drums, panting to catch her breath from the sheer magica outlay required to execute her special attack.

While Cass returned to the ground and recovered from her own move, Hana rushed over and smashed what was left of the construct's head with the body of her bass.

"I think that's enough beer for one evening," she said, her smile shining. "Are the rest of you okay?"

"Sore, but standing," I said.

"Good here," Cass said.

Sara took a deep breath and nodded. "I'm fine."

"Alive, no thanks to the sorceress and her pet," Bloom said.

Nova called out from her spot near Makula. "Tired as heck, but good!"

Sara marched past in the direction of Makula and motioned for the rest of us to follow her. "Come on. We need to have some words with our old friend."

Makula lay groaning on the ground, with Nova now standing over her. I had only heard stories and read after-action reports about Makula, since all of the sorceress's encounters with Magica Riot had been before my time. She had just been one more mark in my mental book of magical antagonists.

Having only fought corrupted magical girls and the totally inhuman Pandora Corruption before, the statuesque elven-featured Makula made me realize just how impossibly large the magical world really was.

The rest of us joined Nova in a circle around Makula. As the sorceress moved to stand again, Cass pointed her guitar and held the headstock against Makula's chest.

"Been a while since we took you down," Cass said. "I missed the satisfaction."

Makula rubbed her shoulder and grimaced. "I see your irresponsible harnessing of so much magica has made you somewhat more formidable."

"A lot of things happened in three years," Hana said.

"Yeah, we got even better," Nova said. "And we told ya we didn't make the flammin' robots! Now do ya believe us?"

"Hmph," Makula frowned. "I suppose your story is somewhat more believable now, which does present me with a new mystery to solve if I am to eradicate those mechanical pests."

"Alright, that's enough, Makula," Sara said. "You're going to need to come back to the Vault with us, so we can—"

"Think again, Riot Red," Makula laughed. "We still have quite a performance ahead of us. This was merely the overture. For now, though …"

Suddenly, Makula raised her left hand, snapped her fingers, and a concussive magica blast exploded from her palm. The force threw me back through the air as the sound of Makula's laughter filled the patio once again.

With a thud, I landed on the pavement. I scrambled back to my feet, only to see Makula stand, lift her staff, and vanish in a cloud of black mist.

I looked behind us, through the windows looking back into the brewery, and saw a crowd of people coming back in to gawk at the carnage and get a glimpse of Portland's magical girl rock band in the flesh. It was par for the course since we'd been outed, and I knew that soon, cameras would be rolling.

Sara raised her wrist link and opened a channel back to the Vault. "Commander, this is Riot Red. Do you read?"

"We read you, Riot Red," Commander McCoy answered. "We saw a Marelian incursion alert. What's your status?"

"Complicated. Sorceress Makula destroyed the robots at the

brewery and caused a scene with a magica construct. Nobody's hurt, but we have some property damage. Construct is down. Makula escaped. Situation is safe, but the brewery will need assistance."

"*Copy that. We'll call the contractors and transfer remediation funds, and I'll call the business personally. Good work avoidin' injuries.*"

"We'll be inbound to the Vault soon. There's a lot to talk about."

"*Understood. See y'all back at the ranch. McCoy out.*"

Sara walked over to me and motioned for the other girls to join us. "Alliance cleanup contractors are inbound. If you're all okay, we need to roll out and debrief at the Vault."

"Sure," I said. "So that's Sorceress Makula?"

"That's Makula," Sara confirmed.

"Charming," Bloom said.

The sound of debris crunching under boots announced the arrival of the bartender from inside. He walked up, looked around at the destruction, and let out a long, low whistle.

"Everybody make it out of here okay?" he asked.

"Yeah, we kept it contained," Cass said. "Nobody's hurt."

"Good," the bartender said. "I'm grateful for what you all did."

Hana raised her hand. "Before we leave, it would be useful to take one of these robots back with us, if you would be okay with that."

"Right," Sara said. "There's some things we don't understand about them, and we believe they could be more dangerous than Rhapsodyz is letting on."

The bartender nodded. "Sure, take whatever you need, I'm down with that. Main thing I wanted to tell you is that the cops are on their way, so you better scoot if you want to get away with it."

Cass smiled. "Thanks for the heads-up, man. Appreciate it."

"Anytime, for real," the bartender said. "Name's Len, by the way. Thank you, all of you. Magica Riot, and your friend here. For saving people, and for freeing me from those crappy robots."

"Uh … it was no trouble, Len," Bloom said. I'd never heard her sound so unsure of herself before.

"We're glad we could help," I added.

On the way back out of the brewery, we passed through the main room near the bar. The robot bartender that had been the subject of so much deserved scorn was slumped lifelessly over the bar top.

Sara pointed at it. "Everybody, let's load this thing and get out of here."

"Not that I'm objectin', boss lady, but is that company gonna come lookin' for one if it goes missing?" Nova asked.

"Maybe," Sara said.

Cass laughed. "Do you care?"

"No way!" Nova said. "We just gotta keep our eyes peeled!"

"You mean to tell me I have to help cart one of these metallic monstrosities to the van with my bare hands?" Bloom asked.

"Just help us pick the robot up, okay?" Sara shot back. "Between them and Makula, our time off is definitely over."

CHAPTER 7

We drove down the access tunnel and parked Vancent Price in the Vault's garage, where Commander McCoy was already waiting for us.

"We brought back a surprise," Sara said as she led us around to the back of Vancent.

She swung the double rear doors open to reveal the deactivated bartender robot lying motionless in the back of the van. Commander McCoy stared down at it for a few long moments, frowned, and shook her head.

"Sorry," the commander said. "He ain't exactly my type."

"No argument there," Cass said, "but this could be big."

Hana nodded. "This is one of the Rhapsodyz robots that were being demonstrated at the brewery. It was acting as a bartender."

"A real flammin' bad one," Nova added.

"Makula seemed to believe these things were using magica," Sara said.

"I ain't especially fond of that possibility," the commander said. "Fortunately, we've got the right two people to find the facts. C'mon, let's lug this thing down to the armory."

Sara wheeled over a nearby utility cart, and we loaded the

robot onto it. After a trip down the Vault's main corridor, we reached the armory and rolled the cart inside.

Saoirse and Hikari sat at the workbench, fiddling with the interior of what appeared to be a prototype guitar as they gazed into it through thick goggles. We wheeled the Rhapsodyz bot over and parked it next to the bench.

Saoirse looked down at the bot and brushed her long ginger hair away from her goggles. "What's this thing?"

"A robot made by the Rhapsodyz corporation," Sara said. "They were being demonstrated at the brewery when Sorceress Makula showed up."

"Rhapsodyz? What's that buncha tools doin' ... wait, did you say *Makula?*"

"Vacation's over," Commander McCoy said.

Hikari looked up from the robot. "Would it be correct to assume that a Sorceress Makula is a bad thing I mean I don't think you're all saying it like that because she's super awesome and chill."

"Definitely not chill," Sara said.

"Makula kept saying these robots were using magica," I said. "Does that make sense to you?"

Saoirse frowned and raised her goggles up onto her forehead. "Nobody but the Alliance should even be capable of makin' devices with magica. That said, I wouldn't be surprised if some fool corpo spanner's got it in their head to juice their numbers by tampering in things they ought not to."

"We thought you two would enjoy taking it apart," Cass said.

"It ain't even half as cool as that robot you've been designing," Nova said, "but maybe you can tell us what it's doing!"

Saoirse laughed. "Why, even Miss Nova's flattering me now? A lady could get used to this. Aye, we'll take a crack at it." She flexed her impressive muscles and gestured at Hikari. "Me and the kid here'll sort it out."

Hikari nodded as they pulled off their goggles and put their glasses back on. "For sure for sure if there's spicy secrets hiding in those circuit noodles we'll dig them out and give you the recipe this is my promise to you I love ripping into a weird computer in a skullduggerous fashion I will crack that shiny technology bone open and slurp up the the delicious information marrow inside."

The commander nodded. "Good to hear. Let me know what you find out."

We left the robot with Saoirse and Hikari and walked back out to the corridor to continue on to the commander's office.

"We'll need whatever edge we can get," Sara said. "Makula's back, and she's upset."

The commander sighed as we reached her office and led us inside. "What'd she say, exactly?"

"Her usual spiel," Cass said. "Humans dabbling in magical things in a way she doesn't like."

Sara nodded. "She thought we were responsible for the robots. We disabused her of that notion."

"Guess it all comes down to what Agents O'Carolan and Tomori find in that bot," the commander said, as she sat down behind her desk.

"There was something going on with the robots, for sure," I said. "We could feel a strange sensation at the brewery, and it went away when Makula deactivated them."

"Bloom here was downright nauseous around them," Cass said.

The commander looked over at Bloom. "What's that?"

"It was deeply unpleasant," Bloom grumbled. "My stomach did flips when those mechanical menaces were running."

"Makula also wasn't happy about our true powers," Sara added. "Although that's not a shock."

"Don't forget Claire and Bloom gettin' zapped to another dimension!" Nova added.

I sighed. "That did happen."

"That blasted sorceress trapped us in some kind of mind space," Bloom said. "It angered me a great deal."

"Yeah. She put me in a giant keg, and then she made us fight hop plants and brewery constructs."

"That woman does love her little tests," Commander McCoy said.

Sara nodded. "We've all been sent to one of Makula's mental realms before."

"That's how she gets to know ya," Nova added.

I frowned. "It was very strange. I didn't enjoy it."

"It's never a great experience," Hana said, "but we have some countermeasures you can take to stop it next time."

"Yep," Cass said. "Mental exercises. I can teach you before we go out again."

"That would be good," I said. "I'd really appreciate that."

"Don't expect me to thank you, exactly," Bloom said, "but I also desire this knowledge. Please."

Cass smiled. "Hey, we've got your back. Always!"

"Alright, let's take stock" the commander said. "We've got an angry sorceress back after three years to stir up trouble. We've got a tech company that might be trying to harness magica. And we've got no idea how or why that would be. We've got us a threat and a mystery, so it's time to work the problems. I want all of y'all to go get checked out by the doc. Agents O'Carolan and Tomori will analyze your sensor readings and take a look at that bot y'all recovered. Let's be ready for anything."

"Understood, commander," Sara said.

The commander smiled. "Good work out there, Magica Riot. You too, Bloom. Keep it up."

———

Dr. Barrera laid me out on a medical bed and clacked a few of the old mechanical keys on the diagnostic station nearby. A scanner mounted on a bar across the bed whirred to life, slowly inching its way down my body as she peered into the glow of the banks of CRT monitors mounted to the wall.

"Is everything okay?" I asked.

"Oh sweetie, I think so," Dr. Barrera said. "Don't worry. It's just good to check whenever you've gone cross-realities, especially if it wasn't your idea to do so. Makula yanking you out of this world for that little jaunt could have been quite a shock to the system!"

I laughed nervously. "Yeah! You can say that again."

"Poor thing. I just want to make sure you didn't come down with dimensional dysmorphia."

"Dimensional ... what now?"

"Well, it's a physical reaction to—" The scanner beeped, and she smiled at me. "Don't worry about it! You're fine. Just let me know if you experience any itching, redness, or dark spectral clouds at the edges of your vision, okay?"

"Um, I will, yeah."

She swung the scanner bar away from me. "That's done! Now, I just need to ask how you're doing. Mentally, I mean."

I sighed. "The way Makula was able to just instantly send me so far from everybody was, well, a lot."

"The other girls expressed similar sentiments in their early encounters with her," Dr. Barrera said.

"Yeah. I don't know if it hit me in the moment so much, but I really didn't like being ripped away from everybody. It's rough to feel like you aren't going to see the people that mean a lot to you. Magica Riot is, like, my family." I chuckled. "Listen to me, I sound like Nova."

Dr. Barrera smiled. "Dear, you sound like a human. We *are* a family here. Did you talk to the rest of the team about the mental exercises they use against Makula?"

"Cass said she can teach me some."

"Good. And if you'd like, I have some advice, based on my years of experience assisting magical girls."

"I'll always take advice from you, Doc."

"In times of great magica-related mental duress, find something in you that means a lot. A positive memory, or a spark of love."

"Love?"

She nodded. "Something that lets your mind stay centered against the storm. It can help. The life of you magical girls is one of magic *and* emotions, after all."

I smiled. "Okay, yeah, I think I can do that."

"I know you can," she said as she reset the scanner. "Bloom's up next. I've got another round of tests for her. Could you let her know to come in on your way out?"

"Sure," I nodded.

"Thank you! Now go get some fresh air topside. Doctor's orders. Oh, and before I forget ..."

She stepped over to a storage cabinet and rummaged around for a few moments before returning with a bright red lollipop wrapped in clear plastic.

"For being such a brave girl!"

"Thanks," I laughed as I took it from her. "I thought I was too old for these."

She shook her head. "You're never too old for a lollipop, Agent Ryland."

Fresh air *did* sound appealing. After telling Bloom where she could get her own lollipop, I walked down to the main elevator, rode it up to the access tunnels, and made my way out of the Vault's now-mostly-secret door under the Burnside Bridge.

I looked around, searching for fans or photographers. Being known to the public meant that we more frequently had people hanging around the park, waiting for us. Today, though, the coast looked clear. I stepped out and walked over to the railing along the riverfront, making sure to not get too close to the part that was being repaired after getting crushed by the enormous Pandora Corruption bug monster from four weeks before.

A breeze brushed across my face, and I took a deep breath as I looked out over the water. *Four weeks.* Four weeks since we'd fought Rennia's army and saved the world. Four weeks since I'd unlocked the true powers of magical girls again. That moment of cosmic clarity seemed like it had happened only four *hours* ago, considering how large it loomed in the back of my mind. Yet the world kept turning, heading down whatever new path it was now on. And we moved with it, toward our next challenge.

At least this one didn't seem to be related to the end of the world. Not as far as I could tell, anyway.

Before I could get too comfortable, I heard a familiar—and very welcome—voice approaching from from the direction of the Vault entrance to my left.

"Hey, rock star," Hazel said. "Welcome back!"

"Hey, Haze," I said as I turned to her. "What's u—"

I froze as I got a look at her. She'd received one of the new Alliance jumpsuits, too, but she'd apparently been *customizing* the fit while we were on our mission. Like tightening the waist strap and leaving the front zipper open a few inches more than was strictly necessary.

She knew exactly how to target me, not that I was complaining.

It was at that moment that I realized Hazel was talking. "—et some food?"

"Huh? Oh, food?" I asked.

"Yeah, silly. Food." She grinned at me. "I was gonna hit up the Kaiju Carcass Food Cart Pod, and who better to join me than my magical girlfriend?"

I nodded vigorously. "Yeah! I'd like that!"

She motioned toward the core of downtown and offered me her arm. "Alright! C'mon, cute stuff."

Blushing hard, I slipped my arm through hers and let her lead me off. We headed out of the park and west toward food, and the site of another remnant of Magica Riot's previous big fight.

A month ago, Magica Riot dropped a massive insectoid Pandora Corruption monster into a dimensional gate at the top of the unfinished Grand Sovereign Hotel. The resulting magica explosion sealed the gate, prevented the return of Rennia, erased nine floors of the skyscraper, and blasted all of us off of that rooftop to land several blocks away.

That included the corpse of the giant bug monster, which had come to a final rest at the intersection of Tenth Avenue and Burnside Street, across from famed tourist destination Howell's Books. The remains completely blocked traffic, and reshaped the energy of downtown Portland as a result.

It quickly become apparent that nobody knew what to do with the bug. Disposing of an interdimensional insect the size of a small ship was a challenge, so Portland had adapted instead. People banded together and turned the intersection into a new public square. A tunnel had been carved through the bug's carapace, allowing the streetcar line to resume operations.

In true Portland fashion, a cluster of food carts soon followed.

They formed a ring around the intersection. At its center, the cart operators assembled a seating area of large picnic tables beneath canvas shades. A sign welcomed visitors to the Kaiju Carcass Food Cart Pod, with a hand-painted addition hastily nailed to the bottom promising "ALL VAPORS FOOD SAFE." The giant carapace watched silently over the pod, slowly accumulating layers of graffiti on its chitin.

One of the carts that had moved in was a familiar favorite, and the one Hazel and I now waited beside: Juice Wench.

Delilah, the Juice Wench herself, leaned out of the window of the cart and handed us large clear cups filled with a thick purple concoction, the cart's newest special.

"Here ye go, my good queens! Two Spacebug Smoothies, made just for you!"

"Thanks, Delilah," I said, taking the smoothie from her. "This looks great."

"How's business been here?" Hazel asked.

"Gettin' in here has been big for me," Delilah said. "Best sales in our history! Plus, I met myself someone special."

She gestured toward the cart beside hers, named POTATO KNIGHT-ERRANT.

"What's that place?" I asked.

"That's Lorelai's cart," Delilah said. "She was a customer, and had an interest in running a cart! We met for drinks a few times to talk business, and then we *kept* meeting, if you get what I'm saying."

A striking, toned butch woman with short orange hair leaned out of Potato Knight-Errant's window, wearing a tight white T-shirt accentuating muscles that made me think she might actually *be* a knight in her free time.

She saw Hazel and me talking to Delilah and flashed a smile that could start a fire.

"Hello there, girls," Lorelai said. "I've heard a lot about you. Any friends of D's are friends of mine."

"Hi," I said, more starry-eyed than I'd intended.

Hazel smiled. "Hey, Lorelai. What do you make in there?"

"Belgian-style double-fried French fries, served up in a paper cone with your choice of two dipping sauces," Lorelai said. "Hot and enticing. Guaranteed."

"Yum," Hazel said, her expression shifting into a grin. "I bet your flavors are incredible."

Lorelai laughed and smiled back at us. "I'd give you and your magical girlfriend a taste anytime."

Hazel was so skilled that she'd gotten us into a flirting situation before I'd even realized it. I was surprised, but not unpleasantly so.

"Oh, wow," I said, feeling the heat rising in my face as I tried to deploy what passed for my "game." "I, um, that would be—"

"I *highly* recommend getting a taste, queens," Delilah said, her eyes sparkling with mischief. "My lady's work is *incredibly* satisfying."

Hazel looked over at me and subtly bit her lip. "Hear that, Claire? I'd love to see you enjoying what Lorelai can do."

My eyes scanned back and forth between the three of them tossing me around like a cat toy, and I yelped out a vaguely comprehensible answer.

"Um, hehe, I would, that is, um, I think that I, um, yes!"

"That's my girl," Hazel said.

Lorelai laughed. "Tell you what, I'll whip up cones for you. Spicy peanut sauce for Hazel, and a nice smooth bourbon honey mustard all sweet and gentle for Claire. I'll take it easy on her, this time."

"That sounds good to me," Hazel said. "We'll ease her into it."

I could only stare back with a dazed grin on my face. "T-thanks!"

"I'll call you over when they're ready, if you want to find a seat," Lorelai said.

Delilah gave us a wave. "Eat well and be merry, my queens!"

Thusly blessed by the Juice Wench and her Potato Knight-Errant, Hazel and I made our way to the main seating area. Just as we sat down, a teen girl approached us from the crowd with a look of anxious awe on her face.

"Um, sorry, I don't mean to bother you, but you're Claire, from Magica Riot, right?"

I smiled back at her. "That's me!"

"Riot Purple herself," Hazel added with a wink.

The girl looked like she was about to burst. "Oh my gosh, wow, okay! I'm a huge fan! And, um, you're a really big inspiration. For me, I mean."

"Aw, yeah?" I asked. "An inspiration?"

"Y-yeah!" she nodded. "Seeing you, and Nova, helped me be more brave out in public. So, um, thank you."

Tears teased the corners of my eyes. "I'm glad we helped. For real. What's your name?

A huge smile spread across the girl's face. "Um, I'm Chloe!"

I recognized the tone in her voice, that potent combination of anxiety and thrill that came with using your new name in public.

"Nice to meet you," I said. "That's a really nice name, Chloe."

She beamed at me, her cheeks red. "Really? Um, thanks! Anyway, um, I didn't want to interrupt, but just ... thank you!"

I smiled. "You're welcome!"

As Chloe walked off into the cart pod, Hazel nudged me. "You're getting good at that. You deserve the adoration, you know."

"Aw, Haze," I said, "I'm just being myself."

She took my hand and gave it a squeeze. "Sometimes, that's exactly what someone needs to see."

In stark contrast, two middle-aged women gave me disapproving frowns as they passed. Hazel spotted them immediately and shot an angry glare back at them, which successfully drove them away.

I sighed. "Not everybody's a fan."

"Screw 'em," Hazel said. "Some people just hate anybody who's not like them."

That was the moment a new voice entered our lives, from behind me.

"Truly, it's unfortunate. People can be so cruel!"

I turned around to find a pale woman standing behind me in a black suit and tie, with a crisp white button-down shirt underneath. Her hair—bleached blonde with dark roots—was gathered into a bun, with swept bangs hanging down above intense blue eyes. Flawless makeup further accentuated her features. She stood with her hands clasped together in front of her, and a small, pleasantly fake-feeling smile on her face.

"You girls, though," she continued, "Magica Riot, I mean— you're brave! The way you live your truth is just so very *valid*."

"Um, thanks," I said. "We are, I guess, yeah."

The woman continued to stare at me. Something about her energy made me feel uncomfortable.

"Sorry," Hazel said, "was there something you—"

"It's just *so* good to finally meet you in person, Claire," the woman interrupted, not acknowledging Hazel. "After seeing you in action, I knew I had to come meet the real thing. Fortunately, my supervisors agreed! I finally get to look at you with my own eyes."

"Your supervisors?" I asked. "Who are you, exactly?"

She held out her hand. "My name's Allison. Allison Webb. And it's a pleasure to finally share this space with you, Claire Ryland."

The name flashed through my brain. I remembered something about an Allison Webb sending multiple emails to the team after the Rennia incident, but Commander McCoy had held off on engaging with her. She hadn't liked the woman's vibe; now, in person, I couldn't help but agree.

Not knowing what else to do, I reached up and shook her hand. Her expression changed subtly, as if she got some kind of satisfaction from that.

"You've been trying to reach us," I said.

She nodded. "I have! You're quite a hard group of girls to get ahold of."

Hazel glared at her. "You a fed or something?"

Allison laughed. "A fed? Oh, no, no! Though I suppose I do have a forceful approach to contact."

"If you're not a fed," Hazel said, "then what are you?"

Allison sat down next to me, more closely than was necessary. "I'm a public relations representative for Rhapsodyz. I assume you're familiar with us?"

Oh, I'm familiar, I thought.

"Yeah, um, I've heard of you," I said. "Is this about what happened at the brewery?"

Allison took my hands in hers, which made me scoot back away from her a little. "Oh, Claire, no. That was a terribly unfortunate incident. Among other things, Rhapsodyz is a leader in robotics and AI development, and we deeply regret any situations where our products behave outside of accepted standards.

I'm just glad you girls were there to prevent any serious injuries!"

Hazel eyed her suspiciously. "You're not upset about all the money you burned?"

"Not at all," Allison said, still looking directly at me. "In the innovation leadership space, it's expected that there will be write-offs. Truthfully, it was an honor to have our products involved with Magica Riot. I happen to think you girls are just *fascinating.*"

The way she said that made my skin crawl.

"Listen," I said, "I don't know what it is you want, but—"

"I don't want anything today! I just saw the opportunity to meet one of you remarkable girls and get my foot in the door," Allison said. "As honored members of the Portland Business Council, Rhapsodyz is excited to participate in this new, unprecedented era of our city! You magical girls are changing the conversation, and I'm so very excited to watch you, Claire. You're breathtaking."

From behind her, a familiar—and much more welcome—voice announced itself.

"I think that's enough," Sara said. "Step away from our keyboard player."

I looked past Allison to see Sara, Cass, Hana, and Nova approach. None of them seemed especially pleased to find Allison Webb in front of them.

Allison stood and turned to face them. "I can't believe my luck! I get to meet all of Magica Riot at once. It's a dream come true!"

"Okay, now you can say you did it," Cass said. "It's time you backed off and went through proper channels. I'm sure your bosses know how to reach us."

"We'll let Commander McCoy know that you're in town. I'm sure she'll be willing to respond to you," Sara said.

"It's nothing personal," Hana added.

Nova frowned at Allison and clenched her fists. "As long as you get outta Claire cutie's personal space!"

Allison laughed and shrugged. "Well, so much the better! I'm going to be in town for a while, so I'll take you up on that. You girls are worth the effort!"

Sara stepped closer to her. "Alright. Time's up."

"Enjoy the rest of your day, my friends," Allison said. Her voice changed in tone subtly, in a way that unnerved me. "We'll be in touch. Don't worry about that."

As quickly as she had arrived, the mysterious Allison Webb walked off into the crowd.

"Claire, are you okay?" Cass asked. "She didn't do anything to you, did she?"

"I'm okay," I said. "She didn't do anything but creep me out. How did you all know to come?"

"Thank Hazel!" Nova said. "Ain't that right, babe?"

Hazel held up her wrist link and grinned. "I set off a silent alert. Hikari showed me how the other day!"

"Thanks for that, Haze," I said. "I wouldn't want to run into her by myself again."

"I feel you on that," Cass said.

Sara nodded. "After you eat, we'll go back to the Vault together and fill the commander in. Something tells me Webb is going to be a problem sooner or later."

"I think you're right about that," Hana said. "We do have one of her company's robots on the dissection table."

From the row of food carts, I heard Lorelai call out to us. "Two orders for the lovely Claire and Hazel!"

"I'll get them," Hazel said. "Be right back!"

As Hazel ran off to grab our fries, I thought about my encounter. Allison Webb had made herself known, and despite her cheeriness, she was unsettling. She was just a little *too* friendly and touchy-feely.

Whatever it was she was after, I decided I wanted nothing to do with it.

CHAPTER 8

After we'd all reported back to Commander McCoy about the appearance of mysterious corporate creep Allison Webb, we decided to call it a night and get an early start on facing our new problems the next day. The commander, Dr. Barrera, Saoirse, and Hikari all had plenty of work of their own to do with the wrist link data we'd brought back and the Rhapsodyz bot we had procured, after all.

Which is how I found myself headed back to my apartment accompanied by Hazel *and* my new roommate.

Since this living arrangement was clearly going to be my new normal for the foreseeable future, I wondered what that said about how Bloom viewed me. After seeing her put up a version of her old persona around the rest of the team, I was coming to understand how much more complicated a being she was now that she was free of Rennia. That made me consider her reasons for wanting to stay with me. Was it convenience, just the path of least resistance that let her avoid awkward moments around Sara?

Of course, she and I had shared a moment after we'd beaten Rennia. Maybe I truly was the closest thing to a friend she felt like she had right now.

Hazel, Bloom, and I rode back to the Hollywood station on the MAX and walked back to my place. As we climbed up to the apartment, I paused on the landing.

"Um, Bloom? I just wanted to make sure you're okay with this."

Bloom gave me a puzzled look. "Okay with what?"

"With Hazel, you know, spending the night."

Hazel gave her a small wave. "If you don't want me hanging around, you can totally say so. I won't be upset! It's a big adjustment for you, and—"

"Do all of you prattle on about feelings this much?" Bloom asked. "I thought it was strictly limited to the magical girls."

"It's not like that," I said. "We're just trying to respect you, and your boundaries."

Bloom chuckled and shook her head. "Claire, you may be a magical fighter, but you are soft. Don't give so much. It can be seen as weakness."

"Sorry, I don't agree with that," I said. "Kindness isn't weakness."

"Well, whatever, whatever," Bloom said. "Yes, I am fine if your companion stays with us. Just don't expect me to participate in some feel-good nonsense."

"No promises," Hazel grinned.

We went up to my front door, and entered the apartment. With speed that surprised me, Bloom immediately walked over and face-planted on my couch.

"Urgghhghgh," Bloom moaned into the cushions.

"Are you okay?" I asked.

She turned her head and frowned at me. "No, Claire, I am not okay. On top of your cloying niceness, I told you before that I never had to deal with biological processes."

"Yeah, I remember."

"Well, I do not care for the feeling of being crushed beneath the wicked weight of tiredness. How do you humans deal with this wretched sensation?"

"Sleep," Hazel said, "and caffeine, not that it always works."

Bloom groaned. "So your choice is to go catatonic for several hours each night, or cram your flesh with low-grade stimulants."

"That's pretty much it exactly, yeah," I said.

Hazel laughed. "Bloom, you make sleep sound so terrible! As you get used to life in the human world, you'll come to love it."

"I doubt that," Bloom said.

"Trust me. You just need to get yourself some nice cozy blankets, brew some tea, snuggle up with a good book or a TV show you love ..."

Bloom grumbled. "Oh, what next? Shall the magnificent leader of the dark armies get herself a plush toy?"

"You might surprise yourself," Hazel said. "Could be your new favorite thing!"

"That makes me realize I still haven't gotten a plushie," I said. "It's been a busy few months."

Hazel grinned at me. "Ooh, yeah, you haven't! You and Bloom should go shopp—"

"Out of the question," Bloom interrupted. "Unlike Claire, I am not soft!"

"There's no shame in being a softie sometimes, Bloom," Hazel said. "Self-care is important, you know." She turned to me. "Claire, do you have any tea we could make for her?"

"I think so, yeah," I said. "It's strawberry flavored."

"Strawberry Sleepytimes! That's my Claire, alright."

I blushed, and walked into the kitchen to plug in my electric kettle.

Bloom rolled over and sat up on the couch. "Do I have a choice in the matter?"

"No," Hazel said. "Consider this part of your human education."

Even from the kitchen, I could see Bloom roll her eyes. Interestingly, she didn't push back any further.

After the water came to a boil, I placed the tea bags into mugs and poured the water in. While it steeped, I listened as Hazel did her best to keep Bloom engaged in conversation.

When the tea was ready, I brought it into the living room and sat it down on the coffee table. Bloom picked up her mug and peered down into the depths of it.

"So this is tea," she said.

"This is tea," I confirmed.

She sniffed at it. "You humans soak plant leavings in water and call it a drink?"

"A *wonderful* drink," Hazel said. "Tea is soothing. It's like a nice warm hug in liquid form."

"Give it a try," I said. "Just sip it slow. It's hot."

Bloom grumbled. "Very well. I will not enjoy it." Very cautiously, she brought the mug to her lips for a long sip.

As she drank, her eyes closed. Her expression softened, and the tension in her face melted away. It hit me that while this would be the first time Bloom had ever experienced tea, Iris would already know the sensations. I could only imagine the complexity of the two of them sharing the experience together.

And then, for a few moments, Bloom smiled. It was a small, soft thing, a far cry from her gleeful grin of destruction.

But it looked just as real.

As quickly as it came, the moment passed. Bloom opened her eyes and, seemingly aware of the emotions she was showing, returned her expression to a vague frown.

"Um, well, if you *must* know," she grumbled perfunctorily, like she knew she wasn't fooling anyone, "I would say this hot plant water buoys my warrior spirit."

Hazel and I glanced at each other and exchanged grins.

"They should put that on the box," Hazel laughed.

———

We finished our tea in the sort of pleasant, awkward silence new friends sometimes share when all the small talk has been spent but nobody wants to talk about their worries yet. After Bloom finished, Hazel and I washed the mugs while Bloom readied herself to sleep on the couch. I dug out the third pillow from the closet, which Bloom accepted "under duress." I took my night dose of hormones and made sure Bloom took the ones Dr. Barrera had given her. Then, despite the protests about our messages of "goodnight" and "see you in the morning," I turned the lights off, and we all went to bed.

Hazel dozed off right away, but I tossed and turned. I simply couldn't calm my brain. Snippets of that mysterious melody snuck in around the edges of my consciousness, and they kept me unsettled. I didn't know what to do with them; part of me wanted to make a song out of them. But would the band even want that? And if I turned it into a song, what would it do when we performed it as magical girls? Would it cast some sort of spell? Was this the Maidensong speaking to me, or just something that my brain—which had, after all, been through a lot in the last month—came up with on its own? I'd thought it felt important; was I hearing it correctly, or was I imagining things that weren't there? Was this melody even *safe* for magical girls to perform? I had no way of knowing.

Eventually, I gave up on sleep and got up to get some water, just to give myself something to do other than let my own thoughts consume me.

As gingerly as I could, I slid out of bed and snuck out to the living room. As it turned out, I wasn't the only one having trouble sleeping.

Bloom was stretched out on the couch, propped up on the pillows I'd given her. The TV was on, and she'd clearly been exploring my video library, but what she'd settled on surprised me. She was bathed in the glow of an episode of *Jetstar Voyager: The Next Era*. I'd been a fan of the show since I was a kid, but it seemed like an unlikely choice for Bloom.

She didn't notice me right away, so I walked over to the couch and waved at her. "You can't sleep either?"

"Very perceptive of you," Bloom said. She looked up at me and sighed. "My brain, or Iris's brain, *our* brain, however you wish to look at it, can get a bit loud and busy."

"I'm getting some water. You want any?"

She nodded. "That would be agreeable."

I went to the kitchen to pour us a couple of glasses. As I did, my eyes drifted back to the TV. The episode she was watching was "A Soul Doth Ride With Death," and she'd reached a pivotal scene in which the starship's captain has to decide what to do with a saboteur who rigged a star freighter's fuel system to explode to stop a weapons shipment.

"This is a good one," I said as I brought our glasses back to the couch.

Bloom frowned. "It vexes me." She took a sip of water and shot me a begrudgingly grateful glance. "And, uh, my thanks for the hydration."

"You're welcome," I said. "Why does it vex you?"

She gestured at the TV. "The saboteur is clearly guilty, yet the captain chooses not to terminate their existence. I had thought this was something peculiar to you and your cohorts, but it seems to be a recurring theme in your media."

"Well, terminating the existence of other people is normally frowned upon."

"You say that, and yet your society does kill people. Often in great numbers."

I nodded. "You've been reading up on us."

"The endless sessions with your doctor provide me with ample time. I simply struggle with understanding you creatures, despite being a resident inside one of you."

"Bloom, I don't know if anybody really understands humans."

"That much seems obvious," she said. She turned and looked at me. "This captain wants to give the villain a second chance, to reform them. You magical girls don't try to kill sentient beings, either. You seek a similar outcome with enemies like this Sorceress Makula. Or with me."

"I guess that's the hope, yeah."

"And yet humans murder each other constantly, quite frequently with the backing of institutions of power, even the very states that govern your lives."

I sighed. "Yeah, that's true, too. A lot of people don't support that, though."

"So why does it happen?" Her voice carried genuine curiosity, even a hint of exasperation.

"That's a really hard question. Sometimes it's a lack of power to change things. And sometimes, some people accept cruelty if they think they can get something out of it that benefits them."

She pointed at me. "Well, then, you can understand why I'm skeptical when you people tell me you have my best interests at heart. When you get Iris back, what value am I anymore? Some of that human cruelty might just turn itself toward me."

Ah, there it is, I thought.

"I know it's hard to believe that we're being sincere," I said.

"Indeed," Bloom said. "I know what I was prepared to do when I was Rennia's agent. Had I succeeded—had you not awakened Iris's conscience inside me—I would have handed the lives of billions over to the armies of darkness. An act many magnitudes worse than what this character in your science fantasy program did. Knowing that, you would still choose to help me?"

I thought for a moment, searching for the best way to put my answer. "You *didn't* do that, though. You learned and grew, and even wound up helping us stop her."

"Yes, but it was very nearly not so." Her voice was nearly inaudible.

"And that's why we look at intent, as well as action, right? And whether or not somebody wants to get better, wants to *become* something better. We saw that in you. It's what made you different from Blaze and Burst."

"A side effect of Iris's nagging. Were it not for her, I would not have betrayed my sisters."

"No," I said, and shook my head. "I don't believe that. I think you're more than you were, Bloom. You've fought alongside us already. I've seen you do the right thing."

She leaned closer. "So if you actually hold up your end of the deal and free me from Iris's body, and I turn around and resume my villainous ways, what will you do? Finally put me down?"

"I can't speak for everybody, but I think we'd stop you, and then try to give you a path to get better." I shook my head. "Nobody wants to hurt you, even if we have a responsibility to stop you from hurting others."

"That could be a grave mistake, Claire. I could be my own variety of monster, just laying in wait for the opportunity to rampage."

I stared back at her, trying to put together the right words. I might not have Sara's skills for heroic monologues, but I'd become more confident in myself as a magical girl since unlocking our true powers, and I very clearly needed to try.

"No," I said. "I'd rather believe you're not a monster and be wrong than believe you *are* a monster and be right. There are people out there who assume magical girls are monsters, or trans people are monsters, and I'm not going to do the same to you. And *that's* the difference with us. Magical girls believe in kindness and hope."

"But you're still human, are you not? You still have the capability for cruelty somewhere in you." She furrowed her brow. "What does hope have to do with that?"

"Everything," I said. "It's because I have hope that I believe you can become your own person. If I gave up on you, it'd be because I lost that hope. I had hope that I could be a girl, and I gave up on that hope for years until the Maidensong and the other girls helped me. Being a magical girl has showed me that I never want to lose hope again."

"Pretty words, I'll grant you that," she said, rolling her eyes. "Why should I believe you?"

"You're just going to have to trust us as we prove it to you, however we can."

Bloom leaned back on the pillows and sighed. "Well, you will forgive me if I lack bottomless reserves of trust."

I nodded. "I do forgive you, actually."

"Corny as ever, aren't you, Claire?"

"Just honest. If I'd been hurt as much as you, I'd probably feel the same way. I've been lucky to have the rest of Magica Riot, and Hazel. And I just hope we can be that for you, Bloom. Maybe one day we'll be there to help Blaze and Burst, too."

"You shouldn't concern yourselves with them," Bloom scoffed. "Given the opportunity, they'd end you girls without a second thought."

I paused; whatever progress Bloom had made, she still hadn't entirely formed her sense of empathy. "Some might have said the same kind of thing about you, Bloom. Something I've come to believe is that nobody is beyond saving."

She frowned and grumbled. "Go to bed, magical girl. We shall see how events unfold."

I downed the last of my water and stood. "We will. And you'll see that we won't give up on you."

Bloom looked up at me, started to speak, then stopped herself and turned back to the TV. Finally, begrudgingly, she mumbled back at me.

"Such a surprise would not be entirely unpleasant."

I gave her a tired smile. "Goodnight, Bloom."

———

I laid down, but sleep still eluded me.

The mysterious song fragment popped back into my head and wouldn't leave. For a long while, I tossed and turned as it played over and over, as clear as if an instrument were playing it in the room beside me. In the dark of my bedroom, it seemed more insistent, more present than it had ever been.

Eventually, I did fall asleep. At least, I think I did, because I dreamed.

I soared over the planet at a tremendous altitude. A gorgeous harmony surrounded me on all sides, thousands of voices singing wordlessly in perfect sync with each other. A grand collective song of power and joy.

The Exalted Harmony. The sound of all magical girls.

It struck me that this was a longer version of the moment I'd experienced when I unlocked our true powers. If I concentrated, I could slip backward and forward in the stream of time, the voices of magical girls past and future shifting the tone and timbre of the harmony, but always in glorious unity.

With more focus, I sensed the presence of melodies. I could tune into different expressions of the Exalted Harmony, some from magical girls on other sides of the planet in forms of music I wasn't familiar with. I realized in that moment that the Exalted Harmony was a resource, and our individual expressions of it were ways we could shape it to our will, just as we did with less powerful variations of our magica.

Songs were the key. Songs were always the key.

I picked up on the sound of Riot Harmony Chordal Cataclysm, the variant we performed on the roof of the Grand Sovereign Hotel. It was aggressive and energetic and sharpened. The style befitted a song that had helped cause a magica explosion so powerful it had sealed a breach between dimensions.

And then, there was the song fragment I'd been hearing. The fragment was gentle, beautiful, and glimmering like soft crystal in the light of a summer sun. A different expression of power.

Yes, that was it. Power had different forms. It didn't have to be a punch to the face. It could be something softer when the need arose.

Kindness isn't weakness.

For a single, radiant moment, I understood. I heard the new song. I felt its emotion, and I wanted to weep.

And then, the dream turned fuzzy. Like vapor, it passed between my fingers.

SIDE B
HELPING HANDS

CHAPTER 9

The next day, Dr. Barrera intercepted Bloom as soon as we walked into the Vault and insisted on a new round of tests and analysis. Hazel and I parted ways with her, then made our way toward the command center. As we passed by the Vault's lounge room, Cass poked her head out and waved me over.

"Hazel, you mind if we borrow your girlfriend?" Cass asked.

"Oh, not at all," Hazel grinned. "Just don't wear her out before I can."

I felt my cheeks go nuclear as Cass laughed and grabbed my arm.

"Don't worry," Cass said. "We've just got some things to discuss."

"Should I be concerned?" I asked.

"Not unless Nova's had too much caffeine."

I followed Cass into the lounge and closed the door. "Lounge" was a bit of an ambitious word for a room that was just as windowless and metallic as every other room in the Vault, but it was the place where some couches had been placed near a fridge, so it was the closest thing we had. Since Hikari arrived, they had added a stack of old CRT displays they'd found in the dustiest corners of the Vault, along with some vintage video game consoles, so the room had almost reached an identifiably collegiate level of coziness in the last few weeks.

Hana and Nova sat together on one of the couches, and Sara sat on the arm. Cass led me over and sat me down in a chair across from the couch before she took a seat on the other arm of the couch.

As I settled in, I let out a loud and elaborate yawn.

"Claire, we've been … uh, did you sleep okay?" Cass asked.

"Not entirely," I said. "Bloom and I got into a late-night talk." In the moment, I chose not to mention the dream about the melody. I still wasn't sure if it was even magica-related.

"A talk? What about?" Sara asked.

"Um, the nature of empathy?"

Hana smiled and made a sound like she'd just seen a kitten roll over.

"The timing's perfect, then," Sara said. "Grab some coffee, if you need it, because Cass has put together a plan."

"Oh yeah?" I asked, looking over at Cass. "What kind of plan?"

Cass nodded. "Okay, so, you know about the community aid group I help run, yeah?"

"I know about it, but not firsthand yet."

Cass nodded. "We haven't had the chance since the whole Rennia thing to go get directly involved, as a group. So now that we're a *little* less busy, I figure Magica Riot should resume our work with them."

"Makes sense to me," I said.

"And so, I was thinkin' we take Bloom along. Get her out into the world, interfacing with regular folks, see if we can't get that inner fire stoked with the satisfaction of helping people in a non-magical context, too. The timing's right, since it's gonna take Hikari and Saoirse a little while to deal with that robot and all our sensor data."

It was an admirable goal, but I had to wonder what Bloom

would think of it. Was she ready to put our discussion into real-world action? Even if she ended up annoyed, it would probably do her good to see us do good, too.

And we could keep her out of trouble, as long as she didn't get her hands on any sharp implements.

"Yeah," I eventually said. "I love it."

Sara must have heard the hesitation in my voice, and understood. "Obviously, the wrinkle here is Bloom. We don't know how she's going to feel about it."

Cass nodded. "Iris was always a real believer, super dedicated to the work. Between her and us, maybe we can show Bloom the path."

"You've been living with her, Claire," Hana said. "What do you think?"

I realized in that moment that the other girls hadn't seen the Bloom I'd been seeing. They hadn't been there for the conversations, the quieter moments, the day-to-day life. Bloom's tendency to retreat behind her old, prickly antagonism when she was around the rest of the team had kept her comfortably safe from engaging with the emotionality she mocked while at the Vault, but it had also prevented the team from understanding her better.

She still seemed like "the consciousness occupying Iris" to them, not a person trying to find her way in her own right. Not like I had come to know her.

"If you want to know my opinion as Bloom's, um, roommate," I said, "I think it's worth a try. I've seen her in ways I don't think y'all have, when it's quiet and we're alone. I really do think she's growing."

"Awesome," Cass said. "Once she gets out of the med bay, we've got our plan. I've got some folks who need yards mowed, hair trimmed, food delivered, all that kinda stuff."

"Hey, uh, Cass, babe," Nova said nervously, "teaching Bloom about helpin' people's one thing, but ya think we can give her a bunch of spinning motorized blades?"

Cass laughed. "We won't know until we try!"

The five of us walked down to the medical bay and waited outside the door for Dr. Barrera to finish up with Bloom. After a few minutes, the door slid open and Bloom stepped out. Unsurprisingly, she immediately realized something was going on.

"Come to check on me?" Bloom asked. "How *very* thoughtful."

"We actually *do* want to make sure you're doing okay, after the last couple of days," Sara said. "There's something else, though."

Bloom laughed. "Let me guess, it's time to put some bows on my outfit, right? Make me an official magical girl!"

"Oh, we're gonna to make you an official magical girl," Cass said, "but we're gonna do it the right way."

Bloom's expression slid into suspicion. "I'm afraid to ask."

Cass grinned. "We're headed out to do some real work, and we thought you might want to come along."

"Did you now?" Bloom narrowed her eyes. "What makes you think that would interest me?"

"Iris always loved doing it," Hana said. "We thought you might appreciate getting to experience it for yourself! You know, as you're figuring out who you are."

"And, somehow, you expect performing menial tasks will make me realize I'm a person who enjoys helping people?"

"I mean, that's kinda the hope!" Nova laughed.

Bloom scowled. "That seems unlikely."

Knowing how much Bloom disliked the confines of the Vault, I tried approach it from that angle. "If you don't want to come along, you can hang out here. I'm sure Dr. Barrera can find some more tests to do."

As if manifested by magica, Dr. Barrera appeared in the doorway. "Oh, yes, quite! I've been pacing you, Bloom, but you've been taking to the procedures so well that I think I can increase the workload. What would you say to a double regimen today?"

"Double regimen?" Bloom asked warily.

"Indeed! Now, I must warn you, some of these might be a touch invasive, but I'm nothing if not known for my bedside manner, and—"

"I will accompany the band," Bloom said through gritted teeth, glaring daggers. "It will be a delightful outing for all. Golly, magical girls, let's go help people."

"That's what I like to hear," Cass said. She clapped Bloom on the back as she gestured down the corridor toward the garage. "Let's get going. We need to swing by the co-op's house and pick up the lawn mower."

Bloom seethed and nodded slowly. *"Fine.* Lead the way."

As the rest of the girls marched off down the corridor, I hung back and gave Dr. Barrera a thankful smile.

"That was smooth," I said quietly.

"Well, Claire," Dr. Barrera said, "some folks need to live before they're ready to fight for their life. Even if they don't think they do."

———

We stopped at Cass's co-op house off Prescott Street and retrieved several boxes of supplies and an electric mower, which fit neatly in the back of Vancent Price. Though Bloom grumbled about having to help load boxes for the trip, she seemed to be taking it well otherwise. It only took a couple of minutes to arrive at our first stop.

Delia Thompson lived with two cats in a modest blue cottage on the northeast side of town, not far from Alberta Street. Cass had mentioned she'd lost her husband some years back and now lived off Social Security and a small nest egg they'd saved up before he passed.

When we arrived, Cass had us unload some food and other supplies for Ms. Thompson and her cats; once that was done, we went back out to the van. Cass retrieved a small box and turned to the other task at hand.

"Alright, that's that. Now, we just need to give Ms. Thompson a trim."

"A trim?" Bloom asked.

"You know, hair. Somebody from the group always gives her a haircut every couple of months. Today's the day."

"Is it not possible for this woman to go to a professional for such a task?"

"She lives on a fixed income," Sara said. "This helps her stretch that a little further."

Bloom seemed confused. "You mean to tell me that even your elders require money for existence?"

"They do, yeah," I said. "They get a little from the government, but it's not much."

Bloom thought about this and frowned. "If your society suffers from such an ongoing power imbalance, why do the people not simply wrest control from those who hold it?"

"That's a whole subject we don't have time to get into right now," Sara said. "The point is, this is one way we help where we can. Ms. Thompson's only got so much money, and her arthritis makes it hard for her to do it herself."

"And you're the one who's gonna handle the job, Bloom," Cass said.

Bloom flinched. "Me? What do I know about cutting the hair of a human?"

"I don't figure *you* know, but Iris does," Cass said. "She's always been Ms. Thompson's favorite. So you're gonna do the honors this time. It'll be good for Iris *and* you."

For a moment, Bloom looked like she was going to push back again, but she paused. Her expression was hard to read, but a few moments later, the reason became clear.

"*Very well,*" she sighed. "I do get the sense that Iris remembers this woman and would like to see her again."

"Good," Cass said. "This box has the scissors, a brush, a drop cloth for the floor, and a cape to put over her. Claire, would you mind helping out? You can put the cape on her, put down the cloth, and sweep up the trimmings when Bloom's done. Rest of us are gonna go around and straighten up the house."

"Oh, sure, of course," I said. "Happy to help."

Cass grinned. "Alright, let's get it done! Bloom, just watch those scissors, okay?"

"Please," Bloom said. "I have no desire to harm elders. There's no challenge in that."

"We'll work on your reasons, but you're hitting the right result," Cass said.

———

Delia had a head full of curly gray hair and a kind face. When she entered the room, she lit up with a smile.

I laid out the drop cloth on the floor of her kitchen and positioned a chair in the center of it. As Delia took a seat, I looked around at the knickknacks and keepsakes lining so many surfaces of her old home. She had clearly lived a long, full life.

"Here you go, Ms. Thompson," I said as I put the barber's cape on her. "This should keep your clothes clean."

"Oh, thank you, dear," she said. "And please, call me Delia! Everybody does! Are you the one cutting my hair today?"

"Oh, no, not me," I said. "We're going to have Bloom do that for you."

I motioned for Bloom to join us from the other room. She walked in and stood, begrudgingly, in front of Delia, scissors and a comb in hand.

"Uh, greetings," Bloom said.

"Bloom! Why, that's an unusual name," Delia smiled. "Quite pretty, though! It's nice to meet—" She paused and stared at Bloom with a quizzical look. "You look so familiar, dear. Like that girl who always used to cut my hair before!"

"Iris," I said.

Delia nodded. "Yes, that's it! Do you know her, Bloom?"

Bloom shuffled nervously. "Iris and I are very close."

"They're, um, sisters," I added quickly.

"Yes," Bloom sighed, "Thank you, Claire. We're sisters, though I'm the more prominent one these days."

Delia was apparently satisfied. "I thought you looked familiar! You're just as pretty as your sister, although the red eyes are certainly unusual!"

"Err, they're a recessive trait," Bloom said. "Shall we get started?"

Bloom moved around behind Delia and held the scissors and comb just above her hair, but stopped before she made an actual cut. I scooted in next to her and whispered in her ear.

"You going to be okay?"

"Claire, I do not know how to do this," she whispered back.

"I know, but everybody says Iris does. You're just going to have to work together with her."

"Are you suggesting I voluntarily give up control of this body just for a haircut?"

I frowned at her. "Not give up. You're cohabitating right now. It's where you *and* Iris live. Work with her, Bloom. It's what magical girls do."

"You magical girls never turn off the saccharine fluffiness, do you?" Bloom asked.

Delia glanced back over her shoulder. "Is everything alright, dears?"

"Oh yeah, everything's fine," I said. "Right, Bloom?"

"Yes," Bloom said. "*Fine.* I was simply, err, preparing myself for the work."

"That's good," Delia said. "You must be a very thoughtful young woman!"

Bloom laughed. "Thank you, Delia. More people should recognize that about me."

I wasn't entirely sure if Bloom would actually cooperate with Iris, but she closed her eyes and, gradually, I realized she seemed to be listening to something only she could hear.

Then, she opened her eyes again and her hands began to move.

She was a little unsure at first, but Delia's haircut needs weren't complex, so whatever guidance she was receiving from Iris was enough to keep her on track.

"What is it that you do, dear?" Delia asked. "Are you a musician like your sister?"

"Err, yes," Bloom said. "Perhaps a bit louder and angrier than her."

"Do you make the kind of music where they scream?"

"Screaming can most assuredly be part of it. When one is leading the charge of the armies of darkness and corruption across dimensions to conquer the planet, one must be able to project power and confidence!"

"Bloom," I said, "uh, maybe you shouldn't—"

"Such a vivid imagination you have, dear!" Delia said. "You must be very creative. It's so lovely to see young women express themselves."

Bloom's face softened, and for several long moments, I wasn't sure what she was feeling, or which part of her was feeling it. When she finally spoke, her voice was quiet, but her own.

"I thank you, Delia."

———

We worked our way down Cass's list, assisting other folks around Portland with a wide range of needs. Eventually, this brought us to the home of Frank Waller on the southeast side of the city. Frank was an older man who had trouble walking, so we arrived to take care of some home maintenance for him.

As Sara, Hana, Nova, and Bloom worked on other parts of his property, I helped Cass. I was kneeling on the kitchen floor, shining a flashlight under the sink as she worked on a pipe fitting with a large wrench, when she paused and glanced over at me.

"How'd our girl do with Delia?"

"Pretty darn well, actually," I said.

"Oh yeah?"

"Yeah. It took her a minute to accept Iris's help, but after that, she handled the whole thing better than I expected. Even kept Delia entertained."

From her expression in the glow of the flashlight, Cass seemed surprised. "No kidding? That's some good news."

"It's the wildest thing. She seemed downright emotional a few times."

"That *is* wild," Cass said as she wrestled the pipe back into place and secured it again. "Think it's sincere?"

"I do. I'm not sure Bloom knows how to fake *anything.*"

Cass laughed. "You're right about that. Whatever else you wanna say about her, Bloom does not have a filter."

With a few more strong-armed turns of her wrench, Cass secured the pipe and slid herself out from under the sink. She sat up and wiped her hands on the towel she'd brought along, propped up one leg, and draped her arm over the knee of her jeans, wrench still in hand.

"That ought to fix the slow leak Mr. Waller complained about," she said.

"That's good," I said. "You know, I never thought about there being plumbing involved in this. I didn't even know that you, uh, plumb."

Cass smiled. "What, this? I'm no expert or anything, but you do pick up a lot of skills doing this." She held her wrench up and flexed her arm; the rolled-up sleeves of her yellow T-shirt strained against her muscles, and for a moment, I caught myself swooning.

"You're showing off," I said.

"Yeah, I am," Cass said. "Without Hazel around at the moment, somebody's gotta pick up the slack."

"Uh-huh," I said, "and did Hazel put you up to it?"

Cass laughed. "Yeah, but she didn't have to twist my arm or anything. You're cute, and you're my friend. It was an easy yes."

"See, this is one of the great things about coming out," I said. "I never had friends like *this* before."

Cass chuckled, and then, after a few long moments, she sighed. "I really hope this helps her."

"Bloom?" I asked. "Well, I think it's a good idea."

She smiled. "Thanks. It's important, y'know? For her, and us. Especially Sara."

"How's she been handling being around Bloom so much?"

"Sara doesn't always like to let on. You know how she can get."

I nodded. It had taken Sara some adjustment time to open up again and showcase her warmer side after I'd joined the band. "Yeah. I do."

"I'd say she's hopeful, but kinda tense," Cass continued. "Understandably, of course. She's got her girlfriend running around the Vault again, but Bloom's up front the entire time. It's putting her on edge, waiting for the other shoe to drop. So we've gotta have hope that our good doctor figures out a way to save them both."

I thought about my late-night chat with Bloom, and smiled. "Yeah, hope. I never want to lose hope, ever again."

Cass gestured at me with her wrench and grinned. "You really are sounding like a magical girl now, you know that? I'm proud of you."

"Thanks," I said. "I've got the best teachers."

"Flatterer," Cass said. "Speaking of hope, you been thinking about how we're going to get Bloom and Iris out of this situation of theirs?"

I shrugged. "I don't even know where to *begin* thinking about that. It's a little above my experience level."

"That's fair," she laughed.

"How about you? You've got a few years on me."

Cass nodded slowly. "I dunno what's *gonna* happen, but I have an idea about a possibility."

"Yeah?"

"Yeah. I think Saoirse is gonna suggest putting Bloom into that robot of hers."

It took me a moment to recall what Cass was referring to, but then I remembered. In my early days with Magica Riot, I'd found myself in the armory, having a conversation with Cass and Hana. Saoirse had been there, too, working on Hana's bass, and I'd noticed a robotic arm jutting out of a pile of parts. Cass had joked about it being Saoirse's "robot girlfriend."

"I sort of forgot about that," I said.

"She keeps making progress on it," Cass said. "And if you think about it, it makes sense. Where else are we gonna get a body, know what I mean? Magical girls aren't gonna go grave robbing."

I shook my head. "No, definitely not."

Cass stood back up and stowed her wrench in the portable toolkit she'd brought along. "I guess we'll see! Anyway, let's go check in on our girl."

The two of us headed out to the backyard and stopped dead in our tracks at the ridiculous sight that waited for us.

Hana, Nova, and Sara stood around Mr. Waller, seated in his lawn chair. All four of them had their eyes locked on Bloom, who was racing around the backyard behind the electric push mower we'd brought along, cackling with glee as she cut down every blade of grass before her.

"Oh, she's having *fun*," Cass said.

"I never seen anybody enjoy mowing so flammin' much," Nova said. "It's bonkers!"

"Oh, I'm not so sure," Hana said. "If there was ever a yard chore designed just for Bloom, that seems like the one!"

"Should we be worried about her?" I asked.

"Probably not any more than we already are," Sara said.

"Honestly, this isn't too different from what Iris would have done if she'd thought she could get away with it."

Cass laughed. "She's always had that streak to her."

Mr. Waller's head tracked Bloom back and forth in her lawn assault path. "Well, I'll say this for her, she's the fastest lawn mower I ever did see."

"And the most enthusiastic," Hana added.

Bloom annihilated the last strip of tall grass and careened over to us, coming to a stop and switching off the mower directly in front of me.

"That was *magnificent*," she said. "The power! The carnage! The sheer volume of green viscera! Claire, it called to mind my battle against the giant evil hop plants!"

Mr. Waller looked up at me, seeking clarity. "Giant evil plants? What was that?"

"Um, she's a creative writer," I said. "So, you had fun, Bloom?"

"Fun does not begin to describe what I experienced here," Bloom said. "I had no idea your society had a socially acceptable way to wield a deadly weapon such as this!"

I laughed. "I mean, of all the ways our society lets you wield deadly weapons, this is definitely one of the more constructive ones."

"This is great, Bloom," Cass said. "We're gonna be finished ahead of schedule if you keep this up."

Bloom puffed up a little and smiled. "Naturally! It is a predictable byproduct of my superior abilities and keen, battle-hardened mind!"

"It's good to provide enrichment for your Bloom," Hana giggled.

CHAPTER 10

After completing the work on Cass's schedule, we headed back toward the Vault and parked Vancent Price in the garage. Bloom had been surprisingly quiet on the ride back, and it was at this point she decided to break that silence.

"So, when do you receive payment for the services you conducted?"

Cass shrugged and shook her head. "We don't get paid to do community aid, Bloom. That's the whole point."

The confusion on Bloom's face was obvious. "But your society here is built entirely around the acquisition of money and payment."

"Society might be," Sara said. "We aren't."

"The point of doing this stuff is to do it because it's the right thing to do," Cass said. "We don't do it for money."

Hana smiled. "We help make life better for people who struggle. Sometimes, that's fighting monsters. Sometimes, it's fixing a kitchen sink."

"I simply don't understand," Bloom sighed. "Using your powers is one thing, but these small efforts like this ... why do you bother when you get no concrete reward?"

Sara stepped toward Bloom and stood directly in front of her, staring down into her eyes. "No, Bloom, I think you *do* understand, and you're afraid to admit it to yourself."

Bloom glowered back at her. "What are you talking abou—"

"You lived it today," Sara interrupted. In the moment, I saw the Sara I'd gotten to know come to the forefront with Bloom again, the dedicated leader of a magical girl team. "Selflessness, kindness. You had to get in touch with Iris's best qualities to do it, and you did. Those feelings you experienced, the satisfaction from helping somebody? That's what it means to be a magical girl *and* a good person. I want you to remember that feeling the next time you wonder if we're actually going to help you gain your freedom."

"There's a bit of a difference between helping some old woman and helping somebody who would have once split your body in two," Bloom said.

"That was Menagerie Bloom, not you. We're going to believe in you, even if you don't yet, because that's what we do. And it's going to inform everything we do for you."

"She's speaking the truth," Cass said.

"Oh, really?" Bloom sneered. "And I suppose she speaks for all of you, does she?"

"Yes," Hana said, "without reservation."

"She does," I said.

Nova nodded. "Totally! Why would we wanna stop there from bein' *two* cool cuties running around? You and Iris is even better than Iris by herself, 'cuz it's double the girlies!"

"But in this case, you do have a material reward for helping," Bloom said. "You would have Iris back."

"Believe us, or don't," Sara said as she laid her hand on Bloom's shoulder. "We'll still be there to hold your hand when you take your first steps, in whatever form that takes. And I hope with all my body and soul that you learn something from that."

Bloom pouted. "Iris is saying much the same thing in my

head. I can't get away from you corny magical girls, no matter what I do."

"If every magical girl you know is telling you the same thing, you should consider that there might be a reason for it," Cass said.

"Exactly," I said. "A reason that *isn't* us tricking you."

The sudden chirp of our wrist links waking up with a call broke through the moment, such as it was.

"Agents Ward, Coates, Hasegawa, Nova, and Ryland, and Bloom, we've got some developments in that little mystery of yours," Commander McCoy's voice said. *"If y'all want to come down to the command center, we can fill y'all in on what we've sleuthed out."*

Sara raised her link and answered, not breaking eye contact with Bloom. "Acknowledged, commander. We're on our way."

We walked into an all-hands-on-deck meeting in the command center. Commander McCoy and Saoirse stood beside Hikari, who was seated at the computer terminal running the giant wall of screens. Dr. Barrera and Hazel stood nearby, waiting for the report to start.

"Welcome back, girls," Dr. Barrera said. "Bloom, I trust everything went smoothly for you out in the field again? No issues, health-wise?"

"Just peachy," Bloom said, "in spite of the magical girls' sappiness."

"She did real well, actually," Cass said. "In the field, and elsewhere."

Dr. Barrera looked at her curiously, but must have realized the implication and decided not to press it. "Wonderful news. You're making good progress."

"Yeah, that's great to hear," Hazel said. A sly grin crossed her face. "By the way, Cass, did you and Claire get some time to work together?"

"Oh yeah," Cass smiled. "Mission accomplished."

I felt my cheeks grow warm as the rest of the girls chuckled.

Just how many people had Hazel been asking to tease me, exactly?

Commander McCoy stepped forward. "Now that y'all are back, we can get into it. Agent O'Carolan and Agent Tomori here have made some progress on our two major issues."

"Aye, commander," Saoirse said. "For starters, we cracked into that Rhapsodyz bot you girls retrieved from the brewery, and I have to say, there's some absolutely manky work in that hunk of junk. Just dire."

"They're promoting those things like they're the next evolution of technology," Hana said.

"More like the next evolution of garbage! So many cut corners and trash design decisions."

Hikari nodded and launched into one of their monotone explanations. "From a computing and logic perspective they're little more than some general routines like 'don't step on people' and 'try to avoid walls' combined with a half-working large language model trained on a bunch of Reddit posts and even with my low opinion of tech companies I was surprised by how lackluster it was."

"That doesn't entirely surprise me," Sara said. "The bartender had mentioned that the bots had a lot of problems, and they kept asking to see birth certificates to serve drinks."

"Flammin' creepy, if ya ask me," Nova added.

"They mostly stick to whatever they've been programmed to do," Saoirse said, "but that LLM will fall back into that stuff when it hits a bug, which is often. So the software side's unimpressive, and the hardware's mostly not any better."

"Mostly?" I asked.

"Aye, here's where things get weird," Saoirse said.

Bloom scoffed. "Is that a technical term?"

"In this case," Saoirse said. She nodded at Hikari, who punched a series of commands into the computer. A few moments later, the screen wall called up an image of the Rhapsodyz robot on the workbench, with its chest opened and a particular section of its interior highlighted.

Saoirse pointed up at the highlighted section. "That there's where the bot's power source is located. I was expecting that to be some kind of battery pack or a conventional fuel cell, and from the outside that's what it looks like. It's even marked with an identifiable part number that comes from Rhapsodyz's battery subsidiary, SparkLogic."

Hikari nodded. "That didn't add up though the readouts I was getting from testing the logic core didn't match the conventional power sources there were a lot of strange references and identifiers in the logs so I began to suspect there was something totes sketchy afoot like just the shadiest goings on in a technology sense."

"So, we cracked that compartment open," Saoirse said, "and this is what we found."

The display changed to a photo and three-dimensional schematic of a strange, futuristic-looking piece of hardware covered in circuitry, wires, and computer chips, with a very distinctive—and familiar—mass of pale green crystals at its core.

"Is that what I think it is?" Sara asked.

"Aye, it is," Saoirse nodded. "It's thaumatite. Turns out our dear friend Makula was right. These things *are* powered by magica."

The room fell silent for several long moments. It didn't make sense; how could a tech company even do that?

"Well, that's not great," Cass finally said.

"You know, this all makes sense, sort of," I said. "We find out these robots are powered by magica, just after I had that run-in with a Rhapsodyz employee who's a certified magica fangirl."

"You mean Allison Webb," Sara said.

I nodded. "Yeah. It proves at least one person at the company knows something about it."

"I think you're right," Sara said. "Good insight, Claire."

"Oh, um, thanks!" I said, grinning a little.

"The thing is, this can't be a recent development," Saoirse said. "For all my problems with their engineering choices in the rest of the bot, this thing's too advanced. This has to be something they've been working on for decades, even if it's still sloppy otherwise."

"You called it both advanced and sloppy," Hazel said. "What do you mean, exactly?"

"There's some tech in here that's next-level, especially regarding energy consumption. It's hitting power-to-efficiency ratios I could only reach with my own thaumatite generators if I had years of time and billions of dollars to throw at it."

"Sounds like something you could take notes from," Cass said.

"Oh don't worry about that we've already reverse-engineered the schematics and found places to improve them," Hikari said.

Saoirse nodded. "That's because in other aspects, this thing's poor work, the work of a company that doesn't care about collateral damage. They're not shielding things effectively. Those bots dump out a lot of residual magica frequencies. It's like radiation, 'cept most humans aren't sensitive to it."

"But we are," Sara said. "That's why we all felt uncomfortable around them."

"And why I felt like I was going to retch," Bloom added.

"Exactly," Saoirse said. "I don't know where they learned to shape the magica in this thaumatite, but the closest match for these signatures is corruption magica, so it's gonna hit Bloom like a van. At least, that's our thinking."

"It's quite plausible, yes," Dr. Barrera said. "Though if they're working with something like corruption magica, it raises some troubling questions about what research they've been doing."

"Y'all know as well as anybody what the consequences of playin' with corruption magica can be," Commander McCoy said. "These corporate clowns could be one accident away from another Pandora Corruption outbreak, or worse."

Hana frowned slightly. "So, Sorceress Makula wasn't lying about feeling something amiss in the flow of magica in Portland. She just didn't have all the information."

"That does *not* make up for her other unpleasant qualities," Bloom said.

"There's something I don't get," I said. "How is it that a battery company could have access to thaumatite and magica? There has to be another layer there."

"Right, that's where things get more complicated," Saoirse said. "The outer case was a SparkLogic battery, but the actual thing inside? No way they're the ones who built it."

Hikari tapped a few more keys, and the display changed again. A close-up photo of a circuit board on the thaumatite generator popped onto the screen. Printed on the board alongside one of the chips was a single word in white text: Sinnes-löschen.

"Sinneslöschen?" Nova asked. "What the flam is a Sinnes-löschen?"

"This is where our computer expert takes over," Saoirse said.

Hikari spun around in their chair to face us again. "Right okay yeah I've been doing a lot of digging real dark web stuff going to the places where the digital dragons dwell and all that and so there's a few answers to that question so Sinneslöschen for starters is fake German."

"Fake German?" Cass asked.

"Yeah or I guess to be more accurate it's made out of some real German but not in a way any actual Germans would use it see it comes from a couple of real words stuck together like an awkward Songcloud mashup if you take it literally it means 'sense delete' or something like that but it's all fake it's like getting a tattoo in a language you don't speak."

"Even if it's fake, it sounds vaguely sinister," Hana said.

Bloom laughed. "It's trying *far* too hard. Real menace should come naturally. People can tell when you're forcing it!"

"Not sure that's the lesson to take from it, Bloom babe," Nova said.

Hikari nodded. "Actually I think that was the intention because you see Sinneslöschen is a defense contractor or more specifically a subsidiary of a subsidiary of a defense contractor and I know you'll be surprised by this but if you follow the companies up the chain eventually you get to Rhapsodyz they're just stinking up the place everywhere you want to be."

"Rhapsodyz has defense contractors?" Hazel asked. "Aren't they just a tech and media company?"

Hikari shrugged and nodded. "Oh yeah for sure for sure you'd be surprised how deep that whole thing goes Rhapsodyz is a tech company and it owns an aerospace company named Yoyodyne which owns an avionics company named GlobalEx which owns a series of other companies until you get down to weapons manufacturer Aegis Dynamics which owns a little company called Sinneslöschen it's all this big shell game to hide accountability and not pay taxes you know how it goes but perhaps I'm editorializing."

"No, that makes sense," I said. "Every media company does seem to own three weapons manufacturers nowadays."

Saoirse gestured up at the magica power cell. "Anyway, the other news is this whole thing gave me an idea and I wanted to present it to you all."

"What sort of idea?" Sara asked.

"An idea to help Miss Bloom. Maybe."

Bloom cocked an eyebrow. "You have captured my attention, armorer."

"Thought I might," Saoirse said. She nodded at Hikari, who tapped out more commands on their keyboard. The image of the Rhapsodyz bot on the big screen slid to the right, and another humanoid figure appeared beside it.

It was clearly another robot, but one that looked nothing like the Rhapsodyz bots. It was much more elegantly designed, covered in gleaming white body panels apart from a bit of exposed framework at what I could only call its midriff.

Most striking of all was its head; unlike the Rhapsodyz bots, this had a human face, with the appearance of a cute woman. That remarkably human face was set into a white frame between two circular attachments where a person's ears would have been, with blade-like fins extending up above the top of its head.

Cass looked over at me and winked. "Called it."

I looked back up at the screen. "That's your robot?"

"Aye," Saoirse said. "Miss Claire, that is the Experimental Support Model One, or XS-1 for short."

"Saoirse's robot girlfriend," Nova said.

"Android support unit, thank you very much," Saoirse said. "It's capable of operating with some percentage of the fighting power of a magical girl. There's just a couple of problems."

"Like what?" I asked.

"Well, first, it can only run for about five minutes at a time. She's a thirsty one, and I haven't cracked that problem just yet. That is, until now."

Hikari spun back around. "Since we reverse engineered the Sinneslöschen power cell that means we can make a better version that doesn't have all the inconvenient magical radiation problems we care about quality here you see none of that move fast break things attitude that the tech weirdos have."

"Just so," Saoirse said. "We're putting together a cell that'll let *my* robot run for weeks on a charge."

"That's impressive," Sara said. "What's the other problem?"

"Right," Saoirse said. "There's also the matter of making it do what it needs to do on its own."

Hikari nodded. "It's hard to create logic routines complex enough to account for all the possible variables that come with running around and using magica right like it's way too much for even advanced CPUs to handle that much cognitive load our best autonomous routines don't have anything on magical girls."

"I think I see where this is going," Hana said.

"This is the idea," Saoirse said. "We can't make an artificial processor that can handle the demands, so we don't try to. We put Miss Bloom in the XS-1 instead."

Cass laughed. "I love this job."

"Is that even possible?" I asked.

"Well, we don't know," Saoirse said. "This is all theoretical. If we can make some kind of magical containment unit, then aye, it might be possible. Of course, that depends on getting Miss Bloom out of her current body."

Bloom stepped toward the video screen and stared up at the image of the XS-1. "That automaton could be me?"

"How do you feel about that, Bloom?" I asked. "It's your life."

Bloom silently studied the XS-1 for several long moments. I could only imagine the feelings running through her head. For a moment, I thought I saw her frown, and felt a pang of worry. Was she going to say no? Given all the risks, she had every right. But eventually, she nodded. As she turned back to us, she gathered herself up subtly and took a long, almost noble breath before speaking.

"What I want is freedom," she began. "I want to exist as my own entity. If taking over the armorer's creation up there is how I achieve that, then so be it. I will adapt, if I get to be myself at last."

I smiled at her. "Yeah, I understand that, for sure."

Commander McCoy nodded and gestured up at the screen. "Fascinating as this idea is, it's all academic if we don't come up with a way to separate Bloom and Iris. Agent O'Carolan, Agent Tomori, please proceed with y'all's work, and coordinate with Dr. Barrera."

"Aye," Saoirse said. "We'll get on it."

"Got it boss we'll tech the pants off this problem," Hikari added.

Hazel raised her hand. "Not to be a downer, but this all brings up the question of our new corporate acquaintance, doesn't it?"

"Allison Webb," Sara said. "I'd bet that Claire was right about her before, and she's directly involved in Rhapsodyz's magica research."

"Sounds like we need to go get up in that jerk's face!" Nova said.

"Let's not run off half-cocked here and get into fights too quick," Commander McCoy said. "I'd like some more information on what Ms. Webb and her company might be up to. Agent Tomori, you think there's anything you can suss out with your technology skills?"

Hikari grinned, or rather, they did something that amounted to a grin considering their barely perceptible facial expressions. "Well here's the dealio getting info on Allison Webb will take a little digging gotta do some real leet hackzorz kind of things but I actually do have something for you on the company though it's maybe not what you'd expect."

"What did you find?" Sara asked.

Hikari turned and began typing at the computer terminal. "There's not much in the way of morsels about Sinneslöschen in the public record no info about what they do or what they've made but I know the name from another whole thing so I kinda hit it from a different angle goofy style I cross-referenced the company and my info on Makula in the Alliance database and boom goes the dynamite I found something."

The image of the Rhapsodyz robot on the video wall vanished, replaced by several rows of text:

STARLIGHT ALLIANCE AFTER-ACTION REPORT
INCIDENT ID: NWUS-PDX-81-001
INCIDENT DATE: FRIDAY, MARCH 13, 1981
INCIDENT LOCATION: STARDUST ARCADE, SE BELMONT

PERSONNEL:
MAGICA AGENT(S): JADE EVERGREEN
SUPPORT AGENT(S): CATHERINE R. CHASE
SUPERVISING AGENT: CMDR. DOROTHY HAVELOCK
NW US REGIONAL COMMAND, PORTLAND BRANCH

"Dang," Cass said. "Jade Evergreen herself."

"I know that name," I said. "You all mentioned her when you told me about Vancent that first time."

Sara nodded. "Portland's original magical girl, and the closest thing we have to a legend around here."

"What's so great about her?" Bloom asked. "Was she extra corny?"

"She was a solo magical girl, and she served for a long time," Hana said.

"Basically wrote the book on magical girls in Portland," Cass said. "She awakened before the Alliance even showed up in town."

"Yep," Commander McCoy said. "I remember her."

"But you only became the commander a little before I joined," Nova said. "How do you remember her?"

The commander nodded. "I remember her as a musician. She was a singer-songwriter." She paused and scratched the back of her head awkwardly; to my surprise, I detected a blush in her cheeks. "I, uh, might've been a fan, when I was a kid. Never met her in person, though. Same goes for Commander Havelock up there. There's a few more commanders between me and her."

"That date," Hana said. "That would have been before the Vault was even built! What a piece of Portland magical girl history!"

Hikari turned back around from the computer terminal. "So yeah this is the first time Makula appears in the database and the only time Sinneslöschen appears the only problem is that it's a little bare in the details sense."

"The old reports are a bit thin," Commander McCoy said. "Especially the few from before the Vault was built."

"Yeah it hits the high points but I have some of what you might call enthusiast knowledge I'm kinda a connoisseur of gaming like a sommelier of pixels anyway it's all about Polybius," Hikari said.

"What's Polybius?" I asked.

Hikari's grin-like expression grew. "So it's a weird game that showed up in a Portland arcade in 1981 it's this whole urban legend thing with mind control but the thing is Sinneslöschen was the company in the legend and well you can see there's an Alliance report from 1981 that mentions Sinneslöschen and that address is an arcade we're really through the looking glass here it's all real and magical girls were involved which just makes the urban legend even cooler if you ask me I'm kind of geeking out about this."

"Hold up, they had video games in 1981?" Nova asked.

"Yep," Commander McCoy said. "Electricity, too."

"Real funny, big boss," Nova said.

I read over the text on the screen again. "Okay, so, if the report doesn't have everything we need, can we, uh, call up Jade Evergreen and ask?"

"Well, that there's a bit of a problem," the commander said. "When a girl retires, for privacy reasons, her location and contact information are locked away in a secure file. We can call up retired girls on an emergency line, which we did during the Rennia incident, but Jade was marked as out of town that day specifically. Which means she's still local, but I don't have a way to reach her directly."

"You don't, commander," Dr. Barrera said, "but I do."

"You do?" I asked.

Dr. Barrera nodded. "Even after a magical girl retires, Alliance doctors keep in touch."

"I don't suppose you can give us her phone number?" Sara asked.

"I can't," Dr. Barrera said, "for the aforementioned privacy reasons. But I *can* give you a bit of advice. You girls might wish to get drinks at Dark Water, out on Northeast Sandy." She smiled. "I think you'll be pleased to meet one of the bartenders."

"Nice," Cass said. "Subtle."

"I'm nothing if not discreet, Agent Coates."

Commander McCoy cleared her throat and shuffled awkwardly. "If y'all are going over there and doing this, uh, could you do me a favor?"

"Oh, sure, of course, commander," I said. "What is it?"

The commander held a finger up and ran to her office. A few moments later, she returned, carrying something rectangular in a clear plastic case.

"Could, uh, y'all get this signed for me?" she asked as she handed me the case.

Inside was a flawless issue of a comic. On the cover, in dark urban fantasy–style art, a girl with wavy red hair in a long side-shave cut, an old 19th century-style green military coat, black skirt, and black pirate boots was locked in combat with a spectral monster emerging from a playing card. She wielded an acoustic guitar that she held like a bow as she pulled back the strings and prepared to fire a magica arrow.

Across the top of the cover in a bold illustrated logo treatment were the words "JADE EVERGREEN." In the corner sat the logo of famed local publisher Night Mare Comics, along with a note reading "ISSUE NO. 1" and a date in 1987.

I looked up at the commander and raised my eyebrows. "She had a *comic?*"

"A portion of the Alliance's funds have traditionally come from turning magical girl incident reports into comics, manga, and anime," the commander said. "It's been a big success in Japan, but it's been more of a rare thing over here, because the market's always been more about superheroes. Jade had a twelve-issue run, kind of a cult hit sort of thing."

"Not to be pryin' or nothing," Nova said, "but how come you don't just ride over there with us and ask her yourself, big boss?"

"Oh, uh," the commander stammered, "well, I ... naw. I could never. I'd be too nervous."

"Don't worry, commander," Hana said, suddenly sounding as serious as Sara as she took the comic from me and cradled it like a precious artifact. "We *will* get you that autograph."

CHAPTER 11

The six of us piled into Vancent Price—along with a tablet loaded with Hikari's findings, and the commander's comic book stashed in Hana's messenger bag—and cruised across the Burnside Bridge to the east side of the city. Dark Water was located out past where my apartment was, on Northeast Sandy Boulevard at 51st Avenue, so I relaxed and enjoyed the ride until we pulled up outside the bar.

We arrived just after lunch; as we stepped through the front entrance, business seemed relatively slow. It took me a minute to adjust to the dim lighting, but I could instantly recognize Quarterflash's "Harden My Heart" as it poured out of the bar's sound system. A handful of scattered customers sat in booths or at the bar.

And then, there was the bartender.

A woman who I guessed was in her fifties stood behind the bar, drying and putting away pint glasses in front of a "Republic of Cascadia" flag on the wall. She wore a black T-shirt with art of skeletons holding roses splashed across the chest, and black-framed glasses. Her hair, wavy and red, featured a prominent streak of white in front that ran down the side of her face.

"Ya think that's our magical girl?" Nova asked.

Bloom smirked and nodded. "If she has a sugary, intolerable aura, I'm certain that is your target."

Hana pulled the comic out of her bag and glanced down at the cover. "If this art is accurate, she could be."

The bartender looked up from the pint glasses and made eye contact with us across the room. She smiled, a smile so bright I could feel the warmth even from a distance, and waved to us.

"Don't be shy now, Magica Riot," the woman called out. "I don't bite!"

"I think that's our answer," Cass said.

We crossed the room and slid onto barstools. I rested the commander's comic on my lap and hoped the right opportunity would present itself. The woman walked up to us, slung her towel over her shoulder, and offered us her hand.

"Jade Everly," she said, "though I bet you know me by my stage name."

She moved down the line, shaking our hands as she went. When she got to me, I felt a subtle but noticeable warmth of magica in her touch. She made eye contact with me, her green eyes catching the light behind the bar, shimmering emerald brilliance, and gave me a knowing look.

"That's right," Sara said. "We ran into a situation that pointed back to one of your old incident reports, and Dr. Barrera thought we should talk to you about it."

"She let me know you girls would be on the way over," Jade said. "I'm glad I can help. What are you drinking? It's on me."

"I'll have a porter," Sara said.

Cass nodded. "I'll have a red."

"Marionberry cider for me," Hana said.

"Um, lager for me," I said.

Nova grinned. "Ooh, I want a—"

"Actually, that reminds me," Jade interrupted.

She walked over to Nova, whipped a Sharpie out of her jeans pocket, and with well-practiced speed, marked the back of Nova's hand with an X.

"I saw you coming, Nova," Jade laughed.

"Aw," Nova pouted. "Well, it ain't like I don't have my favs! I'll have a Shasta!"

"Works for me," Jade said before she turned her attention to Bloom with a warm smile. "And that must mean you're Bloom. What's your fancy?"

Bloom frowned. "I'm not sure."

"Iris likes dark beers," Sara said. "You could start there."

"Hold up," Nova said, "is Bloom old enough to drink?"

"My mind contains the wisdom of thousands of ages of dark warriors, I'll have you know," Bloom said.

"Yeah," Nova said, "but are ya twenty-one?"

"Iris is over twenty-one," Hana pointed out.

"But does that count for Bloom?" Nova asked.

"We don't know how alcohol would affect her," Sara said, "so let's keep it non-alcoholic for now."

Jade nodded. "I can make a mean mocktail."

Bloom considered this, and nodded. "If you can make me something which properly speaks to the very heart of my inner fire, a drink to topple empires, I will be impressed."

"I can do that," Jade said. "You girls just give me a few minutes here. In the meantime, make yourselves comfortable!"

"We appreciate you taking the time to talk with us," Sara said.

Jade smiled as she pulled the first beers from the taps. "It's no trouble at all. To be honest, I've been hoping to meet you girls sometime."

"Why's that?" Hana asked.

"Because I felt it when you gave all us magical girls our full powers," Jade said, flashing me a grin. "I might be retired, but I never lost the magic. Suddenly getting a power up at my age was kind of a shock."

"That was Claire's doing," Cass said.

"Yeah, Claire cutie really gave everybody a big flammin' boost!" Nova said.

"It was just as big a surprise to me," I said.

"And believe me, kid, I'm not complaining," Jade said. "It was an honor. I was down in Monterey visiting an old friend when I got the emergency signal during your big fight. I wished I could have helped you." An expression heavy with memories crossed her face. "Of course, you girls had it handled, in the end."

"It's the thought that counts," Hana said.

Jade slid Sara's and Cass's beers across the bar, followed by Nova's Shasta, my beer, and Hana's cider. She then pulled out a glass for Bloom and started work on her non-alcoholic drink. "So, what's this old incident report you girls needed to talk about?"

"Do you remember Friday, March 13, 1981?" I asked.

"Like it was yesterday," Jade said. "Sorceress Makula, and that damn arcade game."

"Language, legendary babe," Nova said.

Jade paused, and looked at her quizzically. "Sorry, what was that?"

"Heroes don't curse," Hana said, subtly nodding in Nova's direction.

"Oh! Right, of course," Jade smiled, and nodded back. "Sorry about that. That *darn* arcade game, I mean."

"You're talking about Polybius," I said.

Jade nodded. "Corporate slime experimenting on Portland teens. That was the worst thing I'd dealt with at that point in my career."

"We've fought Makula before," Cass said. "Well, all of us except Claire, anyway. The other part of this is new to us."

As Jade finished Bloom's drink and handed it to her, Sara placed the tablet on the bar top and called up Hikari's report. The image of the Rhapsodyz robot and its strange Sinneslöschen core appeared on the screen.

Sara took a sip of beer and motioned toward the tablet. "Makula was after these robots, because she said—"

"What is this beverage you've given me?" Bloom interrupted.

"My own special blend of ginger soda, bitters, and spices," Jade said. "If you don't like it, it's not a problem! I'll make you something else."

Bloom leaned over the bar and stared into Jade's eyes. "You will do no such thing. This drink." She took another sip, and almost growled. "It is robust, passionate." She glared at Jade, her eyes open a little *too* wide. "It is angry!"

"Wow," Jade laughed, "I'm not sure anybody's ever told me that before."

Bloom laughed and patted Jade's shoulder. "I'm glad that at least one of you magical girls understands that which burns inside me!"

"I never seen somebody so excited about ginger soda," Nova said.

Jade smiled. "See, this is why a good bartender's worth her weight in gold."

Sara returned to the tablet. "Now that we've established Bloom's taste in drinks, this is what we found. Makula was after these robots because she said they were causing an imbalance in magica. We got one back to the Vault and found this thing inside it."

Jade looked down at the image and zoomed in on the Sinnes-löschen device. "Now *that's* a name I haven't heard in a long time."

"You're familiar with it, then."

"Uh-huh. Sinneslöschen was the name on the Polybius cabinet. The insides of it looked a lot like this, just not so fancy."

"The report said Polybius was some kind of mind-control experiment," Cass said.

Jade sighed. "Yeah, and a really crude one. They were blasting magica out of the game screen into the face of the players. From what I saw, and what the Alliance scientists thought, it was barely even controlled."

"That seems incredibly irresponsible," Hana said.

"It is," Jade nodded. "I got my theories, based on everything I remember being told back then."

"We'd love to hear them," I said.

"Okay," Jade said, "here goes. Till you girls blew the doors off, magical girls have been this big secret, but I don't think that goes for thaumatite. It's just a natural thing that exists. People could find it, even if they don't know what it really is or what it can do. I figure the government *and* some companies have known about it for decades, but they don't know *how* to use it, except like a blunt instrument."

"Like handing a bomb to a child," Hana said. "That's the phrase Makula used."

"That does sound like her," Jade chuckled. "Anyway, I think they just sort of stumbled into the mind-control thing and decided to try to weaponize it. I don't know what kind of magica it was, and I don't think they knew, either."

Sara nodded. "So this means Sinneslöschen has a long history of dabbling in things they don't fully understand."

"Yeah, 'cept we do kinda know what magica the bots are using," Nova said. "It's close to what the Pandoras use!"

"Pandoras?" Jade asked. "This thing is using Pandora Corruption magica?"

"Not one-hundred-percent," Cass said. "Our scans say it's related, but not exact."

"A pathetic imitation from people who could never hope to understand," Bloom spat.

"Huh, well, that's interesting, then," Jade said. "Sounds like they've been studying it a lot in the last four decades. And *that* is scary."

"That means somebody at Sinneslöschen understands magica at least a little," I said, "but it still doesn't make sense why they'd be using something like corruption magica to power a robot bartender."

"How sure are you that it's *just* a robot bartender?" Jade asked. "Polybius wasn't *just* an arcade game."

"Good point."

Cass nodded. "Yeah, that bot, and those dog waiters, it isn't hard to imagine them with guns."

Jade thought for a moment. "Do you know how they've been studying corruption magica?"

"We don't," Sara said. "There's never been any known examples of Pandora Corruption creatures captured alive. They either dissolve, or die and go inert like the bigger ones did after the Rennia incident."

"It would be extraordinarily bad if Sinneslöschen has found a way to capture living Pandoras," Hana said.

"Even if they hadn't yet," Cass said, "they could be using corrupted thaumatite, or samples from dead Pandoras."

"But why ain't we gotten warnings about the bots before now?" Nova asked. "They shoulda been showin' up on the sensors!"

"It could be that they've been working on this for a long time, but using a variant of corruption magica to power them is a recent thing," Hana said. "Something they figured out in the last several months, as the Pandora Corruption activity got worse."

"It sounds like you girls have a lot on your plates," Jade said. "You mind some advice?"

"Never," Sara said, "especially when it's coming from somebody who's been through it all before."

Jade smiled. "If there's a way to get through this situation with Sinneslöschen and Makula, you have to do it without ever losing your hearts. You girls have something I didn't have: each other. Nobody has to stand alone. Never forget that."

I nodded. "We won't forget."

Hana leaned over the bar. Her expression became deadly serious. "As long as we're talking about harmony and cross-generational respect, I have something to ask of you, Miss Evergreen."

"Ask away!" Jade said.

"Would you be willing to sign this, for our commander?"

Hana asked as she pulled Commander McCoy's comic from behind her back.

Jade paused. "Not for you?" She shook her head, her expression sympathetic rather than dismissive. "I'm sorry, girls, I don't sign autographs for third parties."

"How mercurial of you," Bloom laughed. "I respect that!"

"No, I get it," Hana said. "Some idols only sign autographs for the fan that gives them the item. It's part of the bond between them. Jade deserves to see the smile on the commander's face when she signs this comic."

"I'd love to meet your commander," Jade said warmly. Her expression lit up with a grin. "Maybe we can get together sometime."

Hana leaned closer to Jade, her expression conspiratorial. "You're absolutely right, and I will help make that happen however I can."

"If you'd like," Sara said, "you could also come to our arena show at the Rose Garden. We'll get you a front-row seat."

"I'd love that," Jade said. "And, girls? One more thing."

"What is it?" I asked.

Jade beamed at us. "If you ever get into trouble and need a helping hand, you give me a call. I'd put the costume on again for you, anytime."

———

We left Dark Water and returned to the Vault. After parking Vancent, we went down to the command center, where Hikari still sat at the main console deep in their research. As we walked up behind them, they paused and turned around.

"Hey what's up cool cuties do you have more dead robots for us to look at or is this something else?"

"Cuties, huh?" Cass asked. "Sounds like Nova's rubbing off on you."

Hikari nodded subtly. "I may have been adopting some of

her speech patterns what can I say cuties is a useful word I'm not sure if I'm ready to go full flam though I feel as if that might be a Nova-exclusive weapon."

Nova grinned. "I didn't know ya liked the way I talk, Hikari! That's super rad of ya. We should hang out sometime!"

"Hang out uh are you sure Nova is that something you'd like," Hikari said, suddenly sounding nervous, or something close to it.

"You better danged believe it," Nova said. "You could teach me some video game stuff!"

Hikari froze for a moment before nodding surprisingly vigorously. "Uh yes I think that is uh something I can very much do I will show you all my favorite modded consoles and obscure RPGs and third-person action games that ten people have heard of that would mean a lot to me actually."

"Hikari, we do have a request," Sara said. "Can you find out if Rhapsodyz has another PR stunt scheduled with their robots?"

Hikari gave us a thumbs up. "Oh yeah totally that won't even be hard if the schedule's not public I may have to do some light digital breaking and entering but with the Vault's tech combined with my masking routines that's no big deal let's just say I'm not a stranger to doing things with technology that aren't strictly on the up and up don't worry yourself about it give me just a few moments and I'll have that billion-dollar techno-trash factory figured out for you."

They spun back around in their chair and went to work. I considered myself a pretty fast typist, but I'd never seen anybody's hands fly over a keyboard as quickly as Hikari's did. In the warm glow of the cathode ray tube display, Hikari opened terminal windows, tore through lines of code, and closed the windows before I could process what had happened. Other windows opened in the background with maps, corporate websites, spreadsheets, and assorted bits of data.

Hikari narrated their typing for us without missing a beat. "Alright alright alright let's see here tuning the search routines loading datasets tabulating previous schedules reticulating splines checking against City of Portland permits."

Sara nodded as we watched. "If we can figure this out, we'll be able to predict when Makula will ma—"

"Got it," Hikari interrupted.

"Already?"

"Oh yeah remember who you're talking to this biological construct is designed to process massive amounts of information at speeds no conventional being could handle."

"Even I am begrudgingly impressed," Bloom said.

"What did you find?" Sara asked.

Hikari brought up a schedule on the big screen. "Rhapsodyz has a whole public demonstration at the Kaiju Carcass Food Cart Pod in two weeks with robots talking up their large-language generative AI model that sounds like a nightmare if you ask me but there's your answer a whole big crapbot ad right in the middle of the city."

"Sounds like the perfect place for a flashy statement by Makula, too," Cass said.

"I doubt very much that arrogant woman would be able to resist such a display," Bloom said.

"No kidding," Nova said. "It's like they're layin' out a whole big ol' buffet for her!"

I sighed. "It also means that Allison Webb will probably be there."

"She's in public relations, right?" Hana asked.

"That's what she says, at least," I said.

"I don't buy it," Cass said. "Not willing to give these corporate types any benefit of the doubt. For all we know, she 'works for Rhapsodyz' at Sinneslöschen, building those bots. They're all the same company these days, after all."

Sara nodded. "Agreed. We can't afford to take Webb at her word. We need to find out exactly what her role is in all of this."

Hikari looked back at us over their shoulder. "If you want me to increase the skulduggery factor a bunch I can follow that rabbit hole for you try to break into some deep HR systems at Rhapsodyz and figure out what Allison Webb's deal is it might take me a little longer though."

Cass laughed. "I'd ask you if you can actually do that, but I already know the answer."

"Personally, I vote yes," I said. "I'd really like to know who I'm dealing with the next time she invades my personal space."

"Do it, Hikari," Sara said, "Let's not leave anything to chance."

————

As we left the meeting with Hikari, a fresh pang of anxiety hit me: I still hadn't mentioned the song fragment.

"Hey, can we stop for a second?" I asked.

Sara, Cass, Hana, Nova, and Bloom all stopped and turned toward me.

"What is it? Is everything alright?" Sara asked.

"I think so," I said. "It's just, well, it's hard to explain."

"That's okay," Hana said. "What's on your mind?"

I nodded. "Okay, yeah. Um, I've been hearing a melody I don't recognize, ever since the Daedalus Theater show. Like, it sounds familiar, but I don't know why."

The other girls exchanged concerned looks.

"Claire, anytime something unexplained and potentially magical happens, you should let us know," Sara said.

"You're right!" I said. "And I would have. But then Bloom showed up, and then Makula showed up, and then there were all the fascist robots, and the brewery monster, and it just didn't seem like a big deal anymore, like maybe that's just the life of a magical girl." I paused for breath. How did Hikari *do* this every time they spoke? "But last night I had a dream about it, and I'm starting to think there's something to it."

"Whatcha mean, babe?" Nova asked.

"My dream had something to do with healing, and the Exalted Harmony. I just don't know the full connection."

"That's interesting, alright," Cass said. "The Exalted Harmony wasn't exactly what I'd call a *constructive* thing. It helped make a real big explosion, as I recall."

Sara nodded. "Indeed. So what's the connection between it and healing?"

I shook my head and concentrated. Everything was atomized and disconnected in my head, but I felt there had to be *something* tying it all together. I thought back to the day on top of the Grand Sovereign, to the moment we used the Exalted Harmony for the first time.

And then, a picture slowly came into better focus.

"We didn't use 'the Exalted Harmony.' We used one particular version of it," I said.

"What do you mean?" Hana asked.

I closed my eyes and focused as I put the pieces together. "What I know is the Exalted Harmony is the ultimate form of magical girl power. That's what I learned from Adia. But we all have our own versions of it. I didn't say 'Exalted Harmony' on that rooftop, you know? I said 'Riot Harmony Chordal Cataclysm.'"

"That's true," Sara said. "So what you're saying is—"

"There's more kinds of Exalted Harmony," I said. "Or, like, different *expressions* of it. Um, does that make sense?"

Cass smiled. "It does, yeah! We channel magica with songs. That's gotta be true of the Exalted Harmony, too."

"So what you're sayin' is there could be all kinds of Exalted Harmonies?" Nova asked.

"Maybe, yeah," I said. "Maybe it all comes down to how you perform it."

Sara thought for a moment and gave me a nod. "While we've got some free time, let's head down to the music room and see what this fragment sounds like. Bloom, you don't have to—"

"Oh no, I'm not missing this," Bloom said. "I've had enough

medical tests for one day already. As much as it surprises even me to say it, I'd rather listen to a bunch of magical girls prattle on about feelings."

"It'll be good practice for when you start doing it yourself," Cass said.

Bloom frowned and pointed at her. "Don't you even start."

———

While the rest of the girls watched and listened, my fingers danced over the keys of my keytar as I played the last notes of the mysterious fragment that had been haunting me. The final tone rang out across the room and faded into silence, and I looked up from the keys.

"So, that's all I have," I said.

Hana nodded. "I can see why it's been stuck in your head! It might not be finished, but what there is of it is very pretty."

"Yeah," Cass said. "I could hear something great coming out of it."

Bloom cleared her throat and shifted in her seat. "Not that anybody cares what I think, but I *suppose* it's not altogether unpleasant."

"Don't dump all the praise on her at once, Bloom," Sara said.

"Well then," Bloom said, "if praise is what you most desire, Iris is positively smitten with this melodic fragment."

"Yeah? She is?" I asked.

"Yes, but don't expect me to gush in a similar fashion."

Nova grinned at me. "I think it sounds great, babe! I can imagine it all arranged and full band-ified!"

"Maybe that's the reason it came to our Guardian of Harmony," Sara said.

"What do you mean?" I asked.

She smiled. "We're going to make your fragment into a song, Claire. And you're going to get your first Magica Riot songwriting credit."

"I mean, I haven't really written anything."

"Not *yet*," Cass said.

Hana nodded. "Take that melody and run with it, Claire!"

"Plus, ya got all of us to help out!" Nova said.

Bloom rolled her eyes and looked away, shaking her head before finally sighing. She gave me a half-pump of her fist. "Yes, go Claire, et cetera."

The notion was a bit frightening. I'd loved being in the band, and I'd never felt anything but loved and accepted, but putting my creative stamp on Magica Riot felt almost like a transgression, considering how new I was.

"You all don't mind letting the new girl write a song?" I asked.

"No way," Cass said. "You're part of the family, Claire. Take the lead and get your moment!"

"Besides, you're following in Iris's footsteps," Sara added. "I'm pretty sure she supports you writing your own Magica Riot songs." She glanced over at Bloom. "Isn't that right?"

Bloom groaned. "Ugh, *fine*. Yes, Iris is excited about the prospect of 'Claire songs,'" she said, making sarcastic quotes with her fingers. "Please, I beg of you, don't make me express any more affection. It's *exhausting*."

"See, babe?" Nova asked. "We're all on your side! Even Bloom!"

"Now wait just a moment," Bloom shot back. "I never—"

Hana reached over and covered Bloom's mouth with her hand. "Yes, we all support you! Bloom just makes it unanimous."

Silently, Bloom nodded.

"Thanks, everybody," I said, "including you, Bloom. I'll try my best."

CHAPTER 12

Over the next several days, the rest of the girls and I settled into the early stages of building up my mysterious fragment into an actual song. For everything else I'd done as a member of Magica Riot, I had never before been a party to their songwriting process; it was a reminder that, apart from their skill as magical girls, Magica Riot was also a hell of a set of musicians.

Writing time was factored in alongside rehearsal and combat practice, and it started with Sara and Cass. The two of them had been the engine at the core of Magica Riot's songwriting since the early days, alongside Iris on lyric duty. Despite logically knowing I belonged, it was still intimidating to sit in the music room and behave as a peer to them.

I quickly realized that fear was unfounded. Sara and Cass were pros, and treated me with respect. As we worked with the melody fragment, the two of them quickly built up a chord progression to serve as a foundation beneath it, one that left space for Cass and me to accent it with melodies and counter-melodies.

There was plenty of trial and error, along with a healthy application of music theory, especially from Cass. Her knowledge was truly impressive, and came alive even more when Hana entered the mix.

Once she and Nova joined the work sessions, the fragment gradually started sounding like an actual song. An embryonic song, sure, but a song. There was plenty of work ahead to refine it into something that could stand alongside Magica Riot's catalog—and there was still the matter of writing lyrics for it, too —but it no longer seemed like the echo of something unknown in my mind.

Through it all, Bloom was mostly occupied with Dr. Barrera's tests. Gradually, though, I began to notice that she was hanging around the music room when taking a break from those tests. She never engaged directly with the process, and mostly kept to herself at the periphery of the room, but I could tell she *was* paying some amount of attention.

Was she curious about songwriting, or just bored and looking for something to do? Either way, I decided not to call attention to it. I was just happy she was there, and *wanted* to be there.

When we'd go home to the apartment, she never asked directly about the song, but she also didn't seem to mind me talking about it. That felt like progress.

Our unusual home life had become an oddly comfortable routine. Breakfast in the morning—coffee and a bagel for me, and Peanut Butter Crunchlins for Bloom—before a lengthy session at the Vault, then home again for dinner. Which, for Bloom, usually meant more Crunchlins. A peace had settled over my apartment.

But it wasn't to last.

We'd just returned home after a particularly fruitful day of songwriting. I'd planned to work on the song a little more before it got too late, but I soon discovered an absolute disaster had struck.

"Claire!" I heard her shout from the living room, "We have a dire situation!"

I ran back in from the bedroom, half-expecting to see a horde of Rhapsodyz bots or Pandora Corruption monsters busting down the front door. "What? What's wrong?"

Bloom stood just outside the kitchen, holding an open, upside-down box of Peanut Butter Crunchlins. "We have no food!"

I exhaled. "Oh, is that all?"

"What do you mean *is that all?*" Bloom asked in disbelief. "We have no *food*, Claire! I will starve!"

I tried to stifle a laugh. "I mean, we do have food. There's a whole kitchen full of things to eat."

"All of which is distressingly inferior to the crisped orbs!" She shook the box again. "The *orbs*, Claire! This is an affront to me personally!"

"Can't you hold out until my next grocery day?"

"If you wish me to suffer and writhe in agony, just attack me directly, magical girl. Otherwise, I require sustenance!"

I stared back at her. "You know, for somebody who didn't even know what she enjoyed just a little while ago, you've gotten to be very demanding."

"You should be thrilled I'm expressing myself as an individual," she grinned.

"Of course I am. It's just—"

"Good! Then I shall await the delivery of my Crunchlins, post-haste!"

I shook my head. "Oh, no, no, no. You're coming with me."

"I'm *what?*"

"It's time you learned how grocery shopping works. Besides, there's a few other things I should grab while I'm there, and I could use the extra pair of hands."

Bloom's expression soured. "I refuse!"

"Then you'll just have to go without your Crunchlins," I shot back.

She fumed silently for a very long moment before continuing. "Oh, very well. You are more cunning than you appear, Claire."

I laughed. "Yeah, people tell me that all the time. Now, you ready to do some shopping?"

———

We walked down to the grocery co-op and picked up Bloom's Crunchlins—three boxes, just to be safe—as well as a few other odds and ends that I knew the apartment needed. Bloom's mood improved noticeably once we acquired her cereal, and I could have sworn she was even starting to enjoy being out in the city with me.

Even though the sun had gone down, the sky was light enough to make the walk back a breeze. We threaded our way back through the neighborhood streets off Sandy Boulevard, a normally uneventful and quiet route to the apartment.

Which was, of course, the moment that sinister tendrils of black mist suddenly sprung out of thin air and encircled us.

The sky darkened as the mist grew thicker. I felt a chill wash over me, enough to give me goosebumps. The mist arrived so quickly that I was momentarily disoriented, but as I found my bearings again, I knew immediately what the cause had to be.

Bloom had reached the same conclusion. "That accursed sorceress is skulking about!"

"Makula!" I shouted, summoning what courage I had. "Show yourself!"

Bloom narrowed her eyes. "I believe we should assume more powerful forms, Claire."

I sat my bag of groceries down on the sidewalk, raised my arm, and felt my microphone materialize in my grip. Bloom ran over, placed her bags beside mine, and glared at Makula's swirling mist.

"Sorceress," Bloom shouted, "if you do *anything* to harm my provisions, you will earn my full enmity!"

"Um, let's worry about that afterward," I said. I brought my microphone to my lips and shouted my transformation. "Maid-ensong harmony power ... go live!"

In a flash of purple energy, I shot up through the dimensional barriers away from Makula's mist. Within moments, I was on the Celestial Stage again. Ribbons of magica wrapped me up and formed my costume, while purple energy surged across me and tinted my hair and eyes.

As quickly as it had begun, the Maidensong returned me to Earth, fully transformed. I stood proudly and stared down the mist as it took shape, and pointed at what would soon be my foe.

"I am a guardian of song and heart," I shouted. "Servant of the darkness, be silenced by the song of Riot Purple, Guardian of Harmony!"

Makula's laughter echoed on the street as she materialized, standing before me in her full seven feet of height. "It's still so strange to hear those words come from *you*, dear girl. I heard Iris say them so many times, apart from this new Guardian of Harmony business." She smirked at Bloom. "But then, I suppose Iris is dealing with her own issues, isn't she?"

Beside me, Bloom snapped her fingers and became engulfed in swirling crimson energy. Moments later, she emerged in her black corset dress and long fingerless gloves. "You'll not be so smug once I'm done with you, sorceress! You deal again with the illustrious Bloom!"

"So very presumptuous," Makula laughed. "Stay your hands, my dears. I'm not here to fight. Not this time, at least."

"I'm not sure I'm ready to trust you about that," I said.

"Likewise," Bloom said. "Do you take us for fools?"

"I wish only to talk," Makula said. She looked around the street and shook her head. "This location is far too pedestrian. We shall go somewhere a bit more interesting to have our chat. Once we're done, I'll let you continue with your errand."

I frowned. "A 'more interesting' place?"

"Indeed," Makula said. "A place quite familiar to you and your little friend here, actually."

"Little friend?" Bloom asked. "I'll have you show me more respect than that!"

I shook my head. "Familiar how? Where are you—"

Before I could finish, she conjured her staff, and with a single motion of her arm, crafted a sphere of magica around us.

The magica faded moments later, and we were no longer in the neighborhood around Sandy. As the wind blew through my hair and I readjusted to my new surroundings, I saw the city stretching out below us in all directions, framed by broken concrete pillars.

We were on top of the damaged, unfinished shell of the Grand Sovereign Hotel downtown, several floors below where the roof used to be.

I knew the place well, of course. It had been the site of our final push to stop Rennia, the place where we'd used the Exalted Harmony for the first time to drop the Pandora Corruption bug monster into the dimensional gate.

"There we are," Makula said. "Much better, don't you agree?"

Bloom glared at her. "I do not take kindly to being transported around all creation on your whims, sorceress!"

"Why did you bring us here?" I asked.

"Because it's quite apt for the situation we are in now," Makula said as she looked around at the unfinished, sheared-off concrete columns that had once supported the rest of the tower. "It's my understanding, from my research, that this structure was a grand edifice to your society's lust for money and status, yes?"

"I can't say you're wrong," I nodded. The Grand Sovereign was supposed to be a haven for the wealthy, after all. Hana and I had talked about it as the kind of change we didn't like to see in Portland.

"All that excess," Makula continued. "The sinking of so much capital into a monument to the glory of the fortunate, and it was laid waste by the power of magica, one of the most ancient forces in all the planes of the universe. But there's more than that."

"Like what?"

"You see, I'm trying to understand you, dear girl, and here— or rather, about ninety of your 'feet' above our heads—was the site of a very formative moment for you."

"I would think magical girls are easy to understand," Bloom said. "Why are you not more fascinated by *me*, sorceress? I am a product of a truly singular power!"

Makula laughed. "Oh, please. I solved you at our first encounter. Another self-aggrandizing minion, lacking any sense of empathy or duty. Your angry bluster is the result of a frankly pedestrian inferiority complex." She leered at us, showing far too many teeth, and stepped closer. "Despite the fascinating nature of your creation, you are merely an irritable passenger occupying a far more capable host." She bent slightly, looming into Bloom's space. "You *bore* me."

I tensed, ready for Bloom to fire back, but the moment never came. Bloom backed away, almost imperceptibly. Her expression softened from her furious glower to something still full of anger, but with a measure of surprise. The hurt was plainly evident on her face.

Makula straightened and turned her attention back to me. "Now, the one who replaced Riot Purple I find to be a more interesting puzzle box."

I felt my blood chill under her gaze. If the rest of Magica Riot had been here, they'd have pushed back. Sara would have stood up to her. Cass or Nova wouldn't let that stand. Hana would have stood up for Bloom. But me? I stood there, intimidated by this villainous sorceress.

Was I less of a magical girl for that?

I swallowed my nerves and managed a reply. "What's there to understand about me? I'm a magical girl like any other, aren't I?"

"Humans truly do lack perspective," Makula sighed. "No,

Claire, you are *not* like every other magical girl, not because of anything particularly unique about you physically or mentally, but because of circumstance."

I shook my head. "I don't understand. What is your problem with me?"

"An amplification of the problems I have with your kind," Makula said. She walked around the ruined skyscraper, gazing up toward where the rooftop would have been, and gestured with her staff. "I imagine this must have been quite the sight. The destruction of the dimension gate, I mean."

"Yeah, you could say that."

"The amount of magica required to collapse a gate between worlds is staggering, you know. It is hard to comprehend that much power resting in the hands of a being who has barely taken her first steps into the world of magica."

"It's not as if that was my choice," I said. "I was selected by Adia, and that power given to me by the Maidensong."

"I understand that it wasn't your choice, girl, but the fact remains that you have it now, and your kind has not proven you are ready for that."

"Ready for it? Says who?"

"I do, for one," Makula said as she stepped closer and glared down at me. "I've been watching your species for a long time now, and every time I see you dabble in magica, things wind up going wrong somehow."

"That's not true, though," I protested. "Magical girls have been around for a long time, even longer than you've been coming here. We keep the world safe!"

"I know you girls were once truly powerful, as you are now, but for many years you were held back. A consequence, as we both agree, of a previous human failure to control your more destructive urges in the presence of magica." She shifted her gaze back at Bloom as she spoke.

"You're talking about Rennia," I said. "She was corrupted, though."

Makula laughed. "Because of your human nature. Your curiosity running headlong into disaster with your lust for power and dominance. Isn't that right, Bloom? If Rennia and her army were more competent, and less susceptible to human weaknesses, they might very well have been ruling this planet at this very moment."

Bloom shrunk back, ever so slightly. "Leave me out of this, sorceress. You know nothing of Rennia, or of me."

"Please do keep telling yourself that," Makula said. "The truth of the matter is, I am *quite* knowledgeable. I am a scholar, in fact! My people have always sought to understand the nature of magica, and the way the different shapers grant their power. From my studies into your world and your Maidensong, I know that Rennia was once a magical girl just like Claire here, a protector and explorer who pushed too far into things she didn't fully comprehend, and paid the price for that recklessness."

"But she was stopped, twice," I pointed out.

"And you think that absolves you of humanity's crimes? Your people can't even tend to your own, non-magical business. Your societies are corrupt and cruel, and spawn the sort of heartless greed that births new Rennias."

"A lot of society *is* terrible," I sighed. "But it's not all of us, and magical girls try to change the world. To make it better."

"And yet, your people are, at this very moment, rewarding those who work to twist magica for wicked purposes," Makula said, shaking her head. "They hand tremendous wealth to people who treat magica like a toy, which is the other reason I'm here. I know the stink of this amateurish magica, for I have fought it before."

I nodded. "Yeah, I heard about that. Polybius."

"Quite right. And once again, your people are insulting magica for profit." She paused for a moment. "How do you know of that fight?"

"It's in the Starlight Alliance records," I said, "and we also talked to Jade Evergreen about it."

Makula's expression softened; in normal circumstances, I might have called it wistful. "Jade Evergreen still lives, then?"

"That's right."

She chuckled softly. "I must admit, that news isn't altogether unpleasant. She was the first of your kind I ever personally encountered. It was there that I knew at least some of your species had the ability to make our confrontations interesting, instead of solely irritating."

"Jade was a great magical girl," I said. "We are, too."

"Greatness among the insects is still an insect quality," Makula said. "The power the Maidensong has given you is among the strongest in all the planes of creation, and yet, *you* were the key to it. A girl with barely any experience at all. Do you have any idea how much raw power you wield every time you call forth your Exalted Harmony?"

"Seems like we handled it fine."

"That time, yes. Can you guarantee it will always be so? That you will never falter when calling forth the great cosmic torrent?"

"We'll always do our best. Besides, I believe I can make new songs, use the power of the Exalted Harmony in gentler ways."

Makula smiled. "My analogy was intentional. Wielding magica is like wielding the oceans, a tremendous force that will crush you and anything you hold dear if it goes out of control. Yes, you can direct the flow, and yes, you can use it for small things, but that potential is always there, girl. Always waiting for you to make an error and wipe away whatever it touches. It is not a power to be taken lightly."

I felt a stirring inside me, feelings that at one time were foreign to me but had grown more familiar, coming to life the longer I lived as both a girl and a magical girl. Bravery. Determination. Strength. With the fire of the Maidensong surging within me, I stepped toward Makula, reached out, and pressed my finger into her shoulder.

"I don't take it lightly. I worry *all the time* about letting people down. About people being hurt because of me, or failing to stop a villain like you from hurting them."

"Villain," Makula sneered. "Such a limited understanding of—"

"*I'm not done yet,*" I interrupted, poking her harder. "Yeah, maybe I barely know what I'm doing, but I'm not going to let that stop me from learning and getting better. I'm not going to stop trying to help people, even if there are people out there who don't understand us! Because I'm not alone. I've got Sara, Cass, Hana, and Nova on my side. We've been given something amazing, and we'll use it to make the world better. We can do it, and we'll prove everybody like you wrong!"

Bloom stared silently at me in genuine surprise, while Makula broke out in laughter.

"I'm impressed, girl," Makula said, after regaining her composure. "You have something of a backbone in you after all! I can see now that you're not so different from Jade. You may be foolish, but you'll make the task ahead of me interesting. For that, I am grateful."

"Whatever you're up to, Magica Riot will stop it," I shot back.

"You're welcome to try. Prove your worth to me, or fall in defeat like my other targets. Either way, I look forward to the day you show me!"

With another flash of magica, Bloom and I were standing once again on the street near Sandy Boulevard, beside our bags of groceries. Makula was nowhere to be seen.

"I'm getting kind of tired of her doing that," I said.

Bloom nodded, but didn't answer. I looked over at her; she stared down at the pavement, looking preoccupied.

Before I could say anything else, my wrist link chirped with an emergency call from Sara.

"*Claire, are you okay? We got a large reading from your location, followed by the Grand Sovereign site. Then everything went dark again. Do we have a situation?*"

"Oh, yeah, that," I answered. "Bloom and I got teleported, but we're okay now."

"So, a visit from Makula."

"Yeah. She's gone."

"Copy that. If you're okay, we can debrief in the morning."

"That works for me. I'll see you at the Vault first thing in the morning."

"Right. Over and out."

I lowered my wrist link and turned my attention back to Bloom. "Are you okay?"

"I'm not injured," she said, her voice soft. I couldn't help but notice that wasn't strictly an answer to what I'd asked. "Claire, I'm impressed."

"Impressed?"

"By you. You defended yourself skillfully. I didn't think you had that much in you."

"Neither did I." I reached over and touched her arm. "Seriously, Bloom, are you—"

"I'm fine," she interrupted. "Just perturbed by Makula's words, I suppose."

"She doesn't know what she's talking about."

Bloom nodded as she walked over and picked up her grocery bags. "Perhaps. May we return to your home now?"

"Sure, yeah," I said. I de-transformed, grabbed my own bags, and set off with Bloom toward the apartment.

I'd have to tell everybody about my encounter with Makula, but whatever else came of it, at least I had a better idea of what she wanted out of us. It was clear now, though, that the next time we met her, our lives would get even more complicated.

CHAPTER 13

The next morning, Bloom and I informed the rest of the team about our surprise Makula incident. Since we were so close to the Rhapsodyz event at the food cart pod—and since nothing had technically *happened* to us, other than a conversation—we decided the best course of action was to stay focused on the cart pod event. The potential for something dangerous to occur there between Rhapsodyz and Makula was too great, and we needed to be ready.

Still, our encounter with Makula kept weighing on my mind. I'd put up my best strong face against her, but her words gnawed at me. I was, after all, trying to harness our ultimate magica with a song of my own creation, rather than the one we'd accessed via the Maidensong's guidance. Maybe I didn't really know what I was doing.

There was somebody out there who had a lot of experience with Sorceress Makula, though, so I decided that talking to her again would be my next goal.

And so, I found myself making the trip down Northeast Sandy again, during a rare lull in the band's daily activities. I grabbed a Cycleburg bike and rode over to Dark Water just after opening, and wound up being the first person through the door.

Apart from Jade Evergreen, of course.

As I stepped through the bar's door and let my eyes adjust to the dark interior, I spotted her immediately. Just as before, she stood behind the bar, but this time she leaned against it, watching the door as I entered. It was as if she knew I was coming.

"Welcome back, kid," Jade said as she waved at me. "Come on over and grab a seat."

"Thanks," I said. I crossed the empty room and slid onto the barstool across from her. "Um, you don't seem too surprised to see me."

She laughed. "Not at all. I expected you'd come back around. You drinking a lager again?"

"Sure, that sounds good. Why did you expect I'd be back?"

"I felt it," she said as she held a pint glass beneath a tap and pulled. "What brings you around today, Claire?"

I laughed and shrugged nervously. "I had an encounter with Sorceress Makula again. Well, Bloom and I did."

She slid my beer across the bar top to me. "Ah, the old Makula one-on-one. Or one-on-two, I guess."

I raised the glass and took a sip. "It's not something unique to me, I guess."

"No way," Jade chuckled, shaking her head. "That woman *loves* to hear herself talk. And I'm guessing she said something that's gotten to you."

Jade was perceptive. I smiled and nodded back at her. "You're good at this."

"Claire, I've tangled with Sorceress Makula more times than I can recall. And I'm *also* a bartender."

"Fair," I laughed. "And yeah, Makula said something about my lack of experience. About how I don't know what I'm doing yet, and I'm trying to command all these giant forces I don't understand. She said it's like thinking I can control the ocean."

Jade nodded. "She always did have a really inflated opinion of herself, and a lower opinion of the rest of us."

"Yeah," I said. I took another, longer sip of beer, and sighed. "I'm just maybe a little scared she's right."

"Why's that?" she asked. "Talk to me. Maybe we can work through it."

"I'd appreciate that a lot," I said.

She smiled. "Of course! I'm here for you, kid. Jade Evergreen is on the case!"

I took a deep breath. "A little while after our true powers unlocked, I started hearing this song. Or, not a full song, but a fragment of one. A melody that's been getting harder and harder to ignore. And one night, I had a dream about it. It's related to the Exalted Harmony."

"Exalted Harmony," Jade repeated. "That's the big giant attack you girls used on top of that hotel, right?"

"Yeah." I nodded. "This melody, it's like it's telling me I can use the Exalted Harmony in a gentler way. So the other girls and I started working on turning it into a song."

"Well, that makes sense," Jade said. "Our songs are spells. Why couldn't you use it that way?"

Unconsciously, my gaze drifted down, and I stared at the bar top. There were times when my anxiety hit me strongly and I wished I could curl up inside myself. "The problem is that the Exalted Harmony is, like, our ultimate power. What if Makula's right? What if I try to use it gently and I wind up hurting people? What if I really don't know what I'm doing?"

I felt a tear roll down my cheek; apparently, this had been affecting me more than I realized. I also felt warmth on my hands, and looked up.

Jade had taken my hands in hers, and was looking at me with an expression of kind warmth, like the sun dappling through the leaves in summer.

"Claire," she said softly, "Makula is not right about you."

"How do you know?" I asked.

"I *know*," she answered, squeezing my hands. "Trust me. One Guardian of Harmony to another."

I shook my head. "Wait, Guardian of Harmony? How do you know about that?"

Jade smiled. "When you awakened the true power of magical girls, I felt it, too. It happened to me. And when it did, I experienced an understanding I never had before. See, one of my powers is healing through song, like a super-empathy sort of thing. Back when I was fighting, without the full powers, I used to hit the wall all the time."

"Oh, yeah," I said, "I guess it makes sense that you'd be familiar with that feeling."

"Constantly. No matter how hard I pushed, there was always something beyond that I couldn't connect to. That is, until you came along and broke through the wall."

"And, um, what did you find?"

"That if all this had happened to me in the eighties, I would have been a Guardian of Harmony. I just felt it in my heart the moment you unlocked the powers. So, I know what you're capable of, Claire. You have to use that power to help and heal, and I *know* you can."

I blushed. "I appreciate your confidence. It's just that Makula—"

"Makula is a lot of things," Jade said, shaking her head, "but she's not infallible. She loves to get in your head, mess with your confidence, try to find all the angles she can to get an advantage on you. Loves to psych you out, and if she thinks she can get away with it, she'll even cut deals to get what she wants. She's not a mindless evil. She's crafty and cunning, and you can't take what she says at face value if she thinks she's got the edge."

I nodded and wiped my eyes. "Yeah. That makes sense."

"When you beat her, that's when you'll see her at her most honest. Until then, you can't let her put that poison in your feelings. She's just trying to win. And yeah, she's powerful and skilled, but she doesn't know the Maidensong as well as she thinks she does. She doesn't know what magical girls can do. Believe me, I know!"

"Yeah," I chuckled, "I guess you would."

"The way I see it," Jade continued, "yeah, calling upon magica is like commanding an ocean, but it's more complicated than that. You've got the Maidensong and the other girls of Magica Riot on your side, and none of them want to see you fail. It's the combination that makes it work."

"Right," I said. "People working together."

"I'm guessing you know a thing or two about that already."

I smiled. "Yeah, I do."

Jade gave my hand another squeeze. "You've got to put Makula out of your head. Believe in your own power, Claire. You're a Guardian of Harmony now. You were made for this."

"Alright." I nodded, and took another long sip. "Yeah. I'll try."

I heard the bar door swing open again. Jade looked up, nodded to the newcomer, and gave them a wave.

"Welcome, friend," she said. "What can I get you?"

A familiar voice answered. "Oh, I heard you had a new sweet Ryland on tap!"

I turned around. Hazel stood behind me, grinning with her hands in the pockets of her jumpsuit, looking adorable and hot in equal measure.

"Hey, Haze!" I said. "How'd you know—"

"Nova told me you were heading out here," she said as she took a seat on the stool beside me and rubbed my shoulder. "I figured I'd come make sure my magical girlfriend is okay."

"That means a lot," I said. "Oh, hey, you haven't met Jade yet."

Hazel turned to Jade with a smile. "I haven't!"

"Jade Evergreen," Jade said as she extended her hand and shook Hazel's. "Original Portland magical girl turned magical bartender."

"Hazel Hoffman," Hazel said. "Claire's non-magical girl-friend, and Magica Riot's booking agent."

I smiled. "I wouldn't call you non-magical, Haze."

"I have my powers." Hazel grinned. "Jade, I've heard so much about you! You've been taking care of my Claire for me?"

Jade laughed and winked at me. "Oh yes. She's quite the sensitive sort, isn't she?"

"I am, yeah," I said, feeling the blush in my cheeks return.

"That's my anxiety girl. You wanna talk about it?" Hazel asked as she leaned against my shoulder. She was so warm.

"Sorceress Makula tried to make me second-guess myself, and the new song."

"Ah," Hazel said. "I hope Jade here convinced you not to listen to that jerk."

"I tried my best," Jade nodded.

"Yeah," I said. "It's just a lot of pressure, you know?"

Hazel squeezed my arm. "Sure, but it's pressure you're ready for."

"I appreciate the confidence. It's just hitting me from two directions, I guess."

"Aw, yeah," she said. "A song for the band ..."

"And a song for the Exalted Harmony," I nodded. "So I've got to make sure it's a good song, *and* that it works as a performance of magica."

"I know you'll be able to do it."

"I've just never had to do anything like this before, and—"

Hazel turned on her stool and took my hands in hers. "Claire, your whole life these last few months has been doing things you've never done before. You literally became a girl, became a *magical* girl, and saved the world. You should consider that your old anxiety is making you sell yourself short, just a little tiny bit."

Jade smiled. "Listen to your girlfriend, Claire."

"Well, I guess that puts it into perspective," I said. "It's just that by writing a song of my own for us, I'll be even more directly responsible for what happens. People's lives might depend on that song."

Jade nodded. "That's why you're going to be a great magical

girl. I think girls like us are especially good at this. We wanted to be girls so strongly that we made it happen, even while the world yelled at us. Who better to become the most powerful girls there are?"

"Exactly," Hazel said. "I might not know all the details of magica as well as you girls do, but I know the Maidensong chose you for a reason, and you've more than proven that it made the right choice."

I blushed and squeezed her hands. "Aw, that means a lot to me."

"Besides, you're not alone. You've got Sara, and Cass, and Hana, and Nova, and everybody else in the Vault."

"And me, too," Jade said. "I'll have your back, Claire."

"And you've got me," Hazel added. She leaned in and rested her head against my shoulder. "And I will always believe in you."

"Thank you, both of you," I said.

Hazel nuzzled against me softly. "Anytime, rock star."

"It's my great honor," Jade said.

CHAPTER 14

The morning of the Rhapsodyz demo, I arrived at the Vault with Bloom and led her down to the medical bay. Due to all the data Dr. Barrera had been assembling on her, the testing rounds were a bit more spread out now, and this was her first in a few days.

"Okay," I said, "good luck with the tests today."

"I grow weary of these intrusions," Bloom said. "It seems as though they truly never reach their end."

"Well, it's a complicated problem. Dr. Barrera just wants to help you."

"One would think that she would have stumbled across the solution by now, even if it were an accident." She shrank a little, like a balloon that'd just been partly deflated. I could tell all of this was sapping her drive.

I reached out and lightly touched her arm. "Going by what she's been saying, this is a kind of science that didn't even *exist* before you came back to us. Bear with her a little, you know?"

Bloom grumbled. "Eh, perhaps. How about you take your optimism and go play your keyboard? Leave me to my agonies."

Her voice sounded flat, the flamboyant edge gone. She was

certainly tired, but Makula's cutting words atop the empty hulk of the Grand Sovereign had clearly rattled her. The sight of her like this unsettled me a little.

I started to reach out to her, but thought better of it. I wasn't sure how much a gesture of affection would be welcome in that moment.

"Alright," I nodded. "I'll come check on you later."

Without another word, she entered the medical bay and closed the door behind her.

With this additional anxiety on my mind, I headed down to the music room to get my work in on the song. I'd almost made it halfway down the corridor when my wrist link buzzed with an alert.

I raised the link up and tapped the screen. A map of downtown Portland appeared, and several blocks west of the Vault, a yellow icon lit up over the location of the Kaiju Carcass Food Cart Pod. Beside it, the words *"SINNESLÖSCHEN MAGICA DETECTED"* glared up at me.

Clearly, Hikari had filled in some data in the sensor system.

A few moments later, a call came in from Commander McCoy, right on cue. *"Agents Ward, Coates, Hasegawa, Nova, and Ryland, please report to the command center."*

I tapped the call to answer. "Acknowledged, commander. On my way."

I got to the command center just as the rest of the band did. Commander McCoy, Saoirse, and Hazel stood behind Hikari at the main console, looking up at the CRT array on the wall. The alert at the Kaiju Carcass Food Cart Pod glowed angrily on the displays.

"Girls, things are getting started over at the cart pod," Commander McCoy said. "Y'all ready to make an appearance?"

"Ready and waiting, commander," Sara said. "Do we know the situation?"

"Nothin' dangerous yet, but we're gettin' a lot of readings

that line up with the Rhapsodyz bots, and that means Sinnes-löschen, too."

Hikari nodded. "The Sinneslöschen magica isn't as clearly defined as other kinds like the Pandora magica but I've been doing some modifications to the routines in the sensor system trying to see if I can isolate the signatures and tell you a more exact number of targets if you'll give me just a moment I should have something for you."

As Hikari typed away at the keyboard, Cass sighed. "You know, whatever goes down today, there's gonna be a lot more innocent folks than there were at the brewery."

"You're right," Hana said. "We'll have to be vigilant."

"Well, at least at the food cart pod there's more ways for people to escape," I said.

"If something does come up," Sara said, "it'll be on full public display. Let's do our very best today, no matter what happens."

"I ain't worried," Nova said. "If somebody tries to mess with our town, we'll teach 'em a flammin' lesson! Don't matter if it's some jerko robot company or Makula herself!"

The computer terminal beeped, and a series of yellow blobs appeared on the map of downtown, centered on the Kaiju Carcass Food Cart Pod. As the blobs came into focus, it became obvious that they were all over the cart pod.

Hikari nodded at the big screen. "Here you go there's a rough count for you looks like at least fifteen to twenty bots there it's not exact due to the nature of the sensors and such but this is a pretty good estimate I think that should give you an idea of what to expect sorry to be the bringer of bad news you've got a lot of junky nuggets to deal with."

"Fifteen to twenty?" Cass asked. "How many of these things are there?"

"Maybe they see this as a big PR opportunity, so they're showing off everything they have," Hana said.

Sara nodded. "It does make me wonder how close these things are to full-scale production, though."

At that, Saoirse perked up. "It's a good question, and if the one I've got down in the armory is anything to go on, they've still got some work to do on the software side. The hardware, though … well, I'd wager they can crank it out pretty easily now."

"Even the thaumatite cores?" I asked.

"There's the big question. Can they make 'em with ease, or are these all they have? No way of knowin' that without gettin' a look at their data. The one I have seems like a hodgepodge of mass-produced and bespoke parts."

Hazel stared up at the big screen and then looked over at me. "You should keep an eye out for Allison Webb, too."

"Yeah, good point," I said. "I'm not super excited about running into her again."

Another chime issued from the main computer terminal, and a larger circle appeared over the food cart pod on the map. There was no specific note next to this one, just a message that read *"RESOLVING …"* in block lettering.

"Hey not to alarm anybody but there's a trace reading showing up now for what looks like a different kind of magica," Hikari said.

"We can pick up trace readings now?" Sara asked.

Hikari turned around and gave us the tiniest smile. "I've been busy optimizing things in the system you know there was some headroom in the sensor grid that could be better taken advantage of it's not that there was anything wrong with it before but you just didn't have somebody wise in the ways of software until now."

"I'll own that, yeah," Saoirse said. "The kid here's done wonders for everything they've touched."

"The analysis routines are still working on it because it's a little too indistinct and subtle right now but it's definitely not the

Sinneslöschen signature and it's not something else like the Pandora Corruption so you know process of elimination and all that I bet you're looking at a certain scary-hot tall sorceress," Hikari said.

"Where there's smoke," Cass said.

Hikari tapped a few keys and a new line of text appeared beneath the *"RESOLVING"* note, that read *"LIKELY SOURCE: MARELIAN MAGICA. MATCH: 36%."* The numbers ticked up slowly as the computer chewed on the data.

"That's close enough to fire for me," Sara said. "I think it's time we made an appearance, before things get too interesting."

From the command center doorway, a familiar voice called out to us. "If you are returning to action, you know who must accompany you!"

We turned to see Bloom striding into the room, followed by a harried-looking Dr. Barrera.

"She saw the alerts on her wrist link," the doctor said. "I couldn't keep her in the med bay."

"Quite right, dear doctor," Bloom said. "You all know that I can be of use again, just as I was the first time! I demand that you bring me along!" I couldn't help but think she was trying to pump herself up again after what had happened with Makula.

"Well, she did help us before," Hana said.

"Yeah, she might have some attitude problems, but Bloom knows how to punch!" Nova grinned.

"Are you sure about this?" I asked Bloom. "There's a lot of those robots out there. They're definitely going to affect us like last time, and that hits you way worse than it does us."

"Now that I know to expect it," Bloom said, "I can overcome it!"

I frowned. I wanted to believe her.

"Oh come on," she bellowed. "I crave action! It's in my being! Let me get some payback on those metal menaces and that self-important sorceress!"

"She's got a point," Cass said as she looked over at Sara. "What do you think, boss?"

Sara frowned and thought for a moment, before nodding in agreement. "Yeah, okay. Bloom, you're with us."

Bloom laughed. "Finally, the girl prince sees reason!"

"Y'all just be careful out there," Commander McCoy said. "Stay safe, and keep the people safe. We'll be monitoring the whole time."

"Got it, commander," Sara said. "Alright, it's time to go to work."

———

With Sara at the wheel, we rolled Vancent Price out of the garage and up the vehicle tunnel onto the streets of downtown, and made our way west on Burnside Street. Due to the food cart pod taking up the intersection of Burnside and Tenth, the street was now closed as a through street, so we turned off Burnside and parked in the North Park Blocks a couple of streets over.

We ran over to Tenth and headed back toward Burnside. A block away, the dead Pandora Corruption bug monster loomed over the intersection, and in the food cart pod in front of it, large crowds of people dined and watched as the Rhapsodyz robots walked back and forth carrying orders to the picnic tables; a repeat, on a larger scale, of what the company had done at the brewery.

Before we reached the pod, I felt a physical unease inside me, the same I'd felt at the brewery. It was that same sensation of a sound out of tune, resonating in an unpleasant way against my body and the Maidensong. It was already stronger than that previous night, and I even felt it trying to start a headache in me.

Beside me, Bloom looked downright seasick by comparison, as if her Peanut Butter Crunchlins might evacuate her stomach.

I caught Sara's eye and gestured toward Bloom, and Sara nodded back.

"Hold up, everybody," she said. "Let's take stock. We're all feeling the discomfort, aren't we?"

"I feel it, yeah," Cass said. "Worse than before. Could be because there's more of the bots?"

"That'd make sense," Hana said, "and they might also be running them at higher output."

"It feels real gross, yeah," Nova said, "but it looks like it's really hittin' one of us super dang hard!"

Bloom groaned and glared at her. "As astutely observed as ever, yes."

"Bloom, you can turn back, for real," I said. "You don't have to put yourself through this."

"No, Claire," Bloom said, "I will push through. That is what a true warrior would do. These things put off *vile* energy, a desecration of the magica I was born from. Even if I no longer share that resonance, I can't let this stand."

Sara raised her wrist link and opened a comm channel back to the Vault. "Commander, we're arriving on-site and will be scouting the situation. Are there any more signs of Makula?"

"Negative, Agent Ward," Commander McCoy answered, *"it's still an indistinct reading. She could be anywhere. Keep your guard up."*

"Acknowledged, commander. Ward out."

"Well, shall we dive into the corporate nonsense pit?" Cass asked.

We threaded our way into the crowds of the food cart pod. I glanced around the area and took note of the Rhapsodyz bots that I could see; Hikari's sensor adjustments had worked well, as I counted up twenty bots total, equally split between the humanoid models and the dog bots.

At a spot near the middle of the seating area, Rhapsodyz had set up an array of information kiosks. To my complete lack of surprise, I sighted Allison Webb standing by those kiosks.

Well, crap.

"Allison Webb is here," I said.

Sara's eyes followed mine and spotted her as well. "It looks like she's alone."

"That seems odd, considering there's a small army of Rhapsodyz robots here," Hana said. "Shouldn't they have support staff, or at least a few people from their robotics division?"

"Yeah," Cass said. "Almost like she's not just some PR drone."

"You wanna go get up in her business a little?" Nova asked. "Maybe put the fear of magica in her?"

Bloom chuckled dryly. "Oh, I *must* be ill. Nova's suggestion actually sounds good to me."

"No, let's keep our distance for now," Sara said. "I have a feeling she'll come find us soon enough. Let's treat this casually until we have a reason not to."

"Right," Cass said. "Band mode engaged."

We made our way around the periphery of the food cart pod, meeting and greeting the occasional fan passing by as we observed the Rhapsodyz bots going through the motions. Even from a distance, it was obvious the bots were working just as poorly as they had been at the brewery.

In short order, we came up to Juice Wench and Potato Knight-Errant. The smell of frying potatoes wafted out of the latter, indicating Lorelai was hard at work over the oil vats. Delilah, meanwhile, leaned on the small counter at her window, beaming and waving at us as we approached.

"My queens! Welcome!" Delilah said. "Are you here to eat, drink, or be merry?"

"Hi, Delilah," Hana said. "I'm afraid we're not here for refreshments this time."

"Ah, I see! Business, then, I'm guessing?"

Hana nodded silently.

Delilah laughed. "Should I be worried?"

"Not yet," Sara said. "How's it going here with these robots?"

"Ugh, *those* things," Delilah said, rolling her eyes. "Useless trash is what they are! They barely work, they drop food all the time, and they're also straight-up offensive. I hate them!"

Lorelai leaned out of the window of her cart. "They asked me if I was a US citizen before they'd deliver my French fry cones."

"Sounds like they're doing about as well as they were the last time we saw them," Cass said.

"And this woman they've got repping the company is just full of excuses," Lorelai continued. "A total empty suit."

Nova frowned across the cart pod at Allison Webb. "Yeah, we're dang familiar with her."

As if it had been listening in, a humanoid Rhapsodyz robot walked right up to us. I could feel the discomfort in me growing, its discordant magica pinging against the inside of my skull like a badly tuned piano.

The robot's light bar glowed merrily as it spoke. "Greetings! May I offer you a complimentary item, courtesy of the Rhapsodyz corporation?"

"Oh, uh, no thanks," Cass said.

"We don't need anything you're offerin', ya bag of bolts!" Nova said.

"Are you sure? All I need is to see your documentation, including sex assigned at birth," the robot said.

Before any of us could push back against the bot or get away, Bloom gagged and dashed off toward the nearest trash can. She doubled over the side and retched as she groaned in disgust.

The five of us rushed to her side, but she put her arm out to keep us back. I stepped around behind her, taking a chance that she wouldn't refuse my help. Gently, I took her hair in my hands and held it back for her as she recovered. I rested my other hand on her back; she offered no resistance and seemed to relax after a moment.

Bloom wiped her mouth and glared back over her shoulder at the robot. "These mechanical menaces will *pay* with their artificial lives!"

"The interference is really awful now," Cass said. "My money says they're doing it on purpose this time."

From behind us, an all-too-familiar voice approached. "Oh no! Is your friend doing okay?"

I turned around and came face-to-face with Allison Webb. She had a veneer of concern worn like a ceramic mask, radiating cold corporate courtesy.

"We have the situation under control," Sara added.

"Well, I just hate to think that somebody could be having such an unpleasant reaction at one of our events," Allison said. "Please let me get her a complimentary food item and ten free streaming credits for DyzR, our all-new generative AI music service!"

Bloom stood up, marched over, and poked Allison in the chest. "You and your ramshackle robotic risks are the reason for my retching!"

Allison smiled the practiced, artificial smile of somebody who had been in business far too long. "I'm afraid I don't know what you're talking about."

"Do not play coy with me," Bloom said. "I know how you drive these abominations. You do not understand the power you are warping to your profit-minded whims!"

"You've been misinformed," Allison said. "The Rhapsodyz robots are powered by energy cells from one of the other companies in the Rhapsodyz family: SparkLogic!"

"That's a ding-danged flammin' lie," Nova said. "You've got thaumatite in these things!"

"You can drop the act," Sara said. "We know exactly what your company has been doing with these robots."

"I'm sorry, Miss Ward, but I really don't know what you're talking about," Allison said. "To my knowledge, there's nothing unusual at all about our robots, apart from their incredibly advanced market-leading AI technology and—"

She did not get the chance to finish her sentence. With a

digital klaxon, our wrist links blared an alert. I raised mine and glanced down at the words on the screen, confirming my fears.

MARELIAN INCURSION EVENT.

A sudden swirling vortex of black mist encircled the food cart pod, a smoky obsidian wall that rose up above the carts. The crowds gasped and screamed as another familiar voice echoed across the space.

"The magical girls have a point, human! Lie all you want, for it will not matter in the end. I know all your magical sins."

Allison seemed strangely calm. "So, she came back. Optimal."

"Wait, how do you know about her?" I asked. "Were you at the brewery?"

Allison didn't answer, except for the smallest hint of a smile.

I shivered. This was a trap, but not for us.

The black mist swirl flowed into a point above the food cart pod, and then shot across the street to the rooftop of Howell's Books. Most of the giant city-block-sized bookstore was multiple stories tall, but the section looking out at the food cart pod was only a single floor, and our Marelian friend no doubt recognized it as a potential stage.

With a final, dramatic swoosh, the mist organized itself into humanoid form, and a moment later, congealed into corporeality. Sorceress Makula towered over the corner of the Howell's Books rooftop, her height making the building seem smaller in proportion. She gestured with her staff, sweeping it out across the food carts. Her laugh projected a little too well to be purely acoustic.

"Portland!" she said, her voice drowning out the din of the city as the crowds of cart pod customers looked up in surprise. "I have come to set right the wickedness and recklessness of those who dabble in powers beyond your tiny minds."

Sara raised her wrist link and tapped the comm line. "Commander, it's Ward. We've got a situation now. Requesting permission to go hot."

"We see it on the grid," Commander McCoy's voice answered. *"Permission granted. Riot mode authorized. Good luck, girls."*

Up on the bookstore rooftop, Makula's monologue continued. "Humanity's irresponsibility threatens us all, but your betters are ready to correct your misbehaving. A new day dawns, for you are in the presence of the seventh-generation diviner of the twelfth-dimensional House of Marelia. The keeper of the arcane d—"

"Arcane dark arts of the Undertow," Cass said, as the six of us stepped past the food carts and stared up at Makula. "Right? Life-sworn wielder of the blah-de-blah-blah."

"I'm not surprised to find your naive arrogance here, my old foes," Makula said. "But yes, Portland finds itself humbled by the majesty and unparalleled mastery of Grand Cosmic Sorceress Makula!"

"All those fancy words ain't got nothin' on us!" Nova shouted.

"Oh, I expected you would stand in opposition today, as usual," Makula said. "Let us not waste time! I'll just remove one major irritant right now, as a demonstration of my power!"

Just as she'd done at the brewery, Makula swirled her staff above her head, causing a roiling wave of magica to wash out across the food cart pod. In its wake, the Rhapsodyz robots emitted a tortured digital shriek, seized up, went dark, and fell over, lifeless hunks of metal that clanked hard against the pavement.

My eyes darted around the cart pod at the chaos as the robots collapsed. A few people in the crowd cheered, not that I blamed them. And then …

I saw Allison. She had stepped back away from us during Makula's monologue. She seemed completely unfazed by the shutdown of the bots, as if she had expected it the entire time. I watched as her hand darted down to the pocket of her skirt; it was quick, but it looked as if she had pressed something.

From the rooftop, Makula laughed. "Just as before, these

creations are pathetic! Now, to turn my attention to the magical gi—"

The robots lurched in unison. Each emitted a truly nightmarish-sounding dissonant groan of digital noise as they whirred back to life, forcing their way back up onto their feet. The glow of the light bars on the humanoids and the dog bots had switched from a neutral white to an angry red.

"Uh, y'all?" I asked.

The other girls spun around just as the robots had all risen, their metallic heads scanning the scene.

"Oh *no*," Cass said.

"What the heck is happening?" Nova asked.

The robots answered.

"DO NOT RESIST. RESISTANCE INDICATES COMPLICITY. YOU WILL BE DETAINED."

With pure, mechanical determination, the robots advanced toward whatever group of people they were closest to. The humanoid bots began ransacking the food cart pod, smashing and flipping the heavy wooden picnic tables as they pursued their prey. Intimidating-looking devices with long barrels rose from the backs of the dog bots, which I immediately clocked as guns.

"Allison!" I yelled, "stop these things before people get hurt!"

"Oh, this is unfortunate," Allison said, smooth as ice. "The robots appear to have activated their defense protocols."

"Why is that a thing they can do?!" Cass shouted.

The interference from the robots was pinging around in my head, as if I were inches away from a speaker playing the worst sounds imaginable at top volume.

Bloom had it much worse.

With a groan, she fell to the pavement. She gripped the sides of her head, and curled up in a fetal position, screaming in pain.

I ran over and kneeled beside her. "Bloom! Bloom, can you hear me?"

She forced her words out between gritted teeth. "Stop this! Stop it! It's all wrong, wrong! STOP!"

On the roof of the bookstore, Makula glared down at the nightmare unfolding in the food cart pod. "How *dare* you pathetic humans undo my work! Your mechanized minions are no match for a true master!"

She swirled her staff again, sending out another wave across the food cart pod. It rolled over the robots just as before, but now, the bots seemed completely unaffected.

"What is this trickery? I will not be humiliated by the likes of humans!"

"They must be hyper-driving the thaumatite in the robots somehow," Hana said. "Makula's spells weren't prepared for that!"

Makula continued to bellow from the rooftop of the bookstore. "You creatures are all a danger! If you won't abide by my better judgment, I'll craft something that will *make* you!"

She raised her staff again and a thick black mist appeared around the head, crackling with magica. It grew into a massive torrent, and with a flick of her wrist, she fired it across the food cart pod.

Directly at the giant bug monster corpse.

"Oh heck, she ain't gonna bring *that* thing back to life, is she?" Nova asked.

As Makula's magica arced toward its massive target, it passed over the food cart pod and the concentration of Rhapsodyz robots. It grew twisted and distorted, veering off-course. Instead of blasting straight at the bug corpse, it curved and traveled down and to the left, and for a moment it looked as if it might harmlessly impact the pavement.

Which is when a Portland Streetcar rumbled through the tunnel in the bug corpse and back into the daylight alongside the food cart pod, directly in the path of Makula's magica.

The shot crashed into the streetcar. Its brakes slammed into action, and the sixty-six-foot-long vehicle skidded to a stop alongside the food cart pod, glowing eerily.

For a moment.

As the people inside the streetcar pressed against its windows in shock and fear, it suddenly reared up off its tracks, the front and middle sections elevating into the air, resembling a serpent intimidating a predator. The overhead wires ripped from their mountings along the street and fell slack to the pavement, sparking as they coiled back from the tension they carried. The tracks the streetcar had formerly rolled down took on an identical glow, and with the sound of rending steel and cracking asphalt and concrete, ripped themselves from the ground and reattached themselves to the streetcar like sharpened spears.

The streetcar—or, more appropriately, the streetcar *construct* —turned toward the food cart pod, its headlights now glowing with the energy of Makula's magica.

"Hey, babes, uh, what the flam is that thing?" Nova asked.

"That's a streetcar monster," Hana said.

I turned and looked up at Makula. "What have you done? Can't you stop that thing?"

Makula grimaced, her concentration clearly rattled by what had happened. I understood then what she'd just realized: The interference from the robots had altered her spell.

No, *corrupted* it. They were using an altered form of corruption magica, after all, wielded by a company that had no idea what they were actually doing with it. And if Makula wasn't in control of her spells, the scene was going to deteriorate even further, and quickly.

Things were already spiraling. Screams from the crowd grew as the situation became more clear to them. Bloom lay on the pavement, still in agony. As the streetcar creature loomed over us and the robots continued their steady advance, Cass bumped my shoulder, bringing me back to attention.

"Time for some magical girl interference, right, girls?" she asked. Her smile, ragged but determined, reassured me.

Even if the situation was chaotic, we could count on each other.

Nearby, Delilah and Lorelai got out of their food carts and waved to us.

"We'll get folks out of the way!" Lorelai shouted.

"Right," Delilah nodded. "Do what you do best, my queens!"

"With pleasure," Sara said. "Ladies, let's go to work!"

We raised our hands as our glittering thaumatite-crusted microphones materialized in our grip, and brought them down to our lips. In unison, we shouted the words of transformation into the microphones.

"Maidensong harmony power ... go live!"

CHAPTER 15

I n a flash of rainbow energy, we shot up through the dimensional barriers to the Celestial Stage once more. Swirling ribbons of purple, red, yellow, green, and blue wrapped us up and filled us with the power of the Maidensong, overriding the cacophony of the robots' mistuned corruption magica.

Our street clothes dissolved in glowing magical embers and our costumes materialized against our bodies, adorning us with our colors. My boots, skirt, jacket, and gloves appeared, one after the other, and as the purple bow tied itself around my neck, I reached out and took the hands of Sara and Nova as they in turn took hold of Cass and Hana. Our circle of magical girl power and togetherness connected us, while the final moments of transformation coursed through our cells and into our hair and eyes, coloring them to match our costumes.

The Maidensong's voice echoed across the cosmos once again —*"THOSE EXALTED BY THE MAIDENSONG SHALL WIELD THE POWER OF HARMONY"*—and we blasted back down through the dimensions to Earth in a grand rainbow tunnel.

We arrived back in Portland with an explosion of light. As it dissipated, we glanced around at the villainous presences all around the cart pod and called out to them to let them know their time was short.

"We are the guardians of song and heart!" Sara shouted. "Guardian of Lyricism, Riot Red!"

Cass stepped forward and placed her hands on her hips. "Guardian of Melody, Riot Yellow!"

"Guardian of Rhythm," Hana said, "Riot Green!"

Nova advanced and pumped her fist. "Guardian of the Beat, Riot Blue!"

"Guardian of Harmony, Riot Purple!" I shouted. "Servants of the darkness, be silenced by the song of Magica Riot!"

The scene around us exploded into chaos. Finally realizing the seriousness of the situation, the patrons scattered, running from the cart pod in every direction as Delilah, Lorelai, and other cart owners tried to guide them to safety. In the maelstrom of bodies, the Rhapsodyz robots became even more frenzied and gave chase to the targets they'd selected, the humanoid models reaching out to grab at arms and shoulders in an attempt to apprehend those they had decided were enemy combatants.

The streetcar monster advanced, scraping along the pavement like a giant metallic snake, its glowing red headlights locked directly on us.

"We need to get control of the situation," Sara said. "Yellow, snipe at the streetcar. Try to draw it away from the crowds. Green, you go with Yellow. Once you've drawn it away, see if you can contain it in one place. We need to get the passengers out, but we can't have it crushing other people in the meantime. Blue, you're with me. We're going to get in and take the bots out before they get somebody hurt. Purple, you take Bloom and get her out of the interference field. Once you're done, come back and engage the bots with us. Everybody got that?"

"Flam yeah," Nova said. "I'm ready to bring the pain!"

The rest of us nodded in the affirmative.

"Alright," Sara said. "Let's go!"

Tasks assigned, I spun around and found Bloom, still

writhing in agony on the ground. I needed to get her to safety, someplace where she could be free of the corruption interference. Fortunately, here in the middle of downtown, there were plenty of possible spots.

It just required a bit of vertical thinking.

I ran to Bloom and scooped her up in my arms. My eyes scanned around for a place sufficiently far away. I settled on the roof of a nearby office and apartment building, a few blocks away and a good twenty-five floors up. That would be enough to get her clear of the untuned corruption magica.

Now, I just had to get her there before the bots or the streetcar monster attacked me.

I focused and summoned a magica sigil beneath my feet. As I concentrated on the distance and angle I'd need to reach the building, the sigil spun up to high speed, and within a few moments, launched me off the ground.

Air rushed past me as I sailed up over downtown Portland in the direction of my target skyscraper. I had never done a launch of this distance before, but I did my best to put any mental images of me slamming into a concrete wall or straight through a plate-glass window out of my head. Confidence was key as a magical girl, after all.

It almost worked. As I neared the skyscraper, it became obvious that the arc of my flight was just a bit too low. My path was curving down to place me square in the middle of somebody's apartment on the twenty-third floor, and I had only seconds to react without dropping Bloom.

Well, no time to be graceful.

I lifted Bloom up and slung her over my right shoulder, holding on to her body like a mattress on top of a car on the highway and trying not to think about how I was aiming her butt-first at whoever was in my way. With my left hand, I reached out and focused on the Maidensong again, calling another sigil disc into existence beneath my palm.

The sigil spun up and pushed back against my direction of

travel. I threw my left shoulder into it, letting it act like a retro-rocket to slow me down. The skyscraper loomed in my field of view, but I *was* coming to a stop.

Hopefully, I'd judged this better than I had my original launch.

Purple magica glowed as the sigil spun faster and faster into a blur. With only inches to spare before I smacked into the windows of the tower, I finally ground to a halt. The sigil relaxed and spun lazily, its presence keeping me from falling straight down to the pavement three-hundred feet below.

I exhaled, forcing my gaze straight ahead into the glass wall I'd nearly crashed through—and into the eyes of a *very* surprised young woman in her apartment living room, looking back out at a magical girl carrying a second magical girl like a sack of potatoes in midair.

I shrugged at her and shouted, hoping my voice would carry.

"Uh, you coming to our show?"

She nodded at me, her face still frozen in disbelief.

I gave her a thumbs-up with my free hand. "Thanks, we really appreciate it!"

She gave me a confused thumbs-up in return.

Thoroughly embarrassed, I summoned another launch sigil beneath my feet and blasted up away from her to the rooftop.

This time, my mental calculations were good. I landed softly on my feet, well away from the trio of rooftop wind turbines that topped this particular skyscraper, and gently laid Bloom down. She groaned and looked up at me; clearly, she didn't feel espe-cially great, but she was noticeably improved from how she was in the midst of the robot mob.

"Claire?" she asked. "What ... where are we? What's going on?"

"The Rhapsodyz bots went nuts and turbocharged some-how," I said. "You were getting hit pretty hard by that corruption interference, so I got you away from it. We're, uh, up on the roof of a skyscraper."

She frowned. "This is now the third time I have found myself atop the roof of a skyscraper with you. What an odd life we lead."

"I had to improvise," I said. "The specifics weren't as important as you being okay." I gently poked at her shoulder. "Besides, first time was your fault."

"A fair point," she chuckled.

I made ready to summon another launch sigil and get back to the fight. "Don't worry. I'll come back for you once it's safe."

"Claire, wait."

I paused. "Yeah?"

Bloom smiled at me, weakly but sincerely. "Thank you for helping me."

"Anytime," I said. "It's what magical girls do."

Before she had a chance to argue the point, I summoned my sigil and blasted off the rooftop back toward the food cart pod, landing at the periphery of the fight.

In the distance, Cass and Hana blasted at the streetcar monster, drawing its anger away from the people trying to escape. Closer to me, the bots had apparently come to the conclusion that magical girls were a bigger threat to them than everyday Portlanders, and several had ganged up on Sara and Nova. Despite being outnumbered, they were holding their own.

A few straggler bots had peeled off to chase down food cart pod diners, so I decided to start with them and protect the innocents trying to flee. They needed help, and I was here to provide it.

I summoned my keytar. It materialized in a sparkling glow of purple, the neck in my open hand, the strap fitting around my shoulder like it had never been anywhere else. I listened to the rest of the band, riffing on the middle eight of "Second Promise, Second Chance," and counted myself in. My fingers flew across the keys of the keytar, and I charged up a blast of magica while I decided on my first target.

One of the dog bots was in pursuit of three food cart

customers. I took aim and loosed a blast of magica that crashed into the bot's shoulder. The metal frame of its body distorted beneath my shot, and the bot lost its balance, crashing to the ground as it let out an electronic shriek.

The escaping customers turned and shot me a look of relief. One of them, a bearded man with elaborate tattoos, cheered and pumped his fist.

"Thank you!" he shouted.

"Anytime!" I answered, as I ran between the fallen dog bot and the escapees.

I turned my attention back to the bot, which was struggling back up to its three remaining functional legs. The best it could manage was scraping along the pavement toward me, its eyes glowing fiery red. The small gun on its back started to turn and twist on its little turret, attempting to track me against the shuddering of the bot's body.

It seemed prudent to not let that gun fire.

I ran wide, keeping low, tracing an arc through the smashed picnic tables and debris as I charged another shot. The dog bot tried its best to follow me, but the damage I'd done to it was too great. Just before it could lock onto me with its weapon's barrel, I fired again.

Magica leapt from my keytar and smashed into the dog bot's face. Its head exploded in a shower of electronics, and the blast pierced into its body, splitting it apart with the sound of rending metal. The remaining components sparked and smoked as they finally collapsed to the ground, completely inert.

For a moment, I admired my handiwork, but my celebration was cut short as something heavy and cold punched me in the shoulder from behind.

I stumbled and spun as pain radiated through me from the impact site. My feet tripped over themselves and I smacked into the pavement, landing on my butt with a dull thud that knocked the wind from me for a moment. I was rattled, but still alert enough to look up into the face of my attacker, finding two glowing red light bars staring back down at me from a pair of the humanoid Rhapsodyz bots looming over me.

The bots raised their arms and brought them down on me at full force. I blocked the attack with my keytar, the magica within it shielding it from damage. Steel and composite alloys clanged against the keytar and bounced off with flashes of purple energy, which only seemed to enrage the AI more. The bots kept pounding their fists with surprising speed.

Smash, smash, SMASH. The attacks felt oddly familiar, but I was in no position to figure out why.

If I could just get an opening to fire my keytar at them or swing the body into one of them, I could break out of the attack, but the assault was relentless.

Two glimmering holographic blue discs materialized above me, pointed at the robots, and fired a high-speed series of blasts into them. The bots stumbled backward, trying futilely to press back against the blasts.

I looked back over my shoulder just as Nova flew over me and tackled the bot on the left.

"Aw yeah," she said, "eat some percussion, ya hunk of junk!"

She summoned two more holo drums, one on either side of the robot's head, and brought her glittering blue drumsticks down against them with a tremendous *slam*. The drums fired blue magica blasts directly into the bot from mere inches away. The bot's head crumpled between the blasts like a discarded soda can, sending a shower of sparks into the air as the robot shut down and died.

"There ya go, babe!" Nova shouted. "Get yer smashy-smashy on!"

I nodded as I got to my feet. "Right! On it!"

The second bot had recovered and advanced on me again. I played a riff in time with the song's beat and felt energy surge back into my keytar, and with a shove of my foot, I pushed off the pavement and flung myself at the bot.

The bot pulled back its arms for another strike, but this time,

I was ready. I swung my keytar straight for its torso, pushing as hard as I could with my magically enhanced muscles. The glittering, glowing purple blade that waited in the keytar's body extended from it as I struck, and it sliced into the bot's chest, ripping apart metal and wiring until it cut straight into the thaumatite power cell in the bot's center.

An explosion of magica erupted from the bot and flung me back. I landed hard on the pavement and rolled away, coming to a stop just in time to see the scorched, mangled upper and lower halves of the bot crash back to the ground, fire and smoke pouring from every hole in its chassis.

Nova ran over, grabbed my hand, and helped me to my feet. "You okay, babe?"

"I'm okay," I said. "Just sore. Those things can hit hard."

"For-flammin'-sure! They're made of metal, and robots are strong!"

"You're right about that. Let's go help Sara put the rest of them down."

We turned and ran back toward the main fight. In the center of the cart pod, several of the Rhapsodyz bots whirled and punched at a shared target while stepping over the broken, smoking hulks of their fallen robotic brethren.

And there, in the center of the metal maelstrom, was Sara.

She muscled one of the robots away with her shoulder, giving her room to swing her guitar's axe-like body into the rest of them with wild ferocity. She sang the chorus, nailing every note as she drew back for another swing. Even without Nova backing her up, she was holding her own; the numbers weren't in her favor, though, and I spotted one of the humanoid bots running up behind her for a sneak attack.

As Nova and I ran up to rejoin her, I played another riff on my keytar in time with Nova's drumming, and fired a beam of purple magica into the bot before it could strike. I hit it just below the neck and completely severed its head from the rest of its body. The bot, now disconnected from its processor, fell to the ground and scraped to a stop beside Sara's feet.

She looked down at it, then back up at me. "Thank you, Purple."

Nova and I dove through the bot crowd and stood on either side of her.

"Always," I said.

"I don't wanna interrupt or nothin'," Nova said, "but we've still got a bunch of metal jerks here!"

A wall of the remaining bots stood in front of us, glaring and clearly recalculating for an attack on three targets instead of one. A trio of the humanoid models stood in front, with two more humanoids and two dog bots behind them.

"I've been getting acquainted with them," Sara nodded.

"These things are relentless," I said.

"Three on seven," Nova said. "That's almost fair! You wanna teach these robo-creepos a lesson now?"

"It's not going to be easy, exactly," Sara said, "but I think if we just—"

A sudden screeching roar interrupted her from behind. Immediately after, I heard Cass call out to us.

"INCOMING!"

We looked up just in time to see the jagged end of a long rail track jab down and skewer the three Rhapsodyz bots in the front row, straight through their torsos. The bots sparked and burst into flames, hanging limp as the rail lifted them from the pavement and up into the air.

Attached to that track was the streetcar construct. It towered over us, its body snaking down and resting on top of two food carts it had smashed to splinters. The headlights on its nose blazed with the fire of angry magica. From within, I could hear the screams of the passengers still trapped inside it.

And its other rail track arm was aiming itself at us.

I tensed and prepared to dive out of the way, but a moment later, a green magica shockwave smashed into the side of the streetcar, knocking it away from us. The skewered robots slid off its arm and fell to a heap on the ground. Another shockwave punched it, and another, and the giant artificial beast fought to stay upright against the onslaught.

We turned around and spotted Hana, slapping the strings of her bass to fire those shockwaves in time with the beat.

"C'mon over!" Hana shouted. "Fall back and regroup! I've got you covered!"

The four other Rhapsodyz robots—now more upset with the streetcar construct than they were with us—turned their attention toward their new, larger target.

"Let's go," Sara said.

The three of us bolted from the robots and ran over to rejoin Cass and Hana as they fired at the streetcar construct.

"This thing's out of control," Cass said. "It's unpredictable!"

"It's as if it has no mind or guidance!" Hana shouted.

I glanced back up toward the roof of Howell's Books. Makula was nowhere to be found.

"I think that's exactly it," I said. "Something went wrong with Makula's spell!"

Nova shook her head. "Well ain't that just flammin' great! Miss I'm-the-Greatest-Sorceress screws up and leaves the mess for us!"

"We can rub it in her face if we stop it before anybody gets hurt," Sara said. "We need options!"

"This thing's wrecking everything in its path, but it's got dozens of people in it," Cass said. "How're we gonna stop it without hurting them?"

"Maybe we can weaken it with some careful hits," I suggested.

Sara nodded. "If you all can slow it down and let me get close, I can try to get it open somehow. Yellow, Purple, hit it anywhere you can that doesn't put the passengers at risk."

"We'll try," Cass said, "but that's almost nowhere!"

"Do the best you can," Sara said. "Err on the side of caution.

Green, Blue, keep it disoriented! If it escapes into the city, we'll be in even bigger trouble."

"We can do that!" Hana said, adjusting her grip on her bass.

Nova shot a thumbs-up. "We'll rattle its noggin for ya!"

"Alright," Sara said. "New song, charge up! Blue, count us in for 'Charlatan'!"

"Comin' right up, boss lady!" Nova said. She clacked her drumsticks together and called out the song's shuffle beat. "A-one, a-two, a-one two three four!"

Sara played the opening guitar chords as Hana locked in with Nova on the rhythm, and Cass and I played our accent riffs. My keytar thrummed with magica as I charged up to fire at the streetcar construct, which was currently occupied with fighting the remaining Rhapsodyz bots attempting to grab hold of its body.

Nova's drumming materialized a circle of shockwaves around the streetcar, slapping it from all directions with every kick and snare drum hit. Hana linked in with her and conjured a series of green waves that smacked against the construct's body from opposing directions. The combined attacks clearly made the construct angry, but they also kept it from focusing on any particular target.

We moved into the song's first verse and Sara sang as she strode toward the streetcar beast, walking steadily and keeping her gaze locked on it as it thrashed about.

"I wish that I could read your mind, 'cause I'm so tired of what's in mine. It's the same old story, and it's getting boring!"

"This one goes out to you, Makula!" Cass shouted as she fired her first bolt of yellow magica from her guitar. It sliced the air and hit the streetcar monster with precise aim, on what I could only call the "forehead" above the windshield that comprised a large portion of its "face."

I fired a shot immediately after, aiming at the mechanical monster's undercarriage. My blast impacted near the beast's wheels, sending a shower of sparks out onto the ground and causing it to blast its horn in anger. The metal where I'd hit distorted and rippled, obviously weakening.

Sara kept her up her steady approach toward the construct, doing her best to avoid its flailing and the attacks being traded back and forth between it and the Rhapsodyz bots. Her guitar glowed with red magica, building up with every chord strummed. And all the while, she sang, loudly and forcefully.

"I'm stuck inside this box you made, waiting to be cut in half with your blade, and the crowd's ecstatic, so why are you panicked?"

She had closed the distance. The streetcar construct loomed over her, and as it struggled against the attacks the rest of us fired its way and the pesky Rhapsodyz robots, it noticed her. Its chassis rocked by impacts, it glared down at her, headlights gleaming with magica, ready to strike.

The five of us moved into the song's first chorus, and at that very instant, Sara broke from a steady walk into a run. She hurled herself toward the construct and pulled back her guitar, ready to cut into the spot on the chassis I'd just damaged.

The impact came swiftly, the axe-like body of her Bread-winner guitar crashing into the streetcar's chassis with a fiery blast of red magica. Quickly, she shifted her weight and changed direction, keeping the construct off its guard as she struck again and again. The sounds of sparking, rending metal and warped beast-like screeches were no match for her voice as it rang out and reverberated against the surrounding buildings.

"You're a charlatan with everything to lose! Your world comes crashing down with a single wrong move! Open your third eye and look at what you've done! Cut your heart out in front of everyone!"

"She's doing it!" I shouted. "Keep it up!"

The rest of us fired away as Sara moved into the second verse and the next phase of her plan. She grabbed the street-car's chassis and swung herself up on the side of its body, next to one of the sliding doors near the vehicle's center. The doors were sealed by the magica of Makula's spell, but with some luck and the rest of us disorienting the construct, there was a solid chance Sara could punch through that seal with her guitar.

As she hung off the side of the streetcar, she swung her guitar up and smashed it into the door, over and over again. Blasts of red magica shot out from each impact, illuminating the faces of the passengers who watched from behind the windows, holding on for dear life as the now-living streetcar bucked and writhed around the street.

"The whole world thinks you're so sublime," Sara sang, *"bending spoons with your beautiful mind, but a black cat told me 'bout your gross skulduggery!"*

We played on, and Sara shifted to the second chorus—but she wouldn't get far.

"You're a charlatan with ev—"

The streetcar whipped one of its track arms around and smashed the tip into her chest. She screamed, and fell away from the vehicle's body. Before she hit the pavement, the streetcar construct grabbed her with that same arm, wrapping the steel beam around her like a boa constrictor. Her guitar fell from her hands and dematerialized as the construct took hold of her.

"Red!" I shouted. "No, no, no!"

The track arm creaked as it squeezed Sara's body. She flailed for a moment, then strained to fight back. She groaned, and the steel of the track bent out from the sheer force of a fully powered magical girl.

The construct noticed this, too, and slammed Sara to the ground, buckling the pavement from the force of the impact.

"We have to help her!" Hana shouted.

"Cover me," I said.

Nova shot me a nod. "We've got yer back, babe!"

"Watch yourself, Purple!" Cass yelled.

I pushed off from the pavement with my right foot and tore off at top speed toward Sara. I didn't actually know what I planned to do once I reached her, but one way or another, I intended to free her.

The construct raised Sara up and slammed her down again. I was closing the distance quickly, but not quickly enough. With every muscle in my body straining as I called upon the Maiden-song, I pushed harder, barreling forward like a runaway train.

Unfortunately, I was running toward an *actual* runaway train.

Moments before I reached Sara, the construct noticed me. I had no time to react; for something over sixty feet long, the construct could lunge like a cobra. It aimed at me and hurled itself forward.

"Oh, this is really gonna—"

SIDE C
HEALING WORDS

CHAPTER 16

Thirty tons of enraged streetcar bulldozed my body. Every bone and muscle and cell inside me screamed out in fire and agony. The wind rushed from my lungs and I felt my keytar dematerialize. I was dimly aware of faces looking out at me from behind a windshield and the glow of the magica that roiled throughout the construct's body, but they grew indistinct as I fought myself for consciousness.

After what felt like an eternity, the force pushing me weakened and I fell away. Crashing into a heap on the pavement and tumbling down the street felt almost like a relief. The surrounding buildings spun around me as I rolled, before I finally, mercifully came to a stop face-down on the asphalt.

So much pain coursed through me, it was hard to even think coherently, to consider anything but injury and agony. Despite it all, I was still alive. The magical girl drive inside me, fueled by the strength of the Maidensong, cut through from my soul.

Get up. You have a job to do, magical girl.

I pushed myself up on my hands, shakily and slowly, as I gasped for air. I felt a trickle of wetness roll down my face from a painful spot on my forehead and reached up to wipe it away without thinking. My hand came back streaked with blood.

The food cart pod was in the middle of the intersection of Burnside and Tenth. Wherever I was, I was not there anymore. I looked to my left; judging by the old red brick building next to me, I was by the Armory Theatre, two blocks away.

I looked to my right, and fell over onto my side as a wave of disorientation hit. The streetcar construct loomed in my vision, approaching me as it judged how badly hurt I was. It still carried Sara, wrapped up in its steel track arm, but in my current state I couldn't tell if she was conscious or not. I was too rattled to focus, but I vaguely saw shapes I could only hope were my friends rushing toward the construct from farther behind.

The streetcar construct reared up over me, and I could sense that it was about to deliver a crushing blow straight down onto my beaten body. I wanted to get away, but I hurt all over and wasn't moving fast. Still, I tried. I forced myself to try to stand, to scramble out of the path of the incoming attack, but I could feel the inevitability of what was about to happen.

Until it was all interrupted by the sudden arrival of a screaming purple and black streak.

A red-violet explosion of magica blasted the streetcar construct at the moment it and the streak made contact. The mechanical monster reeled and fell to the side, and smashed into the wall of an old building that held an event space. Bricks and wood fell across the ground, and in its distress, the construct's rail arm loosened its grip and dropped Sara to the sidewalk.

The streak smacked the pavement and tumbled across it until it rolled into me, sending me spinning again before I stopped in a heap beneath it. I shook the stars from my eyes and looked up to find a familiar face staring back at me.

"Bloom?" I asked. "What are you—"

Her glowing red eyes met mine. She was fully transformed, back in her black corset dress, her long violet hair hanging down around me. With a laugh, she tried to answer me.

And then, she groaned, grabbed the side of her head, and rolled off me.

"Ugh," she forced out. "I'm saving ... your ... magical ... ass, yet *again*, Claire!"

The interference from the Rhapsodyz bots had weakened after so many had been disabled, but as the remaining bots reached the scene of the fight, the atonal corruption magica was clearly still affecting her.

I dragged myself up to my hands and knees and crawled to her side. "Bloom, we've got to get you out of here. It's too dangerous for you!"

Bloom screamed and fought her way up to a knee. *"No!* I can *do* this! I am going to get your illustrious leader out of danger, and then take this mechanical monstrosity and those robotic reprobates apart with my *bare hands* if I have to!"

"But the interference field is—"

"Fuck the interference!" Bloom shot back. "I am tired of watching this *literal* train wreck!"

Before I could stop her, she was back on her feet, running woozily toward Sara. The streetcar construct had recovered, and had spun around to deal with the arrival of the Rhapsodyz robots and the rest of the band.

I fought back to my feet and summoned my keytar again. The situation was a mess, and from where I stood, I tried to take stock.

Cass, Hana, and Nova had obviously decided—rightly—that the streetcar construct was a bigger threat at the moment, both to the city and to its own passengers. They ran up and resumed hitting it from a distance, trying to find weaknesses. The Rhapsodyz bots, meanwhile, were attacking—no, that wasn't right. They weren't *attacking* the construct. They approached it as if they were, and they stayed close to it, but they never actually engaged it in a fight.

What were they *doing?*

Cass ran up to me, firing at the streetcar with her guitar. "Purple! Are you okay?"

"I'll live," I said. "It's Bloom! She went in to rescue Sara!"

"She did what?!"

I pointed at the pile of building debris on the sidewalk next to where the streetcar construct writhed and fought the rest of the girls.

Bloom ran into the middle of the chaos as best she could, still pale and fighting her sickness. She dodged her way past the streetcar, and reached Sara. Visibly unsteady, she fought though it, and tried to scoop Sara up in her arms.

"Now I've seen everything," Cass said.

I nodded. "No kidding. If the construct doesn't see her, she might be able to pull it off!"

Bloom's luck didn't last. The construct whipped its body around and found her as she stumbled back in my direction, carrying Sara. Whatever intelligence the construct had, it seemed consumed by payback now, and it reared back to slam down on Bloom and Sara before they could get to safety.

"Hit it, Purple!" Cass shouted.

"Hitting it!" I said as my hands danced as best they could across my keytar.

Cass and I fired and hit the construct, but we barely made it flinch. It was too single-minded now. We tried again, spreading our shots, hoping that we'd eventually distract it without hurting anybody inside.

Thankfully, we weren't alone.

A glowing blue holo-drum materialized twenty feet in the air against a nearby building. Moments later, Hana and Nova—their arms interlinked—flew into that drum and trampolined off it, ricocheting directly into the side of the streetcar with their fists outstretched.

Together, they slammed into the streetcar and punched it away before it could attack Bloom and Sara. The construct shrieked and recoiled as it weighed the choice of going after its original targets or these new pests.

Hana and Nova landed beside Cass and I, and Nova fist-punched the air as she yelled at the construct.

"There ya go! There ya flammin' go, ya big jerk!"

We finally had a stroke of good luck. Now, if we could just figure out a plan to get the passengers off it safely, we could—

The impact of a steel streetcar track bashing me in the chest brought my train of thought to an unceremonious stop.

Compared to getting hit with the streetcar itself, this wasn't as awful, though it wasn't a sensation I would ever seek out again. I hadn't been prepared for it, hadn't braced for it; I felt weirdly detached as I flew backward from the force. My keytar dematerialized for safety as I moved very quickly through the air, and then stopped moving just as quickly. The next sensation I felt was impacting a wall, and seeing my vision clouded by red brick dust as I fell to the sidewalk and landed in the rubble.

With some effort, I pushed myself back up onto my knees and looked around, still dazed and trying to reclaim my breath. Cass, Hana, and Nova had landed near me and were struggling back to their feet.

Sara and Bloom had been flung farther down Tenth Avenue. They lay in a heap together, directly in the path of the streetcar construct as it rolled toward them, stalking and preparing to strike again.

Whatever Makula had done to the streetcar—and whatever the Rhapsodyz magica interference had done to her spell—it was clearly far more powerful than we'd thought it would be. It simply had too much mass, too much force, too much over-charged magical power. The situation was delicate. We could have annihilated the monster with our special attacks if we'd been able to go at it with full force, but it was filled with dozens of innocent people whose lives depended on us finding another way.

A gentler way.

I called my keytar again, and focused. My mind reached out across space, through the dimensions, to the great cosmic sound of the Maidensong. If I was the Guardian of Harmony, commanding the powers of empathy and kindness, maybe those powers could stop this, despite the new song not being ready.

Just as they had on the roof of the Grand Sovereign Hotel that day we fought Rennia, my mind and heart searched through the aether for the Exalted Harmony. I felt for my connection to it, as the member of Magica Riot tasked with commanding its resonance. Though I'd only used it once before, I had to put my hopes in it coming through to help us, even if I really had no idea what would happen if I summoned it as an unfinished piece of music.

Magica flowed into me as my fingers moved across the keys and sought out my fragmentary, tentative song. As my essence as a magical girl got closer to the Exalted Harmony, a faint purple glow radiated from my keytar and crept across my body.

"Purple," Cass said as she stood back up and ran over with Hana and Nova, "what are you doing?"

"Trying to stop this before anybody else gets hurt!" I said.

"Yeah but whatcha actually *doing*, Claire cutie?" Nova asked.

"I'm using my new song," I said, "or what there is of it! I'm going to try to use the Exalted Harmony to calm and disable the construct!"

Hana resummoned her bass. "It's worth a try! We'll back you up!"

I focused my mind and searched, reaching out with my heart. Not blindly grasping, but I couldn't simply see it plainly either. It was like capturing smoke. The moment lingered, and just as the first tremblings of panic crept up my spine, I found it and grabbed hold.

The Exalted Harmony and I linked, and magical energy slammed into my core like a battering ram. Just as before, the collective, radiant voice of all magical girls throughout eternity coursed through every atom of my body. Makula was right; it did feel like an ocean, but I also felt energized, clear headed, buoyed by the waves of raw magica.

I had no words for this new shape the Exalted Harmony was

taking. Our normal, destructive attack version was "Riot Harmony Chordal Cataclysm," but the new song had no title yet, and no special name to shout. I'd need to shape it myself, and hope my instincts were right.

And so, I played.

Silently, I counted myself in, trying to focus on riding the foaming edge of the wave. My tentative notes grew more confident as I played, and after a few bars, Hana and Nova came in with a basic rhythm, their notes and beats winding around the chords like scaffolding. The skeleton of the song solidified as we played, and I could feel the melody well up inside me, cosmic knowledge imparted from powers beyond myself. As we came around to the beginning of the progression, I tried to play that melody.

Commanding the Exalted Harmony with an unfinished song, though, was an intimidating prospect. The flow of magica bucked and strained against my willpower, even as I directed it toward the streetcar construct and the Rhapsodyz bots.

I focused on the song, on the Exalted Harmony, and on empathy. To my relief, something started to happen.

The streetcar construct had reached Bloom and Sara, but it abruptly halted its advance, poised above them but hanging in limbo. I could see the beast fight the effects; it *wanted* to strike, but its magical guidance was being interrupted by my song.

Bloom and Sara had come to by this point and sat up on the pavement. They stared up at the construct in surprise, before Sara looked my way and put the pieces together.

"Purple! Whatever you're doing, keep it up!" Sara shouted.

Bloom got back to her feet and grabbed Sara. "Yes, Claire! At least until I'm out of the way!"

I couldn't answer them. The concentration I needed to pull this off was too great now.

Strands of pure purple-hued magica reached out from both my keytar and my own body, streaming out over to the streetcar construct and the bots. The magical energy flowed around them in tightly wrapped braids, shaking them and lifting them very slightly from the ground.

As the braids settled gently around them, I felt something—*were they emotions?*—feeding back to me along those strands. They were confused, ragged, and incoherent, but I recognized the feelings they expressed all the same. Anger, violence, need, and hate closest to the surface, but underneath I also felt a kind of profound sadness. It was hard to sort out where they were all coming from; some were definitely coming from Makula's magica in the streetcar, and some were coming from the robots, somehow, perhaps from the corruption magica that the robots were recklessly channeling.

Even that bit of distraction was too much, and before I knew it, my concentration on the song had lapsed. The torrent of magica fought back.

I lost full control of the Exalted Harmony, and the strands encircling the streetcar construct and the Rhapsodyz robots constricted. The robots, being the smaller and more fragile targets, didn't stand a chance. Their metal alloy bodies squealed and snapped beneath the force, sparks and smoke blasting out of them as my magica torched their frames and crushed their thaumatite hearts to shards. Explosions of warped corruption magica exploded from them as those cores died, but the force was entirely contained, unable to break through the magica engulfing them.

The streetcar was far larger and sturdier, and had the benefit of a skilled magica user's work powering it, but even it could not hold completely against the Exalted Harmony. The streetcar's articulated body groaned and crashed as it gave way, looking like a soda can after it had just begun to crumple. It wasn't much—there was too much counter-acting force, too much rigidity in its magically enhanced body—but the implication of the inevitable crush was clear. Even over the din and the song, I could hear the people inside scream as they realized what was about to happen.

I froze. Terror shot through me and curdled in my heart and stomach. Dozens of innocent lives rested in my ability to wield a cosmic force I had never tried to wield like this before, using an unfinished song. The margins of error were microscopic, and I was now stumbling over them. If I didn't get control of myself, I was going to kill every single person on that streetcar, gruesomely.

Makula was right.

I was out of my depth. Not only was I commanding something beyond any Earthly conception of "powerful," I was doing it with incomplete tools, and with little experience. It really was the hubris of humankind, the recklessness of a magical girl who hadn't even made it through her first year.

Those people were all going to die, and it would be my fault.

The panic saturated me and tore at my insides. My breathing quickened, turning ragged and shallow, and my vision tunneled in on the streetcar and the thread of magica connecting me to it. My hand faltered on the keytar. I missed notes, hit bad chords, felt everything slide away from me as the Exalted Harmony went dissonant. Darkness crept in at the edges, and the magica strand tightened, sickeningly slowly, around the streetcar. It felt like a crash I was powerless to stop.

I became dimly aware of shapes in my periphery. Faces and voices calling out to me. It was almost impossible for me to focus, but words started slipping through the firestorm of panic in me.

"Purple ... okay ... hear us ... listen to ... voice ... calm."

My mouth barely worked, but I stammered out a reply.

"Wha—what?"

Cass's face suddenly snapped into focus. Nova's followed.

"Purple ... Claire ... can you hear our voices?" Cass asked.

"C'mon, babe," Nova said. My vision had cleared enough to notice she was crying. "Focus on us, okay? You're gonna be okay! You gotta be!"

Hana appeared beside Nova, her kind and calm face no

doubt hiding her concerns. "If you can hear us, Claire, take deep breaths. Concentrate on slowing your breathing. You're going to be okay, you just need to slow down."

"That's it, yeah," Cass said. "You're gonna be okay."

I shook my head. "I don't think I can ... those people are going to get hurt! I can't—"

"You *can*, Claire," Sara said as she came into view beside Cass. "You're chasing the magica. Slow down, keep those breaths steady, and get back on top of it. You can do it."

"Calm ... right, calm," I said, though I wasn't sure I entirely believed it.

To my surprise, alongside Sara, Bloom popped into my field of view. "Magical girl, listen to me, for I will say this affirmation but once. I have come to trust you, Claire Ryland. If I can do that, then you can as well. Take hold of that magica and do what you must! But do it *now!*"

In spite of the panic that still held on to me, I forced myself to close my eyes and take deep, steady breaths. Slowly, note by note and chord by chord, my hands caught back up to the beat and started hitting the right keys. The Exalted Harmony fell back into key, just enough to feel correct again. It was still a tremendous, surging ocean of magica, but I could also feel something deeper beneath the waves, something to hold on to.

I was still on the edge of control, but I was on the right side of that edge again. Makula might have been right about the difficulty of wielding that ocean, but it no longer seemed impossible. I didn't think I could hold it long, but I had to try to bring this song to its conclusion.

I was a magical girl. I *could* do this.

As the song fell back into place, I opened my eyes. The streetcar construct still hung above the pavement, the strands of magica still encircling it, but no longer constricting. That would be enough.

I concentrated again, and willed the song to calm the streetcar construct, to soothe the anger and violence that had fed back into me through my magica. And then, from deep inside me, I felt a familiar warmth.

Peace flooded across my neurons, filtered down into my cells, and soaked through every atom of my body. It was the peace I knew from using the Exalted Harmony, amplified far beyond what I experienced in the Rennia fight. It filled me with calm, and strength, and above all ... *clarity.*

I understood what the Maidensong was telling me. The job of the Guardian of Harmony wasn't simply to wield the ultimate song. It was also to heal, to soothe, to use the song to mend the wrongs of the world. Jade's words reverberated in my mind as I played on.

"I know what you're capable of, Claire. You have to use that power to help and heal."

Makula's magica was very different from the Maidensong, but empathy was empathy, no matter what. I continued to play, and to soothe, the mechanical beast that had attacked us. Slowly but surely, it lowered to the pavement.

The rear segment of the streetcar touched down first. The glow of Makula's spell faded, not completely gone, but clearly weakened. Gently, I willed the rest of its body to lay down, and with a metallic clang that reverberated through the Pearl District, it settled onto its steel wheels and came to a stop.

"Is this it?" I heard Cass ask. "Can we go?"

"It's enough," Sara answered. "Let's move in! Purple, keep playing!"

"I shall assist!" Bloom called out.

The three of them ran toward the streetcar.

I played what there was of the melody. Hana and Nova picked the rhythm back up as I focused on the Exalted Harmony and my emotions. Time was of the essence, as I had no idea how long I could hold out.

Sara, Cass, and Bloom summoned their instruments and hacked away at the doors on the side of the streetcar until they finally pierced through Makula's magica and got to the inanimate object beneath.

"Alright, that's it!" Sara shouted. "Get the doors open!"

The three of them grabbed the sliding doors and pulled. Their magical girl strength peeled the streetcar open like a can of sardines, and Sara motioned to the passengers inside.

"Everybody out right now! It's not safe yet!"

Cass waved to me. "Keep it going, Purple! Buy us time to evac!"

"On it, Yellow!" I shouted back as Hana, Nova, and I played on.

The passengers in the streetcar piled out, two and three at a time. I was too locked-in on the song to fully process things, but I heard mixtures of crying and cheering, and murmurs of heartfelt thanks from the people inside as they hit the street and took off running back toward the food cart pod.

Finally, mercifully, the final passengers exited the streetcar. I waited until they were safely clear of the area before I let go of the song, my strength and mental power exhausted. My hands fell from the keytar and I dropped to my knees, utterly spent. I panted and gasped for air until I coughed, tasting my own sweat as it dripped down my face. My soul was an ember, still glowing after the fire had moved on.

I could only watch now.

The streetcar construct groaned and started to move, much more slowly than before. It was hurt, but trying to get back up and attack.

"Let's end this now, before it has a chance to get its strength back!" Sara shouted. "Green, put it in its place for Yellow and me!"

Hana smiled and nodded. "With pleasure, Red!"

She stepped toward the streetcar construct and readied her hands on her bass. Her smile faded into a stare of serious, menacing intent, and as the construct tried to recover, she unleashed her special attack upon it.

"Riot Rhythm Seismic Shock!"

Multiple strings made of glowing green magica materialized on her bass beneath the low E string. Hana raked her fingers across those magica strings and a series of deep, rumbling tones far below normal hearing shook the street around us. The rumble grew in volume and intensity as magica flowed across Hana's bass and up over her body.

Phasing up from beneath the pavement, a massive geyser of thrumming green magica erupted below the streetcar. The construct let out a tremendous roaring groan as it soared, riding the geyser up toward the tops of the surrounding buildings even as the force of Hana's attack started dismantling it. Chunks of debris flew off as the blast flung the streetcar higher and higher.

Hana's attack reached its peak, and the geyser weakened. The streetcar hung in midair, about to crash back to Earth, but Sara and Cass had other plans.

Before the streetcar could fall, Cass—her body glowing with yellow magica—shouted her spell: "Maidensong Melody Severance!"

She levitated into the air as her fingers flew across the frets of her guitar, playing a blistering guitar solo. Forks of yellow lightning crackled around her and generated eight shimmering copies of her guitar in a ring around her that aimed up at the streetcar. As her solo shredded across downtown Portland, the guitars fired.

A barrage of gleaming yellow projectiles of radiant magica blasted up into the streetcar, perforating it with smoking, jagged holes. The streetcar's body started to break apart, its three articulated sections disconnecting as it lost its structural integrity.

"Finishing it off!" Sara shouted. "Riot Chorus Sonic Blade!"

She played a massive, overdriven chord in a key to match Cass's solo and sang out a wordless melody over the top. Razor-sharp glistening rings of red magica appeared around the broken sections of the streetcar's body, interlocking down its length until it was nearly impossible to see the construct itself.

Tremendous, world-shattering music blasted in every direction, and the rings constricted. They sliced through the streetcar as if it were made of tissue paper, shredding what was once a formidable foe into a ragged mess of metal and plastic that finally fell to the pavement. The last twinges of Makula's magica faded from the debris, and the construct's remains lay lifelessly in the middle of Tenth Avenue.

The fight was over.

Nova kneeled beside me and ran a hand up and down my back as she wiped her eyes with the other. "Hey, babe? You doin' okay now? You kinda had me scared for a sec."

"Yeah," I said. "Yeah, I'm okay. I was scared for a minute, too. I really thought I'd screwed up."

"But ya didn't! You saved everybody!" Nova said. "You did real good, Claire cutie!"

Over at the wreckage of the streetcar, Sara and Cass looked over the debris to make sure it was completely dead. Then, suddenly, Sara turned around and made a beeline for Bloom, fire in her eyes.

Bloom noticed and smirked at her. "You're *welcome*, Sara. I saved you, and I—"

Sara barreled into her and grabbed her by the straps of her corset dress. She lifted Bloom off the ground, and slammed her into the wall of the Armory Theatre behind us, staring daggers into her from inches away.

"You could have been killed, you reckless jackass! What were you thinking? *Were* you even thinking?"

Bloom grabbed Sara's jacket sleeves and glared back. "Don't you *dare* criticize me when you got your sorry hide handed to you by a glorified trolley!"

Hana, Cass, and Nova ran over to them. I forced myself back to my feet and followed.

"Everybody just take a deep breath here," Hana said. "That was a close call, and we're all going to be feeling it."

"Yeah, c'mon, no fighting!" Nova said. I could hear a familiar panic seeping back into her voice. "We don't gotta fight!"

Sara and Bloom were hearing none of it.

"You don't get to gamble with your life right now," Sara said. "You're not alone in there, and I'm not going to let you get Iris killed, too!"

Bloom laughed. "Ah, the truth comes out! You really *do* only care about her!"

"Of course I care about her! I fucking love her, and you took her from me once already!"

Cass put her hands up. "Whoa, whoa, everybody take it down a notch, alright?"

Nova was starting to become beside herself. "Hey, hey, c'mon, babes, watch the language, okay? Let's just all chill out a little and—"

"And how do *you* think she feels," Bloom shot back at Sara, "watching you nearly die on the street because you had to play the hero? I feel everything, too! She can't lose *you*, you arrogant little girl prince! *I* can't lose you! It would kill us both!"

Sara froze, her mouth hanging open before she stammered out a reply. "What … say that again?"

Bloom's expression softened, her cheeks reddened, and tears welled up in her eyes. "I've spent weeks and weeks feeling every blasted emotion that Iris has! They bleed all over my consciousness! She *loves* you, and that makes me feel it, too. And I don't even *like* you! But if … if you die, it would annihilate my soul, Sara Ward! So you have no right to lecture me about *my* recklessness!"

Sara dropped Bloom back to her feet and let go of her dress. She stepped back and shook her head. "You … love me?"

"Yes," Bloom said. "No! I don't know! But *Iris* definitely does, and she's made it my problem, too. Do you know how awkward that makes *all of this?*" She gestured wide. "I'm not sure I *know* how to feel on my own! The closest I've felt to this love Iris insists on feeling is when Claire—"

Bloom clasped her hands over her mouth. She shot me an uncomfortable look, eyes frozen in fear. I heard Nova laugh, a relieved yelp.

"Wait, you feel love for me?" I asked.

"Hrmph." Bloom removed her hands from her mouth. "Let's not make this even more complicated, okay, Claire?"

"I'll second that," Cass said. "Why don't we just stow ... *everything*, and wrap this whole thing up and head to debrief?"

Hana smiled. "I don't know, I think it's sweet, if a little out-of-the-ordinary because of the circumstances."

"Heck yeah, I'm feelin' the love again!" Nova grinned. "Hey Bloom, tell Iris I love her, too, even if she cusses too much."

"It's not that ... *ARGH!*" Bloom shot back. "Just, don't even start, okay, magical girl?"

CHAPTER 17

We rode back to the Vault in a tense, shocked silence. Even when we'd fought the Pandora Corruption and the bug monster itself, none of our encounters had ever taken so much out of me. I still felt winded, despite my enhanced endurance. I could only imagine how the others were handling their roles in the battle.

As we pulled into the Vault's garage and parked Vancent, I noticed that Bloom—who was seated by herself in the back of the van—looked worse than the rest of us. I wondered if there were some lingering effects from the dissonant magica of the robots, or if it was something else. Possibly something related to what happened after the fight.

I swallowed hard and put aside my thoughts about what Bloom had almost said. That particular awkwardness could wait; I needed to check on her.

"Uh, hey, Bloom?" I asked, my voice as quiet as I could manage. "You doing okay?"

"I'm fine, Claire," Bloom said. Her voice had less of its usual cutting edge. "I'm simply tired."

"You look a little more than tired."

She didn't answer. Instead, she looked down at Vancent's floor and sighed softly.

"Maybe you should check in with Dr. Barrera," I offered.

To my surprise, she didn't fight me. "Perhaps I will."

We got out of Vancent and shuffled down the main corridor in silence. Bloom peeled off when we passed the med bay, and the rest of us made our way to the command center, where Commander McCoy and Hikari were waiting.

As we entered, the wall screens played the local news coverage. Video from the Kaiju Carcass Food Cart Pod showed a pale man in a hoodie and an expensive smart watch talking to reporters. I knew I'd seen him somewhere before, and the chyron beneath him confirmed it: He was Zach Tachyon, the CEO of Rhapsodyz.

"We absolutely regret the incident here in Portland today," he said, his voice laced with the irritated disdain of an executive addressing those he'd normally never give the time, *"and Rhapsodyz will be making it right. I'm directing the company to donate seven million dollars to the City of Portland municipal cleanup fund, and will also be starting a complimentary pilot program to integrate our advanced Future of AI 8K Metaverse autonomous robot technology into the city's—"*

Commander McCoy tapped a button and cut him off midsentence. "That's about all I can stand of that man for one day." She shook her head. "Who names themself 'Zach Tachyon' anyway?"

Nova laughed nervously. "Yeah, uh, who'd ever come up with a name like that?"

Hikari glanced back over their shoulder, blushing slightly. "Hey it's okay when you do it Nova it's cute um not that I'm saying you're cute and I'm definitely not saying you're not cute you exist in a superposition of cute and cool and it's just uh well you know it's charming on you because you're Nova you're a lovable rascal and an actual star that shines so bright all creatures great and small are blinded so the name fits perfectly on you but Zach Tachyon is just a slimy jerk I read about him he used to go by Zach Tatum but he started saying Tachyon because he thought it was more marketable and cool even though it's not when it's stuck on a CEO-bag like that."

Commander McCoy turned to us and offered a tired smile. "Right, Agent Nova here can get away with it. Anyway, that was a whole dang mess, wasn't it, girls?"

"Yeah," Cass said. "Everything that could go sideways, did."

"And y'all handled it incredibly well, all things considered," the commander said.

Sara stepped forward. "Not all of us, commander. I let my emotions get the best of me at the end."

Commander McCoy's eyes drifted to Bloom and back to Sara, and she nodded. "This is about you and Bloom."

"Yes," Sara said. She took a deep breath and looked away for a moment. "I didn't keep my head straight, and I—"

The commander's voice took on a gently forceful edge as she raised her hand and interrupted. "Agent Ward, put away that sacrificial sword. Yes, you and Bloom gettin' into it in the field ain't great, but you didn't let it affect your duties to the people of the city."

Sara's gaze fell to the floor. "I still feel like I let everybody down."

"I know you do," the commander said, her tone softening. "Just don't let it happen again, and we'll call it square, alright? If all goes well, we won't have to deal with this forever."

Sara sighed, and nodded. "Right. Thank you, commander."

"We'll address the tension later, once we've sorted everything else out." The commander turned her attention to me as her expression turned skeptical. "The person I really want to talk to right now is you, Agent Ryland. What in the world was *that?*"

"Well, um, I've been writing a new song," I said, shrinking back a little like I'd just been disciplined in school. "A new version of the Exalted Harmony."

"That was the Exalted Harmony?"

I shook my head. "Not like before. This one's more gentle. Or, well, that was the idea. It went a little out of my control for a minute."

The commander frowned. "I'd say so. That was a very risky move, using it in the heat of the moment like that."

"Commander," Hana said, "we were out of options. I believe Claire did the right thing."

"Yeah, me too!" Nova said. "It coulda been way worse without Claire cutie!"

"I agree," Cass said.

The commander put her hands up. "I ain't sayin' I disagree. You girls were handed a real dog's dinner. Let's be grateful it worked out, but I think maybe you should hold off on tryin' out experimental songs until you've finished them."

"Right," I said. "It won't happen again, commander. It was too close for comfort."

Sara nodded. "Still, I think it's clear that you were right. We can alter the Exalted Harmony with songs."

"And that is a powerful tool in y'all's toolbox," the commander said. "So, get into it further. Finish that song and research how it can be used. Just hold off on using it in an actual fight until you do."

"We'll do that, commander," Sara said. "Once we've rested up, we can make some recordings to polish the song up."

Cass grinned. "Now you're talkin'. Been too long since we got to knock out a fresh track."

Nova reached her arms around me and gave me a squeeze. "Flammin' right! We'll make Claire cutie's song into somethin' great!"

"Alright, then," the commander continued. "The data we got on everything is confusing. We've been loading your wrist link scans in, but it's hard to make sense of it. When Makula cast that spell, what'd y'all see?"

"I watched her magica pass over the robots and get twisted up," I said.

"Yeah," Nova said. "It went all screwy! Got messed up and did a whole curveball thing at the end."

"She was clearly aiming for the bug carcass," Hana said.

Cass nodded. "Those bots definitely had an effect on the spell."

"There's a lot that Rhapsodyz isn't letting on about them," Sara added.

The commander nodded at Hikari. "Agent Tomori's got some news on that front."

Hikari turned around from the computer terminal. "Yeah that's right I've been doing some hacking and stuff and I've learned more about your new corporate friend and surprise surprise she's not telling you the truth I know that's definitely totally shocking to you."

"Allison Webb," I said. "What did you find out?"

"Right okay yeah so the hunch we had was right Allison Webb works for Rhapsodyz in that she's actually a Sinneslöschen employee," Hikari said.

"As expected," Cass said.

Hikari nodded. "For sure for sure but there's more I know exactly what her job descriptions are like now it's amazing what you can find if you just break into some of the highest-security computer systems in corporate America."

"You say that like it ain't a big flammin' deal," Nova said.

"That's just how I roll Nova you know I'm a console jockey jamming the cyber highways I'm a rebel a real hacker heartthrob plus Sinneslöschen is running an outdated firewall firmware once I realized that it was pretty trivial not to take away from my very real rakish gender-indeterminate charm or anything."

"So what did the records say about her?" Sara asked.

Hikari turned around and punched some keys on the keyboard. "Here you go Sara get your magical eyeballs on these words."

The big video screen switched to a personnel file for Allison Webb from Sinneslöschen. Her department and job information read ADVANCED THAUMATITE WEAPONS and MAGICA ANOMALIES APPLICATIONS RESEARCH.

"There we go," Cass said. "Rhapsodyz is covering for thaumatite weapons research."

"If they're so smart and already have all this stuff going, why'd this Webb chick try to sweet talk us when she met Claire?" Nova asked.

"Data," I said. "Sinneslöschen wants data on magica users. It's like Jade said, they've only known how to use thaumatite like a blunt instrument, so they're trying to get as much information as they can from actual magica users. She wants to get close to us. And I saw how the robots behaved around Makula's construct today. They were gathering data."

"To what end, though?" Hana asked.

"Building thaumatite weapons for the government, maybe." Commander McCoy said. "Or private military contractors."

Cass shook her head. "It could be even worse than that."

"So, what, we gotta go in and bust some corpo heads?" Nova asked.

Commander McCoy sighed and stared up at the video wall before turning back to us. "That's real tricky territory, Agent Nova. We fight supernatural, magical threats. Goin' after people, even when they're this sketchy, gets complicated. We gotta be dead-on sure of *everything* if we're gonna take on one of the biggest corporations in the world."

Hikari turned back around to face us. "This biological construct might be the newbie vis-à-vis magical business but in my research I know that the Starlight Alliance has dealt with similar things before isn't that right?"

"Storm Maiden, over in Tokyo," Sara said. "Not exactly the same thing, but in the ballpark. There was a businessman trying to build an android army. I read the report their leader, Narumi Katou, filed."

Nova frowned. "What's the deal with all these creeps and robot armies? Get a new evil plan!"

"It'd make our lives easier," the commander said. "In the meantime, Agent Tomori, keep your digital eyes and ears open for anything you can find about Sinneslöschen. And let's keep crunching the data on the corruption magica those bots are using."

Hikari nodded. "Right consider it done I'll nail them to the wall it's like I always say fight the man till you're in the ground."

The commander turned back to us. "You girls will have to play the waiting game again, I'm afraid. Until we can get everything we need on Sinneslöschen, and until Makula makes herself known again, we're gonna be playing defense. You've still got that arena show to practice for, so be ready. Agent Hoffman's been dealing with the arena staff today, getting some final details in place. I have a feeling it might not go off exactly like we hope, at this rate."

"We'll be ready," Sara said. "From a performance *and* a magical girl standpoint."

"Good. In the meantime, I'm gonna do a little thinking on how to help us all get through this stress. Until then, carry on."

With the debrief done, I went to check on Bloom. I figured that once she'd been checked out, she'd be wanting to go back to the apartment and get some rest.

I entered the medical bay to find Dr. Barrera at her desk, her attention buried in her computer monitor. Bloom was still lying in the examination bed. She glanced over at me, but quickly averted her eyes and busied herself with idly fidgeting with her bedsheets as I walked over.

"Uh, Bloom? How are you feeling?"

"Fine, just fine," Bloom said, still not meeting my gaze. "Simply keeping myself busy. You understand."

"I'm heading home. You ready to go?"

"Actually … I shall remain here tonight."

That answer stopped me in my tracks. Bloom *hated* spending too long in the Vault.

"Is something wrong?" I asked.

"I simply wish to remain under the doctor's care," Bloom said. "She advised me to. As a precaution."

"Oh," I said. "Well, if Dr. Barrera says so …"

"Thank you for your understanding, Claire," Bloom said. "Now, if you will excuse me, I must rest."

She rolled over and turned her back to me. It was obvious I wasn't going to get anything else from her tonight. Since that avenue was closed, I walked over to Dr. Barrera's desk and tried to get her attention.

"Doctor, can I—"

"Ah, Claire, yes, yes," Dr. Barrera said. She stood and gestured toward the door. "Come with me, please."

We walked back out into the main corridor and Dr. Barrera closed the door behind her. She took a deep breath and shrugged.

"Bloom's not feeling up to going back to your apartment tonight," she said.

"Is something wrong with her?"

"The physical stress of having two active magica-using entities in the same physical body *is* taking a toll on her, yes. However, I can monitor her basic life signs remotely via the wrist link." She paused, and her voice softened. "I think she's, well, embarrassed."

"*Our* Bloom? Embarrassed?"

"That is my quite scientific guess, yes. Did something happen on top of the physical toll of your last combat encounter?"

I sighed. "Um, yeah, a bit. Some, y'know, emotional stuff. I guess it was more than a little awkward for all of us."

"Ah. Well, that would explain it," she nodded. "Bloom isn't used to feeling so emotionally vulnerable. It must be frightening for her. And I believe she still feels alone. Undefended."

The word cut into me and made my heart ache.

"Undefended …"

She patted my shoulder. "She's more delicate than she lets

on. Let her rest tonight and do some healing. I'll keep an eye on her, just to be safe."

"Okay, yeah," I said. "Thank you for keeping an eye on her. Do you need anything from, uh, the store, or something? Supplies to make the night pass more smoothly?"

Dr. Barrera smiled. "That won't be necessary, Claire, but I appreciate your thoughtfulness. Truth be told, I have spent many a night in this medical bay over the years, and am already well prepared. After all, the demands of pandimensional super-science wait for no woman." She reached over and squeezed my arm. "More importantly, *you* need to rest as well. Doctor's orders."

"Right," I chuckled. "I'll do that."

The doctor and I parted ways, and as she returned to the med bay and I headed toward the Vault's exit, a sight I was deeply thankful to see appeared in the corridor ahead of me.

"Hey, rock star," Hazel said, smiling as she approached me. "I saw your big moment on the news."

"You don't know the half of it, Haze," I said. "It was a lot."

"I'll bet." She wrapped me up in a hug and gave me a kiss before pulling back. Unsurprisingly, she seemed to notice the stress on my face. "You holding up okay, sweetie?"

I tried to tell her, but I couldn't put it all into words yet. Instead, I shrugged. "Just really tired. I was actually going back home for the night."

"Perfect timing. I'll go, too. You look like you could use some friendly company."

I managed a smile. "Honestly, Haze, I could really go for some of those famous cuddles of yours."

"Good thing I've got an infinite supply of 'em for you," she grinned.

———

After we'd put on some sunglasses and masks to keep ourselves reasonably anonymous, Hazel and I left the Vault and went back up to the surface. We hopped on board a MAX Blue Line train at the Skidmore Fountain station and rode it out to the Hollywood station near my apartment.

When we got to my place, the stress and exhaustion of the day finally caught up with me. I staggered into the shower and let the water rush over my head and down my back, hoping it'd take some of my thoughts with it. When I finally emerged, still finding my way into an old T-shirt to go with my panties, the pizza Hazel had ordered was sitting on the table. We ate in silence, the apartment so much quieter without Bloom.

Finally, with nothing left to do, I brushed my teeth, took my meds, and collapsed on the bed.

My body felt like a lead weight, my head like it had been stuffed with cotton. And yet, despite my exhaustion, sleep didn't come to me. I tossed and turned as my mind wracked itself about the streetcar fight and what had happened afterward. Bloom suddenly *not* being in the apartment now seemed even more strange than her sudden arrival had been.

I felt a hand slip under my T-shirt and softly stroke my back, sending electric tingles up my spine. Clearly, my restlessness had caught Hazel's attention.

"You got somethin' on your mind, rock star?" she asked.

I sighed into the mattress. "You wanna start with how I almost got a streetcar full of people killed, or how Bloom accidentally told everyone that she has feelings for Sara *and* me? And now she's so embarrassed by that, she's camping out with Dr. Barrera in the Vault?"

"Wow. You really did have a full day!"

I rolled over and looked at her. "I feel like I shouldn't complain too much, since I've already faced the end of the world and all that."

She reached out and squeezed my hand. "You're allowed to

vent, Claire. It doesn't matter if you're not stopping the literal apocalypse every time."

I laughed tiredly. "Thanks, Haze."

"Where do you want to start?"

"I was looking into the eyes of all the people on that streetcar when I nearly crushed them. What if I hadn't gotten things under control?"

"You can't live on what-ifs. You know that."

"I know. It was still terrifying."

"But you *did* get control." She moved her hands up and rubbed my shoulders. Another blast of sparkles shot through my nervous system. "You're not alone out there. The other girls are there to help you. And, as hard as it might be to admit it sometimes, you *are* a talented magical girl, experience or no."

Her hands felt incredible on my body. It had been a while since we'd gotten physical, a consequence of Bloom's presence in the apartment. As her hands caressed me, I involuntarily moaned and shifted under her touch, before I regained my senses a bit. "I just hope I don't bite off more than I can chew and get people hurt."

She leaned closer. "Look at it this way: What if you *hadn't* used your new song? A lot of worse stuff would have happened, right?" One of her hands dove down from my shoulders across my chest before returning to my collarbone. Sneaky of her. Another little moaning whimper escaped my lips.

I recovered, if only just. "Well … yeah, I guess so. Sara and Bloom might have been hurt. And the people in the streetcar might still have been, too."

"See? There you go. Things are better because you took a chance."

I smiled. "Don't fight regret."

"What was that?"

"Just something Sara told me once." I sighed. "She kind of blew up at Bloom because of everything that happened today. Bloom risking herself, and Iris, to save Sara, I mean. I didn't stick up for Bloom and I feel awful about it. Dr. Barrera said she felt 'undefended' when I talked to her about it."

Hazel squeezed my shoulders again. "It was a charged moment. And Sara's the team leader. You were just unprepared. Now that you know, you can make up for it next time."

"You think so?"

"Yeah, I do. You care about her, and you'll get another chance."

I nodded. "Yeah, I'm sure that's true."

"Speaking of Sara," Hazel said as she scooted up the bed and laid back on the pillows, "what were you saying about her and Bloom and you?"

"Well, Sara had some feelings about Bloom endangering herself, because she's also endangering Iris."

"That makes sense, yeah."

"And Bloom said Iris had feelings about seeing Sara in danger, which meant that she—Bloom, I mean—*also* had those feelings."

"Oh."

"Like, love. Maybe." I paused there to emphasize the implication.

"*Oh.*"

"Yeah. And then Bloom said the closest she'd felt to love herself was when I ... did something? She clammed up then, so I don't know what she was talking about."

Hazel grinned at that. "Aww, Claire, that's adorable."

"You think so? I figured you wouldn't be happy to know that another woman had any kind of feelings for me."

"Claire, oh my god, I'm not some tradwife," Hazel laughed. "You're my girlfriend, but we're both *alive lesbians*. It's okay for you to cast your gaze around and take in the rich bounty of Sappho's blessings. I encourage it, in fact. I mean, how many times have I told you how much I love women?"

"Yeah, but it's different when it's me."

"No it isn't! You're a girl with a pulse who likes girls. It's okay!"

I pushed myself up on my elbows and looked at her. "But I don't want a different girlfriend. I want you."

"And I don't want a different girlfriend, either, silly. I'm just sayin' that it's okay to talk about this stuff! It can be fun! You aren't hurting my feelings. I don't get jealous, as long as everybody's open about what's happening. I *have* had polyam relationships before, y'know."

I laughed. "I forget you have experience with stuff like this that I don't."

"And hell, you have people in the band who know it. Cass is polyamorous, too."

"Wait a sec, hold on," I said, shifting over to my right side, "we're not talking about a polyamorous relationship with Bloom *right now*. There's some complications you haven't really considered here."

"Yeah, I get it," Hazel giggled. "It *is* a little weird when she's occupying the body of Sara's girlfriend."

"Exactly," I said. "I think you can understand me being a little reluctant to talk about Bloom being into me when she's also Iris."

"That's a good point, sure," Hazel said. She smirked and elbowed me gently. "But she's not going to be in Iris's body forever. Isn't Saoirse getting that cute robot girl body ready for her?"

"Let's not put the girl cart before the magical horse, okay? We don't know what's going to happen there. I think we can probably wait until Bloom's a person of her own to discuss the ethics of her having a crush on me."

"I guess you have a point," Hazel laughed. She shot me a wicked grin. "You *do* know I'm gonna tease you about this, though, right?"

"Oh, I had no doubt," I said, breaking into a smile; she could always make me feel better. "Good thing I'm pretty okay with you teasing me."

Hazel smiled and leaned in close to me. Very gently, she kissed the exposed part of my collarbone and slowly worked her way up along my neck. My heart thumped and my head spun into a soft pink haze. I let my hand move to her thigh as she spoke low and smokily in my ear.

"You seem pretty okay with most everything I do to you, Claire Ryland. I'm starting to think you and I were made for each other."

I leaned my head over to give her better access as another, more urgent moan escaped my lips. "You're not wrong there, Haze."

Her lips reached my jaw and I could maintain my composure no longer. I felt lightheaded, in the best way, and the sensation of Hazel's kisses and her soft skin beneath my touch pushed me into bliss. I flopped over onto my back, and she climbed on top of me, straddling me and running her hands down my chest as my own danced up her thighs and caressed her hips.

Sleep was overrated, anyway.

CHAPTER 18

O nce we had all physically recovered from the fight with the streetcar construct, Sara had us meet up in the Vault's music room for song recording. Disappointingly but not surprisingly, Dr. Barrera informed us—with the tone of a mother saying her daughter couldn't come out to play—that Bloom wouldn't be joining the session.

Although the song wasn't fully finished yet—Sara had come up with lyrics for the verses and pre-choruses, but hadn't found a chorus lyric she liked yet—getting what there was onto a recording would let us iterate and build upon what we'd done already.

And with Bloom still keeping her distance from the rest of us, I was grateful for the chance to focus my mind on something else.

We started with a rough guitar and vocal melody demo by Sara, which formed the foundation for the arrangement. After some explorations, we hit upon a structure for the song that felt good. It clocked in at just over three minutes, the perfect length for a Magica Riot song.

With Hikari running the recording process from their computer, the five of us sat together with our instruments, a barrage of microphones, and cables snaking over to an input plugged into the computer. We'd be taking it one track at a time.

"Okay, let's go for drums," Sara said. "Nova, do you have some ideas already?"

"Heck yeah I do!" Nova said. "This song's like your empathy spell, right? A gentle hug that can stop a dang train!"

"Yeah, exactly," I said.

"Gotcha, babe! So I'll play a little gentle-like." She slipped her headphones on and waved to Hikari at the computer. "Gimme a two-bar count-in!"

"Two-bar count-in set up Nova you're good to go I've got the mics on your drums and the overhead room mic hot and ready," Hikari said.

Cass laughed. "This is so much easier with a dedicated engineer."

"Hikari's worth their weight in gold," Hana said.

Hikari blushed slightly. "It's no biggie I do this kind of thing all the time with my own music I'm happy to do it besides you're all pros game respect game you know what I'm saying anyway Nova I'm ready when you are."

Nova nodded. "Ready, babe!"

Hikari hit a key on their keyboard and Nova immediately counted in, clicking her drumsticks together as she nodded to the metronome in her headphones. "One, two, one two three four!"

The song began, and Nova played through the intro, a minimalist arrangement of hi-hat and kick drum to establish the beat before she reached the first verse and added her snare drum to the mix. As I watched her, I was struck by her precision; Nova might be a barely contained ball of energy, but her drumming was always absurdly tight. She rarely played with this much delicacy, but she had no trouble pulling back for a song that required it.

With a soft fill on her floor tom, she moved into the pre-chorus, and then into the chorus, adding flourishes and turning the energy up a notch. As the song progressed into the next verse, she steadily increased her fills and accents, making the track bigger and more driving with each section.

I glanced over toward Hikari and couldn't help noticing that their attention was not on their monitor. Their eyes were, instead, absolutely glued to Nova as she played. While Hikari's expressions were hard to read even at the best of times, it was easy to tell that they seemed totally entranced by the emotionality of Nova's playing.

Interesting, that.

By the time Nova reached the bridge and final chorus, she was fully in the zone, bringing the song to a climax before pulling back into a gentle outro. At the end of the final bar, she gave her crash cymbal a final soft hit and let the sound decay naturally while Hikari caught the tail end of the audio. After several seconds, Hikari shot her a thumbs-up. Nova silenced her cymbal and pulled her headphones off.

"How was that, babes?" she asked.

"Sounded great to me," Cass said.

Hikari nodded. "Yeah shiny and chrome as they say basically flawless Nova I don't know how you do it you're amazing uh I mean uh anyway yeah I think I got all that we can do some punch-ins later if there's anything you want to change."

"Flam yeah, sounds good!" Nova said.

"Okay that's drums done in record time thanks to the incredible one-take wonder that is Nova uh anyway we can do bass if you're ready Hana get that thump and slap in there you know what I mean," Hikari said.

"Yes, please," Hana said. "I've already got a bass line figured out, based on Sara's demo melody."

Cass put her hand up. "Hey, when you get to the bridge, you wanna skip it for now?"

"Do you have something in mind there?" Hana asked.

"I'm hearing something," Cass nodded. "A solo's coming to

me. I want to figure it out with you and record it together so we can play off each other."

Hana giggled as she put on her own headphones. "You're always so good at dancing with me. Okay, deal!"

Hikari started the recording again, and Hana closed her eyes. Her head bobbed gently as she listened to the drum track Nova had just laid down, keeping her bass still during the intro. Then, at the start of the first verse, she began to play.

Hana's bass line started fairly simply and not too flashy, a gentle descending series of plucked notes that turned around into an upward flourish partway through the verse. Just as Nova had done, though, she gradually fed in more energetic playing, feeding the song's tension as it progressed through the choruses and verses. Hana was never the sort of bass player who showed off, but her effortless performance served the song perfectly while still sprinkling in accents at key moments.

She left the bridge blank for now and proceeded to the final chorus, never losing an ounce of precision as she thumped away harder than before. It was then that I took notice of the parts she added to the ends of the choruses, an ascending line that played against the still-wordless melody in those sections.

And it gave me an idea.

As Hana finished, I spoke up. "Um, would it be okay if we did keyboards next?"

"Oh yeah, I don't mind," Cass said. "It'll give me and Hana a chance to figure something out on the bridge."

She and Hana unplugged their instruments and moved over to the side of the room, sitting down together as they worked on the solo while I prepared to record.

"You have an idea?" Sara asked me.

"I think so, yeah," I nodded. "I'm going to stick to pads, mostly, but I hear a chance to do something neat at the ends of the choruses where Hana's playing her ascending part."

Sara smiled. "Go for it."

"Okay," I nodded. "Hey, Hikari?"

Hikari looked up from their computer. "Yo Claire-monster what's up what can I do you for?"

"I need your help for this, I think. At the ends of the choruses, I'm going to play a descending set of notes against the bass. Once I do, can you lay something in over the top of them?"

"For sure for sure I've got a MIDI interface over here I can do whatever you need what do you want me to add?"

"Cool," I said. "I want you to do the notes, too, with a vibra-phone sound."

Hikari nodded. "Oh yeah vibes for sure very Brian Wilson of you Claire I like that I'll take care of it for you."

"Ooh, fancy," Cass said from the other side of the room. "Think this'll be the first time the vibes have showed up on a Magica Riot track!"

"Well, I mean, only if it's okay," I said.

"It's okay," Sara laughed. "Get your vibraphone sound."

"You have our permission," Hana added.

"Yeah, babe," Nova said. "No rules, just right!"

"Okay," I said, smiling. "Thanks."

I pulled my headphones on and listened as Hikari started the track over from the top. To give more of a spotlight to Sara's eventual vocals, I decided to hold off on playing at all during the first verse. Instead, I punched up an organ-like tone on my keytar and held off until the pre-chorus.

When the pre-chorus arrived, I played a steady, soft chord pattern that followed Sara's rhythm guitar, adding a rich texture to the backing track. For the chorus itself, I added a vibrato to spice the sound up a little more, laying on the chords again before switching to a descending series of notes at the end that played against Hana's ascending bass line.

My part was mostly uncomplicated, serving as an enhance-ment to everybody else, so I made my way through the rest of the song without a problem. I dropped out completely on the bridge, knowing that Cass and Hana would take a starring role there, before coming back in for the finish on the final chorus.

After Hikari stopped recording, I pulled my headphones off. "How was that?"

"Perfect texture," Sara said. "Good job, Claire."

Hikari glanced up from their computer. "Give me just a second Claire I'm adding in those vibes now for you I think it's gonna work it's a tasty little sound nugget okay here you go take a listen."

They switched on the monitor speakers and turned the volume up as they called up the end of one of the choruses. The parts we'd recorded so far leapt from the speakers and filled the room. My keyboard part transitioned into those descending notes, and now, a matching series of bell-like tones harmonized with them, subtly adding another layer of interest to the sound.

"Yeah!" I said. "That's exactly what I was hearing in my head. Thank you, Hikari!"

Hikari saluted me. "Happy to be of service Claire just getting to perform on a Magica Riot track is a thrill not unlike pulling off a perfect finisher against Godfrey the first Elden Lord I know you aren't a Soulsborne kinda girl just trust me it's an exciting thing," Hikari said.

"Alright," Sara said, "now let's see what Cass has cooked up."

Cass and Hana walked back over from their joint practice session. Both of them looked very satisfied with their work.

"I'm ready," Cass said. "Think we've got something good. Hikari, can you give me a nearly clean tone with just a tasty little bit of drive and spring reverb?"

"For sure for sure seasoned to chef's orders," Hikari nodded.

"Sweet. Let's do it."

She and Hana put their headphones on as Hikari began recording. Eight beats passed. As the other tracks came in, Cass played her line, a melody she'd written during rehearsals. Her precision, focused as a laser, caught me off guard. It weaved around the song I'd been hearing in my head perfectly, elevating it beyond what it had been on its own.

And she wasn't done yet.

Cass backed off for the verse and pre-chorus, but added a subtle set of accents to the first chorus to create another layer of richness. Now, with the song fully off and running, she played her intro melody again over the next verse and slid into a totally new set of accents in the second pre-chorus.

She repeated her chorus riff and played along with my descending notes at the end. Just before the bridge, she glanced over at Hana as the two exchanged grins; when the bridge began, they dove straight into the solo they'd worked out together.

I sat in quiet awe of Cass. The guitar solo she'd created wasn't overly flashy or too complicated for such an emotional song, but rather, a graceful elevation of the song we'd built and the cosmic melody at its heart. And she played it *flawlessly*. As she and Hana locked in together, each pushing the other to greater heights, I felt tears involuntarily well up in my eyes.

It was incredible to watch the two of them work, especially in service of something I'd made. And beyond their musical skill, their work made the song feel powerful, but warm and vulnerable, too. Exactly what we needed for an Exalted Harmony song about empathy.

Cass finished out the final chorus, her guitar singing out over the rest of the tracks, and then it was over. The song had gone from a fragment fed to me by the Maidensong to a nearly fleshed-out piece of pop songcraft.

"That was amazing, Cass," I said as she pulled her headphones off.

"Aw, thanks," she said. "It's such a nice song! Made it easy to come up with something good."

Sara smiled. "Really good work, all of you."

"Felt just like the old days," Hana said.

Nova grinned and pumped her fist. "You better flammin' believe it! We wrote a new song, babes!"

"Almost," Sara said. "I'll knock out vocals for what

lyrics I have." She paused, and softly sighed. "It might be a good idea to leave this off the setlist for the arena show. Even if we get it finished, it would be best to practice it some more before we start playing it live. Let alone using it in fights."

Cass stood as her guitar dematerialized. "After you're done, what do you all say to getting drinks at Dark Water? I could use a break."

"Good idea," Sara said. "It won't take me long. I've been practicing to the demo."

The rest of us moved to sit by the computer terminal as Hikari turned on Sara's vocal microphone. After getting the mic adjusted, Sara pulled on her headphones as Hikari returned to their place at the controls.

"Okay Sara if you could give me some of that sweet sweet vocal sauce I'll get your levels dialed in do you need reverb or anything?" Hikari asked.

"A little reverb, yeah," Sara nodded. "Check, check, check! Mic check! Checking the microphone. One, two, three, four. Check. Check." She gave Hikari a thumbs up. "Sounds good in the headphones."

Hikari reached over and clicked the "record" button again, and after the intro rolled, Sara sang.

"Frightened or anxiety, an answer only you can see. Living in the framework of the factory, holding on for something new."

Combined with all of the instruments already on the track, the addition of Sara's vocals pushed the song to a new level. Despite us not being transformed, I could *feel* the charge of magica in the room. The song felt like a hug of healing comfort to somebody going through a dark time. As Sara moved into the pre-chorus, I got goosebumps.

"Fact or fiction or fantasy, who's the person you present to me? Rushing headlong into calamity, I hope your aim is true."

When she transitioned into the chorus, she switched to a wordless melody. Though she hadn't written lyrics yet, the chorus melody was soaring, and even in this unfinished form, it tugged at my heart.

After recording the second verse and pre-chorus, Sara was done for the time being. Hikari stopped recording and saved the file in their audio workstation software.

"Okay cool cool that's a wrap I'm gonna do a quick mix on this just get some of that real sonic flavor on there and when you're ready we can do that chorus and any other instruments you want to add," they said.

Nova grinned and patted their shoulder. "Thanks, Hikari cutie! You did a flammin' great job! I might wanna add some tambourine later, if ya wanna do a private sesh!"

I had never seen Hikari's eyes go as wide as they did in that moment.

———

We left Hikari to their mixing duties and drove out to Dark Water. Jade was working the bar, as usual, and we ordered a round of beers and a Shasta for Nova. That first round led to a second, and a third, where I found myself sitting at the bar contemplating the bubbles rising up through my pint glass.

The experience of recording with the band had been exhilarating. Creatively fulfilling, yes, but also more than a bit awe-inspiring. This was the band that I'd fallen for even before I became a girl, a magical girl, or a member of it. Watching Sara, Cass, Hana, and Nova work made me want to push myself harder to keep up, and hope that I was filling Iris's old role well.

I'd almost screwed up big-time and caused a disaster at the streetcar fight. Logically, I knew that accidents were inevitable, but it was difficult not to be upset with myself for letting that almost happen. Now, we were finishing that song, helping it grow into something more special than I'd dared dream; but still, I wondered if it was good enough. If *I* was good enough. Sara and Iris had written so many songs I'd loved; now, I was part of that writing team, instead of Iris. It was hard not to feel a little anxious about that.

My anxiety must have shown on my face, because when I looked up from my beer, I found Jade smiling warmly at me from across the bar.

"Claire, you seem a little troubled," she said. "You need to talk about it?"

I shrugged. "I had a close call in our last fight."

"So I hear. Sara and Cass told me about it."

"Yeah," I nodded. "It was kinda reckless of me to use an unfinished song. We're finishing it now, but still, you know."

"I remember you telling me the last time you were here," Jade said. "You're worried that your song won't measure up."

"Can you blame me? It's Magica Riot."

Jade shook her head. "You know *you're* a member of Magica Riot, right, Claire?"

"Yeah, but I've never written a song before."

"First time for everything," Jade said. "I know, I know, this is extra scary, because it's your first song for the band *and* your first Exalted Harmony song as the Guardian of Harmony."

"Exactly. And what happened at the streetcar fight, well, it rattled me."

Jade nodded thoughtfully. "You know, when I faced Makula for the first time and dealt with Polybius, my best friend got caught in the crossfire. Polybius brainwashed her for a few minutes."

"Really?" I asked. "I didn't know that."

"It's true. I freed her, but I was still new at everything. Those few minutes were terrifying. I was convinced I'd failed, and she was gone forever."

"That's awful. I'd be terrified, too."

"It's a natural reaction," Jade said. "And it wasn't the last time I made a mistake that almost got somebody hurt. But the thing is, Claire, as a magical girl, you know what you have to do.

You pick yourself up and keep going. It's the job, and nobody is better at it than we are."

I nodded. "Reminds me of something somebody told me not too long ago."

From behind me, a familiar voice spoke up. "You get back on the bike, and you keep going."

I looked over to find Sara sliding onto the barstool beside me, beer in hand.

"That's it, yeah," I laughed.

"You should listen to your team leader, kid," Jade said. "Girl's got a good head on her shoulders. And so do you."

Sara sipped her beer and looked me in the eye. "What happened with the streetcar *was* scary, but you pulled out of it. You fixed the problem and saved lives, just like a magical girl should."

"It's just terrifying when you can watch the faces of the people in danger," I said.

"Yes, it is," Sara said. "That's why we're all going to make that song the best it can be. You're learning to shape the ultimate magical power we have, Claire. That's a big deal, and you should be proud of it."

I took a hefty drink of my own beer and sighed. "I just want to be worthy of Magica Riot, as magical girls *and* as a band."

Sara squeezed my shoulder. "You already are. When that song's done, it will be obvious." She took another sip, and frowned. "I'm sorry I haven't finished the words yet."

"No, it's okay!" I assured her. "It takes time, I know that. It'll be worth it."

"Thanks," she said. "Iris was always better at writing choruses than I was."

"Choruses are hard," Jade said.

"They are," Sara agreed. "I'm good with the verses, but Iris knew how to write a chorus hook that you couldn't forget."

"Is that so?" I asked.

Sara nodded. "Yeah. All the big songs have Iris choruses. Of course, that skill and knowledge is a little preoccupied with a certain unexpected guest."

I hadn't thought about it before, but it made sense, especially considering that the band had only released one single in the two-year gap after Iris disappeared. And I thought about Bloom, now cohabitating with Iris's songwriting skills.

For a moment, I considered what it might be like if Bloom wrote a song, but the thought flew away almost as quickly. She'd never expressed any interest in such a thing—but since she had Iris's thoughts, maybe the problem was that none of us had ever asked her.

That notion teased at me a few more times as we finished up our last round of drinks.

CHAPTER 19

We spent the next week or so practicing for the arena show and trying to ignore the transparently self-serving damage control that Rhapsodyz was doing, but there was still a bit of tension going around. Sara hadn't yet cracked the new song's chorus lyric, which I knew was bothering her. Meanwhile, Bloom had remained at the Vault and not come back to the apartment since the streetcar fight, and it had been eating at me the whole time.

I realized that I really, truly missed her.

And I wasn't alone. Hazel was clearly missing my new roommate as well. Bloom had become a presence in our lives that neither of us wanted to lose.

Since we had Saturday off, Hazel and I spent the day together, tending to our shared melancholy as we walked around the neighborhood, enjoying each other's company while we ran errands. The mood was subdued, but being together made both of us feel better. It helped ease the heartache around our unexpected new friend.

Eventually, we returned to my apartment. The relative quiet of our day together made the message that popped onto our wrist links even more surprising.

Outside, it read. It was sent from Cass's link.

"Uh, did you get a message from Cass just now?" I asked Hazel.

"I did, yeah," she said. "What does she mean by 'outside,' though?"

I moved over to the living room window and raised the blinds just in time to see Vancent Price pull up on the street outside the apartment.

"Literally, outside," I said. "C'mon."

Hazel and I left the apartment and descended the stairs. Before we made it more than a few feet onto the sidewalk, Cass rolled down Vancent's passenger window and motioned for us to hop in.

"Hey, you two," Cass said. "Commander wants all of us to meet her somewhere, together."

"What's going on?" I asked. "Is something wrong?"

Cass shook her head. "She won't say. We're just supposed to come to a marker on the map."

I pulled open the side door and was met by nine pairs of human eyes, and one set of feline eyes.

Sara and Cass occupied their places in the front row of Vancent. In the next row, Hikari, Nova, and Hana sat together. A fluffy white cat held a place of honor on Nova's lap.

"Aw, you brought her!" Hazel said. "Hi, Nebula!"

The cat meowed happily at us.

"Yeah, I figured this might be a good day to bring her along," Nova said. "She hasn't had a nice magical family hangout in a while!"

"And she's just *so soft,*" Hana said, her eyes glowing with rapturous joy.

From Nova's side, Hikari regarded us with a microscopic smile.

"Hey Claire Hazel welcome aboard we're heading to the party zone at least presumably I don't know maybe the commander has something more mundane planned but I choose to believe it's the party zone anyway I hope you're ready to get wild in a consistent and thorough sense."

"I'm not much for getting wild, but I *am* curious what this is all about," I said.

In the next row sat Saoirse, and it struck me that this was the first time I'd seen her outside of the Vault. She offered a polite nod as Hazel and I sat down beside her.

In the back row behind us, Bloom sat, gazing out of Vancent's left-side windows and frowning. My pulse shot up as soon as I saw her, and a million questions flooded my mind.

I swallowed my panic as I noticed Bloom wasn't alone in the back of Vancent. She sat with Dr. Barrera and another unexpected guest: Jade Evergreen.

"Hey there, you two," Jade said, practically beaming. "Hope you don't mind me tagging along."

"Are you kidding? Not at all," Hazel said.

"I'm surprised the commander invited you," I said.

Then I realized what I'd just said.

To *Jade Evergreen*.

I panicked slightly. "Oh, flam, that came out wrong."

Nova's face lit up, and she squealed. "YOU SAID IT, CLAIRE CUTIE!"

"Oh, uh," I stammered, "it's just—"

Jade laughed. "No, I get it. Commander McCoy didn't technically invite me."

"That was me," Dr. Barrera said. "While I'm not privy to the commander's plans for today, I saw the opportunity to break through her anxieties and let her meet her hero."

"Ooh, this should be good," Hazel said. "I've never seen Commander McCoy faint before."

Dr. Barrera grinned. "Well, if she does, she'll have medical attention on-site."

Hazel turned her attention to another matter. "And it's good to see you again, Bloom."

Bloom glowered and glanced at us. "I simply did not wish to be in that metal can of yours alone."

"Well, um, whatever your reason," I said, "I'm glad you came."

Bloom looked away. "Think nothing of it."

"Alright, everyone," Sara announced as she shifted Vancent into gear. "With us all assembled, it's time to go. We're apparently off to Sauvie Island."

"Sauvie Island?" I asked. "Um, we're not going to the nude beach, are we?"

"Doubtful," Cass chuckled. "The map marker's on the farmland, and I don't think the commander's the type, to be honest."

Hazel nudged my arm. "We can always go later."

I stifled a yelp at the wicked grin that accompanied Hazel's suggestion. From behind us, I heard a familiar snort of derision.

It was oddly comforting to hear that from Bloom again.

"The commander's being cagey about this," Sara said, "so whatever she's got planned, we won't know until we get there."

Nova clapped her hands. "Well then, what're we waiting for? Let's get this mystery show on the dang road!"

As Vancent Price pulled away from the curb, I leaned over to Hazel and whispered to her.

"Did you really mean that? Uh, about the beach, I mean?"

"Aw, why are you so nervous, rock star? We've seen each other naked plenty of times now."

"Yeah, but not in public! I don't know how people would react to me."

Hazel reached down and squeezed my hand. "If they've got any sense, they'll be amazed by my hot trans girlfriend. And if they don't, then I can kick their butts."

———

After a half hour or so, we turned off Highway 30 and crossed the Wapato Bridge onto Sauvie Island. As we wound our way through the roads on the island, I took in the scenery, which was about as far from my place in the city as you could get without going into the actual wilderness. Fields of crops of various hues separated by the occasional fence rolled past as white, puffy clouds drifted lazily across the sky.

After several minutes, Sara pulled Vancent up to a nonde-script gate in front of a long gravel road splitting two fields. The road disappeared into a grove of trees, through which I could just barely make out a house and other structures.

By the gate, a simple wooden sign attached to the fence read "MCCOY BERRIES."

"No way," Cass said. "No *way*."

"Is this right?" Hana asked.

Sara nodded. "This is where the marker told us to come."

"Anybody ever hear the big boss lady talk about growin' berries?" Nova asked.

"She used to be a rancher," Saoirse said.

"That's quite true," Dr. Barrera said. "I've never heard her speak of what she does with her free time now, though."

"Maybe it never came up," I said.

"Maybe," Hazel said. "Or she's just a little private about her home life."

From the back row, Bloom scoffed. "What need has your commander for berries?"

Hazel grinned. "Berries are good, Bloom. I'll make you some-thing we call a 'smoothie' sometime to prove it to you."

"Hrmph," Bloom grumbled.

Hikari leaned their face against the window and peered out across the fields. "You know this is kind of cool I have to say I've never been on a farm or any other food-production installation for that matter this is basically the opposite of my habitat."

"Aw, that's flammin' tragic, Hikari babe," Nova said. "I'm more of a high desert kinda girlie, but I bet I could give ya a little tour of the nature here!"

It might have been my imagination, but I swore I saw Hikari

blush, just a little bit, as they spoke. "Thank you Nova that's very kind of you and it makes sense I teach you about gaming you teach me about ruralness."

As if acknowledging our presence, the gate in front of us swung open on motorized hinges. Sara shrugged and put Vancent back into gear.

"Guess that's our answer," she said. "Alright, let's see what this is all about."

Sara drove Vancent through the gate and down the gravel road. As we passed through the stand of trees at its end, we arrived in a clearing ringed with a few structures. There was, of course, a barn, with white metal walls attached to a red steel frame and matching roof. Nearby, another white and red metal structure with its sliding doors open revealed an assortment of agricultural machinery I couldn't even begin to identify. Across from those buildings on the other side of the clearing stood an old two-story farmhouse, beautifully maintained despite its age, painted in matching white and red. An enormous fire pit in a sunken circle finished with stone seats lay in the center of the clearing, a long heavy wooden picnic table standing near it.

And on that picnic table, Commander McCoy had laid out a veritable feast. She stood beside it, wearing jeans and a khaki safari shirt with the sleeves rolled up. She waved at us as Sara parked Vancent at the end of the driveway beside what I figured was the commander's personal vehicle, a well-used Ford pickup. It looked like it had been candy apple red when it was new, which, judging from the unassuming lines, couldn't have been more recent than 1986.

The commander strode over to greet us as we exited the van.

"Welcome," she said. "It's a pleasure to finally have y'all here."

"This is your place, commander?" Sara asked.

"Every acre," the commander said. "The Alliance knew I was a country gal at heart, so when they recruited me, they helped me find th—"

She stopped dead in her tracks mid-sentence as she noticed Jade step out of Vancent. Her eyes went wide, and for the first time since I'd known her, Meredith McCoy was at a loss for words.

Jade smiled and reached her hand out. "So you're the commander I keep hearing about."

The commander stammered and, after a few seconds of processing, finally took Jade's hand and shook it. "I, uh, yeah, that's me, uh, yeah, yeah." She laughed the kind of nervous, flustered laugh I was all too familiar with from being around Hazel. "I didn't expect you to be here, Miss Evergr—uh, Everly. I would've dressed a little nicer if I'd known."

Jade laughed softly. "Call me Jade, Meredith. And you're dressed exactly right."

"Well, uh, I … thank you," the commander said.

Dr. Barrera stepped up and waved her hand. "I must confess, commander, this was my doing." She lowered her voice to a stage whisper. "I simply could not abide watching you deny yourself any longer."

The commander shot her a look somewhere between sincere thanks and apoplectic rage before turning back to Jade, her smile genuine but her eyes wide with fear. "Well, it's real good to have you here, Jade." She cleared her throat, recovered some of her usual cool composure, and looked at the rest of us. "It's good to have all y'all here. Welcome to my home."

"This is an amazing setup you have here, commander," Hana said.

"Yeah, it is," I said. "I don't think any of us knew you were a berry farmer."

"Sure am," the commander said. "Marionberries, specifically."

"Classic Oregon," Cass said.

"So, hold up, what do ya do with all them berries?" Nova asked as Nebula hopped down out of Vancent and proceeded to rub against her leg.

"You'll see," the commander said. "C'mon over to the table."

We followed her around Vancent and past the fire pit to the picnic table, where we got a better look at the food spread. She'd made a truly heroic amount of cookout food, with plates full of burgers both meat and vegan, grilled corn on the cob and sweet potatoes, mashed potatoes, biscuits, and—once I started to notice them—marionberries. Marionberries in the salad, garnishing the sweet potatoes, scattered about the tablecloth simply for contrast. Dishes of dark, tart-smelling sauces near the corn. Bottles of marionberry cider spaced along the table's length. And at one end, a couple of mouthwatering marionberry pies, with several small mason jars near them.

The commander took one of the jars and handed it over to Nova. "I've been sellin' them at the farmer's markets in town, when y'all aren't making me work weekends."

Nova turned it over in her hands and showed it to the rest of us. A label on the side featured a cartoon drawing of the commander holding a bushel of marionberries, along with text that read "McCoy Berries: Genuine Oregon Marionberry Preserves."

Nova grabbed a spoon from the table, scooped out a bit of the preserves from the jar, and took a taste. Her face lit up. "Holy flam, big boss lady! This tastes bonkers good!"

The commander beamed at her. "Grown and produced with nothin' but love, Agent Nova. Well, love, and several pieces of specialized equipment."

"Um hey Nova would you believe I've never had marionberries somehow," Hikari said, as they picked Nebula up and cradled her in their arms.

"That ain't gonna stand!" Nova said. "Every cutie deserves a tasty treat! C'mere and get a bite!"

Hikari moved closer and stood beside Nova, shoulder to shoulder. Nova dipped the spoon back in and brought out another bite of preserves, and slipped it between Hikari's lips.

"Whatcha think?" Nova asked.

Hikari was never easy to read, but I didn't need to be a Guardian of Harmony to recognize how their expression changed. "Wow uh okay that's uh wow that's really good how have I never eaten marionberries in the entire time I've lived in Portland I feel like I've neglected my education in all things Stumptown this is an egregious error on my part."

Nova nudged them and grinned. "Like I said, stick close to me, Hikari cutie! I got ya covered!"

This time, I knew I saw it. Hikari blushed ever so slightly, and the corners of their mouth moved up a little more. Adorably, they brought Nebula up higher and tried to hide their face in her fur a little bit.

Hana's expression lit up as her eyes jumped from one dish to the next, eventually settling on the cider bottles. "This looks wonderful, commander! And marionberry cider is my absolute favorite."

Cass looked from the jar of preserves out across the fields. "I can't believe you've been holding out on us, commander!"

The commander shrugged. "I've been waitin' for the yields to improve. I would've been embarrassed if I'd shown y'all and then it didn't pan out."

"Well, I'm impressed," Hazel said, "but I'm guessing you didn't call everybody here to promote your berry business."

"You'd be right, Agent Hoffman," the commander said. She stepped around behind the picnic table. "I wanted to do something for everybody, 'cause I know we've all been under a bit of stress lately."

"To say the least," Bloom muttered.

"Usually, it's Agent Hasegawa who takes care of everybody in situations like this," the commander continued, "but I figured it was my turn. It's the least I can do to show y'all that you mean the world to me."

Hana put her hands over her heart. "Commander ..."

"I think some of us have some things we gotta work out, so this here's your chance," the commander said, as she gestured at the food. "Eat up, drink up, be together, and talk. I want y'all to leave here a fully functional team again."

"I ain't much for the touchy-feely stuff," Saoirse said, "but I've got a fierce appetite, so I vote we dig in."

"I find myself agreeing with the weaponsmith," Bloom said.

"Don't get too cocky there, Bloom," the commander said. "You're one of the ones I expect to make some progress today."

Bloom glared at her, stepped forward, and plunked herself down at the table without another word.

"Well, I think this is a noble goal, commander," Dr. Barrera said. "I approve of this therapeutic use of bonding and food."

Hazel sat down next to Bloom, much to Bloom's surprise. "Right on! Let's get to it." She nodded at me, and then at the other seat next to Bloom.

I took a deep breath and sat down. I could feel the heat of conflicted feelings radiating off Bloom the instant I made contact with the bench.

"Well ... alright, yeah. I'm in," Sara said. She moved around the table and sat across from Bloom as Cass and Hana joined her.

Nova sat beside me, and Hikari by her. Nebula, not content to be left out of the action, hopped up on Nova's shoulders and draped herself across them, purring so loudly that I could hear.

As Dr. Barrera and Saoirse joined us, the commander clasped her hands together. "Now, who wants some cider?"

"I'll give you a hand," Jade said. "I *am* a bartender, after all."

The commander didn't offer a coherent answer, but the goofy grin on her face spoke volumes.

"Must we do this?" Bloom groaned. "I know how complicated you humans get with alcohol in your system."

"Sometimes we need a little motivation to open up," Cass said.

Bloom scoffed. "As if you magical girls need anything to become sappy messes."

CHAPTER 20

The commander's cooking was, as it turned out, delicious. That was the opinion I arrived at even *before* the marionberry ciders took their toll on my cognitive functions, and things only got tastier from there. By the time pie was on offer, I was well and truly buzzed. With approximately three tons of home cooking in me, I eventually made my way over to the fire pit, nursing a bottle of cider as the pleasingly warm fuzziness of inebriation sloshed through my brain.

As the warmth of the fire blanketed my exposed skin, I looked around the farm, taking in the sights of the whole setup as well as scouting out what everybody else was up to.

Commander McCoy and Jade were in the barn, where the commander was gesticulating excitedly at the goats she also kept as part of the berry farm operations. Her enthusiasm for Jade was obvious; Jade, for her part, seemed to be sincerely appreciative, even flattered. I wondered for a moment if there was something going on there beyond mere fan admiration.

Back at the picnic table, Dr. Barrera and Saoirse were deep into some conversation I could barely understand, from the bits and pieces of words I picked up at the edge of hearing. Something about containing "bio-essence" within mechanical devices and thaumatite, which sounded several rungs above my level of specialized knowledge. I'd heard Saoirse use that term—"bio-essence"—before, in relation to binding magical girls to musical instrument weapons, so I assumed that was the subject they were discussing and decided it'd be best if I didn't try to figure it out beyond that.

Over at the edge of the trees, I spotted Nova and Hikari together. Nova appeared to be demonstrating a tree-climbing technique to Hikari, who held Nebula safely in their arms as they watched with rapt attention, despite giving no indication that they would be trying it themself. I smiled as I watched, amazed by Nova's ability to turn anybody she met into her new best friend. Being that outgoing was something that had never been a part of my personality, and apart from Hazel, I'd never had a lot of friends.

Until, of course, I awakened, came out as trans, and joined Magica Riot. One of many aspects of my life that being a magical girl had completely changed. I had actual *friends* now.

I craned my neck around and searched for Cass and Hana, and found them sitting under another tree. They'd summoned their instruments, and were playing something together, too quietly for me to hear. Whatever it was, it seemed to be going well, judging by the way Cass enthusiastically nodded as fingers danced along their respective fretboards.

I relaxed again and enjoyed the fire, letting the warmth seep into my bones. Beyond the dancing flames, the commander's berry fields stretched out in long rows beneath the Sauvie Island sky. There, I finally spotted Sara and Bloom on a stroll through the fields.

It was more than a little surprising to see Bloom out there, actually participating. She moved differently; from a distance, she seemed open, or as close as she ever came to it. I'd noticed she hadn't avoided the cider. Maybe it had cut through whatever inhibitions she carried from her time in the Menagerie. It did have a way of dulling the sharp edges for some people, and Bloom was somebody made entirely of sharp edges.

Or, maybe it had reached Iris, and she was the one helping her body-mate to open up. I only had speculation, but whatever the case, it was a pleasant surprise to see.

Whatever Bloom was feeling at this point in her short life, I knew it had to be complicated—to say nothing of what Sara must be feeling.

Which only left Hazel. Where had she gotten off to? I looked around to my left and didn't spot her, then turned to my right, and—

"Hey, rock star."

Hazel's smiling, slightly reddened face drifted into view as she stepped down into the seating area around the fire pit and sat down beside me. I felt her shoulder brush against mine, and she moved in closer and wrapped an arm around my waist. Pure warmth, accompanied by the gentle scent of her washing over me. My heart rate picked up and I slipped my own arm around her in response.

"What do you think of the commander's farm?" I asked.

"It's nice. A girl could get used to this," she said, leaning her head against my shoulder.

"Never figured you for the country lifestyle."

"Oh, I don't think I could do this if we weren't just a few miles from the city," she laughed. "You know me. It's just, the quiet and the fire is nice sometimes."

"It is, yeah," I said. I snuggled up against her more closely and let my senses drift off happily in the flickering firelight. After several long, quiet moments, a thought snuck through my mind and escaped my lips in my hazy inebriation. "I'm sorry this has all been so nuts."

Hazel looked up at me with confusion on her face. "What are you talking about?"

"This. Me. Being a magical girl. Fighting monsters and evil sorceresses and robots and dark mistresses. I'm guessing I'm the weirdest girlfriend you've ever had. Definitely the most stressful."

Hazel chuckled softly and shook her head. "Oh, Claire. If I didn't want to be here, I wouldn't be."

"Okay, but I know I'm—"

"Stop it right there. Yeah, this is the most unconventional relationship I've been in, but it's also the best one."

"You're kidding."

"I'm not! I think this whole life of ours is fucking wild, and awesome, and I wouldn't trade it for anything."

"You really mean it?"

She reached over with her free hand and rested it on my leg. "I really mean it. Because of *you*, Claire. You're kind, and caring, and I know you respect me."

"Aww, Haze. I always did, and I always will."

"I know." She smiled and squeezed my thigh. "Plus, you're really fun in bed."

I felt my cheeks turn thermonuclear hot, and my language skills fell apart. "Uh, I, well, you know, uh—"

Hazel giggled, stretched up, and kissed my cheek. Her lips danced across to my ear, and her voice dropped to a teasing whisper. "That's my good girl."

By that point, my head was spinning out into a lesbian vortex so powerful that I didn't even realize it at first when Sara and Bloom made their way in from the fields and stood in front of us by the fire. I panicked, sat up, and tried to compose myself from the sensations that had been flooding my body.

I cleared my throat and looked up at them. In my bleariness, it took me a moment to realize it, but they both appeared to have been crying.

"Sorry to interrupt, you two," Sara said.

"It's totally okay," Hazel said. "Nothing we can't do later."

I let out a small yelp and a nervous laugh. "Yeah! Yeah, uh, we're good."

"Claire," Bloom said, "if I may, I require your company for a moment."

"Um, my company?"

"Yes. I wish to have a conversation."

She really is feeling something. "Yeah, sure thing."

I stood, and followed as Bloom turned and walked off again. As I passed Sara, I paused and leaned in close to her.

"So, uh, you two, are you okay? You and Bloom, I mean, after all that."

Sara smiled and nodded. "Yeah. Yeah, we're good."

"I'm glad to hear it," I said. I moved on, leaving Sara and Hazel back at the fire pit as Bloom led me back toward the berry fields.

We walked for quite some time, wandering into the farthest acreage of the commander's property. Bloom didn't speak once during the trek, but as I walked beside her I could see the turmoil on her face, and in her body language.

Finally, as we reached the farthest point in the fields from the house, she stopped and turned to face me.

"Claire, you understand already how … *difficult* it is for me to be personable."

"I do, yeah," I said. "You've never been shy about telling me."

"Correct. So you will appreciate how hard it is for me to say what I'm about to say."

"If it's hard, just say it. Rip that bandage off quickly."

She took a deep breath and sighed. Her expression was one of sour candy. "I am … very … grateful. That you hit me with that van."

I couldn't hide my surprise. "Of all the things I expected you to say to me, that was nowhere on the list."

"Perhaps I should elaborate."

"It might help, yeah."

She bit her lip, and her eyes glanced down to the ground. She seemed to be searching for the words to explain herself. "In a literal sense, this consciousness has not existed for very long. Two years, as you know."

"Right."

"But that was only the creation of Menagerie Bloom. The moment that Rennia crafted this consciousness and placed it within the body of Iris Carr. That was not *me*."

"It sounds as if you're saying that there was a cleaner break with Menagerie Bloom than any of us realized."

She nodded. "Indeed. I have struggled with many aspects of this existence, but I have come to realize that whoever I am, I am not Menagerie Bloom. I haven't been since the day you threw Vancent Price into me. I exist in this form *because* of you, Claire. As a being of my own. And so, I want to thank you for that."

Her pure, raw sincerity caught me off guard. It was a strange sensation to feel, coming from Bloom, and yet I could tell she meant every word. "I don't know what to say, Bloom."

"I am not a human expert, but I believe that people typically say 'you're welcome' when thanked."

"Right, of course. You're welcome. I'm just not used to saying that about vehicular assault."

Bloom gave me a tired smile. "I know a kind of freedom now, because of you. Freedom to decide for myself, and to be myself. At first, I wasn't sure how to feel about that, being free of Rennia's control. But I ... well ... I have come to appreciate it. Need it, even."

"I understand," I said. "Being able to figure yourself out and shape a version of you that's really yours, that's the kind of freedom that not everybody finds."

"Claire, I did not know you had become such a philosopher as you matured into your magical girl role."

I laughed. "I don't know about that. Being a magical girl *and* trans just gives you a lot of stuff to think about."

"That is very true. I have a much more complete under-standing of the kinds of—ugh—*feelings* that you, and Nova, and, indeed, Iris have about such things."

"Yeah, I bet so. You've done a speed run of transness and, like, life in general." I paused, and looked her in the eye. "Which is why I'm guessing there's more to this than just getting hit with a van."

Bloom sighed. "I would also like to apologize to you for making the situation complicated."

"You're talking about the aftermath of the streetcar fight."

She nodded. "I told you before that my sense of self is a mess. That extends to my emotions. Trying to figure out which are mine and which are Iris's, and if there is even a difference, has been extremely difficult."

"I'm sure. Feelings are hard for people who *aren't* two people in the same body. It's understandable that they'd be even harder for you."

"I feel every bit of Iris's love for Sara, which means that in some way, I love her as well. A woman I don't even *know*, and yet, I've known her for longer than I've been alive. That ... well, I don't know how to handle that. And then there's you."

I gulped. "Right, uh, you said you felt something for me."

"I owe my existence to you," Bloom said as she stared off across the island. "You took me in, when I was at my lowest point. You helped me. Claire, I can no longer deny that I have positive feelings toward you. The true *I*, the individual known as Bloom, apart from what I inherited from Iris. You're the first human I've felt such things for, apart from what I have developed for Iris herself."

A new sensation crept up inside me. The edges of my vision went blurry and I wiped away the tears. "Bloom, that's genuinely really sweet."

"This experience has been overwhelming at times," she continued, "but you have given me some modicum of calm in it. I would even dare to call you my ... *friend*. Do you know how strange that is for me to say?"

"Well, I'm honored to be your friend." I hesitated, but decided this was the best opportunity to continue and sort something out. "Um, is a friend all you see me as? I wasn't sure how to interpret what you said at the fight."

She shook her head and shrugged. "I don't know how to process everything I feel. So much of it is new to me, or mixed up with Iris. However, I ... Claire, I ..."

"Whatever you want to say, just say it. You aren't going to be in trouble."

Bloom stammered a few times. I'd never seen her so nervous. Finally, her eyes met mine again.

"Sometimes, I wish to know what it would be like to be held by you. Or to hold you. To know the feel, the scent, the taste of you. Is that wrong of me?"

I shook my head. "It's not wrong. People experience feelings and desires. As long as you're open and honest about it, it's something we can talk about. Um, Hazel and I have already talked about it a little, even. I mean ... there's a complication right now, but—"

"There is, yes," Bloom said. "I would imagine acting upon such feelings would be awkward while I occupy the body of your leader's partner."

"It's a little unusual, yeah."

Bloom stepped closer to me. "But, perhaps, if I have my own form one day ..."

"When, not if," I said. "We'll get you there. And when we do, maybe we figure something out? You, and me, and Hazel. Together."

She laughed softly. "Assuming I am even remotely the same person I am now."

"I bet you will be."

"How can we know that?" she asked and turned away again to look out across the fields toward the river. "How can we know *anything* of what's in store for me? I am so tired of not knowing what my future holds, Claire. And I'm scared."

"When you're scared, it helps to talk about it."

She sniffled. "I'm scared of dying. Of barely knowing myself and then being snuffed out."

"That's a fear I can relate to," I said as I walked over and joined her. "I still worry sometimes about something happening to me now that I'm out. I spent twenty-two years denying myself, and now that I'm here, I don't ever want to lose it again."

"How do you not let that fear eat away at you?"

"Well, you keep living," I said, looking over at her. "You do the things you always wished you could, the way you wished you could do them. You live as big and loud as possible. Be the most yourself you can. And you find people who care about you and will stick with you."

"That has its appeal." She hesitated again, as if she were stumbling through something else that was hard to say. "I'm scared, too, of what I'll be if—when—Iris and I separate."

"I mean, yeah, she's the person you've been closest to. Literally."

"More than you realize. I have access to quite a lot of her life. Iris and I share thoughts, feelings, memories. They are, in a way, my thoughts and feelings and memories, too. And the ones I have made in my short time here, they are hers as well." She turned to me, tears rolling down her cheeks. "I am truly so scared, Claire. What if I wake up in a body I don't know, and she is not there anymore? What if my mind has none of her? Years of emotions and memories that I have come to feel as my own, just gone?"

I had no good answers for her, so all I could do was offer kindness.

"I wish I could tell you it's all going to be okay, but I don't think any of us know how it's going to go. Whatever happens, you'll have me, and Hazel, and Iris, and the rest of the band and everybody in the Vault. We won't abandon you. That's not what—"

"Not what magical girls do, I know," Bloom interrupted. "You truly mean that, don't you?"

"Of course. I care about you, Bloom."

An instant later, I experienced the strangest thing that had ever happened to me, either in my life as a magical girl or before.

Bloom's tears flowed more freely, and her lower lip trembled. She turned to me and dashed forward, and her arms wrapped around me and squeezed so tightly I nearly stumbled over.

I put my arms around her, too, and felt her bury her face in my shoulder. After a moment's hesitation, she sobbed, and I squeezed back.

"It's okay, Bloom," I said. "You can cry."

Bloom's shoulders shook and her chest heaved as she sobbed into me. "I don't want to be alone, Claire. I don't want to be alone! Please don't let me live or die alone!"

I rocked her a little, where we stood. "You're not alone. I'm here, and I'm not going anywhere. I promise."

I felt her arms squeeze me more tightly and responded in kind. My hands rubbed up and down her back. I let my eyes close, and gradually nuzzled into her hair as I felt the boundaries between us crumble. Beneath the headstrong and standoffish warrior consciousness, she was a girl like me, trying to secure her identity. The moment lingered in our shared warmth.

Bloom had a lot of tears in her, but gradually, her sobs relaxed into quiet crying, and finally into gentle sniffles. I held her through it all, feeling our shared connection and closeness, until she spoke again.

"Now I know, at least."

"Know what?" I asked.

"What it feels like to hold, and be held by, you."

I chuckled softly. "I hope it lived up to expectations."

"Beyond expectations, in fact."

"Wow, I didn't know I was *that* good."

"Don't get a big head about it, Claire." Before I could process what she was doing, she moved up and kissed my cheek. "I did enjoy it, though."

I couldn't hide my blush. "Me too."

We held each other for several more long moments. Gradually, we relaxed, and as we pulled apart, Bloom wiped her eyes.

"We should probably get back, huh?" I asked.

"Yes, probably," Bloom said. "I suspect the others have more sappy monologues to deliver before the commander will be happy."

I laughed. "You're one to talk."

"Keep it to yourself, magical girl," Bloom said. This time, it felt like an inside joke shared with a friend. Or more. That didn't feel so far away now.

We made our way back toward the house through the berry fields. I thought for a moment about taking her hand as we walked, wondered what it would feel like.

Bloom looked over at me, breaking the bubble.

"Claire, may I ask you an unrelated question?"

"Sure, always," I said.

"What exactly is your new song supposed to do? If it were finished, I mean. What is its purpose?"

"I wanted to shape the Exalted Harmony into something ... more kind, I guess? You saw it used for destruction on the roof of that hotel, so I wanted to see if it could be constructive. You know, empathetic, life-giving, calming."

"An empathetic special attack?" Bloom asked, laughing softly as she shook her head. "That is very on-brand for you, Claire."

I laughed back. "I'm glad to know I have a brand, at least."

"It is an interesting thought, though, turning destructive power into empathy like that. Obviously, as somebody facing uncertainty about my own mortality, and who seeks to find her own way after once serving the darkness, the concept intrigues me."

I paused as an idea re-entered my head. "Hey, Bloom, if the song interests you, maybe you could take a look at the chorus?"

Bloom looked confused. "What do you mean by that?"

"Well, Sara's been working on the words, but she hasn't come up with a chorus lyric she likes yet. I was thinking, maybe, possibly, you might like to give it a try."

"I couldn't," Bloom said. "What makes you think I have any ability to do such a thing?"

"Because you have feelings," I said. "And you already know how to write songs, because Iris knows."

I expected she'd dismiss the idea again, but to my surprise, she scrunched her face up like she was deep in thought, and nodded slowly. "If you would allow me the opportunity, then ... I would relish the challenge!"

"That's awesome!" I said, beaming at her. "Thank you, Bloom."

"Don't thank me yet, Claire. We do not know if I shall be able to do it."

I smiled. "I think you will. Besides, we probably won't have to use it to save any of us anytime soon."

"Hopefully not," she agreed. "I do not wish that much responsibility so soon!"

Bloom and I reached the fire pit as the rest of the team was assembling there. Commander McCoy threw more wood on, and the flames roared up to full life again. From where she sat before, Hazel waved me over; I circled around and sat beside her.

To my pleasant surprise, Bloom sat down on my other side, not as close as Hazel but still very much with intent. Sara joined her, followed by Cass and Hana. Nova—with Nebula again riding on her shoulders—and Hikari followed suit, the two now seemingly joined at the hip.

Saoirse and Dr. Barrera sat down together and clinked their cider bottles, and finally, the commander and Jade took their seats as well.

"Alright," Commander McCoy said as she looked across the fire at the band and Bloom, "how'd it go for y'all today?"

Sara looked down at the ground, nodded slowly, and returned her gaze to the commander. "I think we've come to a better understanding, commander."

"That so?"

"Yeah, that's so." Sara looked over at Bloom and me. "Wouldn't you two agree?"

"I would, yeah," I said. "I feel good. Bloom?"

Bloom gave a theatrical sigh. "Well, if I *must* engage with the sappy heartfelt do-gooder—" I reached over and nudged her with my elbow and flashed her a smile. She stammered, then cleared her throat and continued. "—then I would say that, yes, understandings have been reached. Feelings ..." She made a small, pained sound. "... have been mended."

"Excellent," the commander said. "That's what I like to hear. Fixin' your problems by talkin' it out. Y'all are magical girls, after all."

Bloom mostly suppressed a groan.

Hana nodded in agreement, more enthusiastically than I expected. When she spoke, her words were a little slurred. "Yes! That's right! That's so right! We're magical girls! Magical girls fight with feelings! Feelings are soooo *good!*"

The rest of us all slowly turned to her, and Cass patted her on the shoulder.

"Hey, how many of those ciders have you had, exactly?"

"I don't know!" Hana said. "They were all so sweet and good! Just like you, Cass! So sweet and good!"

Cass grinned and shrugged. "I mean, she's not wrong!"

Jade laughed. "With this kind of response, I might have to look into carrying Meredith's cider at the bar. You wouldn't mind that, would you, Ms. McCoy?"

The commander became downright flustered. "Well, I, that is, we ... uh, yeah, I'd be in favor."

Dr. Barrera raised her hand. "I feel that, in my capacity as a medical professional, I must point out that almost everybody here is, at a minimum, what we in the field call *rather sloshed*. I insist that, if most of us wish to return to our homes tonight, we hand transportation duties over to one of the people who remained sober! It is the responsible thing to do, after all!"

"Good point, doc, thank you," the commander said, regaining some of her composure. "Which means—"

"It means tonight is my time to shine, babes!" Nova said as she pumped her fist. "I finally get to hop behind the wheel of *the* Vancent Price!"

Nebula meowed in affirmation as she jumped down to Nova's lap.

"Hey now, I might be scuttered, but I ain't sure I wanna hand my life over to Miss Nova," Saoirse said. She pointed at Hikari and leaned toward them conspiratorially. "New kid, can *you* drive a van?"

Hikari nodded. "Oh yeah totally it's no big deal at all I mean I don't technically drive on a regular basis and I've never driven anything bigger than a hatchback before but what is a fifteen-passenger conversion van loaded with super-science technology if not a hatchback that's had a growth spurt."

"Naw, don't worry, cuties," Nova said. "I gotcha covered! Yer gonna get a big ol' dose of Nova Highway Action!"

Bloom leaned over and whispered in my ear. "Claire, you recall what I was saying about facing uncertainty about my own mortality? I didn't think it would be *tonight*."

"Don't worry," I said. "I don't think Vancent would let us get hurt."

Bloom shot me a look.

My eyes met hers. "Again, in your case."

I thought I saw the faint traces of a grin creep into Bloom's expression.

CHAPTER 21

Having healed—or at least mended—the awkward feelings between Bloom and the rest of us, we passed the remaining days leading up to the show at the Rose Garden Arena by doubling down on rehearsing the setlist and training for a fight. This would be the biggest show Magica Riot had ever played, by far, and the last thing any of us wanted to do was get up on a stage in front of twenty thousand people and whiff it.

And of course, most bands didn't practice for a huge show with the knowledge that it also might turn into a gigantic fight against supernatural forces. We truly had no idea what was in store for us on that front. Makula had vanished after the fight with the streetcar construct; not only had there been no more sightings or readings on the sensor grid, I also hadn't gotten any further late-night visitations. I kept thinking back to how rattled Makula had seemed when her spell had gone wrong during the fight. Clearly, whether it was out of arrogance or ignorance, she hadn't prepared for something like that to happen. She'd almost certainly want to save face, and the next time, she'd probably try to do something so big that it couldn't be broken by any outside force.

That likelihood, combined with the fact that she was probably very upset about the whole thing, only served to make her more dangerous.

Rhapsodyz, and its shadowy counterpart Sinneslöschen, was another matter. The company's public-facing side had shifted hard into damage control, since watching a fleet of prized robot servants flip to "kill all humans" mode was probably bad for their stock price. Unsurprisingly, they had succeeded in pacifying the city and the press with empty platitudes and glitzy promo videos, but the Starlight Alliance now knew beyond a shadow of a doubt that they were up to something more than the baseline level of sinister that all tech companies were underneath their corporate facades. Unfortunately, beyond knowing Allison Webb's job title and the physical makeup of the bots, we didn't have many other details to go on. Their exact motivations remained in shadow.

The uncertainty wasn't great. At least with the Pandora Corruption, I generally knew what to expect. This situation just put me on edge whenever I thought about it.

I tried to keep such thoughts out of my mind and focus on the task of preparation, but as we got closer to the big day, they became harder to ignore. I started to see billboards for the show go up around downtown Portland, and seeing my own face on the side of a building was surreal. The more we'd concentrated on our magical girl duties, the easier it had been to forget that Magica Riot was now quite literally the most famous band on Earth, due to being the first—and so far only—publicly out magical girl band. The billboards, and the associated amount of public recognition, made that impossible.

Which meant that when the night finally arrived, I was a bundle of nervous energy being held together with estradiol and any coping mechanism I could find.

We were given a dressing room that was far more spacious than the ones we were used to at the small clubs around town. Sara and Cass sat at the row of mirrors along the wall, going over the set list one more time. Hana camped out on a couch in the corner, taking long, deep breaths to calm herself. And Nova, having decided that caffeine was the best thing to go with her pre-gig nerves, was slamming a Shasta while listening to Hikari talk about Tekken.

There were times I envied Nova's ability to roll with nearly anything.

Commander McCoy leaned against the wall, nursing a whiskey, while Bloom paced nervously near her.

"What's got you in such a tizzy, Bloom?" the commander asked.

"I don't know, exactly," Bloom said. "I feel anxiety about this musical performance, even though I am not involved."

"Maybe Iris has stage fright," I said.

Bloom considered this, and nodded. "That is quite plausible, I suppose."

"That's exactly it," Sara said. "Iris always paced before a show."

"I always wished I could help her relax," Hana said.

"Look at it this way, Bloom babe," Nova said. "At least ya don't actually have to go on stage!"

Hikari nodded. "Yeah you can just be like the rest of us and experience sympathetic anxiety in support of the band all of the stress with none of the fame isn't it great?"

"You feel anxiety?" Bloom asked. "You do a staggeringly impressive job of hiding it, then."

"It's a feature of my biological construct I sequester the anxiety in a subroutine so that it can run itself out without affecting my main emotional functions but believe me when I say it's raging underneath this cool dare I even say suave exterior that you see before you."

The dressing room door swung open and Hazel stepped in, wearing her Starlight Alliance jumpsuit and carrying a tablet. It was the first I'd seen of her since dawn; she'd been running around all day and evening, coordinating the show with the arena staff and the promoters. In spite of how busy she'd been, she was downright glowing with excitement.

"There's my favorite gals," she said. "How's everybody doing?"

"Nervous," I said. "Very nervous. But excited, too."

"Well, if it helps take some of the stress off," Hazel continued, "everything on my side is going as smoothly as we could hope. The sound techs got Hikari's audio settings loaded in, lighting and logistics are all ready, and the crowd ... well, there's a lot of real Magica Riot fans out there."

"It's really happening, isn't it?" Sara asked.

"You better believe it," Hazel grinned. "And don't forget, you girls earned it."

Commander McCoy nodded. "I'll be rooting for y'all from backstage."

"And you've got lots of friends out there in the crowd," Hazel said. "Dr. Barrera and Saoirse are all situated in the special VIP guests section. And I ran into one more on my way in ..."

From behind the dressing room door, Jade Evergreen emerged. Even though she'd been retired for years, I was struck by how she still effortlessly carried herself like an indie star; she wore jeans and a leather jacket over a T-shirt, a VIP access badge on a lanyard around her neck, and looked like a million bucks doing it.

"You girls have one incredible crowd out there," Jade said.

"Memories of your days on stage, Miss Everly?" Hana asked.

"Oh, no, you've got me beat. I played some big gigs, but never like this. I'm proud of you."

"We're honored that you're here for the show," Sara said.

Jade smiled. "I wouldn't miss it. How could I say no to seeing you on the big stage?"

"Well, we'll do our best," I said.

"I know you will, kid," Jade said. "I'm gonna be front-and-center down there in the VIP seats. It'll be nice to be in the thick of it again after all these years."

Hazel tapped her tablet and sighed. "Gotta go again. Somebody's asking about soundboard recordings. Back in a bit!"

As she turned and rushed back out of the dressing room, I moved to leave, too. "If it's okay with everybody, I'm going to take a walk real quick. Burn off some of these nerves."

"Sounds good, Claire," Sara said. "See you in a few."

I stepped out into the concrete hallway outside the dressing room and slipped past the various arena staffers running to and fro preparing for the concert. On our way in, I'd seen another section of the Rose Garden Arena's backstage facilities that looked a little calmer and quieter, so I made my way in that direction and did my best to focus on keeping my anxieties in check.

I had so deeply concentrated on that, in fact, that I didn't even realize I'd walked farther into the bowels of the arena than I'd intended to.

Dark hallways bled together into a contextless maze of gray around me. Even the distant noise of an arena full of people dulled into a low din that sent constant gentle vibrations through the concrete. Wherever I was, I was too far, and I needed to find my way back to something resembling human activity.

I turned around in the direction of the distant, dim light radiating from a corner in the web of corridors. All I needed to do was follow that light, and I'd surely be able to find my way back from there.

Which is when the silhouette of a woman stepped into the corridor ahead of me.

I froze. From a distance, I couldn't quite make out any of her features, though it was clear she was conventionally human-sized and thus not Makula. I assumed, at first, that she was an arena staffer, and my caution felt a bit silly. Still, there was something familiar about her silhouette.

And then she spoke, and I knew exactly who she was.

"Hi, Claire!" Allison Webb called out. "It's a big night for you tonight, isn't it?"

"Yeah, it is," I said as I approached her, trying not to get *too* close. "What are you doing here?"

"Well, naturally, I needed to see how you girls were doing. Your last public appearance didn't go too smoothly." Her voice dripped condescension. "Besides, I am a fan, after all."

I shook my head. "No, you aren't. We know exactly who you really are. You turn magica into weapons for Sinneslöschen."

Allison stared back at me. Her corporate smile didn't waver, but the look in her eyes turned colder. I felt a chill in the air. "That's an awfully simplistic way to describe it."

"I don't think it is. You're messing with something you don't really understand, and it's going to get people killed."

"Give us some credit. We're learning more every day."

I laughed. "Come on, you've been doing this for more than forty years and still haven't figured out how to do it right. Is that why you've been trying to study Sorceress Makula?"

Her smile twitched, just a bit. "What makes you think we're studying Makula?"

"I was at the food cart pod. I saw how you reacted to her."

She chuckled softly and I felt my muscles tighten instinctively. "Well, aren't you perceptive? We've come a long way since Polybius, Claire. It's just a matter of iteration until we've fixed the problems. In this business, you have to move fast and break things sometimes."

"Magica isn't that simple."

She stared into my eyes and stepped toward me. I retreated, but my back hit the cold concrete wall behind me. Allison placed her hand on the wall by my head and leaned in close to me, brushing her chest against mine, her voice dropping to a purr.

She was too close, and I did not welcome the physical contact, but if I ran I wouldn't get any more information out of her.

"Claire, you truly are a breathtaking creature, but you're still a bit naive about the way the world works." I shuddered at her overly intimate familiarity. "Idealism is a pretty little thing, but it's money and success that command influence. Once we solve magica, we'll be uniquely positioned to dominate, and I intend to be the one leading the charge. I *will* learn all the secrets there are, I promise you that."

She was so close I could smell her perfume, cloying and smoky, and feel the heat of her on my skin. Where I welcomed that when it was Hazel, here I felt like I was being coated with slime.

"If you're so interested in magica, why are you doing this?" I asked, trying to regain my focus. "Working for something as crooked as Sinneslöschen and Rhapsodyz? Why not use that knowledge for good?"

"I *am* using it for good," she said. "I'm doing this to benefit humanity, just like you and your little girlfriends. I just intend to be properly rewarded for that work."

"You sound like your CEO," I shot back. "Is he building fascist robots for the good of humanity, too?"

"Mr. Tachyon believes in helping humanity in his way, and I believe in doing it in mine. He's useful to me. For now, anyway. And who knows?" She paused, and leaned in closer; I felt her lips tease my cheek, her breath softly blow across my ear. My skin crawled, and anger boiled deep inside me. "Maybe one day you girls will understand why I do what I do. You should be more friendly, you know? You might even end up helping me. The more magical beings I can examine, the smoother this will go."

"Not likely," I said. "And I doubt Makula would go along with you, either."

She let out a soft laugh. "Well, there are other ways to get what I need."

"What's that supposed to mean?"

"Oh, it's not important right now." She stepped back from me and I breathed a small sigh of relief. "Regardless, I genuinely hope you have a great show tonight, Claire. I'm sure it's going to be spectacular."

My eyes narrowed. "You're planning something."

"Not at all," she said as she turned to leave. She glanced back over her shoulder one last time. "Good luck! And break a leg."

With that, she walked away in the opposite direction of the dressing rooms and disappeared around the next corner of the corridors. For a moment, I considered chasing her, but I knew time was getting short. I turned the other way and headed back toward the dressing room to finish getting ready, and to warn everybody about our unfortunate guest.

———

"Soooo, if this Allison chick is here tonight, does that mean there's gonna be more of those creepy robots?" Nova asked.

"I don't know," I said. "She said she's not planning anything, but when was the last time she told the truth?"

"There's no way to know what Rhapsodyz is up to until they make themselves known," Sara said. "We aren't picking up any readings yet. Isn't that right, Hikari?"

Hikari, who had busted out their well-worn laptop, looked up from the screen and nodded. "So far everything's clean nothing that looks like corruption magica or anything like that on the sensors yet not a single sign of any of the Rhapsodyz junk bots."

"And if you need a biological indicator," Bloom added, "I'm not feeling sick at the moment."

"Maybe Webb's just here to play mind games," Cass said.

"That could be the case," Hana said. "She's clearly got more going on than she admitted to before."

"Or the robots could be powered off, just waiting for the right opportunity," Sara said. "We can't take anything for granted, so let's be on the alert for the first sign of trouble."

The commander nodded and sighed. "As if we didn't have enough goin' on. Agent Tomori, keep active scans running through the whole show. If a Rhapsodyz bot—or Sorceress Makula—so much as flinches, I wanna know about it."

"Right on it I'm gonna flavor blast this building with so many sensor sweeps you'll be able to taste them," Hikari said.

Sara stood and moved to the center of the room. "The concert is important, but keeping people safe and doing our jobs as magical girls is always the top priority. So the instant we see anything start to happen, don't hesitate for a second to stop the show and transform. A lot of eyes are on us tonight, so let's show them again what magical girls do best."

The dressing room door swung open and Hazel appeared in the doorway. "Ladies? It's time to head to the stage door."

I took a deep breath and exhaled. The time had finally come. Our lives were about to pass another milestone, and nobody quite knew what was waiting on the other side of it.

But there was no group of women I'd rather do it with.

Sara took a deep breath and nodded. "Alright, let's go to work."

CHAPTER 22

At the stage door, the sound of the crowd beyond was nearly overwhelming. We were about to step onto a stage in front of an audience orders of magnitude larger than any we'd performed in front of before.

The five of us lined up by the door. Hazel, the commander, Hikari, and Bloom stood on the other side, ready to follow us out and take up spots behind the curtains at the back of the stage, ready in case of any magical incidents.

"They're going to shut off the stadium lights," Hazel said, "and then you'll go out before the spotlights come on. Are you all ready?"

"Ready," Sara said.

"Ready and feeling good!" Cass said.

"Yes," Hana said, "ready here!"

"I, uh ... ready," I said.

"You better flammin' believe I'm ready!" Nova shouted.

Hikari nodded and shot us a thumbs-up. "I have made sure the sound system is set to appropriately face-shredding volumes but will still maintain a balanced sound stage for everybody in the arena I think you will be pleased."

"You gals are gonna do great," the commander said. "Keep alert, and give 'em a show."

"And as loathe as I am to cheer for magical girls," Bloom said, as she crossed her arms, "I hope your performance goes well."

"Alright, everybody," Sara said. "Monitors in."

We put on our in-ear monitors, the audio changing to Hikari's soundboard of the arena, mixed with our own comm links.

Hazel held up a hand. "It's time. Go out in … five, four, three, two, one, *now!*"

Sara pushed open the stage door and stepped through, and I held my breath as the rest of us followed.

We emerged into near-total darkness, my in-ear monitors reducing the crowd's cheers to a polite rumble, but I could feel the sheer size simply from the sensation of the air itself, a vast chamber stretching up and away from the stage. At the limit of my vision, I saw the vague shape of the arena, and the indistinct masses of twenty thousand people all here to watch us play. The very thought of them all looking down at me overwhelmed my sense of proportion; I simply didn't know how to begin to process it.

We took our spots on stage: Sara at the front with the lead vocal microphone, Cass just behind her on her left with the backup vocal mic, me in the corresponding position on Sara's right—without a mic, since I still didn't feel comfortable singing —with Hana and Nova in the back forming our unbreakable rhythm section.

Following the plan we'd laid out ahead of time, Nova was the first to make a move; with a flash of blue energy, she summoned her drum kit out of thin air in the darkness, causing a rush of gasps and even louder cheers to ripple through the arena.

Nova clicked her drum sticks together and counted off the beat of "Gender Hypocritical," the song we'd chosen to start the set. Her voice called out, barely audible through the crowd noise, but cutting through in our monitors.

"One, two, *one two three four!*"

Nova started with a steady kick drum beat and laid in cymbals and snare drums. By this point, the crowd knew the show was starting for real, and the tension and excitement were palpable.

Hana summoned her bass and slipped seamlessly into the groove, thumping out in perfect sync with Nova's drums. Following her cue, Cass and I were next; I called down my keytar and added the song's synth riff, followed by Cass summoning her guitar and interlinking a guitar melody with me.

Finally, with one fluid sweep of her arm, Sara summoned her guitar, smashed into the chord progression, and sang.

The stage and spotlights snapped on as the song leapt out from the huge sound system of the arena and into the eagerly waiting audience. The crowd roared, and suddenly, we were *in it.*

For me, the song was a blur. My heart raced, and I did my best to ignore the twenty thousand pairs of eyes looking at me from the darkness and focus on playing. I fell back on our rehearsals, my hands moving across the keys by instinct and intuition as the monitor mix played in my ear.

It felt like what I thought riding a bull must have felt like. Fortunately, we had rehearsed the set to near perfection. What few slip-ups we made were minor, unnoticed by the crowd. Two and a half minutes flew by, and as "Gender Hypocritical" rolled through its final chorus, Sara effortlessly transitioned us into the second song—"Second Promise, Second Chance"—and the crowd erupted in cheers again.

My anxiety receded as we played on through the second song. It was easy to be intimidated by the scale of the concert, but the size of the crowd didn't change the fact that Magica Riot was a *good* band. We were tight and polished again, fueled by excitement and the drive to prove ourselves musically.

I even dared to allow myself the kindness of being included in that "good band" description. I'd come a long way since that nervous, shaky first performance at Cosmic Club. Despite my anxiety, *I could do this.*

We reached the end of the last chorus a few minutes later, and as the final chord of "Second Promise, Second Chance" rang out across the arena, Sara stepped back to the mic and spoke her first words of stage banter.

"Hey, friends! Thanks for coming. We're Magica Riot!"

The crowd roared again, and Sara waited for it to die back down to a manageable level before continuing.

"Tonight's a big night for us, and we're so glad you could be here for it. Our next song's for all of you who have ever wondered if you could be something more than you are now, who've wondered what it's like to be—"

"THAT'S RIGHT!" a digital voice interrupted, booming across the arena from every speaker. *"YOU'RE HERE TONIGHT TO SEE MAGICA RIOT! AND THE EXPERIENCE IS ONLY ENHANCED BY THE ROSE GARDEN ARENA'S SPECTACULAR AUDIO-VISUAL SYSTEM, NOW UPGRADED WITH RHAPSODYZ FUTURE OF AI 8K METAVERSE TECHNOLOGY!"*

Above us, the arena's jumbotron lit up with Rhapsodyz logos and a looping advertisement clip for the company's robots and other products.

"You gotta be kidding me!" Nova shouted. "A flammin' *commercial?!*"

"Allison's head games," Cass said. "Keep your composure, ladies."

From backstage, Bloom poked her head out of the curtains. "What is this human nonsense?"

"WE'RE BRINGING YOU THE BLEEDING EDGE OF MULTI-VECTOR ENTERTAINMENT PARADIGMS," the voice contin-

ued. *"RHAPSODYZ: INNOVATION FOR A CONNECTED WORLD!"*

From every corner of the arena, choruses of boos and jeers erupted from the audience. Drink cups flew through the air, trying to hit the jumbotron in a futile gesture of disapproval. People shouted up at the screens, not holding back their anger and irritation.

"Your robots suck!"

"Let the band play!"

"Fuck Rhapsodyz!"

"The audience is going to stop them before we have a chance to," Hana said.

Unfortunately, Allison Webb's advanced technology had a response ready to go.

An ear-piercing electronic shriek blasted from the speakers as the jumbotron's screens turned red. White text flashed, reading SECURITY PROTOCOLS ENGAGED as the digital voice returned, its tone far more unpleasant than before.

"THIS IS AN UNLAWFUL DISTURBANCE. DO NOT RESIST. RESISTANCE INDICATES COMPLICITY. YOU WILL BE DETAINED."

"Aw, *flam*," Nova said.

Sara sighed. "I couldn't put it better myself."

The audience now seemed confused, unsure of whether they were watching an unplanned interruption or a part of the show. I feared they wouldn't have to wait long to get their answer.

I felt my stomach drop, the too-familiar woozy headache returning. Behind us, Bloom fell forward through the curtains, already doubled over and retching.

I ran back to her aid and held her hair back. "Bloom, you okay?"

"Not at all, Claire!" she said, after wiping her mouth. "I am growing *quite* tired of this miserable corporation!"

The chirp of an alarm on our wrist links drew my attention to the screen, where a text box confirmed what we already knew.

SINNESLÖSCHEN MAGICA DETECTED.

"I think we're about to see something unpleasant," Cass said.

"Agreed," Sara nodded. "Let's stop it, before it becomes a problem. Maidensong harmony power, g—"

Before she could finish, the alert switched off, replaced by yet another blaring klaxon, followed by Hikari's voice on the comm line.

"Hey sorry to interrupt but you're about to get an uninvited guest performer."

I looked down at my wrist link screen. Flashing red letters confirmed Hikari's message.

MARELIAN INCURSION EVENT.

"It's Makula," Cass said. "She's crashing the party!"

"Do we have a vector, Hikari?" Hana asked.

"Yeah uh should be right in front of you in the standing section," Hikari answered.

I gazed out into the darkness. If Makula was out there, I couldn't see her.

"Can we get light on that part of the arena?" I asked into my wrist link.

"For sure for sure Hazel's working on it right now I think you should be seeing a spotlight on it in a few seconds," Hikari said.

Right on cue, a new shaft of light shined down from the ceiling of the arena. It tracked across the crowd until it reached the center of the floor, in front of the stage.

And there, in the light, an unmistakable black mist was coalescing into a seven-foot-tall humanoid form.

With the mist now illuminated, the people in that section of the audience scrambled away from it, forming a circle of onlookers around the disc of the spotlight. The mist swirled in tighter and tighter spirals. Moments later, with a dramatic *poof*, it solidified.

Sorceress Makula was here. The crowd gasped, and I even picked up on a few cheers and exaggerated boos from people who thought this was all part of the act, like we were putting on some kind of immersive theater performance.

"Hello there, girls," Makula called out, her voice magically amplified and filling out the entire space of the arena, which didn't exactly dissuade people from thinking this was part of the show. "My apologies for missing the start of your little performance. I felt it was important to make a properly dramatic entrance. Once more, you are in the presence of the seventh-generation diviner of the twelfth-dimensional House of Marelia! The keeper of the arcane dark arts of the Undertow! Life-sworn wielder of the Staff of Sorrows! The one, and only, Grand Cosmic Sorceress Makula!"

Boos and jeers erupted from the arena seats. Sara looked around at the crowd and held her hand up as she addressed the new arrival. "We had a feeling you might show up. What do you want, Makula?"

Nova pointed at her with her drumstick and growled at her. "If you were so flammin' desperate for attention, you shoulda got your own concert!"

"Desperate for attention? Hardly!" Makula shot back. "The only beings I see here desperate for attention in this damp city of yours are the humans arrogant enough to think they can wield the powers of the cosmos."

"Based on how our last meeting went," Hana said, "I'm not sure you're qualified to do it, either."

Cass smirked down at Makula. "In case you forgot, the only people who could stop your screw-up were us!"

"I admit, I was not fully prepared for the depths of human malfeasance," Makula said, "but that is a mistake I shall not make again. It is time for the *real* show to begin!"

"What are you talking about?" I asked, pointing up at the jumbotron. "We were just about to stop Rhapsodyz!"

"Oh, Claire, I shall not leave to children what should be handled by the master," Makula fired back. "I have been waiting for these technological interlopers to make their move again, and now I shall call forth the darkness and cast these wretched snakes calling themselves Rhapsodyz to the ash heap of history! Humanity *must* learn its place, and *I* will be the one to teach you!"

Sara stepped to the edge of the stage and glared down at her. "If you want some ultimate showdown, you should do it in a better venue. These people here are innocent."

Some parts of the audience cheered again, but some had started to suspect something wasn't right.

"I'm quite aware of that," Makula said. "I do not come to harm them. They are but the witnesses to my majesty. These Rhapsodyz vermin tried to humiliate me last time, but I shall reestablish my dominance. This audience shall see, definitively, that I alone can correct humankind's misbehavior!"

Another round of uncertain jeers circled the arena. Somewhere in the darkness, I heard someone shout, *"Get the fuck out of Portland!"*

"You're letting your pride get the best of you," Cass said. "Step aside and let us do our jobs."

With surprising speed, a woman leapt up onto the stage from the side and ran over to join us. As she stepped into the stage lights, I recognized her immediately.

"They're not alone, Makula," Jade said. "I'm here, too, and I'm not going to let you have your way. Just like the old days."

Makula paused and stared up at Jade with a curiously pleased expression. "Jade. My old foe. I admit, it is not disagreeable to see you again. However, the path we are now on is unavoidable."

"I think that's going to go about as well for you now as it did back then," Jade fired back.

A look of pure, uncut smugness fell across Makula's face. "You have no idea what is in store for you all. I have spent the recent days refining and perfecting a spell to annihilate the bastardized corruption magica Rhapsodyz is wielding. And now, it's time to show you what a Grand Cosmic Sorceress can do!"

With a flash of light, Makula summoned her staff into her hand. She raised it skyward, and a beam of magica the color of smoldering ash rushed up toward the jumbotron and blasted into it. The giant digital displays glowed and crackled as energy beyond conception surged through the jumbotron's circuitry.

The crowd gasped, and Makula cackled with glee. "Yes! *Yes!* Burn!"

Sparking magica glowed around the jumbotron as Makula's attack built up to what would no doubt be a tremendous explosion—but then, in the blink of an eye, everything changed.

Energy flew back down the beam and smashed into Makula, knocking her back and breaking her concentration. The massive surge of magica above our heads roiled angrily for a few more seconds, and then collapsed back into the jumbotron itself.

"The flam's going on?" Nova asked.

We didn't have to wait long for an answer. A horrific dissonant groan, far stronger than what we'd experienced at the food cart pod, blasted out through the arena. The crowd—by now picking up on all this not being part of the show—screamed in panic. At the same moment, a glimmering dome of magical energy washed out across the roof and cascaded down its sides; people up in the stands who'd been running for the exits slammed into it and fell back.

"Barrier!" Cass shouted as she clutched at her head. "We're trapped!"

My head ached and throbbed against the cacophony, and the other girls were similarly affected. The unpleasantness of the Rhapsodyz bots suddenly felt like a gentle massage in comparison to what was now emanating from the jumbotron.

Bloom was hit far worse. She collapsed, grabbed her head, and writhed around on the stage, screaming in agony as forces and sensations we could only imagine ripped at her essence. Nova, Hana, and I ran to her aid, and I cradled her in my arms as she suffered.

"We need help!" I shouted. "She needs to get out of here!"

From backstage, Hikari, Hazel, and the commander rushed out.

"We've got her," the commander said. "I called for the doc. We'll take her backstage, as far as we can with the barrier, anyway. She'll be safe."

"Thank you," I said.

"Claire, watch yourself," Hazel said. "We both know who's behind this."

Hikari tapped their wrist link and stared up at the jumbotron, the angry red glow reflected in their glasses. "Yeah we do we've got a massive surge of Sinneslöschen corruption magica right up there in that thing it's like thousands of those bots at once."

As the three of them carried Bloom away, the rest of us turned our gaze back up to the jumbotron. By this point, even Makula could recognize that something was going wrong again; she angrily shouted up at it and swirled her staff in an attempt to adjust her spell.

"No!" she shouted. "No, *not again!* What treachery is this?"

The arena's speakers came to life again, but with a different voice. Though the speaker didn't identify herself, I knew the voice of Allison Webb instantly.

"Sorceress Makula! You're very powerful, but very predictable. I appreciate you giving me so much data to work with! You've advanced our research decades with a single spell. Unfortunately, you'll have to deal with the consequences now. Let me know what you think of my construct, though! Your feedback is very important to us!"

"Of course," Sara said. "Webb had to suspect Makula would show up again. What better way to get all kinds of data than to corrupt another spell *and* kill multiple birds with one giant stone?"

Jade shot me a look from across the stage. "I think we're all in big trouble, girls."

"I think you're right," I said. "We need to stop this, before it gets worse."

Nova pointed up at the jumbotron. "Uh, babe? It's gettin' worse."

The ear-splitting sound of screeching, wrenching metal blasted through the arena and interrupted me. The audience screamed again, but had nowhere to run as the jumbotron, glowing with red magica, detached itself from the arena ceiling and hovered over the crowd. From its top and bottom, thick bundles of cables erupted and snaked through the air like tentacles, stretching out across the space.

We were now staring up at a colossal jumbotron jellyfish, and it had a captive audience of twenty thousand targets.

"No, no, *no!*" Makula shouted. "They ruined my beautiful work again! This isn't how it's supposed to be!"

"But it's how it is," Sara said, "and now, we're going to stop it."

She nodded at us, and we raised our hands into the air. Our glittering, thaumatite-encrusted microphones materialized and we brought them to our lips.

Beside me, Jade raised her hand as well, and a microphone covered with jade-green thaumatite crystals appeared. She shot me a wink.

"You mind a little help, Magica Riot?" she asked.

"Not at all," I said. "Thank you."

"Don't thank me till this thing's dead," Jade said.

I stared back, a bit awe-struck at sharing the stage with a legend.

"Oh my gosh, you're so cool," I said, before I could stop myself.

Jade just grinned.

The situation didn't look good, but we were magical girls. It was time to do what we did best. In unison, we shouted the phrase of transformation into the mics.

"*Maidensong harmony power ... go live!*"

SIDE D
OPEN HEARTS

CHAPTER 23

Rainbow energy engulfed us, and we rocketed up through the dimensional barriers toward the Celestial Stage. From the corner of my vision, alongside Sara, Cass, Hana, and Nova, I saw Jade traveling with us, glowing with rich green magica. It hadn't occurred to me that she would transform with us, but it made sense when I considered the true powers of the Maidensong had unlocked for *all* magical girls.

We arrived at the Celestial Stage. The grand crystalline dome overhead glowed with magica, refracting the view of stars in the inky sky beyond it. Beneath our feet, the massive sigil floor lit up and spun, and ribbons of brightly colored magica snaked in through the dome to wrap us up. Energy surged into me as my everyday clothes shattered off my body. The ribbons weaved my costume around me, forming the angled black skirt with purple trim and lining first, followed by my white blouse beneath the dark purple studded jacket on my torso. My asymmetric purple bow tied itself around my neck, and my black fingerless gloves and boots appeared on my hands and feet.

The Maidensong's staggering power flowed through every cell of my body, washing me with serenity and confidence. The glow rose up through my body and fully captured me. Through the haze of magica, I watched the other girls transform, their costumes materializing just as mine had.

We twirled together and linked hands in a circle as our colors cast themselves into our eyes and hair. Through the mind-expanding sensations of the transformation, I caught my first glimpse of Jade, in all her magical girl glory.

Her costume was completely different from ours. She wore a black miniskirt and a fluffy, ruffled white blouse that cascaded out of the placket and sleeves of a long, formal jade green coat with a black collar, the kind I'd seen in drawings of captains of 19th century sailing ships. The coat wrapped around her, securing itself with glittering golden buttons. Matching epaulets adorned her shoulders. In the center, a green thaumatite crystal fastened her blouse collar. On her feet, black boots with large cuffs folded over the top finished off her rakish swashbuckler style.

Her hair had changed as well: shaved on one side and grown longer on the other, it cascaded down the side of her head in gorgeous waves. The fiery red color now carried long streaked highlights of jade. Her eyes, too, had taken on an even more intense green glow, and stood out starkly from the stripe of black makeup that formed across them behind her glasses.

If I hadn't already known Jade was a legend, I'd have realized it from a single glance at her. She was absolutely striking.

Transformation complete, the voice of the Maidensong called out to us from across the cosmos.

"THOSE EXALTED BY THE MAIDENSONG SHALL WIELD THE POWER OF HARMONY."

With a flash of magica, we blasted down from the Celestial Stage back through the dimensions to Earth. The six of us arrived back in the Rose Garden Arena on a torrent of rainbow light, and as our boots touched down on the stage, we strode forward and squared ourselves against the corrupted construct.

"We are the guardians of song and heart," Sara said. "Guardian of Lyricism, Riot Red!"

"Guardian of Melody," Cass yelled, "Riot Yellow!"

Hana stared up at the beast floating above us. "Guardian of Rhythm, Riot Green!"

"Guardian of the Beat, Riot Blue!" Nova shouted.

I glared at the jumbotron jellyfish and pointed up at it. "Guardian of Harmony, Riot Purple! Servant of the darkness, be silenced by the song of Magica Riot!"

Jade stood beside me. "Agent of malevolence, be silenced by the song of the Guardian of Harmony, Jade Evergreen!"

Makula, for her part, ignored us as she tried desperately to cast spells to regain control of the jellyfish. "It's not right! This isn't how it's supposed to be! *I am a master!*"

"Even a master can be bested," Sara said. "And so, the magical girls of Portland are going to save you from your own creation."

Nova summoned her holo-drums and clicked her sticks together to the tempo of "Like You," and called out the beat. "Let's take this creepo down! One, two, *one two three four!*"

The rest of us called down our instruments, and as Nova rolled into the introduction, we played. Beside me, a beautiful old acoustic guitar trimmed with green thaumatite appeared in Jade's hands, and she looked over at the rest of us.

"What key is this in?" she asked.

"D major!" Cass answered.

Jade grinned and moved her fingers to the fretboard. "Got it!"

The song thundered out across the arena. Cass and I aimed our instruments up at the jellyfish and loosed a series of magica blasts up at it.

In front of us, Sara's microphone reconfigured itself as a headset. As she sang, she conjured a spinning red launch sigil beneath her feet. With a flash of magica, she shot skyward, her guitar glowing as she readied a strike.

"I always do things the hard way, can't fall in line right now, oh

maybe someday, try and smile and do what I'm told, don't step out of line or be a little too bold."

The jellyfish, now fully aware of the magical beings moving to assault it, turned toward Sara as she flew up to meet it. Multiple tentacles reared back and prepared to strike.

Sara careened up at the jellyfish and pulled her guitar back like an axe as her voice carried the song's chorus across the arena. *"What's it like to be like you? What's it like to be beautiful and—"*

A tentacle whipped into her and knocked the wind from her. She yelped, and her velocity instantly shifted in the opposite direction as the strike knocked her from the air. A moment later, she slammed into the stage and left a crack in the surface.

"Red! Are you okay?" I shouted.

Sara pushed herself back up. "Fine! Just angrier!"

The jellyfish's other tentacles snapped into action, writhing outward. Several struck down at the audience, only to be deflected at the last second by Nova and Hana throwing up holo-drums and green defensive shockwaves in their path.

"This thing's going after innocent people!" Hana shouted. "It's out of control!"

Sara glared down at Makula. "Stop this thing! You helped create it!"

Makula fell to her knees, shaking her head as she stared up at the jellyfish in disbelief. "Not like this! Not like this! It's not supposed to be like this!"

"I don't think we're getting any help from her, boss," Cass said as she fired a blast of yellow magica from her guitar at the jellyfish's body.

"Agreed," Sara said. "Alright, we need to fight smarter. Green, Blue, go full defense. Don't let any of those tentacles get the audience! But keep your eyes open, Blue. We need you to pull a trampoline for us."

"Right!" Hana shouted.

Nova aimed more holo-drums and shot a thumbs-up. "On it, Red!"

"Yellow, Jade," Sara continued, "see if you can keep some of those tentacles busy, and maybe damage them enough to slow them down."

Jade grinned at her. "That, I can do."

"With pleasure," Cass said.

Sara turned to me. "Purple, you ready to get up close and personal with that thing?"

"Ready, Red," I nodded.

"Okay. Once Yellow and Jade clear a path, let's run up directly beneath it and launch up into it. We can get those tentacles before they can drop into the crowd!"

I looked over at Jade, and what I saw made me understand how she could have been a successful solo magical girl for so long.

She held her guitar by its fretboard in her left hand, stretched out in front of her while she fretted a chord. With her right hand, she raked her fingertips across the strings and drew them back as they glowed with magica, much farther than guitar strings would normally pull. Six glittering green arrows materialized along them, nocked and drawn back like a longbow.

With a flawless, fluid motion of her arm, she pulled the strings back to the limit and let those arrows fly. They soared into the arena and spiraled out in different directions, striking six different tentacles. Blasts of magica rippled from them and knocked the tentacles back as shockwaves buffeted the air around them. Six notes in perfect harmony rang out with each explosion.

Jade looked over at me and winked. "Go, Riot Purple! I've got your back, kid!"

I nodded, and returned my attention to the jumbotron jellyfish. It was huge, but Sara was on to something; if we could strike at the base of that lower mass of wire tentacles, we might be able to do some damage.

My legs tensed and I took a deep breath. I clutched my keytar tight, playing the progression of "Like You" as it charged up with magica. This wouldn't be easy, but with some luck, we could turn the tables on it before things got even more out of hand.

"Alright ... *now*, Purple!" Sara shouted.

I didn't think or hesitate. I shoved off from the stage and rushed toward the jellyfish. I could feel Sara beside me as we ran, adrenaline and magica pumping through us.

Whatever senses the jellyfish had, they picked up on us immediately. Everyone was doing their best to keep it busy, but it had so many tentacles that a few could still get through the barrage. I leapt from the stage, hit the arena's concrete floor, and kept running. Ahead of me, the jellyfish whipped a tentacle down. I zagged out of the way just as the prehensile metal cable slammed into the concrete, sending chunks and dust flying as I ran past.

Another tentacle hurled at me from the left. My muscles burned as I hurled myself around it just as it hit and left another crater in the concrete. Sara dodged past me out of the way of a third attack, missing me by inches. I dodged more pulverized concrete as I kept running, focused on the goal ahead of us.

Sara and I glanced up; we were almost beneath the jellyfish, and that meant it was time for a change of direction. I focused, waiting for Sara's command back to Nova.

"Trampoline, Blue!" Sara shouted into her wrist link. "Count us in!"

"One, two, count on Blue!" Nova answered.

Streaks of blue magica sizzled past Sara and me, and glowing holo-drums materialized on the concrete ahead of us. A few steps later, we hit them; with sudden force, Sara and I launched skyward, straight up toward the jellyfish's underbelly.

We closed the distance in a flash. As the jellyfish's body grew to encompass our entire field of view, we pulled back our instruments to strike. I felt the magica in my keytar thrum beneath my hands and swung it up. The gleaming purple energy blade that lurked inside it materialized from its body and sliced against the jellyfish in perfect sync with Sara's guitar axe strike.

Our attacks struck home, leaving shallow cuts in the writhing mass of metal tentacles erupting from the bottom of the jumbotron. We'd hit it hard, but the construct was extremely tough, and a single strike wouldn't be enough.

Sara cast a spinning magica sigil beneath our feet, giving us a place to stand.

"Again! Keep it up!" she shouted as she pulled back for another attack.

"Right!" I replied. I pushed with all my strength and swung the keytar up again into another blade attack. The blade lodged in one of the tentacles. Sparks showered down out of it, and I leaned in harder. It was like shoving a knife through brick; the metal and rubber and wiring of the tentacles combined with the construct's magica to create a formidable substance to cut. Still, I kept going. Sweat beaded up on my forehead, and I yelled word-less rage toward the construct's body.

I was so focused on trying to sever the tentacle that I didn't notice when another one snaked in beneath the jellyfish straight toward us.

Suddenly, I felt constricted. Sara's body smashed up against mine; our weapons slipped from our hands and dematerialized. It squeezed us like a steel boa constrictor, and swiftly yanked us away from the jellyfish's body. I strained against the cable and gasped for air, to no avail.

The concrete floor of the arena rushed up at us. We impacted hard, leaving another crater in the floor. The tentacle raised us back up and smashed us down again, even harder than before. It clearly didn't intend to stop until we were utterly pulverized.

"P-Purple," Sara sputtered, "focus ... on me! We have ... have to share ... our magica ... and break out!"

I groaned. "R-right," I managed. "Ready!"

I tried my best to tune out the impacts. There, at the edge of my consciousness, I sensed Sara's magica glowing, burning hotter than I imagined. She was a veteran; she knew how to channel her power.

And she was reaching out with it to link with mine.

I pulled up as much magica as I could in the face of the relentless assault and felt it wash across me and into Sara where our bodies touched. The fire of power surged into me, and from me into her. It was easy to sense that we could only manage this for a few seconds without burning out our physical forms, but that would have to be enough.

Sara pressed outward, flexing her muscles against the tension of the tentacle. I joined her, my body straining, pushing with the force of a freight train. Our magica glowed in a hazy, ethereal aura around our bodies. That shared power blended and formed a red-violet hue, and fed back into our bodies to boost us even further.

The raw, overcharged magica flared inside me, and I felt the tentacle snap in the heat. The metal tendril split apart with loud, discordant metallic bangs.

Sara and I fell away from the jellyfish. The floor rushed toward us again, and Sara reached out and took hold of me. With only moments to spare, she summoned a sigil beneath us that spun and slowed us into a safer descent.

We might have landed gently, but we were drained. I forced myself back to my feet slowly, struggling against the pain that radiated through my body as the Maidensong recalibrated my magica supply. It would take a few moments to recover. Sara and I would be vulnerable until then.

The jellyfish had clearly decided the magical girls were a bigger target for now than the audience members, and had redirected all of its attacks toward us. I was moving too slowly to avoid the tentacles that whipped down at Sara and me, and I braced for the hit.

"Red, incoming!" I shouted

"Hang on," Sara answered, "it's going to be bad!"

From behind us, another voice interjected.

"Not so fast!"

I looked up just as Cass and Jade somersaulted over our heads and landed on the floor in front of us. Cass aimed and fired a series of shots from her guitar that streaked up toward some of the attacking tentacles. Jade joined her, nocking and firing a quartet of magica arrows at the other tentacles coming after us.

Their shots struck home and blasted the tentacles with percussive explosions. The jellyfish let out an angry synthesized roar and withdrew for a moment, which gave us just enough time to fall back and regroup.

The four of us ran back to the stage, where we joined Hana and Nova as they valiantly deflected the jellyfish whenever it tried to attack.

"Gettin' real flammin' tired of this thing!" Nova shouted.

"That makes six of us," Cass said. "It's built like a tank and hits twice as hard!"

Sara resummoned her guitar and picked the song back up. "We've got to weaken it enough to hit it with our special attacks. If we can't stop it, it's going to get somebody killed."

"Yeah," I said as I called back my keytar, "and if it gets out of the arena, it could do some serious damage to the city."

"We won't let that happen," Hana said.

"No we won't," Sara agreed. "Let's go for one of the screens. Hammer it together, try to punch through. Blue, Green, keep those tentacles busy for just a little longer."

"Right on, boss lady," Nova said.

"Yellow, pinpoint your fire in the center of a screen," Sara continued. "Once it's hit, Jade, fire as many of those arrows as you can at that same point."

Jade nodded and smiled. "With pleasure."

"Purple," Sara said, "you're going to follow me. I'll go first and smash the target point, then you come in, jam your keytar in the wound, and fire."

"Alright, yeah," I said. "Right past the shell."

"Exactly. Okay, get ready, everyone!"

The jellyfish floated toward us, looming overhead with its tentacles drawn back. It looked like it planned to deliver a big blow, but with luck, it wouldn't get the chance.

I concentrated and cast a launch sigil beneath my feet as one appeared beneath Sara as well. The geometric purple magica spun up, ready to release its energy and fling me skyward toward the construct.

Sara raised her hand. "Blue, Green! Hit the tentacles ... now!"

Hana slapped and picked at her bass, firing green shock-waves up toward the writhing tentacle cables. Nova joined in, playing an elaborate drum pattern that cast blue waves from different sides of the jellyfish in an attempt to confuse it.

"Alright," Sara said, "Yellow! Fire!"

Cass's fingers flew across her fretboard as she ripped out a blistering guitar lead. Needle-sharp spears of yellow magica blasted out from the headstock and sliced toward the construct. They flew past the tentacles and pierced into the screen on one side of the jumbotron jellyfish's body, small but precise strikes that scorched the screen and gave the rest of us a target.

"Jade, now!"

Matching Cass's riff with a complementary chord progression, Jade played and then held her guitar out. She drew her strumming hand across the strings and pulled four magica arrows back. With perfect harmony, the arrows flew out over the strings and streaked toward the jellyfish.

"I'm going," Sara said. "Purple, right behind me!"

Sara's launch sigil blasted her into the air and toward the jellyfish. I gave her a couple of seconds' lead time, then commanded my own sigil to fling me after her.

I flew toward the jellyfish in Sara's wake. Jade's arrows smashed into the target ahead of us. The jellyfish's screen was still mostly intact, but the repeated strikes did appear to be opening a small crack. We could exploit that with another attack.

But I wasn't the only one who realized that. A thick new tentacle erupted from the top of the jellyfish and smacked into Sara. Sparks flew around her as she was flung back, and she streaked past me just as the tentacle came my way.

Pain flashed through me. The tentacle was electrified, and the shock scrambled my thoughts, reaching down into my chest. The agony was so strong that I knew I would have been killed instantly if I weren't a magical girl.

I flew back through the air, tumbling out of control. It was hard to focus, but I became vaguely aware of another set of tentacles below me hitting the other girls. It knocked them back in multiple directions, just as I spun back toward the ceiling of the arena and lost track of them.

Moments later, I hit the stage hard, burning off my momentum as I rolled and skidded back through all the cables and audio gear. When I finally came to a stop, it took me several long moments to realize I was now backstage.

CHAPTER 24

azel's face looking down at me was the first thing I saw when I opened my eyes.

"Claire! Oh my god, Claire, are you okay?" she asked.

I coughed and pushed myself up on my hands. "Not really, no. What happened?"

"That jumbotron thing hit all of you," Hazel said. "Jade's back here, too. Not sure where everybody else is!"

I turned and looked around the backstage area. Jade had gotten back on her feet with the help of Commander McCoy, having the advantage of not being nearly electrocuted, and was shaking off the impact.

And in the middle of the backstage floor, Hikari sat with their laptop near Bloom, who was doubled over on the floor in obvious agony. The jumbotron jellyfish's corruption magica had definitely hit her hard.

"Help me up, Haze," I said.

Hazel nodded and took my arm. "Right, yeah."

With her help, I struggled back up to my feet. From out in the arena, I heard screams and crashes as the audience tried their best to avoid the jumbotron jellyfish. Flashes of red, yellow, green, and blue told me that the rest of the girls were at least still on their feet somewhere out in the arena.

"This is going south real fast," Jade said. "We're running out of time with that thing."

The commander nodded as she helped Sara back to her feet. "Whatever those Sinneslöschen monsters have done to mess with Makula's spell has us on our back foot."

"Maybe we need to throw more magica at it," Jade said. "It has to have a weakness, just like everything Sinneslöschen makes. We have to hit it until we find it."

Hikari looked up from their laptop. "The sensors do pick up minor fluctuations in the jumbotron's magica output whenever you attack it so there's something to that for sure for sure but you're going to need to do a lot more to take it down."

"How are we going to do more?" I asked. "What if we hit it with our special attacks and it still doesn't go down? We could—"

The sudden sensation of something grabbing my ankle stopped me. I looked down into the eyes of Bloom, trying to pull herself up to her feet.

"You need … more magica, do you?" Bloom asked, her voice shaky and weak. "Well, there's … there's a … a way you can get it."

I shook my head. "Bloom, what are you talking about? We already have Jade. What other way is there?"

She grabbed the lapels of my jacket and pulled herself up. "I have had a lot of time to think, Claire, while I worked on your song. That has led me to a plan. Of sorts."

"What plan?"

"We're out of time, Bloom," Jade said. "If you've got an idea, let's hear it."

Bloom looked over at Jade and laughed as much of a laugh as she could manage. "Oh, I think *you* will be quite impressed by this plan." She turned her attention back to me and leaned in close to my face. "Claire, your new song. Tell me again what you said about it."

"The new song? Um, empathy, kindness, giving life," I said.

"Yes, that's it," Bloom said. She reached into the pocket of the skirt she'd borrowed from me and pulled out a folded piece of paper. "These … these are the words. The words I wrote for you, and for myself."

"The words?" I asked. "You mean, for the chorus?"

"Yes," she nodded. "I did not think you'd need them, but now you do. I want to hear them, Claire."

I shook my head. "I don't understand! What's that got to do with—"

"Claire," she interrupted, as she pulled me closer. "I am about to do something. And it depends upon you."

I couldn't follow what she was implying. "Bloom, what are you talking about? You're not in any shape to fight that thing."

"You're quite right, Claire," she nodded, "but this does not involve me fighting."

"I don't get it."

She shook her head. "Claire, please try to keep up. I am about to do something possibly ill-advised. I need you to save me."

I furrowed my brow in confusion. "Bloom, you're not making any sense."

"Perhaps not, but you are out of options. I am going to turn the tide of battle, and I need you and your song to keep me alive. You cannot let me die, or this all fails. Also, I do not want to die. So remember that."

"What are you—"

Bloom pressed her forehead against mine and stared deeply into my eyes. "Claire, I trust you. I know you will protect me this time."

Oh.

I reached up and squeezed her arm. "I will. Always."

"Good." She let go of my lapels, thrust the paper into my hands, and then grabbed her head. "Do *not* screw this up!"

Before I could stop her, roiling red magica lit up beneath her hands and surged into her head. She screamed and staggered back, remaining on her feet for a few more seconds. Then, suddenly, she collapsed.

Jade, Hazel, the commander, Hikari, and I all rushed to her side. Hazel kneeled down and took Bloom's head in her lap as a growing panic settled in over us.

"Bloom? *Bloom?* Wake up! What did you *do?*" Hazel asked.

"She doesn't look good," Jade said.

I tapped on my wrist link to the "team status" display and found Bloom's life signs. Or, rather, her lack of life signs.

"Her vitals are flat," I said. "This is bad."

Jade stood beside me and placed her hand on my shoulder. "Claire, whatever she's doing, you need to do what she asked. You need to play that song. Right now."

I didn't know what Bloom was playing at, but whatever she had done, it was forcing my hand. I had to perform the new song, and hope that whatever she'd planned would work.

"You can do it, Claire," Hazel said.

"Go on," Jade said.

"I don't know if I can play it alone," I said. "I ... well ... I don't really do the singing."

Jade leaned in close to me. She took Bloom's lyric sheet and unfolded it, holding it in front of the two of us. As we read Bloom's words, she rested her head against mine. A moment later, I felt the unmistakable sensation of magica flowing between us. It felt different than when Sara shared hers with me. Jade's was calm, even serene, and felt a lot like my own.

Of course, I realized. She and I were both Guardians of Harmony. We had a sympathetic harmony via the Maidensong.

Jade pulled away, summoned her acoustic guitar into her hands, and smiled. "It's okay, kid. I've got you. Let me be your voice this time."

I took a deep breath as my hands fell to my keytar keys. It had never been performed as a finished song. I'd only finished it shortly before the concert, and we hadn't had the chance to fully practice it yet, but it seemed we were truly out of options.

"Okay," I said. "Let's do it. One, two, *one two three four!*"

Jade performed the opening guitar riff over the chords I played as I tapped my foot to the tempo. We transitioned into the first verse, and Jade sang the lyrics Sara had penned, her voice nearly unchanged from her glory days.

"Frightened or anxiety, an answer only you can see. Living in the framework of the factory, holding on to something new."

I sensed the Maidensong reach out to us, and the grand cosmic path to the power of the Exalted Harmony opened itself as we played on.

"Fact or fiction or fantasy, who's the person you present to me? Rushing headlong into calamity, I hope your aim is true."

In my heart, I felt the Resonance in the hearts around me. I could feel the other girls out in the arena, fighting the jumbotron jellyfish. I could feel the crowd, a cold mass of fear. I could feel the jellyfish itself, some warped and rotten core of corruption wrapped up in the confusion of a being pulled into this world and forced into something it never knew. Makula was out there, too, a raging sea of regret and humiliation.

And in the backstage area, I felt the rest of us. Jade and I, Hazel, the commander, Hikari, and Iris and Bloom. Iris seemed confused, and Bloom felt weak and afraid, but also somehow … trusting?

In me. *She trusted me.* I redoubled my focus and moved into the song's first chorus. Jade sang, and for the first time, Bloom's lyrics rang out across the crowd, carried aloft by that magnificent melody.

"So let the rain fall down on the trees that line the street, let the world pass beneath your feet, don't let people take the good in the things you do. You're too kind to be so cruel."

Hearing Bloom's words sung for the first time hit my heart

like a missile. To think that Bloom, who had so expertly crafted a wall of anger and isolation around herself, could open up like this ... well, it was remarkable. I felt like crying tears of joy for how far she'd come, how vulnerable and honest she'd allowed herself to be.

And then, a new and potent connection reached out from me and linked to Bloom. As Jade and I performed, an aura of magica wrapped itself around Bloom's body and reached down into her chest. It was as if the song was cradling her soul.

A moment later, a roiling sphere of an energy I had never experienced before rose out of Bloom's chest and levitated into the air above her.

"Whoa," Hazel said. "What the hell is that?"

"I've never seen anything like that," the commander said.

Hikari stared up at the sphere, their glasses reflecting the red glow against the contrast of their cyan hair.

"Oh flam."

I had never seen anything like this sphere before, but somehow, I knew instantly what it was: It was Bloom. This utterly alien object was Bloom's essence, the construct that Rennia had created two years before. Her entire brief existence, contained in a single object.

One that was now *my* responsibility.

Jade must have sensed my trepidation. As she played the four-bar break between the first chorus and the second verse, she nodded toward me.

"We'll keep the song going, Riot Purple! We'll repeat it as many times as we need to! Don't worry!"

I pushed aside my fear and focused on the song, and on Bloom. The sphere drifted over to me and came to a stop, hovering in front of my keytar as the magica of the song held it in place. I couldn't communicate directly with her in this form, but her emotions came across the connection as clear as a bell. The only thing I still didn't understand was her plan.

But Bloom, and the Maidensong, weren't done yet. Not even close.

A flash of energy flared up from the right hand of Bloom's motionless body. As it faded, it revealed a very familiar microphone, one encrusted with pristine orange thaumatite crystals. A heartbeat later, her hand closed around the microphone, and with a sudden motion, brought it to her lips.

Softly, her voice spoke into the mic, and everything changed.

"Maidensong harmony power ... *go live.*"

A torrent of magica erupted around the body and knocked Hazel, Hikari, and the commander back as the column of energy shot skyward. The body lifted off the floor and, through the hazy-looking glass of the dimensional portal, I watched as it twirled slowly in the magica stream. Bloom's body glowed, first purple, shifting to a warm sunset orange as her street clothes exploded off her. Swirling ribbons of orange energy wrapped her up, as a costume formed itself on her. It looked much like the ones worn by the rest of us, with a unique new hue: a black angled skirt with orange trim and lining, a dark orange jacket, orange bow, black boots, and black fingerless gloves. Her hair and eyes shifted to a vibrant orange, the old purple remaining as an accent on the tips. The same orange color cast into her eyes.

With a final, radiant blast, the magica torrent subsided and her boots touched down on the floor. Though she now looked completely unlike either form I'd seen her in before, I knew instantly who I was looking at.

"I am a guardian of song and heart," Iris said, for the first time in two years. "Servants of the darkness, be silenced by the song of Riot Orange!"

Hikari's mouth fell open. I had never seen them so surprised. "Wait Riot Orange there's a new color is that something you can do how do the rules even work is this a nothing says a dog can't play basketball sort of thing?"

Commander McCoy stared at Riot Orange, recognition flashing across her face. "I'll be damned! Agent Carr?"

Iris grinned. "Been a while, commander. Don't think I've got a lot of time here right now. We'll figure it out later." She stepped over to me, careful not to interrupt my playing as she ran her hands over Bloom's essence. "Claire, it's damn good to see you in the real world. Keep playing. Don't let her go. I still need her, and I know you do, too. Okay?"

I nodded my acknowledgement as my hands danced over my keytar. "Right!"

"Thanks," Iris said. "We can always count on Riot Purple to do the right thing. If you and Jade will follow me out there and direct the song at that jellyfish, I'm gonna give it a piece of my mind. And also find my girlfriend."

Jade, Iris, and I moved through the curtains and back out onto the stage. The arena was pure chaos now. The jellyfish swung wildly at the other girls. Makula still sat on her knees where she'd dropped before, looking utterly shellshocked. Cass fired more blasts up into the construct's screen, and Hana and Nova had resumed their duty of protecting the audience. Sara stood beneath the jellyfish, surrounded by a quintet of tentacles striking at her. She dodged and deflected the attacks and sliced back with her guitar, operating with pure warrior fire.

As we emerged out on stage, the other girls noticed the change of song, and then noticed our new companion.

Sara leapt away from the mass of tentacles and landed on the stage. She stared in disbelief, her jaw hanging open, tears flooding her eyes.

"Iris?" she asked.

"Hey, sweetheart," Iris said. "Need a hand?"

"Holy flam!" Nova shouted. "How's that possible?"

"I can't believe it," Hana said, looking nearly as emotional as Sara.

Cass laughed with sheer unfiltered joy. "Now we're freaking talking!"

"Claire and Jade moved a little further down the setlist," Iris said. She summoned her old keytar, smiled down at it, and looked back up into the arena. "What do you ladies say we join them and give these people a show? We'll have time to catch up later!"

Sara grinned and nodded. "Right! Everybody, new song! 'Too Kind to Be Cruel' is up!"

CHAPTER 25

Jade and I had been repeating the break between the first chorus and the second verse while we dealt with this series of shocking revelations. The rest of the band now joined in, one by one. Nova rolled effortlessly into the beat we'd practiced, and Hana linked up on the bass line. Sara's guitar took over the chord progression, freeing me up to move to the keyboard riffs I'd written. And Cass seamlessly joined Jade's guitar melodies, adding interesting accents as they synced up together.

"Second verse," Jade said. "Riot Red, take the vocal!"

Sara spun and stared up at the jellyfish looming above us, waited for the verse to start, and sang.

"Write the things you'll say to me, engaging in so much hyperbole. So unsatisfactory, keeping count of what you do."

With the entire band playing—including Jade and Iris—the song's connection to the Exalted Harmony strengthened. I was able to keep a part of my attention focused on Bloom's survival, very keenly aware of the glowing red ball of energy floating in front of my keytar. Every other thread of our magica blasted out of the band's performance and washed out across the arena, saturating the space, into the hearts of the audience—including Makula—as it circled around the jumbotron jellyfish.

The construct closed in on us, now absolutely sure we had only gotten more dangerous. If we'd miscalculated, if Bloom's plan wasn't going to work, we would find out in just a few more moments. The jellyfish raised all of its tentacles, as if to strike.

And Sara sang on.

"Fact or fiction or fantasy, what's the product they try to sell to me? Rushing off to the festivities, searching for what's true."

Just as with the streetcar construct before, I sensed the colossal torrent of magica, the ocean that Makula had warned me about. This time, however, the ocean danced for us. It twirled and soared, riding a pure beam of compassion and empathy that gathered strength inside me until it could not be contained. I felt warmth and love in me like I'd never felt before, the grand sensation of the hearts of so many girls across time, across magical girl history, surging out of me like a geyser of pure emotion.

This was it. This is what it meant to be a Guardian of Harmony. Fighting for the future with love, wrenching fate from the hands of the hateful with an unbreakable grip of kindness.

The strike from the jellyfish never came. It hung motionless above the floor of the arena as a glorious rainbow of magica, energy in hues of red, orange, yellow, green, jade, purple, and blue, wrapped around it and constricted it, embracing it with comfort to calm its rage.

Jade sang out the chorus again, using the opportunity to teach it to Sara. *"So let the rain fall down on the trees that line the street! Let the world pass beneath your feet! Don't let people take the good in the things you do! You're too kind to be so cruel. You're too kind to be so cruel."*

Gradually, the magical glow of the jellyfish construct faded. Not to a full shutdown, but clearly dimmed. Very slightly, the beast's body sank in midair.

"It's weakening!" Hana shouted. "Keep it up! We're almost there!"

We played into the bridge and Cass's impeccable guitar solo. Now, with Jade joining in, the pair stepped forward on stage and threw themselves into the performance with every ounce of their talent.

Cass and Jade moved and stood back-to-back as their hands flew across their respective fretboards. Bopping and dancing in time with Nova's beat, they ripped out the melody and improvised additional pieces, extending it for the live show into an entire piece of guitar theater. The rainbow magica surged in brightness, further sapping the jellyfish construct's rage.

As the guitar duet ended, Jade spun back around and stood beside Sara. The two of them locked eyes and smiled, and shared the final chorus vocal together.

"So let the rain fall down on the trees that line the street! Let the world pass beneath your feet! Don't let people take the good in the things you do! You're too kind to be so cruel. You're too kind to be so cruel. You're too kind to be so cruel."

The final notes of the song rang out across the arena. Suddenly, the glowing magica barrier that had sealed the building flashed and fell, and the jumbotron jellyfish sank farther. It took on a sickly tilt to one side, and its screens flickered dimmer. It was now very obviously weak, and we had our opening.

"Hang back, Purple," Iris said. "You just focus on Bloom. The rest of us are going to end this!"

With the song over, I refocused the entirety of my magica to Bloom's essence. My keytar de-materialized, and I took the sphere in my hands, wrapping myself around it protectively. It throbbed, warm against my skin; I clenched my eyes shut, trying to block out any distractions, pouring the entirety of what magica I had left in me into my hands. Into *her*.

I could only think of her now, if I expected this to work.

I thought about her sitting in my apartment, eating her

beloved Peanut Butter Crunchlins out of the box. Of her bravery at the food cart pod, struggling against her own body. Of our hug at the commander's farm. And, finally, an imagined memory, a hope I dared let myself see.

In my heart, Hazel and I held her hands.

I opened my eyes in time to see the orb blaze a rosy pink in my hands, as if I'd managed to make her entire essence blush. The effort, while still immense, felt just a little lighter now, knowing she could feel me up against her.

I hazarded a look up and saw the rest of the girls rush forward toward the stunned jellyfish.

Cass took the first strike. She levitated from the floor, and glowing yellow copies of her guitar appeared around her, aimed at the jellyfish's body. As her magica crackled between them like lighting, she gripped her real guitar and shouted, "Maidensong Melody Severance!"

With a fierce guitar solo, the copies of her guitar fired at the construct. Explosions erupted from its body as the shots blasted out the back, shredding anything inside in their path to pieces.

"That's our cue!" Sara shouted. "Jade, Pur … err … Orange, together with me! Let's knock it out of here while the barrier's down!"

"Way ahead of you, sweetheart," Iris said. "You girls give it the ol' guitar smash. I've got an extra-special present for it!"

"Sounds like a plan," Jade said.

The three of them ran forward until they were beneath the slowly falling jellyfish. Each summoned a spinning magica sigil beneath their feet and launched themselves skyward. Sara and Jade pulled their guitars back as they streaked toward the jellyfish, ready to deliver a massive blow.

Iris, though, had something else in store. She held her keytar aloft, the neck pointing straight up toward the center of the jellyfish's underbelly. As she flew, she stared up at her target and shouted out with all her might.

"Soul Synth Vibrant Bloom!"

A blazing orange aura enveloped her and grew. It expanded into a tremendous glowing iris blossom made of orange magica, the petals of which unfurled and extended above her body. A beam of energy blasted up from the neck of her keytar and pierced the body of the jellyfish.

Moments later, the three of them hit the construct's jumbotron body. Sara and Jade smashed their guitars up into it as hard as they could, and Iris blasted up into the body itself.

The magical iris wrapped around the jellyfish, crumpling its impact-damaged body inside as the petals closed around it, completely enveloping the construct. The blossom glowed with intense light, and within the space of a breath, Iris shot out the top of the construct as the flower unleashed an immense blast of honey-colored magica.

The jellyfish shot toward the roof of the arena, already starting to disintegrate. A second later, it smashed into the roof and ripped its way out into the night sky beyond. The force of all those attacks knocked it into a tumble. It arced out of the arena and disappeared behind the edge of the jagged hole in the roof. Judging by its direction of travel, it was heading straight for the river, something that was confirmed several seconds later when a tremendous splash could be heard from some distance away.

Sara and Jade landed back on the floor, and Iris drifted back down through the hole in the roof on a beam of orange magica. The rest of the girls rushed over to them, and I followed as quickly as I could while maintaining my focus on Bloom.

"We really flammin' did it!" Nova shouted. "And we got a cutie back!"

"Though a bit altered from two years ago," Hana said. "It's good to have you, Riot Orange!"

Sara rushed over to Iris and wrapped her arms around her. "I never expected it like this."

"I'm not even sure what happened myself," Iris said, gesturing in my direction, "and I don't think we're done yet."

The rest of the girls turned and looked at me, cradling a ball of beet-red energy as sweat rolled down my face.

"Hold the dang phone," Cass said. "What is that?"

"It's Bloom," Jade said. "I saw it all happen. That's Bloom's essence."

Hana stared down into the ball. "Incredible," she murmured.

Nova's eyes glanced from Bloom's energy back up to me. "So, uh, how you managin' that whole thing, Purple cutie?"

"Uh … not … easily," I stammered. "My brain … is on fire."

"We don't have a lot of time here, I think," Iris said, "and we still have at least one loose end."

Nearby, still sitting on her knees on the floor of the arena as the crowd slowly closed in around her, was Makula. She looked small, and empty, and sad.

The seven of us made our way over to her. Iris, Jade, and I stood together in front of her as the rest of the girls kept the audience a safe distance away.

"It wasn't supposed to be like this," Makula mumbled, over and over again.

"It's over, Makula," Iris said. "You're beaten."

Makula didn't look up. "Yes."

"You could have gotten a lot of people hurt today."

"That wasn't my intention," Makula said. She pounded her fist on the floor and shook her head. "I have no interest in harming non-magical beings. That hasn't been me for a very long time. I simply wanted to put those abusing magica in their place."

"I know," Jade said. "You didn't account for some humans' capacity for cruelty. Sinneslöschen knows how to hurt you. Just like how they tried to hurt me all those years ago."

Makula looked up at Jade and cried. "Jade Evergreen. Once more, we find ourselves face-to-face."

"Together again," Jade said, as she kneeled down in front of Makula. "Just like the old days, huh?"

Tears fell from Makula's turquoise eyes. "Jade. You grew up."

"Yeah, I did," Jade said with a chuckle. "Tends to happen to us humans."

"I see. Well ... it suits you."

Jade smiled. "Thanks. I see you changed your look a little bit."

Makula laughed tiredly. "Well, you know, Grand Cosmic Sorceresses must keep in style with the times." She sighed as her tears intensified. "Jade, these humans, they ... I didn't mean for it to be like this. I have made terrible mistakes today. I—"

"You felt the song," Jade said, "didn't you? You felt Claire's compassion."

Makula fell forward and sobbed. "This is all wrong! This isn't how it should be!"

Jade caught her and wrapped her arms around her. "It's how it is, though. And we stopped it. It's over."

"You talked a big game, like you always did," Iris said, "but it was us humans who saved you from that ego. I hope that you ... learn ..."

Iris's eyes rolled back in her head and she collapsed to the floor with a dull thud.

The rest of the girls came running as Jade dove for her and checked her pulse.

"Is she ...?" Cass asked.

"No," Jade said. "There's a pulse, but it's weak. She's in trouble."

Sara dropped to a knee beside Iris and stroked her face. "Iris? Sweetheart? Say something!"

I felt a strange wavering in Bloom's essence and looked down at the sphere. Its glow had dimmed slightly, and the magica rippled in ways that seemed ... desperate? Sick? The sensation was hard to pin down, but it wasn't good.

"I ... I think we've got a couple of problems," I said.

Sara raised her wrist link. "We need to get Iris and Bloom back to the Vault, ASAP! Dr. Barrera, be ready to move!"

Jade scooped Iris's body up in her arms and lifted her off the floor. "Let's get her into Vancent."

"Wait," Makula said as she stood back up. "You have a complicated problem here, and you will need a magica expert. I can help."

"No tricks?" Cass asked.

"No tricks," Makula said. "Jade will know I mean what I say. I can save them." Her eyes met mine. "I can save *her*."

Jade stared back at her for a moment, then nodded.

"If you can help," I said, "then I want you to."

"Yes," Sara said. "Please. Help us."

Makula nodded. "Then let us go back to your Vault, right away. We need to stabilize them, and time is short."

CHAPTER 26

ara skidded Vancent Price to a stop in the Vault's garage. With Jade carrying Iris, and me concentrating on Bloom's essence, we rushed down to Dr. Barrera's med bay. I had been pushing myself hard for the entire drive back, and the strain was getting to me. I felt weak and drained, but I had no choice.

I told Bloom I'd be there for her, and I wasn't about to go back on my word.

In the med bay, Jade laid Iris down on the operating bed as the rest of us followed. The commander, Saoirse, Hikari, and Hazel stood back from the bed as the rest of us clustered around it. Dr. Barrera moved in and powered up her various sensors and instruments, while Makula moved to the bed and motioned for me to join her.

"Alright, Claire," she said, "I am going to take your corruption construct friend off your hands. We must be quick, for she cannot maintain integrity on her own."

Sweat dropped down my face, and I struggled to stay standing. "I think ... it's now ... or never. I don't ... feel ... so good. What ... what are you going to do?"

"Putting Bloom back in Iris, temporarily. Now, release your magical hold on her."

I relaxed my focus and let Bloom slip from my grasp. The essence immediately started to fade more severely, and Makula reached out for it. A strand of magica grew from her hand and took hold of Bloom, and with a steady motion, she guided the essence back down into Iris's chest.

I felt faint. My legs started to give out from under me, but Jade caught me and steadied me before I could fall. Where her hand grabbed me felt warm, and I sensed magica flowing back into me.

"Jade," I said, "thank you."

"Don't mention it, kid," Jade said. "I've got you. From one Guardian of Harmony to another."

The sensor readouts of the medical bay suddenly sprung to life, and Dr. Barrera inspected them. "It seems to have worked. I'm getting the combined Iris and Bloom life signs again, but they're still quite weak."

"As expected," Makula said. "We have solved nothing. We have only bought some additional time. I believe now that two things are obvious."

"What two things are those?" Cass asked.

"First, the Iris body is failing," Makula explained. "The strain of two fully powered magica users in a single biological resonator is too great. It's a wonder the body has lasted this long, though I suspect Rennia's influence delayed the problem. It is imperative that Bloom's essence be moved to a new host."

"And the second thing?" Sara asked.

Makula laid her hand on Iris's shoulder, and closed her eyes. She took slow, deep breaths, as a soft glow radiated up her arm and into her body. Then, she removed her hand and opened her eyes. "It is as I suspected. Iris and Bloom have been together so long, and have become so deeply intermingled, that their essences cannot live individually anymore."

A hush fell across the medical bay as the implications settled in. Nova was the first to break that silence, with the question on all of our minds.

"So wait, if they can't live together, *and* they can't live apart, then what the flam are we supposed to do? Just let 'em die? 'Cause I ain't gonna do that!"

"It feels like that shouldn't be an option, no," Jade said.

"It isn't," Sara said. "Period."

"Oh, I agree," Makula said. "I promised I could save them, and I will make good. We simply have to find a path forward."

As I stood by the operating bed catching my breath, I thought back to the conversation I had with Bloom at the farm. She'd been terrified of waking up alone, of not having access to Iris's thoughts and memories. Was there an answer in that fear somewhere? Maybe, but it was all speculation. The answer seemed elusive from the outside.

And that's when an idea hit me: Maybe going at it from the outside was the wrong approach.

"Um, what if we could, you know, talk to Iris and Bloom about it?" I asked.

The rest of the room turned to me.

"Talk to them?" Hana asked.

"Yeah," I said. "Maybe they could help, if they knew what was going on."

"A fine enough idea," Dr. Barrera said, "but neither of them will be waking up. You must understand, the body's systems are on the verge of shutdown. There is no coming back from this without the actual solution."

"Do you have any suggestions, Claire?" Hazel asked.

"No bad ideas at this point," the commander added.

I stared down at Iris's body and thought. If she and Bloom couldn't wake up and talk to us here, there had to be another way. We were magical girls, after all. There had to be a spell we could cast, or maybe …

"A brewery realm," I said.

"A what?" Sara asked.

I turned back to face the room. "Makula, you trapped us in that weird brewery realm! We need one of those, a place apart from this world. Somewhere the normal rules we have here don't apply. But, like, not a brewery. Someplace familiar and comfortable. A way station!"

"Some place that would be calming to Iris and Bloom, so they could communicate without stressing their body," Jade said.

"It could work," Makula said. "You have that ability. But do you have the power?"

"I think so," I nodded.

"Do you know of a place like that, Claire?" Jade asked.

I smiled. "Yeah, I do. I haven't ever accessed it intentionally, but I can try."

Makula frowned. "This is all academic if we do not have the target vessel," she said. "Another resonator for Bloom's essence to live in. Do you actually have such a thing?"

From the back of the room, where she stood beside Hikari, Saoirse spoke up. "You better believe we do."

Hikari nodded. "We've got a good idea it's just a little unconventional is all but I like unconventional."

Saoirse smiled. "We're going to put Miss Bloom in the XS-1."

"And just what, exactly, is an XS-1?" Makula asked.

"Experimental Support One that's the full name but in casual terms it's Saoirse's cool-as-heck robot," Hikari said.

"Wait, you girls have a robot?" Jade asked. "Things really *have* changed since the old days."

"Oh, we have a robot, alright," Saoirse said. "I made a new power core that runs for weeks on a charge, and the kid here whipped up a whole new control interface and central processor using the data gathered by Doc Barrera. If you put Miss Bloom in it, bind her bio-essence to the thaumatite core, well, she can do it. She can *become* the bot."

Makula's eyes narrowed. "You mean to tell me that you are creating *another* abomination of magica, like the ones I have been trying to defeat?"

"Abomination nothing," Saoirse said. "My tech ain't slap-dash corporate garbage like the Rhapsodyz bots. We ain't using corruption magica, and there's no residual energy leakage. My design is solid as a rock!"

"You realize, however," Makula said, "that you'd be putting it under the control of a magical constructed consciousness who is weakened and unprepared. There is no guarantee that Bloom would take to the thaumatite core, or be able to control your robot if she does. This is magicraft beyond what most humans can ever accomplish."

"There ain't a guarantee Miss Bloom *can't* do it, either," Saoirse fired back. "And the way I see it, we're out of options! We don't have another body. If we found somebody to volunteer, we'd just be kicking the can down the road and have to deal with all this again, if she even survived!" She gestured toward Hikari. "And the kid here's done real wonders with the interface side of things."

Hikari nodded. "For what it's worth I have complete confidence in Saoirse's robot and well not to brag or anything but I have complete confidence in my additions as well we knew this was going to be a possibility and we've worked toward it."

Hana raised her hand. "Also, Makula, I'd like to point out that you are an expert at animating the inanimate and giving it some kind of life."

"I've been hit by enough of your constructs to know that," Cass added.

"Right," Hana said. "So we'd have a better chance with your help than without it."

Makula sighed and nodded. "That is so. It is one of my many specialties. Very well, then. If you all are willing to accept the consequences, I believe this is within the realm of possibility for someone with my limitless levels of skill. I would need to have the robot here, of course."

Commander McCoy suddenly stepped forward into the middle of the room. "Alright, I've heard enough. We're out of time, out of options, and somebody's gotta make a command decision. And that's *my* job. Doctor, Makula, Agent O'Carolan, Agent Tomori, get it done. Put Bloom in the robot."

Dr. Barrera sighed and nodded. "Yes, commander."

"We'll go get the XS-1," Saoirse said. "C'mon, kid."

"I can't believe I get to say 'let's go get the robot' this is a dream come true," Hikari said as they and Saoirse headed out of the med bay.

"I will also need Claire, for her way station," Makula said. "And I would also like to have Sara here as well. You two are closest to Bloom and Iris, respectively."

"I'll do anything," Sara said.

"Very good," Makula said. "Everybody else, I would like to wait outside. This will be a delicate process, and as few observers as possible, the better."

The rest of the team left the medical bay as Sara, Makula, Dr. Barrera, and I waited for Saoirse and Hikari to return. Sara and I remained in our magical girl forms, since we were about to have to do some serious magica work. Dr. Barrera changed into her lab coat, hooked up a barrage of sensors to Iris, and pulled up a live bio-readout on the med bay displays.

"This will give us instant feedback on how the girls are doing," she said. "At least, up until the moment Bloom leaves the body."

"I will also be able to monitor them," Makula said. "The basic theory of a bio-essence transfer is straightforward, but if high-level sentient beings are involved, the complicating factors grow exponentially. It is fortuitous that I am here to provide my expert skills!"

"Have you ever done one like this before?" Sara asked.

Makula smiled, but said nothing.

The medical bay door slid open again, and a motorized sled wheeled its way in, with Saoirse at its controls. On the sled lay a sheet-covered humanoid form. Hikari followed, and shut the door behind them.

Saoirse wheeled the sled over near the operating bed and raised it up to the same height. "Alright, here she is."

Makula reached over and pulled the sheet off the sled, and I got my first glimpse at the XS-1 in its completed form. Saoirse had installed the body panels now, and most of the bare skeletal frame that I'd seen before was completely covered. Only some exposed structure around the neck and collarbone area and a section between the robot's chest and hips laid visible.

The rest of the bot now carried sleek, rounded panels of white on its chassis, which I estimated to be six and a half feet tall. The robot's uncannily human faceplate was also installed now, framed by what almost looked like headphone cups on the sides of its head that featured twin blade-like fins protruding up from them. Just as it had appeared on the computer before, the XS-1 had the face of a cute woman around my age, with realistic soft skin and features.

The only unusual element were the eyes, which were also perfectly human apart from their cold gray color. I wondered for a moment if something so intimidating would suit Bloom, who had made such bold steps forward as her own person. Would this be something that enticed her into her old ways?

I pushed the thought out as soon as I realized it had arrived. No, that wasn't Bloom. Not anymore. I believed in her.

In my friend.

"A fascinating machine," Makula said, studying the XS-1 intently. "When I return to the Undertow, I shall adjust your technological quotient slightly in Marelian records."

"It's my finest work so far," Saoirse said. "Well, me and the kid here."

Hikari nodded, and I caught a glimpse of a smile on their face. "Be sure to note that the XS-1 is not just a breakthrough human technological achievement but that it also kicks butt and looks stylish doing it if I know Bloom you can take that to the bank."

Makula smiled and nodded. "Well then, shall we?"

"I'm ready over here," Dr. Barrera said. "Saoirse, could you please power on the XS-1?"

"Aye, on it," Saoirse said.

Hikari handed her their laptop, and Saoirse connected a cable from it to a small port in back of the XS-1's neck. After typing in some commands, the robot sprang to life. Soft lighting around various panel lines all over its body glowed and pulsated, cycling through a rainbow as a nearly inaudible whirr emanated from some piece of machinery inside its body.

"It has gamer lights?" I asked.

"That was Hikari's idea," Saoirse said.

Hikari blushed slightly and nodded. "For sure for sure usually I'd say it's a little gauche like it's kind of excessive and a little stereotypical to do something like that but then I thought when am I ever going to get a chance to help design a magical fighting robot again it would be an insult to coolness to not put as many LEDs as I could get away with on it."

"Good instincts, young one," Makula said. "Magica indeed benefits from a certain level of spectacle. Now, we are ready to begin. Sara, I will need you to take Iris's hand. Claire, you do the same for the robot. And then take each other's hand."

"Right," Sara said, as she moved into place between Iris and the XS-1. She took hold of Iris's hand with her left, and offered her right to me.

I moved over and took her hand, and the XS-1's. "Ready."

Makula raised her hand and took a deep breath. "I shall require the Staff of Sorrows for this procedure. One moment."

A flash of magica surged though her grasp and the staff materialized in her hand. She closed her eyes and breathed steadily.

"Now, Claire," she continued, "I will begin the casting process. You will simultaneously attempt to connect to your way station. You may start when ready."

"Okay," I said. "Here goes."

I focused my magica and reached out with my mind. I wasn't

actually sure what I was doing, since I'd only ever been taken to this place against my will, but I had to believe there was a way for me to access it intentionally.

The Maidensong responded to me, and I probed at the barriers of the dimensional planes, searching for a way to link to the package of magica that had lived in me since the first time Iris had touched me. At the same time, Makula raised her staff and cast the first stage of her spell. As I reached deeper into the great cosmic well, a swirling dome of energy rose from her staff and settled down around us in the medical bay.

It came down to me now. I needed to find that place again, on my own terms. I needed to access the part of me that knew the connection to that place, the distant memory in the hearts of all magical girls. I searched deeper, my magica surging, until ...

Suddenly, blackness crept in around the edges of my vision, and the medical bay stretched away from me. I felt a surge of magica within Sara through our linked hands, a power that reminded me of when she'd rescued me during my first full-group fight. The connection came so easily, I accepted it without thinking.

The sensation of falling overtook me then, and I realized I was pulling Sara along with me as I descended into nothingness.

———

I came to beside a gleaming railing looking out over the endless expanse of the ocean. The sky above shone a flawless blue, streaked with barely perceptible chromatic rays. The air felt fresh and life-giving, and I breathed deep as the sun's warmth washed over me.

It had worked.

Sara stood beside me, stiff with the shock of her first traversal. Her eyes opened wide, and she gasped as she took in the surroundings.

"Claire! What ... what is this ..." she began. As she spoke, she turned to look behind us, and trailed off. Her jaw dropped as she stared up at the scene before her.

I smiled and turned around with her. The glittering towers and lush plazas of the Crystal City stretched out before us with stunning grandeur, and I let her take in the view for a moment.

Eventually, she spoke again, with quiet awe in her voice. "This is where you met Adia?"

"It is, yeah," I said. "I still don't know what it's actually called, so I just call it the Crystal City."

"It's gorgeous," Sara said. She stared out at the skyline for another long moment. "Why do I feel like I know this place?"

"I haven't really figured that out, either. Adia told me it's a memory from magical girl history, but she's never explained what that actually means."

Sara nodded. "It feels sort of ... comforting?"

"Exactly," I said. "Like whatever this place was, it was a happy place for magical girls."

"I can see why you chose it."

I sensed something else coming through the dimensional planes. A moment later, a cloud of mist appeared before us and slowly coalesced into two human forms, revealing Bloom and Iris, resplendent in their magical girl forms, arm in arm.

Iris whistled low as she took in the scene. "Damn, this is a hell of a thing. Is this where you went after I connected you to Adia?"

I nodded. "Yes. Although I've never been to this part of it before, which is kind of weird."

"It reminds me of the park above the Vault," Bloom said. "The railing, and the water, specifically."

Sara looked back toward the ocean and nodded. "There might be something to that. We've spent a lot of time at Waterfront Park, and it was where Iris and I had our first kiss."

"Makes sense to me," I said.

"Since I assume we are not here to wallow in senseless

nostalgia," Bloom said, "would one of you tell us what our purpose here is?"

"What's the last thing you each remember?" Sara asked.

"A very unpleasant self-inflicted pain," Bloom said. "Then, blackness. Vague sensations of warmth." She frowned. "Unexpectedly pleasant thoughts. And a maddeningly catchy song, with quite frankly exquisite lyrics in the chorus, if I do say so myself."

Iris thought for a moment. "I remember being in the arena. We'd just killed the jellyfish, and I was talking to Makula. Jade Evergreen was there, and you were, too, Claire. You were holding a ball of energy."

"Yeah," I said. "That was Bloom."

"Right, yeah! And then I don't remember anything past that."

"You passed out," Sara said. "We brought you and Bloom back to the Vault. Right now, Bloom's back inside you, and you're lying on the operating bed."

Iris and Bloom traded uneasy looks.

"Sooo, I'm gonna guess that means we're out of time, huh?" Iris asked.

"This is where it ends, is it?" Bloom asked. "Is this some kind of afterlife?"

"Nothing's ended yet," I said. "Dr. Barrera, Saoirse, Hikari, and ... um ... Makula, are working on you."

Bloom glared at me. "You let that self-important sorceress work on *my* very being?"

"If we didn't, you two wouldn't have made it even this far," Sara said.

"You can yell at me later about it," I said. "I'll be glad if you can. We don't have a lot of time, and we've got a big problem we need to solve so that you two can survive."

"Bloom's just grumpy," Iris said. "C'mon, let's hear it. I'd really like to not be dead, if I can manage it."

"Okay, alright, yeah," I began. "The strain on Iris's body has gotten too bad, so you can't stay together. But, well, you've been together so long, living in the same body, that you're all commingled now. You can't survive *without* each other, either."

For the second time, I saw tears well up in Bloom's eyes and roll down her cheeks. "We can't survive apart? What does *that* mean?"

Iris shook her head. "You don't have a solution for it, do you?"

"I wish," I sighed. "We aren't sure what to do."

"That's why we needed to talk to you," Sara added.

"Yeah. We thought that if we could talk to you both, we could figure out what to do."

Iris smiled and squeezed Bloom's arm more tightly. The two of them walked over to the railing, turned around, and leaned against it, between Sara and me.

"Bloom and I have actually talked about this a little," Iris said.

Bloom nodded. "You recall our chat at the berry farm, don't you, Claire? After I talked to Sara."

"Yeah," I said. "I remember."

"I was in there, too," Iris said. "I heard all those things Bloom said about me, and we had a chat that night."

"Bloom … do you feel okay talking about this?" I asked. "I know that you don't like to open up."

"I am tired, Claire," Bloom said. "Tired of fighting this. And I am a reasonably intelligent being. I have reached the limits of this existence, and if I am to survive, I must evolve."

I smiled at her. "Okay. Go on."

"As you well know," she continued, "I am deeply fearful of being alone now. Alone in a new body, alone in the world, no longer able to know Iris's memories or emotions. Over the months since she was reawakened, I've come to appreciate Iris, as a companion and a … a f … fr—"

"You can do it," Iris said. "Take your time."

Bloom grumbled. "Ugh. As a *friend*. As Claire and the rest of

Magica Riot helped me from the outside, she has helped me from the inside."

"There's never been a dull moment since Bloom and I were able to talk to each other," Iris said. "I'm really proud of how far she's come. I almost think of her like a sister. Maybe something deeper, I don't know. I want to know she'll be okay."

"Iris and I are both magical beings, of different sorts," Bloom said. "We have discussed using our powers to ..." She made a small, dissatisfied noise. "It is hard to explain. To ... copy some part of the other to keep after we're apart. Does that make sense?"

"She takes what she needs of me, I take what I need of her," Iris said. "That way, we never have to be alone or apart, not really. We get to keep living without destroying my body, and we still get to be together. Head mates, I guess you could say."

"Is that something you know how to do?" I asked.

"Don't know," Iris said. "Won't know until we try. And I think we have to, because from what you've told me, there's no other choice. All I know is that even though I've been out of the world for a couple of years, I'm still a magical girl, and another magical girl once told me something about facing the impossible that I've never forgotten."

Sara smiled, her lower lip trembling, and a tear fell from her eye. "Magical girls face the impossible with love."

"Damn right we do," Iris said. "And I've come to love Bloom, the Bloom I know now, like a part of myself."

Bloom groaned and frowned. "This magical girl sappiness is a part of you I shall refuse to copy."

"Am I wrong, though?" Iris asked, grinning. "Remember, I know when you're lying."

"You ... are not wrong," Bloom said.

Iris nodded, satisfied. "There you go. And that's your answer. Bloom and I will try to pull off our plan while Makula does the transfer."

"Are you sure it'll work?" Sara asked. "I can't go through that ag—"

"Hush, babygirl," Iris said. She cupped Sara's cheek in her free hand. "We're not gonna go there. It'll work. We're Magica Riot, dammit."

"Yeah, we are," Sara said.

They kissed, lost for a moment in each other. I glanced at Bloom and realized she was looking at me. She gave me a scowl that seemed less than genuine, and looked away.

"Are you two ready?" I asked.

"As ready as I shall ever be," Bloom said.

"Same," Iris said. "Let's do this thing."

I looked up into the sky and reached out with my magica to find a route back to the real world. I realized I hadn't worked out a signal with Makula. Did she already know?

I decided to play it safe. "We're ready, Makula! If you're listening."

Subtly at first, then all too quickly, the periphery of my vision darkened. As the Crystal City stretched and faded, I saw Bloom and Iris become translucent, their forms blending together, becoming less distinct, as we slid back toward the plane of our reality.

I wasn't sure if it was a trick of the light, but I thought I saw Bloom's eyes soften to a new pink hue.

I coalesced into the middle of a whirling torrent of magica. It took me a moment to recognize the medical bay in the dizzying light.

A glowing beam linked Makula's staff to Iris's body and the XS-1. Saoirse and Hikari held on to the robot's transport sled for dear life as Dr. Barrera gripped the corner of one of the wall-mounted monitors, fighting to stay standing in the rush of air and energy.

"The barriers have been breached!" Makula shouted over the noise. "Bio-essence transference in progress! We near the moment of kindling!"

"What does that mean?!" I yelled over the din.

Makula laughed. "It is a *very good* thing, Claire Ryland! Just a moment ..."

I noticed her hands shaking as she tried to control the torrent of magica.

"Just a moment ..."

The glow intensified, until it was so bright I had to shade my eyes.

"And we will have ..."

A tremendous flash of magica erupted from Iris and the XS-1, and blew all of us back from the tables. Sara and I skidded across the floor and wound up in a heap together against the wall.

As we recovered, Makula stood back up and ran over to the tables. "Yes! *Yes!* It is complete! *This* is the work of a true master of magica!"

Sara helped me up and dusted herself off. "Does that mean they're both okay?"

"It means the transfer was successful. The next steps are up to them, and to your doctor and technicians."

Dr. Barrera ran back over to her computer display and scanned her eyes down Iris's readout. "Well, I can vouch for Iris being alive. All her vital signs are stabilizing. Brain activity is on the low side, but I would expect such a thing after this experience."

"So, you're saying that's normal?" I asked.

"We won't know right away, but I believe she simply needs time to recover."

Saoirse and Hikari returned to the XS-1. Hikari's beater laptop had miraculously survived the transfer blast, and they reconnected it to the port in the robot's neck.

"Pulling up system status now running a full diagnostic please wait I should have some answers soon," they said.

"Aye, at least from a visual inspection, the XS-1 is intact," Saoirse said.

"How quickly will we know if Bloom is okay?" I asked.

"That ... I don't have the foggiest. Nobody's ever done this before." She glanced at Makula. "On this planet, anyway."

Hikari peered closer to their laptop screen. "Structural integrity is good servomotors and actuators good thermal regulation is a little on the high side but falling back to normal levels power delivery is good voltage steady thaumatite power core stable now checking central processing systems."

"Means the hardware's good," Saoirse clarified. "Now, we just have to see if the new software's taken to it."

The room held its collective breath as Hikari typed away and looked over the results. Eventually, they nodded, slowly and subtly.

"The logic circuits and the thaumatite core are showing readings consistent with what we would expect if they had suddenly become home of an impossibly complicated constructed consciousness and since I don't know any others right here I have to say that the robot has a Bloom on board now."

"So ... does that mean she's okay?" I asked.

Saoirse put her hands up. "You gotta take it slow. It means Bloom is probably alive in there, but it was always gonna take her some time to connect with the systems and be able to interface with the XS-1."

I felt my lip tremble, and a lump in my throat. It was then that I realized I had tears in my eyes. I swallowed and tried to maintain some kind of calm. "That makes sense, yeah. I just worry."

"I know," Saoirse said. "We've got her."

Makula ambled around the room, admiring her handiwork. "It would indeed be wise to allow both of them to recover on their own terms. We have done something remarkable here today, and should now let magica take its course."

"Doctor," Sara said, "if it's alright with you, I'd like to wait here. At least, as much as I can."

"Of course," Dr. Barrera said. "We can—"

Her wrist link beeped and interrupted her. She raised it and tapped the alert, then directed her attention toward me.

"Claire, *your* vitals are not looking especially good."

For the first time all night, I realized how truly exhausted I felt. "I, uh, yeah. I've been through a lot tonight."

"Your magica must be nearly gone," Sara said.

Dr. Barrera walked over and placed her hand on my back, guiding me toward the bed nearest to the robot's—no, Bloom's—sled. "I'm giving you a prescription for sleep, immediately. It's likely neither Iris nor Bloom will be waking up for the time being, so you have no excuse."

I de-transformed as I reached the medical bed. My energy cratered, and as I climbed onto the bed, sleep came for me before I'd even fully settled into the pillow.

My dreams were full of vibrant orange and pink flowers.

CHAPTER 27

Some time later, I woke up. I felt like I always did after staying up too long and trying to make up for it with an excess amount of sleep: still tired, but *differently* tired. My eyelids dragged themselves open, and I realized I was still in the medical bay.

The lights had been dimmed and partly turned off, the few still on fluorescing dull white on the smooth metal Vault walls. I rolled over onto my back and looked around, getting my bearings. The room was empty, save for the occupant of one of the other beds, and the person keeping them company.

Iris sat up in a bed across the room from me, lit by the overhead reading lamp. Sara sat in a chair by her side. They talked quietly together, occasionally laughing, their laughter full of catharsis and relief.

The laughter of two women who knew they'd gotten back their lives together.

Iris took notice of me and waved.

"Claire! You're finally awake!"

"Good morning, Claire," Sara said. She beamed at me, the biggest smile I'd ever seen on her face.

I slid out of my bed and padded over to them. "Hey. I'm not the only one who's awake, I see."

"Yeah, I came to a few hours ago," Iris said.

"A few hours? How long was I out?"

Sara glanced down at her wrist link. "Oh, about eleven hours."

"Wow," I said. "I really was exhausted."

"You did a lot! I think you earned it," Iris said.

"Thanks," I said. "It's a little weird to hear somebody who literally got her consciousness split from a magica construct say that about me."

"That's the life of a magical girl for you," Iris giggled. "I really can't thank you enough for what you did, Claire."

"That goes for both of us," Sara said. "I don't even know what to say, other than thank you."

I shrugged and smiled back at them. "Hey, with Iris here, we all have plenty of time ahead of us to say whatever we want."

Sara reached over and squeezed Iris's hand. "Yeah, we do."

"So," I said, "um, Iris, if you're back, does that mean that Bloom ..."

"Not yet," Iris said. "At least, nobody's told me if she's awake."

"Last report I got was that she looks stable in the core," Sara said. "The XS-1 hasn't started responding, though. So we're still waiting."

"You must really be worried, huh?" Iris asked.

I nodded. "Yeah. I really am."

"I get it. I was there for that conversation at the farm."

"Right," I blushed. "So, if you're sitting here alive, I assume that yours and Bloom's plan worked."

Iris smiled and tapped her head. "It did. She's still up here. Or, some of her is. I can feel her with me. I can even still talk to her."

"Really? You can?" I asked.

"That's amazing," Sara said. "Is that some kind of connection to her in the robot?"

"Not like that, no, I don't think so," Iris said, shaking her head. "It's more like I got a new copy of her that shares my head now."

"How does that feel?" I asked.

"Honestly, it feels good. It feels *right*. I'm not the Iris Carr from two years ago. I lived through this impossible thing between then and now, and now I'm Iris, plus Bloom. And if—when—Bloom wakes up, she'll probably be Bloom, plus Iris."

"Yeah, that makes sense," I said. "And is Iris plus Bloom different from regular Iris?"

"A little," Iris said, grinning and shooting a playful look at Sara. "You know how Bloom is. She and I weren't *that* different in some ways. I was always a little wild."

Sara laughed. "You were."

"Bloom's influence and personality are in me now," Iris continued. "A little more fiery." She grinned. "But with a new perspective on things." Her expression took on a wistful softness. "Feeling both of our emotions has me appreciating things I used to take for granted."

Sara blushed and grinned back at her. "Something tells me neither of us will make that mistake ever again."

Iris nodded. "I got to be there to watch Bloom become a person apart from Rennia. I got to help her. Kinda showed me the value in being relentlessly compassionate, know what I mean? And admitting when you're wrong, and doing better. Weird to think having an evil consciousness in me for two years would make me wanna be a kinder person, but there you go."

"No, I get it," I said. "It shows that if somebody wants to do better, they can. I know that, like, abstractly, but getting a clear example is always nice."

"Yeah," Iris said. "I guess it's a little funny that I'm both a little louder *and* a little softer, thanks to her, but what can I say? Iris Carr is a land of contrasts."

I laughed. "I always heard that, but I'm glad to see it for myself."

The medical bay's door slid open, and Dr. Barrera entered. "Ah, Claire! You're finally awake!"

"That's what people keep saying, yeah," I said.

She pretended to frown. "It's been a while since I saw a magical girl that drained! Hopefully that's not something you'll be repeating in the near future."

"I'm definitely not planning on carrying any magica consciousnesses around in my hands anytime soon, no."

"Good, good," she laughed. "Now, Iris, how are *you* feeling, dear?"

"Still weak," Iris said. "And just feeling normal things, like the air, or temperature, or the bed sheets, it's all still strange. Like, surreal, you know? I haven't felt those things directly in two years, so I guess that's normal, maybe?"

"I'd think so," Dr. Barrera said. "This is, obviously, an unusual situation, one that nobody has any hard data on, but it's only logical to expect such things. You are reconnecting your essence to your physical form. There are countless sensory threads that you will be experiencing again with a fresh perspective. And that will also be affecting your physicality, which partly explains the weakness."

"For sure, yeah," Iris said. "I think it's safe to say I won't be punching monsters or robots again for a while."

"No interest in getting back out there?" I asked.

"It's not like that. I think I just need time to acclimate. Anyway, Magica Riot with five members is more than capable of dealing with things!"

"You'll have the chance again, when you're ready," Sara said.

"Yeah," I said. "A whole new color and everything."

"The Maidensong's not done with me, I guess," Iris laughed. "I didn't expect Riot Orange, but I have to admit, it's nice to be on the spectrum right next to Sara now."

"I'd like to think it's because the Maidensong wants me to keep you safe, forever," Sara said.

"Maybe. Or maybe it wants me to keep *you* safe, sweetheart. Little Miss Beaten-Up-by-a-Jellyfish over here."

Sara nudged Iris's shoulder. "Hey, you saw that jellyfish! I think I did pretty well!"

When I was new on the team, Nova told me about how Sara used to be when Iris was around. That she was a warmer, more cheerful person. Now that I could see that version of Sara with my own eyes, it was one of the most beautiful things I'd ever witnessed.

Sara Ward was, for the first time since I'd known her, genuinely happy. With no asterisks.

Now that I was awake, and knew Iris was okay, I decided it would be best to leave her and Sara to their reunion. I backed away a bit and said, "I'm going to check on Bloom and then go down to the lounge and get some coffee, I think."

"Sounds good," Iris said. "We'll have plenty of time to talk later!"

Sara smiled and nodded at me. "Thanks, Claire. For everything."

"Sure," I said, smiling back. "Anytime, Riot Red."

"If you're looking for Bloom, she's down in the armory now," Dr. Barrera said. "Saoirse and Hikari felt it would be best to keep an eye on her with their tools."

"Makes sense," I said. "Thanks, doctor."

I made my way out of the medical bay and into the Vault's main corridor. The facility was surprisingly quiet, but then, I had been asleep for eleven hours. Everybody else was probably busy with daily functions, what with Iris being awake but resting and Bloom not having come to yet.

When I reached the armory, I slid the door open and peered in. Bloom lay on Saoirse's workbench, a series of cables and sensors hooked up to her new robotic body. Hikari sat beside her, along with Jade; Saoirse, meanwhile, was curled up beneath a blanket on the couch that sat along one wall in the corner of the room near the instrument lockers, sleeping soundly.

Jade noticed me enter and waved as I approached. She waited until I got closer, so as not to wake Saoirse, before she greeted me.

"Good morning, sleepyhead."

"Morning," I said. "Looks like I'm not the only one."

Hikari nodded. "We kind of pulled an all-nighter Saoirse took the first shift and now we've traded she's pretty exhausted I think but you know this was one of her pet projects so I get it it's like when I stayed up all night to make sure my custom Pi-based tracker synth was working after I built it except you know with the whole magical living consciousness thing which admittedly is a little more impressive."

"Speaking of, how's Bloom doing?"

"I've been monitoring the thaumatite core for fluctuations either the bad oh crap oh crap something's broken kind or the oh yay oh yay Bloom's waking up kind but so far it's just been stable so I think she's still figuring her way around in there it's like suddenly having to get used to a whole new transit map except the transit map is your own body," Hikari said.

I looked down at Bloom. The XS-1 body was exactly as it had been the night before, powered up and softly glowing in rainbow colors, but no more activity visible. Its eyes were closed, as if deep in slumber.

"How long can she run on a charge?" I asked. "Um, assuming that's how it works."

Hikari nodded. "It is yeah so in normal operations Saoirse's new thaumatite power core will let Bloom work for weeks between plug-ins it's very efficient and while she's strong it's not taking that much power now Riot Mode is a different story but we'll cross that bridge when we build it."

"What's Riot Mode in this context?"

An almost imperceptible smile crossed Hikari's face. "A little something I've been cooking up the name is an homage of course it's basically a magical girl form for the robot body uh we're still working out the bugs in it by which I mean it's almost all bugs right now but when it's ready it'll be very cool and/or radical but in that form because the power draw is exponentially higher due to all the fun new stuff she'll be able to do it's going to last uhhh fifteen minutes give or take before low-power mode kicks in."

Jade chuckled beside me. "A robot magical girl. The game's changed a lot since my day."

I reached down and ran my hand across Bloom's arm, feeling the unique sensation of her body panels. They were unlike any substance I'd felt before, clearly metallic but with a texture that was a strange blend of rigid and soft. Surprisingly, she was also warm to the touch, in an unexpectedly human sort of way. Apparently, a thaumatite-powered robot magical girl put out some heat.

"Aetheric-charged chromium zirconium copper alloy with carbon nanotube suspension matrix all actuated by Ohara Heavy Industries servomotors before you ask you know only the best for our Bloom here spared no expense," Hikari said.

"Sure," I said. "That sounds like something that exists."

My hand slid down and touched Bloom's. Though her robotic hand couldn't respond in kind, I squeezed it and looked down at her eyes.

Please, please, please wake up soon.

Beside me, Jade gave me a gentle nudge. "I've gotta run for now. Got a bar to check on, after all. Said my other goodbyes already, so would you mind walking me to the garage?"

"Sure, of course," I said. "No problem. Hikari, would you let me know if there's any change in her?"

Hikari gave me a little salute. "For sure for sure you're number one on the list Claire I promise."

Jade and I walked out of the armory and turned down the main corridor toward the garage. After everything that had happened the night before, I felt like I had a thousand things I wanted to say to her, but I also had a feeling we'd be seeing her more often, so I didn't want to overwhelm her. Best to start small.

"Hey, Jade," I said, "thank you. I don't think we would have made it through that fight without you."

Jade grinned and shrugged. "Don't think anything of it. It's what magical girls do, even if they're in their fifties. To be honest, it felt good to transform again."

"How'd you like your true powers?"

"Those sigils take some getting used to, but that's a minor detail. It's great to know what's beyond the wall now. Although I didn't get to figure out what my special attack is!"

I laughed. "You should come back sometime and try it out in the training room. I know we'd all love to see that."

"I might have to do that." Her grin took on a different vibe, the sparkle in her eyes growing. "Gives me an excuse to see Meredith again."

"Meredith ... the commander?"

"The very same. She gets flustered easy. It's cute as hell."

We reached the garage and went inside. Jade walked me past Vancent Price to where another car was parked alongside him: a pristine older Chevrolet Camaro with the T-top removable roof panels, painted jade green with twin white racing stripes down the center of its body.

"Dang, is this yours?" I asked.

"Yeah," Jade said. "For a while, actually. 1983 Camaro Z28, with some Starlight Alliance-approved modifications."

"Wait, so this—"

"Used to be my Vancent, yeah," Jade laughed, "before there was a Vancent. Didn't need a van as a solo act, after all. When the Roses joined up and I gradually handed the job off to them, the Alliance bought Vancent and gave the old girl here to me. Her name is Camarolyn Monroe."

I couldn't help myself, and burst out laughing. "Of *course* it is. So does this mean you're the one who named Vancent? The other girls assumed it was the Roses."

Jade grinned. "Claire, I can't tell you *all* the secrets of magical girls past. Where's the fun in that?"

"I guess you've got a point. Camarolyn looks good. You've taken care of her."

"You better believe it. She might not have had Vancent's time on duty, but she saw a lot of wild stories. Those, I'll happily tell you about sometime."

"Please do, yeah!"

"One thing before I roll out of here, though. Can I offer you some advice, Claire?"

"Of course," I nodded. "Always."

She moved in closer and gave my shoulder a squeeze. "You've got something real special here, and I'm not just talking about Magica Riot or your new robot friend. Somebody who cares about you, who feels for you … *and* is on-board for the magical girl job? That means something."

"Hazel."

"That girl's one in a million, so you have to do everything in your power to keep her safe. You're an extremely lucky magical girl. Not every girl who falls for us can deal with the life." Her face fell, just a bit, and I imagined there had to be another story behind it.

I wasn't about to poke at that old wound, though.

"You're right, and I will. I swear."

Her smile returned. "I know. You're a good girl. Take it from me, one Guardian of Harmony to another."

With that, she stepped away and opened Camarolyn's driver-side door. "Oh, and Claire?"

"Yeah?"

"Don't be a stranger! I'll keep a booth at Dark Water reserved for Magica Riot, whenever you need it."

I smiled. "Deal!"

She slid into the driver's seat, shut the door, and fired up

Camarolyn. With the throaty, burbling roar of an early-eighties muscle car, Jade Evergreen rolled out of the Vault's garage and up the ramp to the outside, not for the first time and surely not for the last, either.

———

I made my way back into the Vault to look for Hazel. I realized as I checked my wrist that someone had removed my wrist link when I'd fallen asleep. Perhaps Dr. Barrera took it to stop the notifications from interrupting my rest. I felt almost naked without it, but at the same time, the quiet after the storm felt safe enough, and I didn't want to bother Sara and Iris. So I walked the halls, disconnected and truly alone.

Without an ongoing emergency, and lacking the ability to know where people were, the facility felt unnaturally quiet. In moments like this, I felt the Vault's size even more acutely. The rest of the girls had told me of the structure's history, how it was originally designed for a larger crew. With our smaller, more tightly knit team, it usually felt like a second home. But the times when we all sought our own space could make it feel intimidating and empty.

I passed the music room and peered inside. After seeing it occupied more often than not for the last month, the dark quiet of its emptiness felt like a held breath.

The training room was similarly empty. I moved on to the lounge and poked my head in. This time, I *did* find something: a sight that would have seemed impossible only a day before.

Sorceress Makula sat on one of our couches, watching intently as a pleasant woman on one of the old CRT displays stood in an expensive-looking modern kitchen and stirred a bowl full of some kind of sauce while talking about emulsion consistency. Hana sat beside her, while Nova occupied a bean bag chair perpendicular to the couch. She noticed me first, and called out as I entered.

"Hey, Claire cutie! You're up!"

"Claire! Hello," Hana said, with a cheerful wave.

Makula looked back over her shoulder at me and gave me a nod. "Well hello, Claire."

I walked over to join them. "I didn't know you were such a fan of internet cooking channels, Makula."

"I required something to occupy my time here," Makula said. "You didn't think I would escape before I confirmed that my handiwork was successful with my own eyes, did you?"

"Bloom, you mean."

"Yes. I may be what you magical girls so charmingly refer to as a 'villain,' a term I consider misleading at best, but I keep my word. It is what distinguishes me from your lesser foils. I intend to remain here until your newly mechanized Bloom awakes from her state of hibernation."

"Well, um, thank you. I'm a little surprised you're being so open about escaping, though."

Hana smiled and shook her head. "Oh, we had this discussion earlier, while you were sleeping."

"Yeah we did," Nova said. "We got a little problem there, babe."

Makula chuckled. "You do not have the *ability* to prevent me from leaving, of course. The Starlight Alliance possesses neither the technique nor the mechanism to stop a Marelian from dispersing and traveling wherever she wishes. You can only do so by defeating me in pitched combat until I am too weak to cast magica."

"Nobody really felt like getting into another battle so soon after the last one," Hana said, "especially considering that Makula saved Iris's and Bloom's lives."

Nova nodded. "So we all kinda figured maybe we'd take a lil tiny rain check on the whole magical butt-kickin' thing till next time. That's part of bein' a magical girl, too! Holdin' up your end of the deal!"

"I get it," I said. "Is the Alliance okay with that?"

"The Starlight Alliance allows commanders operating under special circumstances some independent discretion," Hana recited. She smiled. "And Makula is certainly a special circumstance."

"And so, I yet grace you with my presence," Makula said.

"Okay," I said. "And so you decided to watch cooking videos?"

Makula laughed. "Ah! Yes! You must understand, food is a subject that is taken *very* seriously in the Undertow. Possibly second only to magica itself. For example, the Seventy-Sixth Inversion of Tyrneska was fought over the proper amount of seasoning to add to fried minkartha cakes."

"What are minkartha cakes?" I asked.

"Claire, don't get hung up on details. Now, one of the grandest philosophical debates in our society involves the use of magica in cooking. There are the Delendians, those who follow Delenda, the elder flame of practice. They believe cooking is itself a sacred art on par with sorcery itself, and feel that using magica to aid in the preparation of food is a grave insult to the purity of the act."

"So, a whole sect of cooking hipsters?"

"I do not know these 'hipsters' of which you speak, but to prevent further interruption, I will say yes. Now, conversely, there is the Tacholian League, those who abide by the views of the elder flame of performance, Tachola. To them, cooking is only improved by the use of magica, considering that our entire society's finest accomplishment is our peerless mastery of the grand cosmic torrent. They believe that combining what are essentially two holy acts elevates them both."

"In other words," Hana said, "cooking hipsters versus cooking hackers."

"Sounds like the food version of those computer forums Hikari's been telling me about," Nova said.

"So, naturally, I take an interest in the food preparation rituals of other societies," Makula continued. "Even societies as insignificant as humanity. I am, after all, a scholar, apart from my many and varied other qualities."

I nodded. "That all makes sense, I think. So … which faction are you in?"

"Me?"

"Yeah. You must have an opinion."

Makula sighed and pursed her lips. "I'm not certain, actually. Both sides make fine points."

"That surprises me," I said. "I would have figured you'd be right there on the front lines, one side or the other."

"Within Marelian society, I am known as something of a free-thinker, Claire," Makula said, smiling in a way that spoke to debates I would have no context for. "Besides, I may frequently be at odds with you magical girls, but I am not closed-minded. I can be swayed with careful critical thought and spirited debate. That is the hallmark of all truly great masters!"

I laughed. "I can't argue with that. I'll let you get back to your research, then. I still need to go find Hazel."

"Last I heard, she was in the command center," Hana said. "I bet you'll find her there!"

"Thanks," I nodded. "I'll check."

I headed down to the command center and entered. Just as Hana predicted, I found Hazel there, along with Cass and Commander McCoy, watching local news coverage of the aftermath of the concert on the big video screen.

Helicopters carrying city officials surveyed the Rose Garden Arena and the mangled corpse of the robotic jellyfish as it lay in the river. Off-screen, a reporter narrated with practiced serious-ness: *"City officials aren't sure of a time frame for repairing the arena, or if repairs are even possible. Engineers are examining the damage to the structure to determine their next steps. Travel in the Lloyd District in the vicinity of the arena may be slowed, but officials do not currently expect significant impacts to nearby businesses or the Oregon Convention Center. It is unknown if the Rose City Rollers will open their upcoming season in the Rose Garden this October, though National*

Roller Derby Association representatives say they have been assured alternatives are already being considered. For KION-7 News, I'm Leslie Cho."

The footage cut back to an anchor in the studio. *"Mayor Bradshaw commended Magica Riot for preventing serious injuries and deaths during the attack, but some members of the city council and Portland Police aren't happy with the damage to an important city landmark. The incident has also attracted national attention. A number of politicians have offered tentative support for this latest incident involving the enhanced humans known as magical girls, but some—like Republican Senator Edward Criss of Texas—say that this is, quote, 'another example of the insidious anti-American magical ideology being shoved down—'"*

Commander McCoy smashed a key on the computer console and closed the video stream. "Pfft. Senator Criss. What a little worm."

"At least they don't think we caused it," I said, hopefully.

Hazel's expression lit up and she ran over and gave me a hug. "Hey, rock star! Welcome back from sleepytown."

"Thanks, Haze," I said. "I see the world's not wasting any time having opinions about everything."

That was an understatement. As if I didn't have enough anxiety soaking my mind, the thought of losing the public's support chilled me inside. Dealing with the kinds of threats we faced as magical girls was difficult enough without thinking that a large swath of the population was rooting against us.

"What else is new?" Cass asked. "Rhapsodyz can wave a bunch of money at the city and the feds and buy off some good press."

"The public's not totally buying it, though," Hazel said. "A lot of people in Portland have figured out that Rhapsodyz aren't the good guys they insist they are."

The commander nodded. "Still, the feds gettin' het up about it ain't ideal. Hard not to think this all comes to a head at some point."

"What's *that* going to look like?" I asked.

"That's way, way above my pay grade, Agent Ryland. We do have the Alliance on our side, and that ain't nothing. They're talkin' about sending us a legal counsel to interface with the feds if Senator Criss tries to start something."

It had never occurred to me that the Alliance would have legal representation, but it did seem obvious once I heard it. That had to be a surreal job, considering that until our incident with Rennia the entire magical girl world had been a secret. I could only imagine the shock to that person's system when they found out one of their clients had blown the door open on the entire thing.

Of course, that raised even more questions. So far, Magica Riot was the only group that had come out publicly. Coming out had, naturally, become a pretty hot topic of discussion within the Alliance, but the rest of the planet's magical girls had been advised to maintain caution as the organization dealt with the fallout from us. I wondered about the other girls out there who wanted to go public, or more worryingly, about girls who might be forcibly outed against their will by either government action or members of the public who didn't approve of magical girls.

"The government's a big ship," Cass said, "but it was bound to happen eventually. This is all a big enough iceberg in front of them that they think they need to start steering the ship around it."

"True," the commander said. "Still, don't let it bother you girls too much. Dealing with this is why you've got me, and if anybody wants to come after Magica Riot, they're gonna have to go through me. And I can push back pretty hard."

"Let's hope it doesn't come to that," I said.

"Yeah," Hazel said. "C'mon, Claire, let's take a walk. I need some fresh air, and you're the person I want to grab it with."

I blushed. "Sounds good to me."

CHAPTER 28

We left the command center and, after a quick stop to get my wrist link back from Dr. Barrera, headed down to the Vault's entrance. After an elevator ride up to the underground tunnels beneath Old Town and a quick jaunt through them to the secret door beneath the Burnside Bridge, we emerged into daylight. From that part of Waterfront Park, we had a perfect view of the damaged Rose Garden Arena across the river as work crews and helicopters swarmed it. The jumbotron jellyfish still lay in the river nearby, between the Steel and Broadway bridges, as recovery boats worked on the best way to extract it from the water.

Hazel ran her hand along the small of my back and giggled softly. "Hard to believe that my girlfriend's helped kill two giant monsters already."

For a moment, I just enjoyed the sensation of her touch. How was she so good at making me feel like this with the smallest efforts? "It wasn't even two months ago that we were talking about that 'may you live in interesting times' saying. Hard to find times more interesting than punching a giant flying electronic jellyfish, I guess."

She slid her arm around me and held me as we looked out

across the water, watching the activity at the arena in silence. When she spoke again, her voice was soft, and quiet.

"Bloom's not awake."

The lump in my throat returned; I leaned into Hazel, trying to drive it away with her softness. "No, she's not," I paused, then quickly added, "not yet."

"Not yet," she agreed. "I'm worried about her."

I opened my mouth to agree, but the words were difficult. Of course I was worried, but "worry" seemed impossibly small for what had just happened. Bloom had crossed the boundary of physical form, into a literal robot. Even considering the things I'd seen over the last couple of months, I struggled to contextualize what had happened.

"I'm worried, too," I finally said. I slipped my own arm around Hazel. "I'm going to be worried about her until I see that robot body walking around the Vault."

She nodded. "I feel that, yeah."

I felt a tear roll down my cheek, and the dam inside me started to break. I looked away from the arena and down into the Willamette's water, as my lip trembled. "Every minute that goes by without seeing her makes me scared we did the wrong thing."

"No way," Hazel said as she pulled me into a hug. "That's not *my* magical girlfriend. You'd never give up on her. I watched you become yourself, remember? So I know you'd give everything to let Bloom have the same chance."

I buried my face in Hazel's shoulder and cried, loudly and messily. "I just want her to be okay, Haze. I don't want our lives to not have Bloom in them!"

She sniffled; I knew she was crying, too. "Me neither. That constructed girl has a way of getting under your skin." She laughed softly. "Uh, y'know, I didn't mean that as an Iris joke."

In spite of myself, I laughed, too. "I know you didn't." I squeezed her more tightly. "Who am I kidding? I'm going to be worried about her even after she wakes up."

She stroked my hair and moved back just a bit to let her look into my eyes. "Why's that?"

"What if we trapped her in a body she doesn't want?"

"It's not as if you had a lot of other options."

I shook my head. "I know, but I still worry. I know how that feels, and I wouldn't wish it on anybody."

Hazel pulled me close again and rubbed my back. "I see what you mean, but we won't know until she's awake. And that new body of hers is a blank slate! She can literally change it with new parts whenever she wants. That's trans as hell, isn't it?"

I had to admit, I hadn't looked at it that way before. I sniffled, looked up at her, and wiped my eyes. "That's ... actually a good point, yeah."

"Thanks," she chuckled. "Besides, she's going to have all of us there to help her." A more playful smile crossed her face, and she nudged me. "Maybe even you and me in particular, huh?"

I felt a familiar heat in my cheeks. This was a subject I knew was coming, but I'd had no idea how to approach it. It had felt premature to bring it up before we even knew if Bloom was going to be okay, but it was clearly something we were going to need to talk about sooner or later.

"You and me," I said, as I stepped back and leaned against the railing along the river. "And Bloom."

Hazel slipped her hands into the pockets of her jumpsuit, her grin a mile wide. "And Bloom. You still don't know how to process this, huh?"

"That's an understatement, Haze," I said. "You seem so comfortable with it, though."

She nodded. "You know how I feel about polyamory. I've done it before. Question is, how do *you* feel about it, Claire?"

I took a deep breath. I really hadn't expected my life to take me to a place where I'd be discussing robotic polyamory, but then, I *also* hadn't expected to become a magical girl, or even come out of the closet as a trans woman. Life, as it turned out, was full of surprises.

"I can't deny that I care about her," I said. My eyes met Hazel's again. "I just don't want it to hurt what you and I have, or make you feel uncomfortable, Haze."

Hazel smiled, stepped toward me, and took my hands in hers. "It won't hurt what we have, because I trust you, and I know you trust me. That's the thing about polyamory. It depends on open communication, and trust, and respect."

I squeezed her hands. "I definitely trust you."

She beamed at me. "Likewise! And you're good at communicating. You did a great job of coming out to me. Hell, you told me straight-up about being a *magical girl*. You trusted me enough to handle that revelation, which tells me you respect the hell out of me. I'm not worried about that at all."

My blush intensified, and I glanced away toward the ground. "How are you always so kind and supportive of me?"

Hazel reached up and took my chin between her thumb and finger. She lifted my head up and gave me a tender, gentle kiss on the lips. "Because you mean the whole damn world to me, Claire Ryland."

"Aw, Haze," I said as I felt the tears threatening to come back. "I feel the same way."

"Good," she purred.

"So, um, I guess that means the only question mark is Bloom," I said. "We talked a little bit about this whole thing at the commander's farm, but there were still a lot of question marks then. And I guess there still are. Like ... what's it going to be like dating a living robot?"

Hazel's expression took on that mischievous bent. "I dunno, but I'd be lying if I said I wasn't really intrigued."

I laughed. "Intrigued, huh?"

"Well, duh! C'mon, Claire, don't tell me you're not a little curious yourself. You know, about what that'd be like. What it'd *feel* like." She elbowed me gently in the ribs. "Whether or not she's *fully functional*."

"Um, well, I, uh," I stammered, unsure of what words to

even use in response. "I suppose, um, well, I can't *deny* that, um—"

Hazel laughed. "That's my girl. Useless and adorable as ever."

My blush reached thermonuclear levels. "Hey, not all of us have an advanced lesbian studies degree."

"Oh, don't worry," Hazel grinned back at me. "We'll get you there, rock star."

The sudden chirping of my wrist link saved me.

"Agents Ward, Coates, Hasegawa, Nova, Ryland, Carr, and Hoffman, please report to the armory," the commander's voice said. *"Agents O'Carolan and Tomori report increased activity in Bloom's core."*

"Oh wow, Claire, does that mean she's waking up?" Hazel asked.

"Could be," I said as I tapped my link. "Copy that, commander. Ryland and Hoffman, on our way."

———

We rushed back through the tunnels and down the elevator into the Vault, and made a beeline for the Armory. As we arrived, Sara was pushing Iris along in a wheelchair, on their way from the medical bay.

"I might be a little weak right now, but there's no way I'm going to miss this," Iris said.

"No, I get it," I said. "Let's hope this is it."

"Yeah, let's hope," Sara said.

"Fingers crossed," Hazel said as the four of us entered the armory.

The rest of the team, along with Makula, was gathered around the workbench. Saoirse and Hikari peered into the array of monitors hooked up to the bench's diagnostics systems, and Hikari occasionally punctuated the moment with furious typing as they adjusted things only they and Saoirse had any understanding of.

Cass and Nova moved apart to let the rest of us into the circle. I looked down at Bloom on the workbench; she was still lying there motionless, so whatever was happening must have been strictly internal.

"Is she okay? What's going on?" I asked.

Hikari nodded but didn't look away from their monitor. "There's increased activity in the thaumatite core and the logic circuits of the XS-1 it's hard to say exactly what it is but if I had to guess I'd say it's like the equivalent of increased brain activity so basically I think Bloom is working on plugging in all her various mental cables to the virtual plugs that are the interface system for the body like she's wiring herself up as the strings on the marionette if that makes sense."

"It does, actually, yeah," I said.

"We don't know all that for sure," Saoirse said, "but that's where my head's at, too. I know my hardware, and this was something I wanted to see."

Nova leaned in closer to Hikari's shoulder. "So what you're sayin' is we might be about to have a new robotic cutie for the crew?"

"That's exactly it Nova you have a way with words as always we might be about to have our robocutie well unless I made a mistake somewhere in the coding and design," Hikari said.

"Naw, there ain't no way," Nova said as she nudged Hikari's shoulder. "You're the coolest flammin' hacker cutie of 'em all!"

Hikari blushed ever so slightly and smiled. "With your confidence Nova I will make it work no matter what thank you I will slay the digital gods of challenge and soar high on the skies of robogirl achievement."

"You know how long it'll take?" Cass asked.

"No clue," Saoirse said. "We're so far off the beaten path here that we're basically clearing the brush as we go."

"Y'all are doing good," the commander said. "Keep at it, as long as it takes."

"I would say also be careful of getting too close to her while this process happens because we don't know what she might do with the body's limbs and such as the connections are being made so you know don't try to hold her hand right now or whatever unless you want to have your bones pulverized which is not a fun time," Hikari added.

"Noted," Hana said.

As if to drive the point home, the robot body's limbs jerked upward and settled back down onto the bench. The fingers on both hands flexed in random patterns, and clenched into fists before relaxing again. I was struck by how quiet the movements were, just soft whirrs, whispering in chorus.

Dr. Barrera nodded. "That's it, Bloom. You can do it."

"Do you think she can actually hear us?" I asked.

Hikari shrugged. "The analog-to-digital conversion circuitry is fully operational and I can even hijack the signal as it comes into the XS-1 internal interface but I can't guarantee the magical girl essence has connected to that yet but uh I wouldn't let that stop you from offering aural encouragement to your girl who is a friend so yeah go for it rock on with those words of affirmation."

I felt Hazel squeeze my left hand, and Iris reach up and take my right. I glanced at them both, sharing in our mutual concern and worry, before returning to the robot body.

"Please, Bloom," I said quietly. "Please be okay and come back to us." I felt my stomach turn with anxiety. "Please ... come back to me."

Makula nodded as she watched. "She will make it. Of this, I'm certain."

"She can do it," Iris said. "I know she can."

The silence and waiting—punctuated by moments of more limb movement—stretched on for what felt like an eternity. I just wanted her to be okay, to wake up and talk to us again, to finally be free like I'd gotten to be free. She deserved it after everything she'd been through.

Gradually, the robot body relaxed. A soft chime emitted from somewhere down inside its chassis, and its eyes snapped open, darting around between each of us onlookers.

With a gentle whirr, the robot sat bolt upright on the workbench. It glanced around at us, moving its head and eyes.

"Bloom?" I asked. "Is that you?"

She responded with a soft laugh. The robot's face suddenly sprang to life, controlled for the first time by an actual consciousness. Any uncanniness I'd felt from it was gone. It looked *human*.

And then, Bloom's eyes met mine. She beamed at me and spoke to us at last from her new body.

"I am not alone!"

The room burst into cheers, tears, and relieved laughter.

I almost couldn't decide what I wanted to say to her first, so I went with what felt closest to my heart. "I missed you, Bloom."

"Flam yeah! Bloom's back!" Nova shouted. "You made it, robo-babe!"

"Absolutely remarkable," Dr. Barrera said.

Cass chuckled and shook her head. "Never thought I'd see anything like this!"

Even Hikari let a tiny laugh escape their lips. "Okay this is awesome we've got stable readings in the logic circuits and the thaumatite core operating within all expected parameters I kind of can't believe this worked but yeah Bloom's back Bloom's back."

"Don't try to move too much yet, Bloom," Saoirse said. "You don't have experience operating the body's limbs."

"Indeed," Bloom said. Her voice was remarkably similar to the one she'd affected in Iris's body. "I can tell I don't have full control yet. But I am *alive!*"

"Do you feel okay?" I asked. "Do you feel, um, right?"

"Apart from the awkwardness of movement, I feel ... relieved," Bloom said. "The sensations are different, but not unfamiliar."

"Aye, you've got enough sensors on board that we can map them out to the same kinds of senses a human has," Saoirse said.

"That explains it, yes. Otherwise, I feel surprisingly similar to how I felt before." She looked at Iris. "And I see we both made it."

"Yeah, we did," Iris laughed through a sob. "I still have you with me, Bloom. Is it the same for you?"

Bloom smiled. "Yes. I am not alone, neither in the world nor in my mind. I ... I still feel you. I still have the memories." She shifted her gaze to me. "All of them, with all of you."

I couldn't hold back. Tears rolled down my face, and I laughed. "Welcome to the world, Bloom!"

Makula cleared her throat and stepped away from the work-bench with a dramatic flourish. "Well, this is truly heartwarming. I never expected that the lives of such insignificant beings could bring a song to my heart. Consider me impressed, Magica Riot."

"I suppose this means you're leaving," Sara said.

"Regrettably, yes," Makula said. "I would love nothing more than to take advantage of this moment to advance my own plans, but alas, we did strike a bargain, and I would not be much of a Grand Cosmic Sorceress if I were to break my end of it."

"We won't break ours, either," Sara said. "You're free to go."

"This time," Cass added.

Hana smiled. "Something tells me the next time we meet won't be so calm."

"Yeah, next time ya come around and try to mess with stuff, we'll blast yer flammin' face!" Nova said.

Makula laughed. "I would expect nothing less, Riot Blue. In fact, I would be disappointed if you didn't!"

"I never thought I'd say this, but thank you, Makula," Iris said.

"Yes," Bloom said. "As much as it deeply, deeply irritates me to say it, I only live now through your assistance. So ..." She paused, her mouth working silently as if she'd encountered a burnt Peanut Butter Crunchlin. "... thank you."

"It allowed me to prove my mastery," Makula said. "I should be thanking you for the opportunity. And, Claire, I must begrudgingly admit that you showed me magical girls are perhaps more capable than I expected. I shall adjust my expectations and schemes for next time accordingly."

"So will we," I said.

Makula grinned as dark misty tendrils materialized in rippling swirls around her. "I know. For if there is any constant in this universe, it is that the great torrent of magica never stops flowing!"

With a flash of energy and a blast of black mist, Sorceress Makula vanished into thin air, leaving the rest of us in the armory alone.

Bloom shook her head. "I do not care for that woman."

"That's okay, babe," Nova said. "Nobody ever said ya gotta like somebody just 'cause they magic'd ya into a living robot."

CHAPTER 29

With Bloom now awake and conscious inside the XS-1's body, the first step of her new life had been completed, but she was a long way from fully recovered. She had to essentially relearn how to move, how to walk, how to live with her new form and newfound freedom.

And so, our lives for the next few weeks were spent in rotating shifts with Bloom, as she went through what was essentially a form of physical therapy. Working with Saoirse and Hikari, she started with simple limb movements while laying on the workbench. Once she could reliably actuate her new body's appendages, she progressed to attempting to walk.

Between training and practice, each of us joined in to cheer Bloom on in turns. We found out early that one observer was enough, and sometimes too much, for a still easily embarrassed Bloom. I spent a lot of time with her, and Iris—who had herself physically recovered—also took on a significant role in Bloom's therapy.

For some time, that therapy was a frustrating experience for Bloom. Her skills manipulating Iris's body didn't transfer one-to-one to the XS-1. The robotic body was also taller and heavier than Iris; the new Bloom now stood six and a half feet tall, and clocked in at four hundred pounds of hyper-advanced alloys and compounds. Her initial explorations of mobility ended with her smashing to the floor of the armory again and again. Saoirse insisted that once Bloom got accustomed to the body, she'd be as nimble as a magical girl despite the bulk, but getting there was a long road.

Slowly, though, Bloom became more surefooted. She progressed to managing a few halting steps, then to circling the workbench. After days of that, she managed to cross the armory and return to the workbench. A few days of steadily managing that, and she graduated to taking trips back and forth to the medical bay, with one of us—usually me—accompanying her.

I enjoyed how much it reminded me of our walk at the commander's farm.

After a week of that, Bloom requested our presence in the command center to witness the end of her biggest walk yet: from the armory, down the main corridor, to us.

We stood together around the main computer console, watching the door anxiously.

"If she falls over or whatever, can she call us? Or do we, like, gotta listen for a big noise?" Nova asked.

"She's got a built-in link," Saoirse said. "Of course, if she hits the floor out there, you'll probably be able to hear it from Gresham."

"I must do my duty as a medical professional to remind you all not to try to lift her on your own," Dr. Barrera said.

"She'll make it! We all just need to think positively," Hana said.

"She's been working hard," I said. "I believe in her."

"Me too," Iris said, now back on her own feet full-time as well. "I know how she thinks, and there's nothing she's more stubborn about than proving she's the best."

Sara chuckled. "You're right about that."

"Totally," Hazel said. "This is Bloom we're talking about! She isn't going to stop until she does it. She doesn't want to let us have that on her."

Hikari nodded. "Also if she was having trouble I'd get an alert on her status indicator so I know she's fine I have a whole readout on the XS-1's accelerometers and gyros and everything's in the green so far besides I know my software is good you just gotta have faith."

"Agent Tomori," Commander McCoy said, "you and Agent O'Carolan have already added a bunch of chapters to all kinds of science and engineering books. We have no shortage of faith in your handiwork now."

From out in the corridor, a steady *thump, thump* sound grew in volume, and considering the circumstances, there was only one thing it could be.

Moments later, the command center door slid open and Bloom strode confidently into the room. She was moving so much more fluidly than she'd been over the preceding days and weeks; for a moment, I forgot she'd ever been in another body.

And, for the first time, that new body carried the mark of individuality. A full head of luxuriously soft synthetic pink hair flowed down behind her in long twintails. The color matched perfectly to the newly installed trim pieces accenting her white body panels, and the formerly rainbow-hued lighting between her components now glowed that same bold pink. Even her eyes were now a sparkling pink hue.

Combined with the strip of exposed chassis and hardware just above her hips—which resembled an exposed midriff—her new robotic body looked downright *cute*.

I felt myself blush a little at the realization.

Bloom placed her hands on her sturdy mechanical hips and smiled. "There! I have conquered the main corridor. Am I now fully certified to move about the world?"

A round of applause went up around the command center as we walked over to congratulate her.

Nova pointed at Bloom's hair. "Hey, check it! Twintail twinsies!"

"Do you fancy them?" Bloom asked. "I decided such a fashion was suitably stylish *and* intimidating, truly fit for a warrior such as myself!"

"I'm really proud of you," I said. "You've come a long way!"

Bloom smiled smugly. "Something as pedestrian as 'learning to manipulate a robotic body' was no match for the illustrious Bloom!"

"Yeah, she's definitely feeling better," Cass laughed.

"Indeed," Bloom said, pointing at Cass. "I feel *tremendous*. I still have Iris with me, so in a way, I'm never alone, *and* there is no more conflict about what to do with our body. While I expect this new form will have certain challenges, it is refreshing to once again be free from Iris's incessant biological needs. No offense intended, of course."

Iris laughed. "None taken. I know how hard it was for you when my body kicked back into gear."

"So much *sleeping* and *breathing* and *expulsion*," Bloom said with a shudder.

Dr. Barrera nodded. "Those are things that science has not yet rendered obsolete, it is true."

"Yeah," Nova said, "but ain't ya gonna miss eating and drinking? There's so many flammin' flavors out there!"

"Does this mean I can back off on buying so many Peanut Butter Crunchlins?" I asked.

Saoirse raised her hand. "Actually, I'm not so sure about that. Bloom's mouth can ingest food and drink, same as the rest of you. It goes into an analysis port."

I blinked. "So that means—"

"I can still consume my beloved crisped orbs," Bloom said. "So *no*, Claire, you may *not* cease your acquisition of Crunchlins. Partaking of them is a purely pleasurable act for me now, divorced from any particular need! If anything, I may require you to redouble your efforts!"

"Oh, yay!" Hana said. "We'll have to get you to come visit the restaurant sometime, then!"

"I shall take you up on that offer, bassist," Bloom said. "I wish to sample a great many of this city's offerings, now that nobody can stop me."

Commander McCoy stepped forward and raised her hands to call for attention. "On that there topic, I've got a couple-a surprises for you, Bloom."

"May I presume these to be positive surprises?"

"I'd like to think they are," the commander replied. "And there's one for Agent Carr here as well."

"Yeah?" Iris asked. "I like surprises!"

The commander walked over to the main terminal and tapped a few keys on the console. The big video display on the wall called up a Starlight Alliance database showing everybody's role at the Portland Vault, from herself on down through the list. Below Saoirse and Hikari, the XS-1 body had been listed as EXPERIMENTAL SUPPORT ONE - AUTOMATED UNIT. And, in another line at the bottom, a list of deactivated users led off with AGENT IRIS CARR - RIOT PURPLE (M.I.A.).

"Now, clearly, that ain't accurate anymore, so with the permission of the Starlight Alliance, allow me to update our records."

A few more taps, and the record changed. The XS-1 and Iris moved up to the cluster alongside the rest of us in the band. Iris's record switched to active status and updated to read AGENT IRIS CARR - RIOT ORANGE. Finally, the XS-1's name disappeared, replaced with AGENT BLOOM - ROBOTIC MAGICA DEFENDER ONE.

"Allow me to welcome you back to the team, Agent Carr ... and welcome you to the team for the first time, Agent Bloom."

Iris blushed and smiled back at the commander. "It's good to be back, Commander McCoy."

"You would have me as a team member?" Bloom asked, sounding a bit surprised.

"If you wanna be," the commander said. "Understand, this is here for you if it's your choice. We ain't gonna dictate your life to you anymore, but we'd love to have you."

"Aye," Saoirse said, "and on that point, we've got one more surprise. Hikari?"

Hikari stepped forward and nodded. "Right okay so when the robot body was first designed it was intended to be fully autonomous with an onboard AI but like Saoirse knew it would be dangerous to let something with that much power go do whatever it wanted so just in case the AI messed up or went rogue there was a kill switch to shut down and return the body to the Vault but well that's a little invasive and creepy on the whole 'free will' front now so with Bloom living in it we completely removed the kill switch."

Bloom cocked her head to the side. "So, what you are saying is—"

"We ain't got any way to shut you off," Saoirse said. "You're totally free, Miss Bloom. Other than getting a recharge every so often, you're entirely your own person now. Just one that happens to be a priceless magic robot."

"You're free to live your life," the commander said, "but we'd be honored to have you work with us."

Bloom nodded. "I see. Well, then, I shall take you up on the offer of total freedom, as there are a good many things about the world I wish to experience! As for the Alliance, well … I suppose I quite like the idea of being able to expand my power to its fullest, and your Vault provides the necessary resources to explore that ambition."

"Oh yeah?" Iris asked. "That the *only* reason? Don't forget, we know—"

"—how each other thinks," Bloom said. "Yes, indeed. If I *must*, I will admit to a certain fondness for the presence of the lot of you. A feeling not entirely caused by Iris's remnant consciousness in my head."

Hazel laughed. "We like you too, Bloom."

"I've come around on you," Sara said. "That should tell you something."

Bloom glanced over at her. "Well … the feeling is mutual, girl prince."

"I'm gonna make a suggestion," Iris said. "Why don't we go celebrate Bloom's recovery?"

"I'd be down for that," I said.

"Same," Cass said. "Not to mention your recovery, Iris."

Dr. Barrera sighed. "As much as I would love to, I have extensive reams of data to sort and file with Alliance Tokyo about Iris and Bloom's experience. I will leave the festivities to you all."

"Aye, and I need to upload the newest schematics for the chassis to Tokyo as well," Saoirse said. "I'll send the kid in my stead."

"Yes I'll be happy to go I can't drink alcohol yet but I am down for festivities and revelry and maybe even a shenanigan or two," Hikari said.

Commander McCoy clasped her hands together and nodded. "Understandable. For the rest of y'all, sounds like a great idea. Maybe Dark Water?"

"Interesting suggestion, commander," Iris said. "Almost as if you have a thing for one of the bartenders."

"You've been officially reactivated all of two minutes and you're already giving me sass?" the commander asked. "You really *are* back."

Iris laughed. "Just keepin' you on your toes, boss."

On our way out of the command center, as Cass put in a call to Dark Water to see if Jade was working, Hazel nudged my shoulder.

"Psst, hey, rock star," she whispered. "We should talk to Bloom. You know, privately."

"Oh, yeah, we should," I said.

Hazel and I stepped to the side of the corridor as the rest of the team left. As Bloom emerged from the command center, she paused and gave us a curious look.

"You two look as though you wish to say something."

"Um, yeah, we do," I said. "Can we talk? Away from everybody?"

The expression in Bloom's eyes told me she knew exactly what conversation was looming. "I, well … yes, that would likely be wise."

The three of us walked down to the training room and stepped inside, closing the door behind us. In the bright light of the room's holo-emitters, Bloom's new pink and white body panels gleamed.

"Figured you'd want to talk alone," Hazel said. "We know how you feel about magical girl sappiness."

"Very astute, yes," Bloom said. She looked around the empty room. "You do take me to the nicest places."

"Hey, I had to think on my feet," I said.

Bloom nodded as the moment stretched into an awkward pause. "So."

"Sooo," I said.

"Yeah," Hazel added.

"I do not know how to begin this conversation," Bloom said. "It would have been awkward in any context, but I understand if it is especially strange given my new form."

"Your new form is great, Bloom," Hazel said.

Bloom eyed us back. "You truly mean that?"

"I do! Look at you! You look badass!"

"She's right," I said. "You're a six and a half foot magical robot with head fins and pink twintails. You're kind of the *definition* of cool-looking."

Bloom grinned. "I suppose I cannot argue with that. Nor do I *want* to argue with that."

"And it's still *you*, Bloom," Hazel said. "Whatever form you're in now."

"Exactly," I said. "You were brought into the world in the

body of a trans woman, and you know Nova and me. You know we mean it when we say we understand what it's like to take charge of your own body."

"That … is a good point, yes," Bloom said.

"Listen, there's no point in dancing around it," I said. "We talked about this at the farm. You said you had some kind of feelings for me."

"I did say that, yes."

"So, um, how do you feel about Hazel?"

"We haven't had as much time together," Bloom said, "but Hazel is, well, quite agreeable as well. From a personality and attractiveness perspective."

Hazel laughed. "I'm flattered!"

"I am still not entirely accustomed to expressing myself, alright? Anyway, what are you saying?"

"Claire and I talked about all of this, too," Hazel said, "after the whole thing with the streetcar fight, and we've talked about it more since. And … how should I put this? Do you know what polyamory is, Bloom?"

Bloom nodded. "I am somewhat familiar with the concept, yes. I understand that Cass participates in such relationships, and Iris knew about the concept as well. She said it was a 'very queer, very Portland' sort of thing."

"She's right," Hazel giggled. "I've had relationships like that before. It's something you can do, if everybody involved is open and honest with each other."

"When you say 'you,' do you mean—"

"Referring to you specifically, yes." Hazel's face brightened into a radiant grin. "You know, sometimes a relationship is a cis lesbian, her trans magical girl girlfriend, and her 'living consciousness inside a magic robot' girlfriend."

I looked over at Hazel and we shared a smile before I turned my attention back to Bloom. "If it's something you want to explore, of course."

"Right," Hazel said. "We don't want to push you into something you don't want."

Bloom looked away nervously. "If I may allow myself to be—ugh—*vulnerable* for a moment, I must admit that my pride and my fear that my feelings would not be reciprocated got in the way of my well-being. I stayed away from the apartment, and from spending time with the two of you, for that reason. It was not my finest decision, but the time I spent here in the Vault did allow me to come to a realization."

"What kind of realization?" I asked.

"Not being around you both made me feel worse," Bloom said as she turned back toward us. Her face expressed real pain, in an undeniably human way. "I realized that I never wanted to be apart from either of you anymore. I ... missed you."

"Is that right?" Hazel asked as she smiled and moved over to Bloom.

I walked over and joined her. "We can figure out the details. Right, Haze?"

"Totally! Work out date nights for us in all our different combinations, have check-in chats, all kinds of stuff," Hazel said.

Bloom's gaze drifted back to us. "That would be ... agreeable, yes."

Hazel's expression took on the wicked grin knew very well by that point, and she ran her hand along Bloom's arm. "You know what? I say we seal the deal with a hug. Would you two like that?"

I smiled. "Yeah. I'd like that."

"Ugh," Bloom said, theatrically rolling her eyes. "This magical girl sappiness will be the end of me."

"Hey, I'm not even a magical girl," Hazel said. "I just like making cute girls blush. Whether they're human or robotic."

She nodded to me, and we wrapped our arms around Bloom. Just as before, I was struck by how warm she was. Bloom slowly placed her arms around us and hugged back firmly, but not too tightly.

As the three of us held each other, I heard a whirring noise pick up in volume and pitch.

"What's that sound?" I asked.

"That is the sound of my cooling fans," Bloom said.

Hazel laughed. "Oh, so *that's* what happens when you blush now."

"Do not let that piece of information leave this room," Bloom said. "It would be unwise to let our enemies know of my weaknesses."

"We won't," I said. "Your secret's safe with us."

CHAPTER 30

The ten of us loaded ourselves into Vancent Price. Saoirse and Hikari had installed a custom seat in the back of Vancent for Bloom, where she could lock herself into place.

Sara put Vancent into gear and drove us out of the Vault's garage and up to the surface. As we navigated our way across the Broadway bridge toward Dark Water, I turned around in my seat to check on my new robotic partner.

"You okay back there, Bloom?" I asked.

"I am secure, yes," Bloom said, "but this position makes me feel unsettlingly like *equipment*."

Hana glanced back at her. "Is there such a thing as robodysphoria?"

"If there is," Cass said, "Bloom's probably the first person on Earth to experience it."

Nova beamed back at Bloom and shot her a thumbs-up. "Naw, don't worry, Bloom babe! You're still super flammin' cool and totally not equipment!"

From beside her, Hikari nodded. "Also we can add more in the ways of creature comforts or rather robo comforts well you know what I mean I want to make sure you feel good back there

Bloom vis-à-vis niceties and whatnot you should feel like it's a chassis-mounted high-strength reinforced seat of honor."

Vancent passed over a pothole, and Bloom bounced up and down, locked in place, as she was over the rear suspension.

"Well, I no longer feel like equipment," she said.

Hazel smiled back at her. "Yeah? That's wonderful!"

"Instead, I feel what Iris referred to as 'carsick.'"

"Dang," Iris said. "I had no idea *that* would carry over between our bodies."

We pulled up to Dark Water a short while later and got out. A group of nine people and a pink magical battle robot walking into the bar drew a few surprised looks from the other customers, but Jade's warm and outgoing welcome headed off any awkwardness. Most people went back to their food and drinks with only the occasional stolen glances or surreptitious photos of Bloom.

"It's good to see you all again," Jade said, "and especially good to see Iris *and* Bloom up and on their feet."

Iris laughed. "You have no idea just *how* good! If there's one thing I can't stand, it's being stuck in a hospital bed. Not that the doc wasn't a delight."

"It is still something of an adjustment," Bloom said, "but now that I am truly free, I feel my verve returning!"

"Always good to hear," Jade said. "That's a killer new look you've got."

"Isn't it?" Hazel giggled. "Bloom's one of a kind now."

Bloom beamed with pride. "The color scheme and hairstyle are my first customizations. I expect I will treat myself to further ones until I truly reflect my magnificence, but this is a fine place to start."

"It is indeed," Jade grinned. "So it's a celebration today?"

Cass nodded. "And we wanted to have it here. Wouldn't be anything to celebrate without your help."

The commander leaned on the bar. "She's right. We couldn't have done it without you, Miss Ever … um … Jade."

"Why Meredith, that's so kind of you to say," Jade said. Her eyes sparkled, as if on command. "Between this and the get-together at your farm, I have to say I'm impressed by how thoughtful you are."

"I, w-well, it, um, wasn't anything," the commander stammered. A goofy grin fell across her face, confirming that Jade's charms had hit the target.

Jade smiled with satisfaction and then turned to the rest of us. "Alright, so, what are you all drinking today? Wait, hold on, I know the answer for at least one of you. Nova, present the back of your hand for me."

"Comin' right up, drinks lady!" Nova chirped as she held out the back of her right hand. "I'll take a Shasta, babe!"

Jade pulled out a Sharpie and marked it with a black X. "Okay, that's Nova done. Am I missing anybody?"

Hikari stepped forward. "Just me Miss Everly I know it can be hard to tell from my clothing demeanor and general unknowable nature but this biological construct has not yet experienced sufficient linear time to ingest alcohol so I will also have a Shasta I have come to appreciate them after being around Nova."

"I appreciate the honesty, Hikari," Jade said as she marked their hand with an X. "And that just leaves Bloom, I guess, but I'm not sure how to treat this case now."

"You need not account for me anymore," Bloom said proudly. "Chemicals cannot intoxicate this body! Anything I ingest merely imparts flavor, with no after effects!"

"Bloom, that might be your biggest advantage over the rest of us," Jade laughed.

"Indeed," Bloom said. "So I believe I shall start from the top of your menu and work my way down!"

"I can do that," Jade said. "And the rest of you?"

"Lager for me," I said.

"Same as before," Sara said, "a porter."

Cass sat down on a barstool and nodded. "Red, here."

"I'm a cider gal, as usual," Hana said.

Iris grinned. "It's been a whole long while for me, and I've been craving it. Your finest black lager, please!"

"Rum and diet for me!" Hazel said.

"Good choices all," Jade said, turning back to the commander. "And you, Meredith?"

I was pleased to see the commander get back a little of her swagger as she leaned closer over the bar and answered. "Surprise me, Jade."

Jade laughed and raised her eyebrows. "Oh, that I can do."

As Jade went to work on the drinks, we settled in, some of us sitting on stools and the others standing around the bar. I sat down beside Hazel, and Bloom stood beside us as she began her intoxication-free exploration of Dark Water's menu.

"You know, something's just occurring to me," Cass said.

"What's that?" Hana asked.

"We have, once again, put ourselves in the situation of the only folks being able to drive us home sober being Nova or Hikari."

"Or Bloom," Hazel pointed out.

I looked up at Bloom and tried to imagine her sitting behind the wheel of Vancent Price. "Bloom, do you know how to drive?"

"Hmm," Bloom said. "I know the concepts. Or, rather, Iris knows the concepts, and I know them via her."

"I never liked to drive, though," Iris said. "So even that info's probably kinda rusty."

"There is that," Bloom continued. "In addition, I'm not sure how I would go about it, mechanically. It's not exactly something that was covered in my recovery therapy."

"Naw, don't y'all worry about it, babes!" Nova grinned. "I gotcha covered again! I did okay comin' back from the farm, didn't I?"

Hikari moved over closer to Nova and looked up at her. "Nova for what it's worth I was very proud of you you actually did do a great job and I believed in you the whole time you're pretty awesome well I mean uh we all knew that I guess I'm not saying that because of any particular reason it's just a statement of general fact uh anyway you're cool and I'd ride with you anytime."

The blush in Hikari's face was unmissable.

"See? Hikari cutie gets it!" Nova said, somewhat obliviously. "You're pretty dang awesome too, ya know that?"

Hikari smiled a tiny smile. "That's all the intoxication I need thank you Nova."

———

After a couple of rounds of drinks, most of us were nicely buzzed, apart from our trio of exceptions. While Bloom was now physically incapable of getting drunk, I was enjoying watching her in her magical battle robot body sipping at Jade's specialty cocktails.

Spirits were high. It had been easy to put all of the stress of our recent fights out of my mind, right up until the moment the bar's door swung open and Allison Webb stepped in.

"So *this* is where Magica Riot's been hiding," she said. She looked at Bloom, and a look of unsettling interest crossed her face. "Along with their new metal friend. How very interesting." Her expression returned to its usual corporate faux pleasantness. "What are the odds? Hello, everybody!"

The rest of us fell silent and stared back at her.

"Who's this?" Jade asked.

Allison stepped forward and offered her hand. "Allison Webb, Rhapsodyz public rela—"

"Cut the crap, Webb," Cass said.

"She's not just Rhapsodyz," Sara said. "She's Sinneslöschen."

Jade's expression fell. "Is that so?"

"It's so," the commander said. "Advanced Thaumatite Weapons and Magica Anomalies Research, ain't that right, Webb?"

"The lowest kind of villainy," Bloom said. "A weapons dealer."

"Well, then, I ought to kick you out," Jade said. "Sinnes-löschen isn't welcome here."

"Jade Everly," Allison smiled. "Or, more famously, Jade Ev—"

"Leave that alone, Webb," Commander McCoy interrupted.

"Oh, yes, of course," Allison said. "It's just that Miss *Everly* and my employer have quite the history together!"

"Yeah, we do," Jade said. "You think the kind of people who experiment on kids would *ever* be welcome in my bar?"

Allison sighed like a substitute teacher. "Well, I can see my time here will be limited. I just had to swing by and tell you all the good news!"

"What news?" I asked.

"Our parent company Rhapsodyz, and our CEO Zach Tachyon, feel absolutely terrible about what happened at the Rose Garden Arena."

"Hmm, I'll bet they do," Hana said.

"Miss Hasegawa, we had no way of predicting any of the unfortunate events that occurred there," Allison said. "We were simply enhancing the arena with our Future of AI 8K Metaverse technology, and through an unfortunate coinci—"

"That's total flammin' crap and you know it!" Nova shouted. "You act so smart and slick, but you're just a creepo like the rest!"

"Just get on with it," I said. "What's your big news?"

Allison recomposed herself and gave me her best empty smile. I felt a shiver along my spine. "As a way of showing our commitment to the people of Portland, we're making a major investment in the city. Rhapsodyz will be building a replacement for the Rose Garden Arena from the ground up, utilizing a fully robotic construction force."

Hazel scoffed. "A new arena, loaded down with all your creepy magica tech."

"I assure you, that is only a secondary benefit to us," Allison said. "The company feels like this is the most optimal way to truly give back to the people."

"Right," Cass said. "'Give back to the people,' defined as 'we get a shiny new building to take the heat off our PR trouble,' right?"

"It's simply a matter of investment," Allison said. "Something the Starlight Alliance should possibly consider, since you seem to be involved every time some major magical damage happens to this city."

"If it weren't for the Alliance and magical girls, the world would be a flaming nightmare right now," Sara said.

"Yes, yes, everyone knows how you *saved the world*," Allison shot back. "We at Rhapsodyz are merely doing our part to help the city recover from your 'saving.' The Rhapsodyz Center will be a shining example for the future of technological innovation in an always-online world, and the perfect remedy for all the damage Portland has sustained over the past few months."

Jade stepped out from around the bar. "That's enough. You set foot in this bar again, you'll find out the real definition of damage."

By this point, several of the bar's regulars—who weren't the kind of Portlanders to feel much affection for a giant tech corporation—had begun to shout their support for Jade, and boos and jeers at Allison.

Recognizing the room was turning against her, Allison smiled and nodded. "Message received, Miss Everly. I'll simply have to find another watering hole."

Before any of us could say another word, Allison turned and walked out of the bar. However, I was just inebriated enough to do something possibly foolish, and got up off my barstool and followed her.

"Wait, Claire," Sara called out to me, "don't—"

"I'll be okay," I said. "I'm just tired of this!"

I exited onto the sidewalk on Northeast Sandy. Allison was

partway down the block, though I had no idea where she was actually going.

"Hey! Allison!" I shouted.

She turned around and gave me an altogether more unsettling smile than before. "Claire! What a surprise."

In my state, I approached her more closely that I otherwise would have, and pointed at her accusingly. "What is your problem? What is it that you *want?*"

Allison laughed and shook her head as she moved toward me. "Claire, what I want is unimportant right now. You don't really need to know."

I was getting very tired of her act and felt anger bubbling up in me as I glared back at her. "Screw that! I do need to know! I've seen what your tech is doing with my own eyes. I've *fought* it. What could you possibly be doing that makes you think you have to endanger all those innocent people? It's unforgivable!"

"Don't mistake my goals for those of the company," she said. She was getting closer now, and I smelled that mixture of hair product and perfume that I couldn't identify but which would always be tied to her in my mind. "What we want happens to broadly align right now. That's all."

"And yet you won't tell me what that is," I shot back.

"I simply find magical girls interesting," she said, her expression taking on something I might have called reverence in another context. "You are *enthralling.*" She fixed her eyes on me, that predatory look back on her face again. "And your story, Claire? Simply inspiring!" She was *very* close now. "I want to know every little thing that makes you tick!" After another long moment, she regained her composure and stepped back.

She had me alone again, but I wasn't going to freeze up this time. I fixed my stare at her. "You won't win."

From behind me, Sara's voice spoke up. "She's right about that."

I glanced back to see her, Iris, Cass, Hana, Nova, Bloom, and

Hazel making their way out of the bar. They walked up and stood behind me, staring Allison down defiantly.

"Your nonsense isn't gonna work out the way you hoped," Cass said.

"Magical girls fight on the side of love and kindness," Hana said. "That will always win out over reckless destruction."

Nova punched the palm of her own hand and nodded. "Yeah! We're always gonna be here to stop whatever you're up to!"

"Nothing Sinneslöschen or Rhapsodyz can do will be able to stop Magica Riot from doing what we do best," Iris said.

Bloom pointed at Allison and sneered. "My combat skills were forged in the fires of the corruption realm. You will *not* enjoy fighting me, I promise you that."

"I'd listen to them," Hazel said with a smirk. "They mean it. Sincerity's probably something you struggle with."

Allison slipped back into her empty company smile. "I have no doubt you all believe what you say. Take care of yourselves, girls. I'm excited to show you what we're cooking up next!"

Suddenly, from over the roof of the bar came the percussive *thump, thump, thump* of helicopter blades. A sleek black craft, of a design I'd never seen before, slid into a hover above us. A metallic link ladder unrolled to the street, and Allison stepped onto the rungs. With a *woosh* of rotor wash, the helicopter rose back into the sky and turned to the west, toward downtown, as Allison ascended the ladder to the cabin.

The eight of us watched it depart for several long moments until the noise faded to manageable levels.

"Huh," Cass said.

"What the flammin' flam was that all about?!" Nova asked.

"This all feels like quite an escalation," Hana said.

"You're right about that," I said. "She's got something going on bigger than we know. I just ... feel it." I sighed. "I guess things in Portland aren't going to be getting any simpler, huh?"

"That's for ding dang sure," Nova said. "No rest for the cutie crew!"

Sara nodded. "Adia told Claire that the world would start changing when we got our true powers back. I thought that mostly meant defeating Rennia and coming out, but it's obvious now that there are a lot of things happening in the world that are going to involve us."

"Yep," Cass said. "There's the question of what Rhapsodyz is up to, and how it connects to the government."

"And what that might mean for magical girls all over the world," Hana said.

They were all right. The challenges ahead of us were only going to get more complicated from here on out, but with Bloom and Iris both back in the game, Magica Riot was stronger than we'd ever been. Time would tell if that was enough, but strangely, I felt less anxious than I thought I would.

"As the Guardian of Harmony," I said, "I *know* we can use our power to help and heal. I experienced it with every cell of my body. I have to believe that makes us stronger than whatever Rhapsodyz and Sinneslöschen are cooking up. We *can* change the world for the better. Together."

Sara smiled. "You're right."

"Yeah, she is," Hazel said. "That's my girl."

"I like the way you think, Claire," Cass said.

"Same," Hana said. "This is what magical girls do!"

"And there ain't nobody better at it than Magica Riot!" Nova grinned.

Iris smiled. "I'm so glad I'm back for this!"

We all looked over at Bloom, who rolled her eyes and put her hands on her hips. "You magical girls are always so corny."

"Are we wrong, though?" Cass asked.

Bloom smiled. "No. I suppose you are not."

"You'll come around eventually," Hazel said, her mischievous grin reappearing. "I'm definitely looking forward to helping Claire show you the appeal."

I felt my cheeks blushing and tried to compensate. "Um, well, okay," I said, gesturing toward the bar's door, "how about, for now, we get back to it?"

"Back to what?" Hana asked.

"Finishing our celebration," I said, "and then working to save the world. That's what we do, right? And I know there's no power on Earth that can stop Magica Riot."

Magica RIOT
WILL RETURN

ABOUT THE AUTHOR

The stories of the Maidensong Magica universe are the creation of author Kara Buchanan, a former city planning journalist and musician turned fiction writer.

After a dozen years writing about urban issues for various publications in her hometown, she moved to the Pacific Northwest and finally got to be her real self. Taking her love of magical girl anime, her life playing in bands, and her personal experiences dealing with gender issues, she created the Maidensong Magica universe to bring joyful, action-packed queer stories of self-discovery and adventure to the world.

She lives in a modest apartment with her wife and cats.

ABOUT THE AUTHOR

MORE MAIDENSONG MAGICA ADVENTURES BY KARA BUCHANAN

NOVELS:

Magica Riot

Magica Riot: Full Bloom

NOVELETTES, NOVELLAS, AND SHORTS:

Jade Evergreen and the Perils of Polybius

www.ingramcontent.com/pod-product-compliance
Lightning Source LLC
Chambersburg PA
CBHW010521100726
47903CB00011B/2851